DEDICATION

Approximately three hundred Americans are
known to have volunteered to fly for the British
Royal Flying Corps, Royal Naval Air Service, or
the Royal Air Force in World War One. They
flew, fought, and many died without fanfare.
This book is dedicated to their service and
sacrifice.

Endure the Dawn

by

David A. Bly

Eagle
Bluff
Press

<small>CLINTON, WA</small>

This book is a novel of historical fiction. While the story has its basis in history, it is a piece of fiction. All primary characters and their names are fictitious, and any resemblance to real names or individuals is purely coincidental. For the sake of authenticity, actual squadrons of the Royal Flying Corps and German Imperial Air Service are referenced, and their aerodromes are situated in authentic locations as near as I could determine. However, the actions of the squadrons and personnel in the squadrons are fictionalized. A few exceptions are made for historic figures such as high-ranking officers and high-scoring aces, but even then the depiction of those individuals is in no way intended to be an accurate portrayal of them. No other identification with actual persons, living or dead, is intended or should be inferred.

2016 Eagle Bluff Press

Published in the United States of America by Eagle Bluff Press.

ISBN 978-0-9985227-0-8
ISBN-13: 978-0998522708 (Eagle Bluff Press)
ISBN-10: 0998522708
eBook ISBN 978-0-9985227-1-5
Library of Congress Control Number: 2016921407

Cover art: © 2016 by Adam D. Bly

ENDURE
THE
DAWN

1

TREIZENNES, APRIL, 1917. Phillips told Jimmy he would be dead in two weeks. Second Lieutenant James Arneson had proved Phillips wrong, but now he was himself convinced it was just a matter of time. Taut and a little taller than average with slicked-back flaxen hair, Jimmy liked to think he had piercing blue eyes, but gentleness was more often the impression left on others. Those gentle eyes were now weary from combat just two months after joining 40 Squadron in the Royal Flying Corps.

Flying number three position in the V formation of five, Jimmy felt his nostrils sting in the freezing air as they climbed to twelve thousand feet. He scrunched down in the cockpit of his Nieuport against the cold as he scanned the world around him. The skies were clear, save for scattered puffs of cumulus clouds between ten and fifteen thousand feet. The sun shone brightly close to the horizon in the east, promising a beautiful spring day.

Once at the front, they turned south and started their prescribed patrol route. Their instructions were to follow the trenches southeast at twelve thousand feet to the Arras sector, seeking out German aircraft as they went. They were instructed to attack any enemy observation planes they saw trying to photograph the front lines at or around the big push at Vimy. They were then to retrace their path back home closer to the lines, strafing enemy positions with their remaining ammunition. With any luck, they should be home in time for a hearty breakfast around brunch time.

Archie, the German anti-aircraft artillery, found them shortly after their arrival over the front. Black, mushroom-shaped explosions jerked them out of their reverie, blasted them with cordite fumes, and set them on edge. They adjusted their altitude every minute or so to prevent Archie from homing in on their position. Archie rarely hit anything, but he signaled the German patrols that the British were around.

Sure enough, a German patrol appeared as six dots in the sky up and behind them to the northeast about ten minutes after reaching the front. Phillips saw them first and danced his plane around, jabbing his pointed hand up to let the others know. "Good man, Phillips," Jimmy thought. "Grumpy, jaded, but a good pilot." The Germans saw the British, too, and dove to catch them. Captain Stevens, the flight commander of A Flight, kept flying straight but started climbing rapidly. Trading speed for height meant the enemy patrol would catch them sooner but would have less height advantage.

Soon, Jimmy could see they were DIII Albatros scouts. Fast, sturdy, and heavily armed with two Spandau machine guns, they outclassed the little Nieuports in many ways. The Nieuport 17 carried only one Lewis .303 machine gun and its 120 horsepower Le Rhone rotary engine was less powerful than the Albatros' big Mercedes engine. However, it was lighter, climbed faster, and could turn circles around the Albatros.

Jimmy's heart raced as he watched the Germans approach. He began sweating behind his goggles and breathing heavily. Moments later, they converged. The Huns steepened their dive at the end to strike fast and A Flight turned sharply left to face them. Adrenalin rushed. Jimmy's world slowed. The two flights passed nose to nose, interspersed and jinking as they approached each other with all guns firing. Phillips bought it on the first pass. His engine leaked oil and his kite spun out of control, trailing a thick plume of black smoke. Jimmy could see Phillips' head flopping around in the cockpit, either dead or unconscious.

The Huns dove straight through them and zoomed up for another pass. Jimmy muscled his Nieuport around to the right and climbed as fast as he could toward them with Shorty McGruder in tow. Stevens and Clark did the same to the left. The flights got separated in the pass. Four Huns focused on Stevens and Clark while the other two came straight at Jimmy and McGruder. This time, they had equal height.

Jimmy barrel rolled just as they closed and evaded their fire, gaining a little height in the bargain. The Germans turned left and climbed after the pass. On the top of his roll, he cranked his head around and saw their maneuver. He jerked his stick back and to the right, snapped out of his roll, and pulled into a tight, left turn. The DIIIs pulled hard left but he pulled harder. He could see them swiveling their heads to keep him in sight. They slowed heavily in their climbing turns while he closed on them. They split, one staying in the tight left turn while the other reversed and dove off to the right. Jimmy stayed with the one on the left, knowing he would have a lead on him before the other one could come around to re-engage behind him. He hoped Shorty stayed with him instead of chasing after the other Hun, but was too busy to look behind him to find out.

Jimmy closed on the German to fifty yards while they turned. The Hun jerked his stick around and stabbed at his rudder in his turn to make a more difficult target. Staying with him, fluttering on the edge of a stall, and still closing, Jimmy pulled inside of him. The Hun fell out of sight under Jimmy's nose. At thirty yards, Jim fired his Lewis gun, not knowing if he had a good bead on his enemy. The Albatros flew into the stream of bullets. A few bullets hit the German's engine and the Albatros flattened its turn. Jimmy saw him off his starboard wing, slowed, rolled out behind him, fired again, and saw the German's head jerk as he was hit. The Hun and his plane both went lifeless. The Albatros fell off to the right and spiraled down to the ground. Jim followed the German down and saw him explode into flames on impact. Jimmy had his first kill.

No time to reflect, Jimmy reoriented himself. He had lost a few thousand feet following his opponent to the end. McGruder was still with Jimmy, thank God. Jimmy climbed, looking all around him for the other Albatros scouts and the other two members of their flight. Stevens and Clark were nowhere to be seen. Jim kept climbing, hating the vulnerable feeling he always got in a long, slow climb. He spiraled up in a shallow right turn, swiveling his head constantly.

Jimmy saw the Albatros that had earlier reversed out of the fight diving towards him a thousand feet up and a half-mile to the east. He turned to meet the German and scrunched down in his cockpit, gearing up for another fight. The Hun thought better of it, rolled off to the right and dove to his own side of the lines. There was no way Jim could catch him. When an Albatros ran from a fight, it ran fast.

Jimmy and Shorty climbed back up to twelve thousand feet, looking all around for Stevens and Clark. No sign of them or the other Huns. By now, Jim knew this was not unusual. He decided to continue the patrol, hoping they would find them somewhere along the way.

They did indeed come across them after flying southeast for another fifteen minutes. Having apparently dismissed their Huns, Stevens and Clark were diving on an observation plane over Lens. Their enemy saw them however, and dove away to the east as they so often did. They dropped four thousand feet in the process. Jim and McGruder entered a shallow, full-power dive to catch up to Stevens and Clark as they were climbing back to patrol height.

The rest of the patrol was uneventful with no Huns about, so the flight began a slow, lazy, S-turn descent to the west, clearing their turns at each reversal. They had little ammunition left, so they headed for home. The farther west they flew away from the front, the more Jim decompressed. His adrenalin was shot. His heart rate slowed. He caught his breath and relaxed his stomach muscles.

As he relaxed, he replayed the fight over and over in his mind. He could not shake the picture of the enemy pilot's head snapping forward and back when he shot him. In his mind's eye, Jimmy saw the spray of blood and brains in his slipstream when his bullet hit the Hun's head on its way into the Albatros' control panel. He saw the German's head roll around in the cockpit like a limp doll's. During the fight, he was just an opponent. Now, Jimmy's heart sank. He had killed a man.

All of Jimmy's upbringing railed against him. He could hear his father saying, "Thou shall not kill." No ifs, ands, or buts. He also remembered Pastor Olson saying, "There is no place in heaven for a man who kills another man." Now, Jimmy was not only a dead man waiting his turn, but he was also destined to go to hell for what he had done.

Flying had been Jimmy's childhood passion. He had always dreamed of flying the best airplanes, throwing them around the sky in cavalier fashion doing all sorts of fancy aerobatics. Flying in the war had given him that opportunity. He had shot at the enemy before and missed. He had seen his friends killed in sometimes agonizing ways. But now, for the first time, he felt the sickening horror of killing another human being. His stomach turned as they flew home.

As they descended, the pock-marked mudscape of no man's land with its trenches like the stitch marks of an operation gone bad gradually yielded to farm fields, rivers, and roads that had not been shelled into oblivion. He saw the aerodrome in the distance and looked around for chimney smoke to tell him the wind direction. Stevens lined them up for a nearly straight-in landing into the wind.

The Nieuport settled down as he sputtered the Le Rhone intermittently with the blip switch, interrupting the spark, to reduce airspeed. A few minor bumps and the tail skid settled down. He adjusted the air and fuel mixtures to an idle and taxied into the tarmac in front of the hangars along with the rest of the flight, his

4

wings rocking characteristically from the effects of repeated blips. The ground crew rushed out to grab his wingtips and spun him around to the ready position. Switching off the engine, he was down.

Jimmy slouched in his seat, waiting longer than usual to climb out of the cockpit. "You okay, sir?" Wilson asked as he helped him unbuckle his harness.

"Yes, I think so, Wilson. Thank you." His heart was not in it. He was still dwelling on what he had done.

McGruder came running up to him full of cheer. "Congratulations, Arnie! You got your first kill!"

"Well, congratulations, sir!" Wilson added.

"Yes, thank you," Jimmy replied. He tried to maintain the jolly demeanor of a victor, but he just wasn't engaged. Nonetheless, they cheerily helped him out of the cockpit and McGruder and he walked back for the debriefing.

Phillips was gone. Jimmy couldn't believe it. Phillips was an excellent pilot and had personified British courage. Stevens was shaken, too. He and Phillips were close. The debriefing was an awkward combination of grief for Phillips' loss and congratulations to Jim for his victory. Jimmy was in no mood for congratulations, but he didn't have a choice. Fortunately, it was over quickly. Stevens asked him to report his victory to Captain Hargrove, better known as Uncle, who acted as intelligence officer as well as squadron adjutant.

Jimmy walked slowly over the duckboards to the squadron office. Uncle was seated at his desk as usual, writing a letter as Jimmy approached. Jimmy snapped to attention with a hand salute, "Lieutenant Arneson reporting for A Flight, sir!"

"Ah, well hello Arneson, old boy." Uncle was always friendly, casual, and upbeat like a favorite uncle should be. "Unusual to see you here. Normally, Captain Stevens provides this report. Everything go okay?"

"Well, yes and no, sir," Jimmy replied. "We encountered a flight of six Albatros scouts shortly after arriving over the lines. They dove on us from the northeast. Phillips was lost on the first pass. We split up and so did the Germans. I engaged two with McGruder and Stevens engaged the other four with Clark. I shot down one of them with McGruder on my wing. He will confirm the kill. Apparently, the four that tangled with Stevens were not as aggressive and dove for home after a few turns with Captain Stevens. We rejoined over Lens when Stevens and Clark attempted to attack an LVG. However, the German dove away for home too soon."

Hargrove listened intently and patiently. "Phillips, eh?" He was saddened as well. "Did he burn?"

"No, sir. He was dead before the plane caught fire. We could tell."

"Shame, that. I shall have to write his mother tonight. I see now why you are here. He and Stevens were close. They went to flying school together." Uncle glanced out the window to his right in momentary reflection. Then, he smiled and came back to Jimmy, "And you got your first kill! Congratulations, Laddie!"

"Thank you, sir, but I am deeply troubled by it. I killed a man, Uncle."

"Yes, you did, son." Uncle became more paternal. "You killed an enemy soldier who would have killed you if he could. It is war."

Jimmy stammered and began to fall apart as he spoke, "Frankly, I'm confused, sir. My upbringing taught me to love my fellow man. But now, I'm told to murder my fellow man. Which is it? How can anyone do the latter who believes the former? How can anyone purport to love and murder their fellow man at the same time? To do one, you must forsake the other."

"Arneson, you either shoot them down, or they kill you and your friends. Can't you see that, man?" Uncle sympathized but could not allow it to get in the way of his duty.

"Am I a coward to not want to kill people?"

"No, you are not. Cowards don't get as far as you have. You are not a coward, you are a man with morals who just did his job." Hargrove became sterner. "You are a fighter pilot, Arneson. Your job is to kill Germans. You must not think of yourself a loving, kind-hearted young man anymore. You left that life behind in Minnesota. Here, you are His Majesty's weapon. You must realize that and embrace it. You are not a human, you are a killing machine."

"Yes, sir!" Jimmy braced and saluted. "Thank you, sir"

"You're a good lad, Arneson. Don't let this get to you." Uncle returned his salute. "Dismissed."

Jimmy turned and walked out, disconsolate.

A merry celebration awaited Jimmy in the officers' mess that evening. McGruder, Clark, and Alfie Campbell welcomed him with a tall whiskey. "Hurrah! The Yank drew his first blood!" They all cheered and raised their drinks. Some of the fellows from B Flight and C Flight came over to toast him as well.

He had no choice but to join in, at least on the surface. Jimmy feigned celebration for the sake of his mates. He couldn't let them see what he really felt like inside. The alcohol helped him suppress his feelings.

By the time the sun set he was pretty well inebriated, as were most of the other fellows. His drunk mind's eye looked for Jack Bailey. He thought he saw Jack for a moment, but he faded out. He began to weep. Drunken Alfie Campbell tried to console him, "Hey there, old man. Mustn't let it get to you old boy. Have another drinkie poo."

"Phillips is dead," Jimmy blurted.

"Yes, I heard," Alfie said. "He was a good man, Phillips was. A bit of a grump I suppose, but a good man and a great pilot. How did he get it?"

"He took one head on in the first pass," he sobbed.

"Was it quick?"

"Yes. Took it in the head," Jimmy said.

"Well, that's a blessing then, isn't it?" Campbell sobered for a moment. Then, he raised his glass to no one in particular and shouted out, "Hurrah for the next man to die!" Several of the men around them shouted in repeat and took another swig.

Captain Stevens strode into the room then. His demeanor was always serious but you could tell he had a different, more caring, personality hidden inside the one he let them see. He walked up to Jim, Alfie, McGruder, and Clark. "Well, it appears we will be hosting another pair of boots tonight."

Drunkenly, Jim blathered, "Phillips was a great pilot, sir."

"Yes, he was, Arneson," Stevens said. "He and I went to flying school together. He could outfly any of us but he was too angry to lead. It showed."

"Aye, sir," he said.

Stevens raised a glass of whiskey. "To Phillips!" They all toasted their lost comrade. After this and a moment of silent thought,

Stevens added, "Arneson, you got you first kill today. Congratulations!"

"Th— Thank you, sir," Jimmy stammered. "However, I do not feel good about it. I killed a man, sir."

"Yes, you did, Arneson. I am glad you did. He would have killed others." Stevens grew serious.

"This is not what I thought it would be like, captain." Slurring through the alcohol, he continued, "Vanquishing one's enemy is s'posed to be cause for celebration, advancing a gallant cause against a valiant foe. And yet, I find myself full of guilt. I killed a man and I am going to hell for it." He began weeping again.

"Ask the Frogs about the worthiness of this cause," Stevens said. "For the Frogs, it has nothing to do with fighting for principles. It's about defending their homes from attack. Principles have long gone out the window, Jim, save for freedom and preservation of life. Today you struck a blow for freedom."

"It's my conscience that's killing me, Captain Stevens. I was raised to believe life is sacred, and I just committed a heinous act."

"Straighten up, Arneson." The captain grew angry. "Get rid of your emotions. You are not commissioned in His Majesty's Royal Flying Corps to have emotions. You are commissioned to kill Germans, nothing else."

"Yes, sir!" He braced, wobbling as he did.

"Good. Don't forget it. And, drink up."

The night passed in a drunken stupor. He stumbled into bed and fell asleep, or at least he tried to. Every time he thought he might fall to sleep, he kept seeing the German pilot's skull open up.

2

ST. OMER, DECEMBER, 1916. Private Hank Jacobs sailed to France in December on a troop ship along with thousands of other Canadian soldiers bound for the front. They came from all over Canada and a few from the United States. It was cramped. He was surprised at the lack of privacy.

Of Jewish descent, he watched for anti-Semitic bullies. He didn't make friends easily and this experience proved no different. For the most part, he lay in his bunk reading whatever newspapers, magazines, or books he could find. Highly intelligent, he was a voracious reader. He was average height with a stocky frame, strong forearms, and big hands. He had a coarse beard topped with curly black hair. He walked with bit of a limp favoring his right leg.

This was a dark period for him. He had enlisted with his best friend, Jimmy Arneson. They had grown up together in Gresham, Minnesota and signed up to become pilots in the Royal Flying Corps. Jimmy received his orders for that, but Hank failed the flight physical because of his bum leg. Now, he was destined to be a motor pool mechanic, work he considered menial in comparison. He didn't begrudge Jimmy's good fortune, but he resented his own fate. For the first time ever, he was not in control of his own life. The RFC owned his life. They told him what to eat, when to eat, what to wear, and what to do all day every day. He was a small cog in the huge machine of the British Commonwealth at war.

Upon landing in France at Boulogne-sur-Mer, he was thrust into a world much larger than he had ever known and was rudely awakened to how sheltered his life had been growing up. This was a massive operation. Thousands upon thousands of green-clad soldiers shuffled from one place to another, formed up into groups, and marched away.

When his turn came to disembark from the troop ship, he looked for the RFC Station on the docks. The RFC presence was so minor compared to the Army, he had trouble finding it. When he finally did, a sergeant directed him to a makeshift processing center a couple hundred yards further in. There, he was instructed to wait for the next bus to St. Omer. "How odd," he thought, "The next bus to St. Omer?"

Sure enough, in forty-five minutes or so, a green double-decker bus pulled up to the processing station. He hurled his duffle bag into the back and clambered in. It seated about fifteen of them. He slumped in the back, sullen, brooding, and furrowing his heavy brow as he stared at his shoes.

The ride to St. Omer took a little over an hour on bumpy, muddy dirt roads. The gently rolling farmland of the bucolic countryside contrasted with the messy, muddy world of green soldiers flowing east like a slow-moving river.

When the bus pulled into the St. Omer, a sergeant reviewed Hank's orders and directed him to the maintenance unit. He slung his duffel bag over his shoulder and headed that way.

He looked around as he walked. St. Omer was a large base. It housed the headquarters of the Royal Flying Corps in Europe and served as the primary supply and maintenance depot for European operations. There were many stick-built and Nissen hut buildings formed around the airfield. He must have counted twenty large, canvas and wooden hangars and saw many different types of aircraft parked in front of them. He recognized the BE2 and the FE2b, but others were new to him.

Eventually, he found the maintenance unit building and entered. Sergeant Major Higgins sat at his desk reading through a file. Hank braced to attention and saluted. Higgins casually acknowledged his salute and instructed him to sit down, asked him his name, and asked to see his orders. Hank handed them over to him.

He scanned them quickly and advised Hank to make his way over to building K-42 and pick an empty bed stall there. He was to unpack his kit and report to Sergeant McBride in the motor pool. The motor pool was in building T-24. Higgins provided a rudimentary map to help him get around.

Hank located K-42 easily enough. It was a Nissen hut that slept eight airmen. It was empty when he walked in, but he could tell which bunks were unoccupied by the lack of paraphernalia hanging on the clothing rods and lining the little shelves above the bunks. He singled out an empty bunk at the back and unloaded his kit.

After unpacking, he read a letter from Margaret he had just received. It took several weeks to get to him.

November 22, 1916

Dear Henry,

I hope you have been able to settle into your new assignment in France. I know from your last letter you're going to be working on cars and trucks in the motor pool somewhere in France, but that's about all. I am sorry you are so restricted in what you can say about your work there. I am so relieved to hear you are not fighting in the trenches. Everything we hear about that back here at home is terrifying.

We have big news to share with you. Ellie is pregnant! We didn't know she and Jimmy had relations before he left, but now it's definitely out in the open. I know Ellie loves Jimmy with all her heart so her decision was consistent with that. In her own mind, they were already married and she feared she might never see Jimmy again. I for one do not condemn her and continue to support her in any way I can.

I am sorry to say such was not the case with her father. Old man Johnson was outraged when Ellie told him and her mom. I guess he yelled at her over it and kicked her out, downright disowned her. She came over to my place in tears and spent the night with me. Next morning, we went over to the Arneson's and Jimmy's mom agreed to take Ellie in to live with them.

If you ask me, it's the best thing that could have happened to Ellie. You do know, don't you, that Mr. Johnson beat Ellie and her mom almost daily? He drinks all the time and when he does, he gets mean. Any little infraction would send him through the roof. He is a wicked man cloaked in self-righteousness. That's why Ellie is so sweet. She's afraid of upsetting anyone. That's also why she always sat down so gingerly. He used his belt on her. I found out about it when we were kids and have kept it quiet all this time at her request. Now she's out of there, I think it's okay to talk about it. At least we know she and the baby will be safe.

Ellie lives in Jimmy's old room now. Mrs. Arneson is a lovely lady. She makes Ellie feel welcome. I spend a lot of time there with her. Mrs. Arneson is teaching us how to knit and shares stories about growing up in the Cotswolds. I should like to visit there one day.

We three are also enjoying preparations for Thanksgiving. I wish you could be here with us. I miss you, Henry.

I continue to work at Daddy's bank in town. I am still a teller, but I try to help out in other things to learn more about the bank and to kill the boredom. Daddy has a mean old man running the operations of the bank, Mr. Haraldson. Every time I ask him to learn more about other parts of the bank, he shuts me down. He says I shouldn't worry about such things, being that I'm a girl. I should be looking for a husband, instead. He's such a pig. I want to kick him in the fanny. How am I ever going to run the bank if I can't get this man to let me learn?

Well, more about that later. I imagine you and I will keep up a regular correspondence, yes? I should hope so. Keep yourself safe there, Henry. Don't go getting yourself killed or anything.

With warmest affection,
Your Meg

"Your Meg. Hmm," Hank thought to himself. To Hank, it sounded like maybe she was telling him she was his and loved him but couldn't come right out and say it. "That's Meg for you," he thought. He loved her, and wanted to propose when this was all over.

Hank was astonished to learn Ellie was pregnant. Jimmy told him, while they were on the train to Winnipeg, that he and Ellie made love. Hank guessed all it took was once sometimes and wondered if Jimmy knew yet. He laid the letter in his lap and remembered the day it took place.

He and Jimmy had just agreed to enlist in the RFC. They had discussed it with their parents, listened to their objections, but committed their decision to each other nonetheless. After all, they were twenty years old and able to make their own decisions. They objected to America's policy of isolationism, which had kept the country out of the war for two years.

The next day they had a picnic with Meg and Ellie. Hank and Jimmy had been talking with them about their plans to enlist for months, but the girls were still sad when the boys told them of their decision.

"You're a fool," Meg said. "You're going to go over there and get yourself killed. That's what happens in war, you know."

"Meg, you know this is something I have been wanting to do for some time."

"Doesn't make it right," Meg said.

Hank found Meg had an odd way of showing affection. "Will you wait for me?" he asked. He had grown fond of her, even in her quirky ways.

"I suppose," she replied, raising her chin and glancing down at him through a sideways glance. Hank detected a bit of a grin. "Of course, when you come back, I'll probably be running the bank, so you'll have to get in line with all the other suitors."

"Oh, Jimmy!" Ellie whimpered. "What will I do if I lose you? You're my everything!" She was always sweet and vulnerable. She played the part of the damsel in distress to Jimmy's knight in shining armor quite well.

"Don't worry, darling, you won't lose me. I'm invincible!" Jimmy exclaimed.

Sometimes, Hank thought Jimmy really believed it.

The four of them finished their lunch in contemplation. Each of them tried to think of what to say next, but none of them came up with anything good. The decision had been made and communicated. Now it hung there, unspoken, dampening the spirit of the afternoon.

After lunch, Jimmy and Ellie went for a long walk while Hank and Meg cleaned up and headed home. Jimmy told them he and Ellie would walk home on their own.

Late that afternoon, the boys packed the few belongings they would take with them and headed north to Winnipeg. Their moms and dads saw them off, moms with tears in their eyes and fathers with sadness.

Their jointly owned Indian motorcycle had served them well for several years, but the trip to Winnipeg proved too much for it. It broke down outside of Marshall and they had to give it up. Undaunted, they walked into town with the motorbike, left it with the owner of the town livery stable, and found train tickets to get to Winnipeg through Fargo and Grand Forks.

The train chugged along, spewing out clouds of steam as it rolled north. The territory they rode through was still wild. Miles upon miles of sagebrush dotted the rolling hills passing by their windows in the heat. Scrub grass covered the ground and the horizon simmered like a mirage in the distance. Every once in a while, they saw colonies of prairie dogs alongside the tracks. They also saw dirt roads, little more than trails, run off into the prairie wilderness. Where they led, they had no idea.

Occasionally, they pulled into small towns, some with train stations. Fargo came along later that day, Grand Forks the next. They couldn't afford sleeper cars so they just hunched up in their seats opposite each other. Fortunately, they had packed some lunches in their kits, expecting to eat them as they camped along the roads.

Jimmy and Hank sat for long periods without saying anything on the way to Winnipeg. They were both quiet and introspective. When they did speak, bravado overrode sincerity. Inside, Hank thought each of them was a little afraid. He knew he was. They were on a great adventure, that was certain, but it was an adventure they both knew was dangerous.

After some time on the train, Jimmy confided in Hank that he and Ellie had slept together on their walk after the picnic. Jimmy said it was actually Ellie's idea, that she didn't want him to go without that bond between them. She was devoted to Jimmy and needed his assurance the devotion was mutual. She also feared for his death and wanted to have the memory of them at their most intimate.

3

FARNBOROUGH, OCTOBER, 1916. Jimmy had been fascinated by airplanes since he was a kid growing up in Gresham, Minnesota. It was such a peaceful place and yet, he always wanted more adventure in his life. There was not much of that to be had in Gresham! Still, he missed his home town, his mom, his girlfriend, Ellie, and his best friend, Hank.

When the war broke out, he and Hank followed the development of aviation closely through newspapers and magazines. Airplanes were magical for both of them. They got to ride in one once and built some of their own gliders. Even as a teenager, he knew he wanted to be a pilot.

They were frustrated when America decided to stay out of the war. It just didn't seem right to them. Jimmy's mom was from England and Americans owed so much of their culture to the British. They should be helping their allies. So, when they turned twenty, Jimmy and Hank headed up to Canada to enlist. They parted company after Jimmy got his orders for flight training. Hank didn't make it because of his bum leg and was assigned to the motor pool in St. Omer as a mechanic.

Immediately after his enlistment, Jimmy was put on a boat and sent to the School of Military Aeronautics at Oxford for a four week course in military bearing and the basics of aeronautics. Oxford was close to Cirencester, where his mom grew up, so he got a chance to visit the town on a weekend. They didn't have any relatives left there, however, so he just wandered aimlessly.

After ground school, he was assigned to the No. 1 Reserve Squadron of the Central Flying School establishment at Farnborough for primary flight training. They assigned him to a twelve-man room in Blenheim Barracks. Most of the other cadets were already there when he arrived. He was surprised to see how many of them were transferring from other units in the British military. Four were from the Royal Engineers, two were from the

Royal Guard, and the rest of them were all direct entries to the RFC. The Engineers and Guards, Eton graduates for the most part, stuck together while the rest of them ended up in whatever beds remained open. He bunked next to Gerry Page on one side and Joe Worley on the other.

Brisk autumn air greeted them the next morning as the twelve of them reported to Lieutenant Moss, who escorted them out to the flight line. A gentle breeze blew across the wide open airfield and white puffs of clouds dotted the blue sky. He scanned down the line of aircraft in front of the hangars. What a hodgepodge of aircraft there was. He didn't know what any of them were. There seemed to be thirty or so of them all told and at least four different types. Most of them had the propeller in the back but a few had them up front.

Lt. Moss gave them all a brief lecture on the theory of flight and how the flight controls on the planes worked. It all seemed a bit like magic. Fortunately, he had read up on all of this back in Minnesota with Hank, so it made sense to him. After an hour or so of this, they headed out to go flying.

Lt. Moss introduced them to two other instructors. "This is Lt. Garland and Lt. Young. They are also instructors and will get you flying. Now, count off by threes, starting with you." He pointed at Al Chapman. They did as they were told. "Ones are with me, twos, go with Lt. Garland, and threes, go with Lt. Young." Jimmy went to stand with Lt. Young along with Larry Walker, Charley Gordon, and Frank Newcombe.

Lt. Young walked them over to one of the airplanes. He had a bad twitch in his right eye and seemed more stressed than they were. "This is a Maurice Farman Shorthorn. We all call it a 'Rumpety' because of the funny sounds it makes when you start it up. It has dual flight controls so you will be able to follow me on the controls before you fly on your own. Believe me. You are lucky to have this type of arrangement."

The Shorthorn was large and ungainly. Its lower wing was shorter than the top wing and it had a cage-like set of tail booms that narrowed in a V back to a double-tail assembly in the rear. Wires laced all throughout the structure and between the wings seemed like the only thing holding the plane together. An engine sat at the back of the body of the aircraft with a propeller behind it. This "pusher," as they called it, had a long, open tub called a nacelle in front of the engine where the pilot sat with a student in front of him. There were two big skids that stuck out in front of the wheels.

Jimmy was surprised they were just going to go flying with so little instruction beforehand. He guessed they had no time to waste. With no further delay, Lt. Young looked at Charley and said, "You climb into the front seat and buckle in. The rest of you stand to one side beside the plane. Watch and listen closely. We'll be back shortly. You will each take a turn this morning."

The three remaining on the ground watched as they climbed up into the nacelle, got buckled up, and put on their helmets and goggles. Lt. Young started giving Charley some instructions on the flight controls. They strained to listen in. "Now, as we take off and fly around the circuit, I want you to follow me on these controls. Don't try to fly it yourself. Just follow my use of the controls with your own hands and feet lightly touching the controls so you can feel how they move. Light touches only. It doesn't take much to fly the plane."

With that little bit of instruction out of the way, Lt. Young waved to Walker, one of the ground crew, who helped him get the plane started. As promised, the rough-running engine made a funny sound that sounded like "Rumpety, Rumpety, Rumpety." The whole airplane rocked from side to side while it was doing this, and sprayed up a messy cloud of dust behind the plane.

After warm-up, Lt. Young signaled the ground crew to pull out the chocks. When they did, the plane surged forward. It moved out slowly at first but picked up speed rapidly. Soon, the tail skid rose off the ground and the plane picked up more speed. Ever so gradually, the plane left the ground and began a slow, gentle ascent heading straight out from the hangar. The three young men watched them fly a squared-off circuit around the airfield and come back in to land. Flinging one leg over the side and hopping down, Charley exclaimed, "Brilliant! That was just brilliant!"

Lt. Young also walked toward them, pointed at Jimmy and said, "Okay, you next." His heart raced with anticipation. It was time for him to fly.

He climbed into the nacelle on the left side where a ladder had been set up by Walker, put on the helmet and goggles and settled into the simple wicker seat up front. He found the harness and slipped the straps over his shoulders, buckling them together in front of his chest. He felt like he was sitting in a bathtub sticking out in the air from the way the cockpit was designed. In front of him on the floor was the rudder bar and sticking up between his legs was the control stick.

Lt. Young walked up and got in behind him. He put on his flight gear and harness and Jim found the rudder bar at his feet moving and the stick moving in front of him. He called out to him, "What's your name, boy?"

"Arneson, sir. Jimmy Arneson," he replied.

"All right, Arnie it is then. Let's go through the orientation again. Put your feet lightly on the rudder bar in front of you. Don't try to move it yourself. Just follow along as I use it. Same with the control stick in front of you." Lt. Young walked through the flight controls all over again. This time, however, Jimmy could feel him moving the controls.

After this, Lt. Young started the engine as before, signaled the ground crew to let go the chocks, and away they went. The plane gathered speed quickly and the wind in Jimmy's face grew more intense. He could feel a little movement of the stick and the tail rose. The rudder bar shifted, too. Then, a little pull back on the stick and the plane rose into the air. What a feeling! The plane seemed to come alive in the wind. He could feel the wind pushing on the aircraft and the aircraft rising and falling on the air, sometimes in little dips, sometimes in large adjustments to the air currents. He felt like he was riding a kite.

As they climbed straight out, he was surprised to feel the stick moving almost continuously even though they were flying pretty straight. Before long, Lt. Young began turning to the left. He could feel the gentle, steady pushing of the stick to the left and the rudder bar moving forward on the left. The whole plane rolled a little bit. They stayed in that tilted attitude for 30 seconds or so, and then he felt the stick and rudder being moved in the opposite direction until they levelled off again. All the while, the plane was rising and falling in the air currents. It was glorious.

Before he knew it, they had done three left-hand turns and lined up to land. They entered into a glide, sloping slightly down. He could hear the engine power being reduced. The stick moved around all over the place, apparently to keep the plane steady in the changing air currents. He could see the ground approaching rapidly. Just when he thought they were about to hit, the stick came back, the plane levelled off, and they settled down onto the grass. Lt. Young taxied them back to the hangar so Newcombe could have his go at it. Wow, it was great! They each got three short flights on that first day.

That afternoon, as he lay on his cot studying the handouts from the morning lecture, Jimmy found himself remembering the first time he and Hank got to ride in an airplane. They were seventeen in the summer of 1913 and spent hours on end at the Gresham library reading about flying. The Wright Brothers were taking the world by storm with their European exhibitions and had gotten some contracts with the government to supply them with planes. Glenn Curtiss also fascinated them. He was bound and determined to show the world he could build a plane as well as the Wright Brothers.

In July, they saw an advertisement for the Minnesota State Fair scheduled to take place in Minneapolis in late August. The advertisement showed a big picture of an airplane with the headlines saying Jake Trueblood, the daredevil pilot, was going to be at the fair with his 1911 Thomas Pusher. It said he was going to be giving rides to people who were interested for ten dollars each.

Jimmy and he looked at each other and were immediately set on it. "We can handle ten dollars apiece easy," Jimmy said. "How much does your dad pay you now for working in his furniture store?"

"Five dollars a week. I already have twenty-five dollars saved up," Hank said. "We'll need money for gasoline to get there and back and food, too."

"And the ticket for the fair itself," Jimmy added.

"Let's see, that's about two hundred miles, right?" Jimmy figured. "If we make a hundred miles the first day, we could sleep outside for one night and get there the next day," Jimmy said. "Can we pack all that stuff on the rack you built?"

"Yeah, I think we can make that work."

"That's great. We're going to fly in a real airplane! Yipee!" Jimmy exclaimed.

August came quickly. They drove up the Marshall Road and across the Dogwood River on the bridge next to their old swimming hole. They took a break in Marshall, and headed up to Granite Falls. They came across a few horse wagons and a horse-drawn buggy or two, but pretty much had the dusty road to themselves. They turned east and camped under the stars along the Minnesota River.

Next day, they made it to the fair. It was a crazy, busy place. Neither of them had ever seen so many people gathered all in one place. They wandered around with the purpose of finding the airstrip and the airplane rides and found them on the south side of the fair grounds.

A few people stood behind a makeshift rope fence at the edge of a big field. The airplane sat inside the roped off area and there stood Jake Trueblood by his plane, all decked out in his leather flying coat and helmet, military-style jodhpurs, and boots laced all the way up to the knee.

He was hawking airplane rides. "Ladies and gentlemen! You have before you today an opportunity made available to a tiny few people in this glorious state of Minnesota. Just step right up and let me introduce you to the miraculous world of flight. I will help you get strapped in securely and we will rise into the heavens as on eagles' wings. We can see for miles in the air. Or we can look down and find our loved ones down below on the field looking up at us and waving! Who will join me?" Jake shouted for all to hear.

Like a schoolboy hearing the end of school bell, Jimmy darted out toward Jake yelling, "I will! I will!"

"Well what do you know ladies and gentlemen, we have our first customer, a fine, young, intrepid soul. What might your name be, son?" Jake spoke in a raised, public voice.

"Jimmy, Jimmy Arneson, Mr. Trueblood."

"Very well, young Jimmy!" In a lowered voice, he spoke more discretely, almost conspiratorially, to Jimmy, "You do have ten dollars don't you, son?"

"Oh, yes I do!" Jimmy pulled the ten dollars out of his pocket and handed it over to Jake.

Trueblood smiled, took the money, waved it for all to see, and called out to the crowd, "All right ladies and gentlemen, we are going flying! Hang on to your hats when we get her started up and be sure to stay behind the rope. We don't want any of you getting hurt now do we?"

Jimmy walked over to the airplane. They all watched as Jake settled him in a seat next to his on the wing of the plane and spoke with about what they were going to do.

Jake called over to Hank, "Come over here, young fella."

Hank practically ran over, "Yes, sir! What do you need?"

"Would you be willing to help me get this old girl started?" Jake asked.

"You bet! What do you want me to do?" He was more than eager.

Jake instructed him. "I'll get everything ready to go. When I tell you, I want you to stand in front of the wing by your friend and hold the plane still so I can run back up front and get into the pilot's seat, okay?"

"Sure, I can do that!"

"Okay, when I get settled and wave you off, you let go of the plane and run off to the left to get out of the way. That's all you have to do."

"Yes, sir!"

"Good. Get into position now and I'll get started."

Hank went over to stand beside Jimmy and hang on to the wing as instructed. "Holy crap, Jimmy, you're going flying!"

"I know, I'm so excited!" he squealed like a little kid.

Jake came up to his seat and flicked a switch. Then, he went back behind the wing and crawled into the wire cage surrounding the propeller. He slowly turned the propeller around a couple of times and came back up to his seat. He flicked the switch again and checked with him, "Okay, son, I am going to go back now and start the engine. When it comes on, the plane is going to want to surge forward. You put your weight against this strut to keep it still, okay? She's going to want to come around to the right on you but don't worry, I'll grab hold and prevent that. Then, I come back up and get in my seat. Finally, I'll yell, 'Go!' and you let go and run off to the left. Got it?"

"Yes, sir!"

And to Jimmy, he said, "You just hang on, okay?"

"Yes, sir!" he replied.

"Okay, here we go!" He ran back around the wing to the engine, grabbed the tip of the propeller and yanked it down hard. The engine sputtered and spit oil and smoke, but then came to life.

Hank leaned in against the strut as the engine roared. Quicker than he would have expected, Jake was back up around the wing and getting into his seat.

"Okay, Hank. Go!" Jake yelled and he ran off to the edge of the crowd.

The plane rumbled forward while Jake quickly donned his own seat belt and adjusted some controls. "Fuel mixture!" he yelled over the engine noise. Then, he grabbed the steering wheel in front of him and checked the positioning of his feet on the bar below them.

The plane bumped and jostled over the grassy fairground as it picked up speed. Then, right before Jimmy's eyes, the land fell away from beneath him. He could feel his weight right down through his bum as they lifted off. It was the strangest feeling. The plane danced around as it took flight.

"Air currents are always bouncing the plane around a little bit!" Again, Jake yelled in his ear over the noise of the air flowing past him and the roar of the engine. "You'll get used to it. It's all normal!"

He was mesmerized as he looked all around. The ground was speeding underneath his feet and the air was blowing his hair around like a mop. He looked around at the world flying by, the people at the fair getting smaller and smaller as they rose into the air. "Yee haw!" he yelled out at the top of his lungs and looked over at Jake, who smiled a great big smile.

"I thought you'd like it!" he yelled.

"It's fabulous!" Jimmy yelled back.

They continued to climb and settled off in level flight. Just as Jimmy thought he was getting used to it, Jake started to turn the plane to the left. Jimmy grabbed hold of the strut with both hands in a panic. He thought he was going to fall off! After a second or so, he felt his weight settle back to normal as Jake continued the gentle turn. He watch the world below rotate under the left wing as if they were slowly spinning around.

Jake levelled off again and flew straight for a few hundred yards and turned to the left again. Each time he rolled into the turn Jimmy got a little more accustomed to it. It was an odd sensation like he had never felt before. He clung to the strut with his life.

They did a sort of square circuit to the left around the field. When they came around, he could see the crowd they had left on the ground. Hank was down there jumping and waving excitedly.

And then, before he knew it, Jake started to line up the airplane for a landing. He adjusted some controls again and put the plane into a gentle glide. Jimmy could see the ground getting closer beneath his feet. Just when he thought they would hit the ground, Jake pulled the nose of the plane up a tiny bit back to level flight again and the plane settled gently down onto the grass, bump, bump, bumping as it slowed in its roll back to the waiting crowd on its little four-wheeled undercarriage.

The plane rolled to a stop in front of the crowd and Jake cautioned him, "You sit tight until I can come around to help you out, young fellow."

After a few seconds, Jimmy popped out of his seat and ran up to his friend all bug-eyed. "Holy cow! That was fantastic!" he yelled.

Jake followed up behind him. "Well, young Jimmy, how was your flight?" Jake yelled out in his publicly loud voice again.

"It was amazing! I want to go again!" Jimmy yelled out to Jake and the crowd. They all cheered and applauded.

"Who wants to go next?" Jake called out.

"Me! Me! I want to go!" Hank yelled and ran forward.

"All right, Hank. It's your turn!" replied Trueblood.

He took his money and walked him over to the airplane. "Here, put these goggles on and sit still while I get her started. I need to find a volunteer to crank the prop for me."

"Oh, Jimmy will do it!" he called out.

"Jimmy!" Jake called out, waving his hand into himself to tell Jimmy to come over.

"Yes, sir!" Jimmy responded and stepped forward to meet him.

"Will you help me with the plane just like Hank did for you?"

"Sure thing, Jake!" Jimmy replied eagerly. He came up and stood beside him, just like Hank had done. "You're gonna love this!" he said to Hank.

Jake went through his start-up routine and yelled out to Jimmy, "Okay, son, go!" Jimmy ran off to the left.

The plane rumbled forward and built up speed. Jimmy watched as the plane took flight. Gradually, it turned to the left and straightened out. Then, it turned left again followed by another straight stretch. The plane made a circuit around the field to the left as they all stood and watched in amazement. It went around a few times and glided in for a landing, rolling to stop in front of them.

"Hank, how did you like it?" Jake yelled out to him and the crowd.

"I loved it!" Hank yelled back.

Jake was genuinely happy to see them so thrilled. Hank could tell he sincerely liked taking people up in his plane. Their excitement probably didn't hurt his business either. "Terrific!" Jake shouted. And to the crowd, he yelled, "Now, who else would like to go?"

A good looking young man about 20 years old came out and volunteered. Jimmy and Hank watched as Jake got him all settled. Then Jake came up to them, "Tell you what, boys, if you help me get people up and help me with the plane for the rest of the day, I'll give you each a free flight before you go home."

"You bet!" they both yelled together.

The day passed too quickly. Jimmy and Hank took turns helping Jake launch the plane. The crowd grew as people saw the plane flying around the fairgrounds. Jimmy and he answered questions for people while the plane was up and shared their excitement.

Jake was true to his word and gave Jimmy and Hank each another ride around the fairgrounds at the end of the day. Afterwards, when all the people had gone, he gave them a personal tour around the plane and explained all the controls. They were enthralled, soaking up everything like sponges.

The day came to a close and Jimmy and Hank walked around the exhibits on the fairground before calling it a night. They hardly slept at all, they were both so excited about their experiences of the day. Jimmy knew that he wanted to fly. No matter what, he wanted to be a pilot.

4

FARNBOROUGH, OCTOBER, 1916. "Everybody loves a baby that's why I'm in love with you! Pretty baby, pretty baby!" Jimmy found himself singing while he shaved the next morning, eager to fly again. He wasn't alone. The whole lot of them shared a delightful air of anticipation. They dressed, had their breakfast, and headed out to the field.

"My instructor told me yesterday I had a natural knack for flying," Gerry Page bragged as they walked to the tarmac.

Joe Worley wasn't about to let it go. "Natural knack. More like a natural snack you mean!" as he rubbed Gerry's belly.

Gerry shoved him away, laughing. "I'll show you. You'll still be learning how to land when I get my first kill!"

"Not likely!" Joe retorted and pushed him back. The two began a good-natured round of slap-boxing with each other.

"All right, all right, you lot head over to your instructors now!" Lt. Young chided as Larry, Charley, Frank, and Jimmy gathered by him on the tarmac, anxious for their turns to fly.

The five of them gathered in front of the hangar for their briefing. Lt. Young told them they were going to repeat their turns around the pattern, but this time they were to do the flying under Lt. Young's guidance! He rehearsed every step they were going to take. "Gentle but steady movements of all flight controls are key here," Lt. Young said. "These old crates must be treated gently. They are not made for fancy flying. That will come later on more advanced aircraft. Try to get the feel of the airplane and work with it, not against it. Don't try to force it to do anything by violent movement of the stick or rudder. Work it gradually and let it adjust to your direction. Gentle, shallow climbs and gentle, shallow turns. Let the machine gather speed for take-off. She'll take herself off with enough speed. Once you're in the air, if you feel the plane start to shudder, level off immediately. And, if you feel me correcting you on the controls, do not fight me. I repeat, do not fight me!"

Charley went first again. He did well.

Jimmy got to go next. This time, he had the controls. He knew Lt. Young had his hands on the controls, too, but he was not guiding them at all. This time, he was waiting for him to take control. He held the stick steady and let the craft build speed. With his hand on the stick, he could feel the plane straining to rise from the ground. He let it do that for just a bit and eased the stick back, just like Lt. Young had coached them. They were airborne!

He held the stick back a bit to keep it in a climb. He found he had to manage the right amount of tension in moving the stick. It was a bit overwhelming to keep the side-to-side tension in balance and at the same time keep the stick pulled back just the right amount. The stick controlled both the roll and the pitch. He had to learn to feel both in the stick at once.

He grinned from ear to ear. He was flying! As they climbed, he felt his way into a three-dimensional balance more than anything else. He quickly learned he could not simply hold the controls in a constant position, because the air currents were always shifting and he had to constantly shift in response to keep a semblance of stability. He had never experienced anything like this. His mind was working at full tilt, his eyes and hands were in constant, coordinated motion, and his adrenalin was pumping at full blast. His heart raced.

When the altimeter read 800 feet, he began his turn to the left. He pushed the stick to the left and his left foot forward on the rudder bar. The plane rolled to the left and began to turn. Lt. Young prevented him from oversteering by resisting his movement with his own set of controls. He glanced at the slip/skid indicator and the little bubble was dancing around like crazy. For the life of him, he could not get it to settle down. The best he could hope for was an average position over the center with fluctuations both ways. It was a bit frustrating for him. At any rate, they soon completed the turn. When he could see the field below them to his left and it looked like he might be perpendicular to the line of flight he had taken during climb-out, he rolled it back to level and let up on the rudder under Lt. Young's guidance.

Level flight seemed a bit easier after that. He got better at turning, too, as they made their circuits around the field. His next big test was landing. He had to reduce power to the engine and carefully watch his airspeed so he didn't stall. Lt. Young had told them to be careful here as many crashes take place in the final leg when the plane stalls during descent. He could feel Lt. Young more heavily guiding him on the controls, for which he was quite grateful. The hairs on the back of his neck stood up as he tensed in fear. It all seemed a little too much to keep track of all at once.

Fortunately, they had lots of space to work with. There was a big airfield ahead of them. The ground rose up to meet them faster as they got closer. Just when he thought they would hit the ground, he could feel Lt. Young pull back on the stick. The plane seemed to level off and fall out of the sky just as the wheels touched the ground. This was the flare he had told him about. It was going to take some practice to get the timing down right. He never concentrated so hard in his life, but it was also incredibly exhilarating. "Nothing good in life is ever easy," his dad used to say. This was not easy, but it felt great. He had flown a plane! He could barely contain his excitement as they taxied back to the hangar and he dismounted the plane.

Next, it was Frank's turn. He mounted up after a refresher from Lt. Young. The plane started up and off they rolled. Charley and Jimmy watched as the plane gathered speed. The nose came up and the plane struggled to fly but couldn't quite get there. Not enough speed. The nose came back down and the speed built up again. It rose then and began its climb out. However, it seemed odd. The nose would rise and fall, then rise and fall again, almost porpoise-like. Were Frank and Lt. Young fighting over the controls? Gradually, it climbed after this series of ups and downs.

It was fascinating to watch someone doing what they had just done themselves. The plane banked to the left, but the bank continued and the plane steepened its turn, rolling beyond vertical, almost inverted. The nose came down and the plane ploughed right into the ground with a crack and a smash and exploded into flames! He recoiled in shock. The ambulances sounded their sirens and rushed to the crash site but it didn't look good.

They stood there in shock, their eyes agape, and watched as the ambulance and the fire trucks pulled up and sprayed water on the fire. Before long they could tell it was no use trying to save them. They were goners.

They ran out to the plane along with twenty other folks. When they arrived, they could see there was almost nothing left. The cockpit must have folded up like paper, but the heavy engine just kept coming. The fuel tank exploded as the engine drilled though it and then the engine drilled through Young and Newcombe, driving them into the ground. The ribs and spars of the airplane's wings were just burned sticks lying around, some sticking up out of the ground. Most of the canvas had burned away, except at the ends of the wings.

Jimmy stared at the wreckage, numb and in shock. Moments ago he was on top of the world and now he had just watched his instructor and classmate die doing exactly what he had just done. "How often does this happen?" he asked the sergeant standing next to him.

"Once or twice a week," he said. "Deaths, that is. Crashes happen every day." He had seen charred circles of earth around the pattern and now he knew what they represented.

"You're kidding. Why don't they do something about it?" he asked. "Airplanes cost a lot of money and even more money is spent training all these fellows to fly. It seemed such a waste."

"Well, look at it this way. In the Battle of the Somme earlier this year, we lost tens of thousands of men in a single day, with even more wounded. What does a few pilots matter, here and there?" The sergeant voiced precisely what the generals thought. Lives weren't worth much in this war.

Charley and Jimmy just stood there dumbstruck for a while. The other bystanders trickled away, returning to work as if nothing had happened.

They watched as the orderly packed Newcombe's belongings back in the barracks. Some of the chaps seemed to shrug it off. In true British fashion, they made light of the situation. "On to Valhalla for the lad," Matt Brown offered up. This was the way adversity was handled in public. Shrug it off, be a man, keep a stiff upper lip, and all that. Others expressed their absolute certainty these things happened to other people, not them. Their self-assured invincibility sustained them.

Not so for Jimmy. His invincibility was shattered. This was the first time he saw anyone die and it bothered him deeply. He had seen death before but only in pristine funerals of Gresham townsfolk. Death was what came peacefully to old people, surrounded by their loved ones, after a long and happy life celebrated by friends and family. Death was not supposed to happen unexpectedly and violently to vital, young nineteen-year olds. As soon as he could, he closed himself off from talking with anyone. He went for a long walk, just to be alone. Tears came more than once on that walk.

Jim grew to realize it was up to him to make a go of this. Nobody was going to mollycoddle him. He had just seen Darwin at work, the survival of the fittest. Poor Newcombe had not survived. He determined he would. He would learn everything he could about flying and get better and better until he was the best pilot in the air.

Charley Gordon was assigned to Lt. Moss later that afternoon and Jim was assigned to Lt. Garland. Garland was more serious and impersonal than Lt. Young had been. He expected you to do it right and if you didn't you weren't going to make it. That was all there was to it. When he remarked on the death of Lt. Young and Newcombe, he simply said, "That's war, I'm afraid. You have to learn to accept these things."

Jimmy repeated the pattern work with Lt. Garland a few times and then he told him it was time to solo. Jim only had about four hours of flying time, but Garland didn't seem to care. So, off he went. All Garland said was, "Just go do it, lad. Take your time. Three take-offs and landings. Stay in the circuit. Tell me when you return."

His hands trembled as he worked his way through his pre-flight checklist. As he worked his way through the list, he rehearsed the steps he would take to complete his solo.

Fortunately, the air was still. He followed the routine he had memorized, taking his time to keep his head clear. His spirit climbed as his plane climbed. He was flying all alone, commanding the plane to do his will. He knew also he had to give his steed its due respect or else it would bring them both to an early death.

Oddly, beyond the joy of flying on his own, he had to admit his solo was uneventful. He did his circuit of the field, he landed, and taxied back to immediately take off again. The second time felt better than the first, and the third felt even better yet. Anxiety gave way to budding confidence. He could do this.

Over the course of the next few weeks, weather allowing, they were given increasingly more rope. They gradually flew higher and farther, adding a little more height and distance each day. He made it all the way up to three thousand feet, but it took him forever in the old Rumpety. He also flew around by himself for at least ten miles away from the field. By the middle of November, he had recorded fifteen hours in his logbook and had landed the plane thirty-four times.

They lost two more of their roommates during that period as well. Joseph Worley and Allen Cooper both crashed. Joseph turned too sharply just one time and down he went. Allen had an engine failure. His plane stalled and nosed straight in.

On the fifteenth of November, Lt. Garland called him in to his office. He informed him he had competed all of the objectives for primary training. Then, he handed him a set of orders for him to report to No. 9 Reserve Squadron at Gosport for advanced training in preparation for scouts. "You've done well here, lad. You have good flying skills in the basics. At Gosport, you'll be flying more advanced aircraft and you will be learning aerobatics. Remember to keep a level head about you and don't try to do too much too soon. Good luck to you, boy."

"Hurrah, I'm going to be a scout pilot!" Jimmy could scarcely contain himself. He hurried back to the barracks to pack up his kit and head out.

5

GOSPORT, NOVEMBER, 1916. Jim Arneson gazed out his window hypnotized by the rolling green hills and nurtured fields of Hampshire on the train from Farnborough to the Gosport Air Training facility on the sixteenth of November. The mid-afternoon sky hung low in a thick, gray layer of stratus clouds when he arrived and a stiff sea breeze blew in from the English Channel, frigid, moist, and salty. Hiking his duffel bag over his shoulder, he walked over to the adjutant's office and went inside.

"Ah yes, Arneson. We have been expecting you. Down from Farnborough to become a scout pilot, are you?" He casually returned his salute without rising, as one would expect from a superior officer.

"Yes, sir. It was a pleasant train ride, sir."

"Well, good. I have you slotted into Nissen hut number six, just down the lane to your left as you leave here. Pick out any open bunk. Your instructor will be Lieutenant Higgins. He's a good man. Report to him at eight o'clock tomorrow morning in front of hangar number three. Off you go." He was pleasant but obviously not interested in small talk.

"Thank you, sir!" Jim saluted, did an about-face, and left the office, picking up his duffel bag on the way.

Gosport was primarily a naval sea port by Portsmouth. The airfield was west of the port by the sea, more rudimentary than Farnborough. A row of new-looking Nissen huts lined the east side of the pathway, and five large hangars paralleled them about fifty yards to the west. A few old wooden buildings lay between them, probably the flight office, mess hall and bathing facilities.

He walked down the duckboard path to number six and entered the empty hut. Suspended wiring with blankets sown onto them gave a little privacy between cots, but at present, the blankets were pulled back to make a single, large open space. A small desk and chair were provided next to each cot with an oil lamp for reading and writing. A footlocker was provided for folded clothes and what not, and a free-standing coat rack was provided for uniforms and flying coats. Uniforms hanging on these, plus knickknacks and pictures on the desks, told him which spots were occupied. The third one down on the right side looked unoccupied, so he unpacked his gear into the footlocker.

Eager to get going on things, he took a walk over to the hangars to see what was going on. The aerodrome was smaller than Farnborough, but it felt more business-like. Each of the five big hangars could easily house three aircraft. They all had at least one in them even at mid-afternoon. A team of air mechanics hovered around them and the smell of grease, castor oil, and petrol filled the air.

Out in front of the hangars was the line of serviceable aircraft. They all faced west, ready to take wing. He recognized four Avro 504s and four BE2s in the lineup. However, lots of gaps between them told him there must be several aircraft up in the air. Confirming that, he heard an engine, looked around, and saw an Avro on final approach, landing to the west. He cut his power to idle, blipping it as he glided in. Just above the ground, he flared beautifully and settled all three points of the airplane nicely onto the airfield with nary a bounce. He turned her around and taxied back to the hangars. "Nice job," Jim said aloud to no one but himself.

He shifted his attention back to the hangars and came across his instructor, Lieutenant Higgins, in hangar number three, talking things over with one of the mechanics there. He was a slight fellow with dark hair and a large moustache that curled up at the tips, giving him a quintessentially English look.

Jim walked up to him. "Lieutenant Higgins, sir?"

"Yes?" He turned around and looked at him with intense green eyes.

"I'm James Arneson, sir. The adjutant said I am to be your new student starting tomorrow."

"Ah, yes. Very good. You must be an eager little beaver to show up here a day early."

"I am indeed, sir!" Jimmy's ear-to-ear grin amplified his eagerness. It was true, he was excited to try out the new planes and learn new skills.

"Very well. Here's the order, son. Your job is to build the flying skills you need to move on to a front-line fighter squadron. That's going to be mostly up to you. I will give you orientation flights along the way to demonstrate each set of maneuvers you will learn and you will practice them on your own. When you are ready, you will demonstrate your skills to me in a check-out flight before moving on to the next set of maneuvers. You'll also teach yourself navigation skills from the documents you will be given and demonstrate your learning to me. I have several of you fledglings to look after so I won't spend any more time with you than I have to. Clear?"

"Yes, sir!" he replied.

"Good, we'll fly the Avro first and the BE2 later." He walked over to a workbench on the side of the hangar and pulled a booklet out of a cubby hole. "Here's the flying manual for the Avro. Commit it to memory. Your first set of maneuvers will include slips, skids, stalls, flat turns, and S-turns. Read up on them, too. Report back to me at eight o'clock tomorrow morning." He was all business. Jimmy was dismissed.

He spent the afternoon on his cot reading all about the Avro 504k and the specified maneuvers. The Avro was a tractor aircraft with the engine and propeller up front to pull the aircraft through the air. With two seats in tandem and dual controls, the instructor sat in the rear with the student up front. The front seat was almost completely under the top wing while the rear seat was out in the open. He looked forward to flying a tractor arrangement. It always seemed more natural than a pusher to him.

He met a few of his school mates as well when they came back from their flights. This was different from primary training. Each of the others seemed at different stages of development. Alfred Jones had been there for five weeks already and was doing cross-country flying on his own. Charlie Weeks had only recently arrived so they had more in common. Charlie came from Heathfield in Sussex and was the son of a town merchant. Apparently, there were only two more pilots in the hut at present. Three had just graduated and headed over the Channel to France yesterday.

There was a feeling of expectancy on the airfield early the next morning. The morning sun shone brightly, raising mist across the vast expanse of dew-covered grass and promising excitement in the coming day. Jimmy had wakened early, brimming with anticipation for new flying adventures.

Lt. Higgins found him standing on the tarmac in full flying gear reviewing his Avro Operator's Guide when he walked up. "Alright, Arneson. You follow me on the controls as I fly around for a couple of touch-and-goes. Pay attention to my rudder pedals especially. The Avro needs right rudder on take-off to counteract the torque of the engine. She also wants to dive on left turns and climb on right turns due to the gyroscopic effect of the engine. After two circuits, I'll head out to the northwest away from the aerodrome to begin our practice maneuvers. I'll fly each of them myself while you follow me on the controls and then turn the controls over to you for you to try. I have rigged up a speaking tube so you can hear me in flight. Listen for me to say, 'You have control.' Take over the controls while I follow you on them. We'll start with some lazy turns to get a feel for the Avro. Then, we'll do slips, skids and level turns. When I am satisfied with your performance on a maneuver, I'll take control back to demonstrate the next and so on. We'll return to base for a chat about turns and stalls before our next flight. Got it?"

"Yes, indeed, sir!" he replied.

And off they went. Jimmy was immediately struck by the difference of the Avro. It was much more powerful than the Shorthorn and took off like lightning in comparison. While the Shorthorn seemed to float through the air like a big kite, the Avro punched a hole it. The engine up front gave a distinctively different feel. It gave off a lot of welcome heat, but spit out castor oil profusely. The little windscreen didn't help much. He couldn't help but ingest a little of it whenever he opened his mouth. It tasted awful.

As planned, they headed northwest a few miles and climbed to thirty-five hundred feet. Lt. Higgins did a few shallow turns and yelled through the tube, "Now, you do it. You have control." Jim grasped the stick more firmly. The plane was lighter on the controls than he thought it would be, but it wanted a definite hand to move it around.

He tried a left turn first and noted a considerable tendency to nose down. He instinctively levelled out in response. He tried it again. This time as the nose turned down, he gave it a little back stick while keeping it in a bank. It seemed to work. Just the opposite occurred in a right turn, as predicted by Higgins. The nose rose and he had to apply more right rudder to compensate. Slips and skids were easy.

After repeating the prescribed maneuvers several times, Higgins yelled into the tube, "I have control." Jim could feel Higgins' firm grip on the stick and let him have it. They headed back in, taxied over to the hangars and shut it down. When they climbed out, Higgins said, "Okay, you did all right, Arneson. You need to work on your coordinated turns more and improve your rudder work. Come back in an hour and we'll have our second flight."

Jimmy was glad to hear this. The castor oil had given him the runs. He had things to do and places to go! He headed back to the barracks and lay on his cot afterwards, replaying the flight in his head, committing to memory the key elements.

The hour passed quickly and they picked it up again where they left off. "This time, we'll head northwest straight out. We'll work on some steep turns to left and right, power off stalls, and power on stalls. As before, you follow me on the controls each time, paying special attention to his use of the rudder in the stalls, and then you do the same. Should take us just about an hour and we'll return."

"Steep" was the right word for the turns! They went nearly vertical as Higgins cranked the stick back into their stomachs. Jimmy felt his innards compress down into his bowels with the pronounced g-force produced in these steep turns. The stalls were a little bit scary, too, as it brought back pictures of fatal crashes at Farnborough. It was different with the Avro, however. She was such a stable plane. True to procedure, Jim sensed some rudder adjustment from Higgins just as the wings broke into the stall. The left wing stalled first, pulling the plane off to the left. Hard right rudder brought it back expertly so the stall came straight forward. He had read such a stall, uncorrected, could easily result in a spin, something they had all been warned about at Farnborough.

Jim's turn found him yelled at by Higgins in his turns, "Steeper! Steeper!" he yelled through the voice tube. He kept doing that a little bit more, and he came to appreciate the importance of the rudder to control the altitude. He kept falling off in the left turns. It felt like he had to point the nose to the sky with the rudder as the turn tightened. "When she flutters, back off the stick and roll out a bit!" He could feel the wings flutter in the tight turns. This was going to require practice.

Stalls were even more eventful. He blipped the power off as he pulled the stick back for a power-off stall and felt the wings shudder just as she was about to stall. Just as it had with Higgins, the left wing stalled first and she fell off to the left. He applied right rudder but was surprised how hard it was to keep it level. Power-on stalls were even scarier than power-off. With the power on, the stall was more dramatic and she wanted to fall off to the left. He had to jam the rudder bar to the right to bring her back in line.

"Do that set again three more times, Arneson!" And so he did. He was surprised to see how much altitude was lost before he could pull her back to level flight. If he rushed it, he just stalled again. He was ready for a break when they landed. "An hour for lunch,

Arneson. See me back here at one o'clock and we'll get you to land her on your own."

They stayed in the circuit all afternoon. First, Higgins landed it twice with Jim following on the controls. Then, Jimmy landed it with Higgins following him on the controls. It was actually easier to land the Avro than the Shorthorn. Stall training had helped a lot. He learned to feel the wings and knew when to adjust his slope better. The hardest part was getting the flare at just the right moment to let her stall down gently on both the tail skid and the landing gear at the same time.

"You did well today, boy," Higgins remarked when they shut her down for the day. "Tomorrow, we'll repeat everything we did today and then you'll solo. After that, you'll be on your own to practice all you've learned. I want you to read up on zooms, chandelles and wingovers as well."

Reading about stalls before dinner that afternoon, Jimmy was reminded of his experience with Hank's homebuilt glider. It was a doozy.

"I'm game if you are," Jimmy said as they rolled the glider out to the county road.

"Okay, but you know you're the one with the most to lose here. If this thing doesn't work the way it should, you could find yourself in a crumpled up heap alongside the road."

"Hey, I trust you, pal! This is what, the seventh glider you've built now? Every one of them has done pretty much what you expected it to. This one will be no different." Jimmy was too confident, Hank thought.

This glider was twenty feet across, almost the size of a real airplane. It was big enough to support a real, live person at the controls. Hank had studied and copied the works of the Wright brothers and Glenn Curtiss in building the control systems. They had a place for the pilot to lie down on the wing with a stick in front of him to control the elevators and the wing warping. He would also be able to move the rudder by sliding his feet left or right.

Jimmy was expecting to fly it all along as they built it together. He was familiar with the handling of the controls. However, he couldn't tell if he would be able to control the aircraft in the winds. He was especially worried it was too nose-heavy. They wouldn't know until they got it roped to the motorcycle and towed down the road at enough speed to get it into the air.

"Now listen," Hank said. "When we build up enough speed, it should rise up on its own. If it seems hesitant, pull back on the stick just a little bit. Don't do it too much or you'll snap the pull rope and probably stall into a crash."

"Yeah, yeah, yeah, we've talked about this before." Jimmy got it. "Come on now, let's get this little beauty out onto the road and hooked up to the bike."

They had fashioned a four-wheel cart out of wood to allow the glider to roll along the dirt road until they built up enough speed to generate lift under the wings. Hank hoped thirty-five miles per hour would be enough. If it worked, he should be able to maintain that steady speed for a while.

They centered the glider on the road facing due west. They hoped the breeze that always blew across the plain from the west would help them get it airborne sooner.

Hank walked back to the barn to get the bike while Jimmy held the glider steady. They tied the rope onto the motorcycle to pull the cart and also connected the rope to pull the glider to the detachable hook on the nose of the plane.

Hank continued his instructions. "Remember, if the aircraft becomes unstable, release the tow rope right away. It will help you keep it steady. Then you can just glide down onto the empty field next to the road." They had figured the dirt would be softer in the field for landing instead of the road.

Hank walked the bike out in front to get the tow ropes taut. Once he was comfortable with the ropes, he mounted the bike and pedal started it. With it idling he yelled back to Jimmy, "Okay, climb on!"

Jimmy was already halfway there when he yelled back. He climbed up on the wing, and pulled himself forward into position up towards the front of the wing. Hank could see him reviewing all the controls and practicing using them. The wings warped, the elevators pitched up and down, and the rudder turned from side to side. "Okay, I'm ready!" Jimmy yelled.

Hank climbed onto the bike and put it in gear. Releasing the clutch slowly, he inched the bike forward until it took the full weight of the two lines. He added power and was surprised how much he needed to add before they got moving at any speed at all. Gradually, the speed built. He kept his eye on Jimmy in the rear view mirror, but he couldn't see much.

His speedometer rose to twenty, twenty five, and on up to thirty miles per hour. Still no flight. But a few miles over thirty and he could feel a distinct jolt that pulled the rear of the bike sharply over to the right. He responded in kind to right the bike and looked back in the mirror.

He watched in abject horror as the glider jumped into the sky far too quickly, trying to head straight up it seemed. His bike jerked around even more as the glider banked sharply off to the right as if it were about to crash. Bang! The rear end of the bike flew out from under him and jerked backwards.

He tumbled down the road for a moment before he could look back. He saw the rope fly off the front of the glider as the glider reversed its bank a little bit and start to return to level flight. Just as he thought Jimmy might have been able to offset the bank to the right, the nose dove down to the ground, the right wing fell off, and the glider crashed into a heap in the field.

Limping on his bum knee, Hank half-hobbled, half-ran back to the spot as fast as he could. When he got there, he saw Jimmy lying amidst the rubble, still and unconscious. The plane had disintegrated. The wings were broken off, the front elevators were completely destroyed, and the tail rudder struts had all broken clear through.

Hank climbed in, pushing glider parts aside, to see if Jimmy was okay. He lifted Jim's head. He had blood weeping from a cut over his right eye, his nose was bleeding and he had a split lip. "Jimmy! Jimmy! Wake up, Jimmy!" he yelled.

Nothing. He rolled him over and checked his arms and legs for obvious damage. Everything seemed okay. "Oh, God!" He started to cry. His best friend was dead and he had killed him!

Jimmy groaned, "Uff da!"

"Thank God!" Hank said.

Jimmy turned his head to the left and back to the right. He reached up to hold his head. Slowly, he fluttered his eyes, opened them and looked at Hank. A huge grin broke out. "Wow! That was great!" Hank nearly decked him. And that was Jimmy's first wing stall.

Jimmy missed Hank and hoped he was okay at St. Omer.

Not long after arriving at Gosport, Jimmy received a letter from Ellie that floored him.

November 20, 1916

Dearest Jimmy,

My darling, I miss you so very much. Each day, I rush to the post office box to see if there is a letter from you. I know you are immensely busy, so I don't ask for a letter each day, but I do so love to hear from you. I shall strive to write to you often, as you asked, so we might remain close in spirit while we are apart physically.

I have wonderful news to share with you, Jimmy. I am going to have a baby! Yes, that's right! Our afternoon in the field by the Dogwood River has given us a child. I do so hope you will be happy to hear of this. I am overjoyed myself. The doctor tells me I should give birth sometime in June next year. Do you think the war will be over and you'll be home by then? I pray for that.

I am sorry to say, Jimmy that my father was not happy to hear of this glorious news. As you know, he is quite set in his beliefs of right and wrong. In his eyes, it was wrong that you and I had relations before getting married, and our little baby is therefore not a blessing in his eyes. You know how he can be, don't you? He and I were unable to reconcile our differing views so I have moved out of his house. Mother did not like it, but she is not one to challenge Father.

I spent the night with Meg and the next day, I was fortunate enough to run into your mother in town. When she heard all that had happened, she most graciously invited me to stay with them until you return. I am sleeping in your old bedroom. I love it. Everything there reminds me of you, your clothes, your belongings, your smells. Your mother is so welcoming and calming for me. She has been a godsend to me, just as you are.

My darling, I know this will come as a surprise to you. I hope you feel as happy about it as I do. I simply cannot wait for you to come home safe and sound. We have a child to raise together now!

My love for you has no end nor limit,
Your loving Ellie

He was dumbfounded. They made love just before he left, but he never imagined a child would result. Intellectually, he knew it could happen, of course, but he never figured the odds would land in favor of Ellie getting pregnant.

Nonetheless, it happened and there was no doubt about his feelings. He loved Ellie and knew she loved him. They must get married as soon as they could, of course. It was the right thing to do to honor his wife and child, to give him his name, and to do the right thing in the eyes of his dear mother, father, and village elders. But he would do it also out of love. Ellie was a dear, sweet girl. She would make a good wife. He would love her easily. He knew he would. It was just that it seemed too soon. He hadn't expected it so soon. He would have preferred to live through this war first, and then come home to raise a family.

It would seem fate had a different idea. Okay, he could live with that. If it was to be their fate, he would embrace it and love his fate. He wrote back to her immediately.

December 10, 1916

My darling Ellie,

I got your letter of November 20 informing me of your pregnancy. My love, I am as surprised as you must have been to hear this news. Surprised but ecstatic. This is wonderful news. While I may not have expected it so soon, I welcome it and vow to you to make you my wife as soon as I am able.

I only wish I could come home right now to marry you, sweetheart. I love you with all my heart and I want to be together forever and raise a family together. As it is, unfortunately, I am not able to leave at will. We will have to wait until I can get home. If it's a boy, can we name him James, Junior? I would like that as a sort of a legacy, you know?

I am sorry to hear of your father's reaction. He always has been a hard man, hasn't he? I am relieved to hear Mom and Dad have welcomed you. I will sleep well at night knowing you are in my boyhood room, safe in my parent's house.

I am also glad you have such a good friend in Margaret Lassiter. She is a true friend. Does Hank know the good news? Has Meg written to him already? I'll have to send him off a line. I know where he is but can't get to see him and am not allowed to say at any rate. I'll still write.

My days are filled to the brim with flying now. I don't have much free time, but when I do, I think of you my love. Of course, you know by now I can't say much about where I am or what I am doing. Please just know I love you so very much, Ellie. I am so happy we will have a child!

Be safe, my darling. Take good care of yourself and our child and wait for me.

Love,
Jim

He also wrote to his parents to thank them for taking Ellie in and to let them know he intended to marry her as soon as possible. Then, he jotted a note to Hank to be sure he knew, too.

As his flying proficiency grew, Jim spent more time on his own practicing the maneuvers Lt. Higgins taught him. As they moved on, he learned to recover from spins. They definitely got his wind up at first, but once he learned how to recover, they were more predictable and not quite so scary. He also learned to roll the aircraft, do a split S, and loop it. It's all about airspeed and gravity! Keeping the airspeed up and positive gravity on all of those maneuvers was key. He was determined to be the best pilot he could be so he practiced them over and over again.

The BE2d followed the Avro. It was also a stable plane to fly and he quickly learned to do all the same maneuvers in that type. He gradually increased the altitude at which he flew, taking the BE2 all the way up to 8,000 feet. How small the world seemed at such heights. Small and freezing cold! He could not believe how cold it was at height. Higgins taught him how to apply whale grease to his face as a way to ward off the freezing temperatures. Apparently, this was common practice at the front where patrols routinely took place at altitudes of 8,000 feet or more.

Navigation and cross-country flying followed. Some days he flew the Avro and some days the BE2. What a joy it was to fly around to airfields all over southern England, weather permitting. He grew to enjoy hedge hopping quite a bit and had a few close calls in the process, once nearly knocking off his undercarriage on the roof of a barn that popped up out of nowhere one fine morning.

The last half of January was focused on gunnery practice. He learned all about the Lewis and Hotchkiss machine guns, including how to take them apart and put them back together again. Initially, he fired at stationery targets from a machine gun emplacement on the ground. Then, they had him fire at moving targets pulled across his field of fire on little railroad tracks so he could get a sense of leading targets.

As the final step in his training, he was given an Airco DH2 to fly. This front-line aircraft was a delight to fly. It was a pusher again, however. At first, he thought it would be a major disappointment because it was laid out so much like the old Shorthorn, but he soon learned it was much more powerful and maneuverable. He could do everything in the DH2 he did in the Avro and the BE2, but he could do it more quickly and easily. Lt. Higgins taught him some more advanced maneuvers to try in this plane.

It had a Lewis gun in the nose of the cockpit he could fire with one hand while he flew the plane with the other hand on the stick. At first, he fired on ground targets, but then he learned to fire at a large sock-type target towed behind an Avro. This proved quite difficult at first because he could not maneuver the plane well while at the same time, aiming the gun to hit the target. He did better when he kept the gun stationary and just aimed the plane.

And then he was done. In the space of a few months he had become a pilot. He knew how to fly four different types of aircraft and he could make an airplane do just about every conceivable maneuver in the air. He had accumulated fifty-five hours of flying time and he was ready to go.

Lt. Higgins agreed. "You're a good pilot, son. You have a real knack at flying an airplane. However, there is more for you to learn after you report to your duty station. You must learn to survive. And then, you must learn to hunt and kill. Your survival will depend on chance, and a sixth sense of when to fight and when to run. Get to know your enemy and his airplane. Observe and learn what his aircraft does well and what it does not do well. Learn to avoid situations where he is strong and to create situations where you can exploit his weaknesses. That is the skill of the hunter."

He continued, "You will find two types of pilots in this war, the hunters and the hunted. The hunted fall prey to the hunter. Learn to be a hunter if you want to survive. You will see the difference when you get to the front. The hunted concern themselves only with survival. The hunters concern themselves with the hunt. You must have both the attitude and skill of the hunter. A skillful adversary will turn you into prey in a moment. You must practice and hone your hunting skills as well as your flying skills if you are to survive."

He handed Jim his orders. He was to report to the Movement Section at RFC headquarters at St. Omer where he was to be assigned to a scout squadron as a second lieutenant. "Allow me to give you your first set of wings. Sew them on today and wear them with pride." He had made it! Jim wondered if Hank was still at St. Omer. Maybe he could see him there.

6

ST. OMER, DECEMBER, 1916. Private Hank Jacobs smelled trouble as soon as he walked up to the Motor Pool in Building T-24. Sergeant McBride was standing out in front of the large garage of the motor pool maintenance unit. Hank walked up and introduced himself. "Private Jacobs reporting, sir!" He handed him his orders.

Sergeant McBride was a short, stocky Scotsman with bright, orangey-red hair. He looked Hank up one side and down the other. "Jacobs, is it? Where are you from?"

"Minnesota, sir," he replied.

"Don't sir me, Jacobs. I am a sergeant. You don't sir sergeants."

Yes, sir, err, sergeant," He stammered a bit.

"Minnesota, you say. Are you a Yank then?"

"Yes, I am, sergeant," he replied.

"Fair enough. What I mean is, what stock are you made of, Jacobs? Where does your family hail from?"

"My grandfather emigrated to the U.S. from Poland if that's what you mean, Sergeant McBride," he answered.

"Are you a Polish Jew?" The directness of his query startled Hank.

"Why yes, I am, Sergeant McBride." He stood upright. Hank had never been ashamed of his heritage and he could not understand why McBride pursued this line of questioning so directly.

McBride's face contorted into a grimace. "I hates Jews. You got that, Jacobs?"

Hank's life just went from bad to worse. "Excuse me?" he said.

"I said I hates Jews. You're a Jew. I hate you." He strode forward and stuck his smelly, red, stubbled jaw out close to his face. "I can't choose who I work with here in this outfit but I can promise you, ikey, I will make your life miserable. Now, you get over there and work with Airman Jones in the brakes department. He'll teach you what you need to know. Stay out of my sight and out of trouble and you might get by. Cause any problems, and I will personally make your life a living hell so bad you'll cry to get assigned to the poor bloody infantry."

Shaken but not wanting to show it, Hank walked over in the direction McBride had pointed. He approached the mechanic working there, "Are you Airman Jones?"

Airman Jones seemed a straightforward enough fellow. His face and overalls were caked with brake dust and his hands were dry and cracked. "Yes, I am. Who are you?" he asked.

"I am Hank Jacobs. Sergeant McBride said I was to work with you and you would show me what I need to do."

"Hullo, Hank. Name's Lucas. Everyone calls me Luke. Pleased to meet you, mate," Jones said. "Don't let old McBride get to you. 'E hates everybody."

"Not just Jews?" he asked.

"Not just Jews," Luke consoled. "But Jews probably get the worst of it. Sorry."

"Well, I'm going to have to figure out how to handle it."

"He's not too bright. You'll sort it out," said Luke. "He's a bloomin' Ginger after all."

"Ginger?" Hank asked.

"Yeah, them redheads. Their hair is the color of ginger, see? There hain't no ginger what has a bit of brains. They're all dumb as rocks. McBride, too. We call him 'Ginger Snap' because he's about as bright as a biscuit," he chuckled.

"So, for now, I assume I am to help you and learn from you. What can I do to help?" Hank asked. With that, they set to work on the brakes of the tender raised on jacks in front of them.

It seems brakes were about the only job Luke did. Everyone in the motor pool repair shop had a job or a set of jobs assigned to them. They learned how to do those jobs, but not much beyond them, because they were not given the opportunity. When they finished on one vehicle, they moved on to the next vehicle needing their hands.

This was McBride's way of organizing the work. It was efficient enough in the near term, but it didn't help in the long run. There were few backups if someone fell ill, got orders to go elsewhere, or left for whatever reason. The mechanics didn't like it either because of the repetitiveness of their work without any opportunity to learn new things. The other problem was no one took an overall view of what was wrong with a vehicle or to sequence the work well.

Whenever an undesirable job arose, McBride would single Hank out and assign it to him. He cleaned up several oil spills, scrubbed out oil pans, removed rusty leaf springs, and just about every other lousy job one could imagine.

The one way this worked in Hank's favor was getting to know the other mechanics in the garage and not getting pigeon-holed in just one job. They started calling him, "Hank the Yank" with some modicum of affection, he believed. McBride overheard this one day and started called him, "Hank the Ike." He just tried to ignore him but some days were worse than others. "Bagel Boy" was another name he used to like to call him.

Once Hank learned to do one job, he would quietly seek out another mechanic to work on a different job. If McBride came around, he would just say he was asking for a cigarette and pretend he was only standing there for that purpose. By so doing, he eventually learned most everything there was to know about these vehicles, from tune-ups to engine overhauls.

Neither Luke nor any of the other mechanics minded him doing this. However, they were hesitant to do it themselves for fear of getting in trouble with McBride. Hank found it interesting that these Brits just seemed destined to obey orders, as if it had been bred into them.

Hank found himself wondering what Jimmy would do if he were confronted with this situation. He was sure he knew, based on Jimmy's actions one day when they were in school together several years ago.

Hank's family moved to Gresham in 1904. Hank's dad, Gustaf, hurried the family out of Germantown, Pennsylvania because anti-Semitic German immigrants harassed them and threatened them with harm if they didn't leave. As a result, Gustaf instructed his family to keep their Judaism a secret in Gresham.

No one ever knew how it happened. The Jacobs family always thought it might have been little Maria, the chatterbox, letting it slip out without realizing it. The family secret got out and people learned they were Jewish. Hank was 14 then. Most people in Gresham, a peaceful, Norwegian farming village, simply accepted it without fanfare. It certainly made no difference between Hank and Jimmy. Jimmy was curious and wanted to know more about Judaism, but it was always respectful. Never once did Hank doubt Jimmy's friendship.

Unfortunately, that sentiment wasn't uniform among the residents of Gresham. There were some who looked down on the Jacobs family because of it. Gustaf's cabinetry business lost a few customers. The Jacobs got a few hostile looks from people in town sometimes, especially on Sundays. They stopped going to Peace Lutheran Church once word got out.

Mr. Jacobs was especially sensitive to it all, since he had borne the brunt of it in Germantown. His wife, Anna, handled it better. Her friends were supportive. Women understood better about such things.

They had a couple of uncomfortable incidents in the summer of 1911, but none of these compared to what happened after school one day in May. It was a warm Friday afternoon and the kids were all happy to be out of school for the week and looking forward to summer. Hank was talking in the schoolyard with Jimmy about going fishing in the river north of town while they waited for Maria to come out so they could head home. Most of the kids were milling about, saying their goodbyes to their school friends or making their plans for the weekend before heading out.

Three of the older boys in school came up to Hank and started bothering him. ""Jew boy! Go away, Jew boy!" Jan Selvig spat out while pushing Hank on the shoulder.

"Leave me alone, Selvig," Hank replied. "I never did anything to bother you."

"Why did you keep it a secret, Jew Boy?" Roald Thorson yelled. "Were you ashamed? Little Jew Boy ashamed to be a Jew?"

"Kike!" big Bjorn Nelson joined in. All three of them yelled in Hank's face.

Bjorn pushed Hank down. He started to get up and dust himself off. Bjorn's friend, Selvig, pushed him back down before he could get up. All the while, they were chanting "Jew boy go home!" Every time Hank tried to get up, one of them would push him back down before he could regain his balance.

"Hey, back off!" Jimmy stepped in between Hank and the bullies, and pushed Thorson off before he could push Hank again.

Bjorn laughed at him. "What are you going to do about it, Arneson? Go away so you don't get hurt."

"I said, leave him alone!" Jimmy was madder than Hank had ever seen him.

Bjorn walked up to Jimmy and puffed his chest up against him, forcing him to step back. "And I said go away unless you want to get hurt, punk!" He was a big kid, two years older than Jimmy with a muscular build from working on the family farm.

Jimmy pushed back at him in his chest. "I won't go away and you leave my friend alone, you big dumbbell!"

"Don't say I didn't warn you, Jimmy." Bjorn backed up and made fists out of his big hands. He held them apart, ready to swing forward, and took a step or two to his left, starting to circle.

Jimmy responded by striking a surprisingly classic boxer's stance, his left fist up and forward with his right fist a little farther back to protect his face. He began a little bob as he circled to his left, opposite Bjorn.

"Fight! Fight!" a couple of kids yelled as everyone began backing away from Jimmy and Bjorn, forming a ring of onlookers. Margaret and Ellie were among them. They looked scared, their eyes big as saucers.

The two boys went around the circle a couple of times, checking each other out. Bjorn stepped in, cocked his right arm back, and took a big roundhouse swing at Jimmy.

Jimmy bent to his right like a leaf and Bjorn's punch found nothing but the air over Jimmy's head. It threw Bjorn off balance. Jimmy jumped around to the left and resumed his stance.

Bjorn regained his balance and stepped toward Jimmy. His fists were a bit lower and spread out. He started to cock his right arm again, but before he could start his swing, Jimmy jabbed him on his right cheek and jumped back before Bjorn could react. It hardly fazed him. He took a step closer and Jimmy jabbed again. This time, he hit him twice on the corner of his eyebrow with two quick pumps before Bjorn could even raise his right arm to block it. Bjorn was big but he wasn't fast. Jimmy was smaller but faster. Jimmy circled to his left.

Selvig and Thorson yelled out, "Get him, Bjorn! Get him! Knock his block off!"

Bjorn followed. This time, Bjorn coiled his left arm and swung it towards Jimmy in a big arc. Once again, Jimmy side-stepped it in a duck to his left. Bjorn kept coming, starting to get angry. He cocked his left arm again and Jimmy beat his swing with a straight right to Bjorn's forehead, right between his eyes.

Bjorn shook his head at this, a bit dazed. His eyes crossed momentarily as he stepped back. Jimmy came in quickly, jabbing him twice in the nose and immediately hitting him with another straight right to Bjorn's mouth, connecting on his upper lip. His lip began to bleed as he lifted his hand to rub his mouth.

"Yay!" A big cheer went up from the kids gathered around the big circle. Bjorn and his bully friends were disliked by most of the kids in school.

Bjorn roared, put his head down and charged Jimmy. Jimmy tried to side-step him, but Bjorn rotated just enough to get his right arm around to catch Jimmy on his left eye with a wide-ranging swing. Jimmy went spinning down in the dust, knocked off balance by the blow. He scrambled out of Bjorn's reach before Bjorn could stop his momentum.

Jimmy got up and the two started circling to the left again. Bjorn rushed him again, but this time, Jimmy planted his feet firmly against the onslaught and put his whole weight behind a powerful straight right punch to Bjorn's left eyebrow. The skin split and blood spurted out and began to run down Bjorn's face as he fell off to the right. Jimmy's hand hurt like crazy and he shook it to relieve the pain.

Bjorn put his hand up to rub his eyebrow and was shocked by the blood on his hand. He stumbled, trying to remain standing, his eyes rolling and blinking repeatedly. Jimmy backed off to let him regain some composure.

Just then, their teacher, Mrs. Olson, came rushing out of the school wielding a broom like an axe, screaming at the top of her lungs. "Stop that! Stop that, you two!" She ran right in between them with her broom ready to bonk either one of them over the head. "You boys stop this instant or I will personally show you the stars in heaven right this minute!"

Hands still fisted, both boys backed off a bit and stopped circling. Bjorn struggled to stand still as if he had been spun around until dizzy.

Mrs. Olson lowered her broom and directed herself to the kids around the ring. "What on earth happened here?"

Two or three of them chimed in all at once. "They were picking on Hank!" said one. "They called him 'Jew boy' and pushed him down!" yelled another. "Jimmy was protecting Hank!" a third kid exclaimed.

Mrs. Olson sternly looked at both boys, first Jimmy and then Bjorn. "Bjorn Nelson, you leave this schoolyard right now and take your two hooligans with you!" Mrs. Olson was on fire. "I am going to speak with your father and you can be certain he will have more to say to you about this!"

Bjorn dropped his fists and slouched a little, still rubbing his eyebrow. He knew he was going to get a beating tonight. Selvig and Thorson followed along as Bjorn stomped down the street.

"And you, James Arneson, just what did you think you were doing taking on those thugs? Don't you know you could have gotten hurt? You should have come to me, instead." Mrs. Olson remained stern but softened a bit.

"There wasn't time, Mrs. Olson," Jimmy explained. "I just couldn't stand by and watch them push Hank around an' stuff. He's my friend. Nobody hurts my friend, Ma'am!"

"He was only trying to help, Mrs. Olson!" Ellie exclaimed.

"They were really being mean to Hank," Margaret added.

"I understand," said Mrs. Olson. She addressed the whole gathering. "However, all of you should know that violence is a bad thing. You are supposed to settle your differences peacefully. You do know that, don't you?"

"Yes, Mrs. Olson," The class replied in unison.

"Very well. Now, run along and go to your homes. Mr. Jacobs and Mr. Arneson, you two stay here. I want to speak with both of you further."

She waited for the little crowd of kids to disperse. Her tone softened. "Henry, why were those boys picking on you?"

"They called me 'Jew boy' and 'Kike' and kept pushing me down. They wouldn't let me get back up," Hank replied.

"I am sorry to hear it. I was afraid that might be the case. You have no reason to be ashamed of your faith, you know."

"Yes, ma'am."

"And as for you, Mr. Arneson, It's good to stand up for your friends, but fisticuffs are not the best way. Use your mind, not your fists, Jimmy. You should have tried harder to talk them out of what they were doing."

"But, Mrs. —"

"No buts, young man!" Mrs. Olson remained stern. She admired him for his action, but she had a part to play.

"Yes, ma'am." Jimmy lowered his eyes.

Compassion crept in. "I will be speaking with your parents as well, Jimmy. However, you don't need to worry about it. I understand what you did and I will not be angry as I will be with Mr. and Mrs. Nelson. At the least I will need to explain that black eye of yours." A sliver of a grin grew on her face against her will.

"Thank you, Mrs. Olson," Jimmy replied. He didn't know he had a black eye and rubbed it. "How black is it?"

"Not much yet, but it will be by the time you get home!" She directed her attention to Hank. "Henry, I think I should speak with your parents, as well. We want to discourage such disrespectful behavior in our town. Gresham is a peaceful and loving community. That extends to all who join us here. Your family is a revered and respected part of this community."

"Thank you, ma'am," Hank replied, squinting into the sun, now lowering toward the horizon of flat and treeless prairie grass.

"Now, both of you run along." A determined Mrs. Olson strode back into the schoolhouse.

Jimmy, Hank, and Maria walked home. "Thanks, Jimmy. What you did for me today was, well, really nice."

"Nah, it wasn't so much. Those guys deserved it. They're just plain bullies."

"Nobody ever stood up for me before." Conflicted, Hank honestly didn't know how to feel. He was immensely grateful to Jimmy, but also ashamed he had let them bully him. "I should have stood up for myself better."

Jimmy just seemed to know. "Guys can be bad sometimes. They were big guys. You can't expect to be able to take them on by yourself."

"You did."

"Well, all I did was take on Bjorn. He's just a big, dumb ox. I could tell what he was going to do long before he did it, what with that silly cocking action with his arm." Jimmy laughed. "I think he's got the brains of a doorknob. Have you ever seen him in school when

Mrs. Olson askes him a question? It's like there's molasses flowing around in his brain, he's so slow."

Jimmy was always independently minded and irrepressible. He would not take this McBride thing lying down and neither would Hank. He determined to get even with McBride somehow.

7

TREIZENNES, FEBRUARY, 1917. The rolling hills and dales of Hampshire once again hypnotized Jimmy on the train from Gosport to Reading. He reveled in his accomplishment, repeatedly rubbing the new wings on his tunic and shining the RFC badge and lieutenant's bars on his hat. In Reading, he took a train into Paddington Station in London and from there he caught a cab to his hotel on Craven Terrace for his twenty-four-hour pass. The room was tiny, no wider than the single bed was long. But the radiator was right by the bed so it was warm in the cold night. He spent a lovely evening in the nearby Swan pub on Bayswater Road. Several folks offered to buy him drinks owing to his RFC uniform and his brand new wings. He grew to like Fuller's ales, especially London Pride!

Next morning, he caught a train to Waterloo Station and another to Folkestone for embarkation to France. He spent the night there in military housing along with many other soldiers of all kinds and ranks. As a freshly minted officer, he was provided a semi-private room, quite a luxury he felt.

On February 6, he boarded the boat to cross the Channel. It was uneventful and they soon landed at the French port of Boulogne-sur-Mer. Just one of the cattle train of arriving soldiers, he processed through the busy British Army offices and was directed to board a bus to St. Omer where he was to report to the Movement Section.

The bus was crowded with RFC officers and other ranks. It appeared everyone with the RFC went to St Omer to be sorted into their respective assignments. The ride was cold and bumpy in the rickety old bus. The muddy roads had frozen in an unending series of ruts and holes. The 25 miles took an hour or more, the bus jostling to and fro the whole way.

St. Omer was the biggest air base he had ever seen. It was a beehive of activity with all sorts of personnel scurrying around and a large airfield lined with every imaginable type of aircraft. Nissen huts, stick-built, and brick buildings were crowded around the field, all connected by a latticework of duckboard walkways to help avoid the ubiquitous mud. The air was still and pregnant with moisture and the whole base was blanketed in thin veils of fog.

The bus dropped them off outside the Movement Section building and the whole bus load of them entered in file. Four different processing desks were set up in the large foyer of the building. He found the one for officers and got in line behind a couple of other pilot officers.

The lieutenant behind the desk was most efficient and dispatched the two fellows ahead of him quickly. Jimmy reported in and gave his name and rank. He looked at his list, found his name, and told him he was assigned to 40 Squadron and a car would pick him up at around ten o'clock the next morning. He provided him with a map of the field, a building and bunk number for the officers' transient quarters, and sent him on his way.

Perfect! He had a couple of hours left to find Hank and say hello. He trotted his kit over to the transient hut and dumped it on his cot. The map indicated a block of buildings referred to as Maintenance. That sounded like a good bet for a motor pool, so he walked in that direction. Rudimentary signposts around the airfield helped him find his way.

Hank was working on the brakes of a Crossley tender when Sergeant McBride came up to him. He was gruff as always, "You, Jew boy, get up and dust yourself off. You've got a visitor out front. Keep it short, you hear? I want you back on the job here in ten minutes, no more."

"Yes, sergeant!" Hank replied. He got up off the floor and wiped the brake dust off his trousers and used some gasoline to clean the ground-in brake dust off his hands. Walking out to the front of the building, he saw Jimmy standing there looking sharp as a brand new penny!

"Jimmy!" Hank yelled as he trotted out.

"Hank!" Jimmy yelled back. He gave Hank a big bear hug and Hank hugged him back. It was grand to see his old friend. "You're filthy!" Jimmy laughed.

Hank held Jimmy out at arms' length and looked him up and down. He looked magnificent in his freshly pressed tunic and jodhpurs. "Look at you! A second lieutenant and just look at those wings! My God, it's good to see you!"

"You, too, old friend!" Jimmy replied. "Listen, can you take a break for us to go get a cup of coffee or something? I want to hear all about your life here and I have tons of stuff to share with you."

"God, how I wish I could," he said. "My boss here is a real mess. He treats me like shit and said I only had ten minutes."

"Maybe I could request it," Jimmy suggested. "I am an officer after all."

"Yeah, problem is, if I try to get around it, he'll only make my life even more miserable," he replied. "We'll just have to keep it short, I'm afraid."

"Nuts. Well, how about if we walk out to the tarmac and back to chat?"

"Okay, that should work!" They walked together towards the flight line and chatted as they went. "Do you know where you're going yet?"

"Just found out, actually. I am assigned to 40 Squadron in Treizennes, about fifteen miles down the road."

"Do you know what you'll be flying yet?" Hank asked.

"Nope, not yet," he replied. "My flight instructor at Gosport told me many of the squadrons are converting to Nieuports the British built from French designs. I think I'd like that!"

"Great!" Hank replied. "I hear they are just about the best thing there is now."

"Do you get to work on planes at all?" Jimmy asked.

"God, how I wish. I'm afraid my life is pretty miserable, Jimmy. This guy, McBride, hates Jews, so I am putting up with a bunch of rubbish."

"Want me to go knock his block off?" Jimmy was ready to take him on. Good old Jimmy.

"No, no, no. I'm afraid it's not like school back home, my friend. I'm finding ways to get on. I've made some good friends in the shop and they help out. I'll be okay, but thanks!" He didn't want a mess.

"All right, if you say so," Jimmy replied.

"Listen, I need to get back. I get off work around five o'clock. We could get some dinner together if you're around."

"Yeah, let's do that! Want to come by my hut when you're ready? I'm in the Transient Officers' Quarters."

"Will do!" Hank saluted him and they both laughed as Jimmy saluted him back.

They had a great evening together and talked each other's ears off. Hank was happy to see how well things had gone for Jimmy. They talked about Ellie's pregnancy and Meg's news from home. Hank shared his woes and Jimmy bolstered his spirits. It was great to see him. They promised to write often, but they both knew that would mean once in a long while.

Jimmy had an easy morning and a good breakfast of eggs, beans, and toast in the officers' mess hall. Around ten o'clock, he was all packed and waiting outside the Movements Section as instructed. Shortly after the hour, a Crossley staff car pulled up and Jim was greeted by Captain Hargrove. "Well, hello young fellow! You must be Lieutenant Arneson," Hargrove gushed with boatloads of personality. "I am Captain Arnold Hargrove, the adjutant of 40 Squadron. So glad you could join us. We're a bit short of pilots at the moment."

"How do you do, sir?" Jimmy replied, saluting him awkwardly.

"Very well, thank you." He returned the salute quite casually. "Grab your kit and hop in the back. We have about fifteen miles to travel to Treizennes. It will probably take us the better part of an hour with the lousy roads we have here."

Before long, they were on narrow, country roads, motoring across the peaceful French countryside. They bundled up under tartan blankets to stay warm in the cold February air and bumped their way along. The captain soon pulled out his pipe and began loading the bowl with his favorite tobacco. Occasionally, they passed a farmer walking his horse and wagon, but for the most part, the war had halted all but military traffic. Open tenders drove by carrying cargo of one kind or another, but most of the vehicles they saw were ambulances, making their way back to the hospitals in Boulogne.

"By the sounds of it, you're American, yes?" Hargrove queried. The smoke from his latest puff on the pipe floated away as he spoke.

"Yes, indeed I am, sir. I come from Minnesota."

"Minnesota, hmm. I've heard the name and have seen it mentioned here and there, but I can't say I really know anything about it. What's it like?" Captain Hargrove seemed genuinely interested.

"The part of Minnesota I come from is open prairie land, pretty much flat as far as the eye can see. It's only been settled for about 50 years or so. The Sioux Indians lived there before that. I live on a farm outside a little town called Gresham. It's made up of Norwegian immigrants for the most part. My Dad is Norwegian."

"Ah yes, of course. Hence the name, Arneson. You know, most of the chaps in the squadron end up with nicknames of some sort or other. You tend to be given your name rather than choosing it yourself, you know. I suppose you're likely to end up Arnie, or something like that. I hope you don't mind. I'm not excused from this custom myself, you know. Most of the pilots refer to me as 'Uncle,' no doubt because of my age." Jimmy found Hargrove a rare English officer who actually seemed to care about how a person felt. Most were intentionally cold and aloof.

"Oh, that's alright. My first flight instructor called me that, too. Lt. Young, he was. Nice fellow. He died the day after I met him in a training accident. It was quite sad."

"That happens quite a lot in training school, I'm told. I'm afraid it happens quite a lot here on the front line, too. Say, isn't there some sort of twin city or something in Minnesota?" Captain Hargrove had regretted his comment about death and hurried to change the subject.

The car hit a particularly large bump and jostled them both around. Uncle's cane whacked Jimmy on the knee and he jerked reflexively.

"Awfully sorry about that, old boy!"

"No problem, sir. Just a tap, really. Minneapolis and St. Paul are called the Twin Cities. There are the two biggest cities in the state, each one on opposite sides of the Mississippi River."

"The mighty Mississippi, really? I always thought it was down by the Gulf of Mexico." Hargrove looked askance at Jimmy.

Jimmy chuckled. "It is there, too. But it starts as a small river in Minnesota. It gets bigger each time another river flows into it. I've never seen it down south where it's so big."

They passed through a forest along the way. All the leaves were gone, of course. The brown branches of the trees intertwined and closed around them above their heads on their little country road.

"Well, that's interesting." Hargrove paused for moment, scratched his temple with his pipe's mouthpiece, and said, "I hope you don't mind my asking this, old boy, but there's something I am curious to know about you. Why is a young man from out on the Minnesota prairie over here in the Royal Flying Corps fighting for the English? I should have thought all you Americans were dead set against joining in on the war."

Jimmy thought a moment himself. "No, sir, I don't mind at all. That's actually something my friend, Hank, and I talked about at length before we decided to enlist through Canada. He's a motor pool mechanic at St. Omer. We had a nice visit last night."

"Well, good, glad to hear it," Uncle said.

"Thanks! You're right, I suppose most Americans want to stay out of this war. Why they feel that way though is not an easy question to answer." He paused to collect his thoughts. "How much of this should I really discuss, sir? I mean, I don't want to overstep my bounds, sir."

"Please, elaborate, lad. Don't worry, it's all right. I am indeed interested in this. Why don't the Americans join in?"

"I guess one of the reasons is most Americans are sons or daughters of parents who came to America from somewhere in Europe. Some came from England, but some also came from Germany. For instance, Wisconsin is mostly German-American. Back east, there are a lot of Irish, Italians, and Polish folks, too. We don't all line up on the same side. Instead we have factions that line up with their home countries. Granted, the Lusitania certainly pushed a lot of folks to side with the allies."

"Yes, I can see that," Uncle said. "So, you're saying there are many different opinions and that leads to a policy of staying out of it."

"In part, yes, I think so. Then, there's the whole fiercely independent aspect of Americans. We fought for our independence and now, we don't want to be holding to anyone."

Uncle asked, "Would you say the Americans resent the English over their war of independence?"

"No, I don't really think so. I think most Americans have put that aside and appreciate how much of our culture stems from the English. But, there's an independent streak that runs through Americans. We fought hard to win our country, to build it, to settle it, and to hold it together through a bloody civil war. There are many who would say we should not be pulled into something over allegiances to a country we had to fight for our freedom from."

"I see."

"Mind you, I am not saying I feel that way," he hastened to add, "I wouldn't be here if I did. I am only trying to explain how some others feel. There are also those who feel allegiance to France, for instance, as allies in our war of independence. The name Lafayette stirs strong emotions in some. Indeed, the Escadrille Américaine was just recently renamed the Lafayette Escadrille. If we do come in, it may be out of a sense of gratitude to the French, for all I know. Is this okay, sir? I mean, I'm not making you angry, am I?"

"Quite all right, my boy. Quite all right. Please, continue." Uncle puffed on his pipe as they bumped and jostled down the lane, passing a small farm house off the road. The gray stones of the fence looked like a fortification around the central farmyard. He heard some pigs grunt as they drove by. Clouds were gathering, threatening rain.

"Thank you, sir." He paused to catch his breath. "I guess the final point I would make is that America rather likes its isolation from the rest of the world. We have two big oceans on either side of us and that means we are more isolated from wars raging on other continents. It's like the English Channel only many times bigger. The separation from Europe provided by the Channel shaped and unified the English psyche. I think the same is true of the American psyche. We know no one is going to sail across the Atlantic or the Pacific to invade us. It would just be too hard. So, we tend to think about ourselves more than others. I suppose you could even go so far as to say we're rather self-centered in our views of the world events."

"I doubt you'd get much argument on that last point!" Hargrove chuckled. He had listened intently. "Well, well, you obviously have thought about this a lot. I can't say I necessarily agree with everything you just said, but I am glad to see you have given it some thought. Tell me this, then, given Americans have thus far chosen to stay out of this, why did you, James Arneson, decide to join up? And, why didn't you join the American Escadrille rather than the RFC?"

"Well, sir," he spoke with reconciliation in mind. "Please recognize I don't share the feelings of many of my countrymen on this issue. I don't think this war is any longer a European war. It's already reached to Africa, Constantinople, China, and Japan. This is a global war. I personally feel America is naïve in thinking we have a choice. And, I think our delay in joining is only costing more lives everywhere. We should be in this war decisively and with all the power and might we can muster. Only that will bring this war to a rapid conclusion and allow all of us to all live in peace once again."

"As to sides, it is abundantly clear to me we should side with the British and French. We are all three bound culturally and economically much more so than with the Germans or the Austro-Hungarian Empire.

"I am proud to be an American, but like all Americans, my roots come from elsewhere. You may be interested to learn my heritage is only half Norwegian. My mother grew up outside Cirencester on a sheep farm. So you see, I am also half English!"

Hargrove laughed heartily. "Well there you have it!"

"Yes, sir. My mother still keeps a flock of sheep on our farm back home and knits the family sweaters every year from the yarn she spins from their wool. In fact, I have a warm one in my kit I will be wearing here in the cold evenings."

"By sweater, you mean a jumper, of course."

"Ha! Yes, I mean a jumper." Jimmy smiled a broad smile, enjoying the little tease. "We are two deceptively similar cultures divided by a common language, aren't we?"

Uncle laughed as well. "You use jumper in America, too, don't you?"

"Yes we do. But it describes a type of dress worn by little girls."

"Deceptively similar indeed." Uncle grinned as he relit his pipe.

"Growing up, Mother educated us well on our English heritage. I learned quite a lot about history of England, from the Celts to the Roman occupation, Alfred the Great, and all the way up through the Boer Wars."

"Ah, the Boers," Hargrove said. "That was my war, don't you know. I took a bullet in my right leg in 1901, standing firm on a Transvaal hilltop with my brethren defending against a Boer attack. Damn those Voortrekkers after all. To this day, the blasted thing pains me. That's why I need this confounded cane all the time." He grabbed his right leg at the knee and shifted it a bit, trying to find a more comfortable position.

"As to the RFC, sir, I have long wanted to fly," Jim added.

"How did you know you wanted to fly?" Hargrove asked.

"My friend, Hank, and I have been following the evolution of flying since we were kids, starting with the Wright brothers and Glen Curtiss. We read up on all of the mechanics and aerodynamics of flight with the help of our local librarian and we built several experimental gliders themselves. We even took our motorcycle up to Minneapolis one summer and got to ride in a biplane at an exhibition there. Cost us our whole summer earnings, but it was well worth it."

"Well, I must say, I'm impressed!" Captain Hargrove acknowledged. He was very polite.

They entered a quaint little village along the road. The stone buildings clustered together along the narrow, cobblestone street. The tender slowed as they passed through. Jimmy saw a couple of Frenchmen smoking outside a tobacco shop. They paused in their conversation to stare at them as they drove by. An old Frenchwoman walked along the road with a basket full of food, probably tonight's dinner. She stopped and turned to watch them. Their lives seemed timeless, untouched by the war. But there were no young people to be seen. Maybe they were not so untouched after all.

Captain Hargrove paused to take it in as well. He tapped the tobacco out of his pipe and continued, "Look here, old boy. I have rather enjoyed hearing your views on this awful war. You're a smart young man and we are glad to have you with us. I hope you make it. You must understand, however, that some of your fellow pilots may not be the kindest towards you in the mess. They have been at it now for two and one-half years and have lost a lot of good friends. Some of them blame America's reluctance for their losses. We British count ourselves staunch allies of the United States and many resent what is perceived by some to be America's selfish hesitation, prospering economically off of our dead and wounded."

"Yes, sir. Thank you, sir." Jimmy withdrew.

"Now, look here, lad. Don't worry about it too much. They'll soon get over it once you join in. One or two tussles alongside them with the Hun and you'll be part of the side."

They passed one farmer's field after another as they bounced along the road. Jimmy couldn't tell what was grown on them, however. Most of them were ploughed over for winter. They passed through a few more villages as well as they worked their way out to the airfield.

They finally arrived at their destination about noon. Treizennes was little more than a collection of a few farmhouses near an intersection of two country roads a bit south of Aire-sur-la-Lys. A lonely old inn sat at the intersection. The aerodrome sat southeast of this intersection.

The entrance to the aerodrome was noted by a simple log frame built up and over the drive. A turnstile was manned by a private standing at arms with his Enfield resting on his shoulder. He raised his palm up to us as they approached, warning us to stop. "Halt! Who goes there?"

Captain Hargrove pulled out his ID card, as did the driver and Jim. Satisfied, the private opened the turnstile to let them in and they drove to the squadron office. Captain Hargrove and Jimmy got out and the driver pulled away. Jim followed the captain into the building and set his kitbag down on the floor. "Come with me, lad, and I'll introduce you to the squadron CO, Major Hugh McAllister."

Captain Hargrove led the way but quickly stepped aside when they entered the office so Jim could report. "Sir! Lieutenant James Arneson reporting for duty, sir!" He snapped to attention and raised his hand in salute as he announced himself.

Major McAllister returned a casual salute. "Well, hello Lieutenant Arneson. At ease. Welcome to 40 Squadron." He was a handsome, red-haired Scotsman who seemed tired to his bones. "Do you have your file and orders with you? May I see them please?"

"Yes, sir." Jim handed them to him. McAllister looked them over for a minute or two.

"How old are you, boy?" he asked.

"Twenty, sir!"

"Mmm. How many hours?" he asked without looking at him as he reviewed his files.

"Fifty-five, sir."

"Good, thank you. I see you flew Avro's, BE2's and a bit on DH2's. Good. You'll be flying an FE8 here. It is much like the DH2, a little faster but not as maneuverable. Let's see, I think number R1445 is the plane designated for you."

"FE8's, sir? I was told we would be flying Nieuport scouts." The FE8 did not have a good reputation. It was said to be just okay but badly obsolete compared to the latest German airplanes.

"We fly the planes His Majesty gives us, lieutenant. I don't need young student pilots telling me what we ought to be flying!" Major McAllister flared up quickly. Jim must have hit a sore spot.

"Yes, sir!" He snapped back to attention.

McAllister sighed a deep and weary sigh. "We all wish we could fly a more modern plane, young man. The Frogs have a marvelous plane in the Nieuport, but we must make do with what we have. At ease, please."

He relaxed a bit again. "I meant no disrespect, sir."

"Yes, I know. You'll find all of the pilots here feel the same way about their planes as you do. Their machines are a problem by themselves, let alone fighting against enemy planes that are better in almost every way. You will need to learn your plane's limits and to fly it on the edge of those limits. With a little luck, you might survive longer than most. This is war, son. War asks more of us than we can give sometimes. You must harden yourself."

"Yes, sir."

"We share this field with 43 Squadron, so don't be surprised to find them in the mess. They're good chaps. We often escort their Strutters on their observation missions." The Sopwith 1½ Strutters were reputed to be good aircraft with two seats, a machine gun for the observer in back and a Vickers firing through the propeller up front.

"We operate A, B, and C Flights here. You will by flying with A Flight commanded by Captain Roger Stevens, an outstanding pilot and officer if ever there was one. They're out on patrol now, but should be back in an hour or so. Uncle will point you to your bed in the officer's quarters. You'll be rooming with Jack Bailey, a nice young man only with us a little bit. He is also in A Flight. I'm sure you'll get on.

"Tomorrow morning, find your aircraft and take it up for familiarity. Get used to take-offs and landings. Fly no more than a mile from the airfield. We don't want to lose you on your first day. Captain Hargrove, please see the young man finds his quarters. Good day, Arneson." Major McAllister sat back down at his desk and went back to work signing papers.

Captain Hargrove walked him to the little wooden-framed shed that was to be his quarters nearby. On the way, he pointed to the large, old stone house nearby. "The chateau is our mess and senior officers' quarters. The owner lets us use it in exchange for fighting this war. However, he's not very friendly, so steer clear of him." He then showed him his room in the makeshift hut. "Here you go, lad." Have a good evening. The officers generally take in a drink or two at the mess before dinner. Dinner is at nineteen hundred hours. See you then."

"Thank you, sir!" Jimmy replied. Hargrove left him on his own, tipping his pipe to say farewell as he limped off.

Jimmy's room was sparse but functional. The stick-built hut had no insulation in the whitewashed walls so it was quite cold. It had two single beds on either side of the room with a table and chair between them to serve as a desk. A small wardrobe stood against the wall at the foot of each bed and an old, iron stove sat in the center of the room with a stack of wood next to it. A sideboard with a porcelain wash basin and pitcher on it sat next to one of the wardrobes.

He unpacked his things quickly and struck out to explore his new home. It was a large aerodrome. There were nine large, wooden hangars arranged in a rough "L" configuration in the northwest corner of the airfield. Some of these were workshops for the carpenters and riggers, but most housed a mix of Sopwiths and FE8s being worked on by the air mechanics. Each hangar had one or two aircraft inside to be worked on, but some of them looked like they could house four or five aircraft if they were angled in just right. It appeared each flight of 40 Squadron had a hangar, while four were operated by 43 Squadron. The remaining two looked like shared space for heavy maintenance, one for engine work and the other for major structural work.

Jimmy stopped for a moment to watch some riggers brushing on fresh dope to a wing they had just rebuilt. It smelled, looked and acted like paste from everything he could see. He wondered what kind of damage the plane had sustained to necessitate such effort, but moved on shortly.

He walked up to one of the unattended Sopwiths to look it over. This was an impressive aircraft. It had the new interrupter gear to synchronize the machine gun with the propeller blades so it could fire through the propeller along the line of flight of the aircraft. This was a brand new capability for the RFC. The Germans could do this a year ago in the infamous Fokker Eindeckers, but the RFC had only just come out with it on these Strutters. The pilot sat directly under the top wing and the observer sat in an open cockpit just aft of the wings. It had eponymous A-shaped struts from the fuselage to the top wing and a flexible machine gun mounted in the rear cockpit to give the observer a wide range of fire behind the plane. The Strutter would make a dangerous foe, capable of striking from either the front or to the rear.

He looked to find his appointed aircraft, R1445. He found it in the third hangar he looked in. The wings were painted solid green with tan undersides and the nacelle was painted gray. It looked quite similar to the DH2 with a bathtub-like cockpit out front with a Lewis gun pointing forward. Two spare drums of ammunition were easily accessible in a tray on the outside of the cockpit. The two long wings were situated behind the cockpit, strutted twice on each side. They looked a bit longer than the DH2's. The ailerons were longer than he expected. He hoped this might improve maneuverability. The short fuselage held a large petrol tank behind the cockpit and in front of the rearward facing rotary engine in the back. He was pleased to see it had the more powerful 110 horsepower Le Rhône engine rather than the earlier 80 horsepower version. A large, four-bladed pusher propeller was surrounded on both sides by an open-strut "cage" of tail booms that extended about ten feet back from the trailing edges of the wings to converge at the empennage assembly. The rudder was painted in the standard RFC red, white, and blue stripes. A massive number of cables held the airframe together tightly. The rigger would be awfully busy keeping this plane taught, balanced, and trimmed properly.

Two crewmen were working on just that, tightening a turnbuckle on the left wing as he walked up to introduce himself. "How do you do? I am Lieutenant Arneson. I am to fly this aircraft, apparently."

The two young men snapped to attention. "Yes, sir! How do you do, sir? I am Air Mechanic Wilson and this here is Private Stewart."

"Please, at ease," he offered immediately. "Do you mind if I climb in?"

"Please do, sir," Wilson replied.

He climbed into the little cockpit and imagined flying it. The instrumentation seemed somewhat standard. It had a compass, tachometer, altimeter, magneto switch, turn/slip indicator, air flow control, fuel flow control, and the blip switch atop the control stick. "I'll take it up tomorrow for some orientation flights."

"Very good, sir. She'll be ready for you first thing, sir." Wilson was eager to help. He seemed a good fellow. Stewart didn't say a word, but Jimmy just thought he was a bit shy.

He climbed out and thanked them both. "Do the two of you maintain only this aircraft?"

"No, sir. We have three others we try to keep going. It's not always easy, you see. Parts are hard to come by so we sometimes have to rob one aircraft to keep the others serviceable. It keeps us on our toes."

"Well, thank you both. I look forward to flying it tomorrow morning." He excused himself and started back to his room.

8

TREIZENNES, FEBRUARY, 1917. On Jimmy's way back to his hut, he heard the distant sound of aircraft engines so he stopped to take it in. From a faint buzz off to the southeast, the sound of their engines grew like an approaching swarm of angry bees. This must be A Flight back from patrol. The dots first visible grew in size to reveal two formations, two Sopwiths and four FE8s.

The two Sopwiths lined up first for a straight-in approach while the FE8s executed a lazy 360-degree turn in single file to the left. By the time they came around, they were roughly line astern and the Sopwiths were taxiing toward their hangars.

The FE8s glided in, blipping their engines intermittently. The pilots looked exposed out in front of their wings compared to the Strutter pilots tucked away under their wings. They taxied up in front of the hangar housing his bird. As they approached, the ground crew ran out to meet them and get their aircraft turned around into position on the ready line.

The pilots climbed out of their cockpits and began peeling off their flying suits, aided by the ground crew. Two of them hurriedly inspected their wings and control surfaces, apparently looking for damage they had incurred. They gathered at one of the center aircraft and walked to the hangar together.

He joined them and introduced himself, saluting the stocky, rugged looking captain among them. "How do you do, gentlemen?" he offered. "My name is Jim Arneson. I believe I am the new member of your flight. Are you Captain Stevens by chance?"

"Hello Arneson," Captain Stevens said. "Tag along and listen in while we debrief. These three are Lieutenants Phillips, Campbell, and Bailey."

"Hullo," they said in unison. They walked to the back of the hangar.

"Alright, let's have each of you describe what you witnessed in the fight today." Captain Stevens was concerned about what had happened, but it was apparent no one knew the whole picture.

"The sky was full of Huns out to kill us. That's what I saw." Phillips was grimly sardonic. "They fell on us from above, dove straight through us and took out Exeter on their way. They zoomed and came round to the right for another pass at us from in front."

Campbell added, "I would say they were a good two thousand feet above us and behind us. They had picked up a lot of speed when they hit. There were six of them, I believe. I don't think Exeter knew what hit him. One of them went after the Strutters, but I think he was hit by their gunners. I thought I saw a thin stream of smoke trailing him as he dove eastwards."

"Sorry, sir. I was pretty confused the whole time." Bailey seemed junior compared to the rest. "I saw them dive past us and saw them zoom. I spent most of my time just trying to stay with Campbell."

"That's okay, Bailey. That's what I told you to do." Stevens softened a bit. "I have to say we're bloody lucky they left after their second pass. I don't know why they would do that, however. Any ideas?"

"Time for a Schnapps back home, I suppose," Phillips said.

"Petrol?" Campbell offered.

"Yes, I suppose. Very well. You lot get off from here. We'll have a dawn patrol tomorrow so don't get too hammered in the mess tonight." Stevens released them. "Arneson, stick around."

Phillips, Campbell, and Bailey headed back to their quarters.

"Fresh out of flying school, yes?" Stevens asked.

"Yes, sir. Gosport," Jimmy replied.

"What types and how many hours?" It was a question almost everyone asked straight out.

"Fifty-five hours total. Rumpetys, Avros, BE2s, and a DH2 for a bit towards the end." He figured the short version would do here.

"The DH2 experience will serve you well on the FE8. Let's go up for an orientation flight. We have a little light left. I want you to get in your plane at least once before joining us on patrol tomorrow morning. We'll just circle the field a few times and do a few take offs and landings. Then, I shall want to see what you know."

"Major McAllister had recommended I do that in the morning, sir," he interjected.

"That was before young Lord Exeter went west on us today." Stevens replied.

"Was he really a lord, sir?" he asked.

"No, we just called him that. However, you will find aristocracy in the RFC. Second and third sons of barons and earls have found the RFC to be the new glamour service now that the cavalry has become obsolete. Some carry with them a higher sense of honor and duty than the rest of us, but some also think they'll get a relatively light go of it. We may not lose as many sheer numbers of men as the PBI, but I would venture to say their odds of making it through this war are better than ours."

"PBI, sir?" Jim interrupted.

"Poor Bloody Infantry." He went on. "We seem to be losing close to one out of every two pilots. New pilots like you aren't lasting long. Young Exeter was only with us two weeks. I am growing weary of writing so many letters home. So, listen to what I tell you. I will try to help you survive, but you must do your best and you must not question my authority, my direction, nor my wisdom. Do you hear me?" Captain Stevens was earnest in his appeal.

"Yes, sir!" he replied.

Stevens signaled Wilson to roll 1445 out and he walked over with Jimmy. "You'll find these aircraft similar to the DH2. It has a bit more power but it's not as light on the controls. Left turns take a determined stick. And don't forget your rudder on takeoff. The crew will need to steer you during taxi. These crates have little control on the ground. It's calm this afternoon so we'll head straight out. Watch for my signal."

Stevens headed over to his aircraft and mounted up while Jimmy did the same in his. He donned just the flying coat, helmet and goggles as it would be a short, low-altitude flight. Wilson and Jimmy got the engine started and then Wilson and Stewart shepherded him out from the ready line.

Captain Stevens and his crewman had done the same. He raised his hand and pointed it forward to signal take off. He hesitated just a moment at idle before powering up so he would follow him.

Jimmy's adrenaline started pumping as he released the blip switch and let loose the engine at full power. The plane built speed quickly. The tail rose almost immediately. It definitely craved right rudder to stay straight but before long, he was airborne. He hunkered down in his little cockpit to ward off the wind stream hitting him dead on. This was a damned cold February.

The controls did feel rather like the DH2. They didn't seem quite as nimble, but the plane was responsive to his touch. They climbed to six hundred feet and turned left. It was indeed a bit resistant to turning to the left. She flew like she always wanted to go to the right.

They came around a 270-degree turn to the left and he followed Captain Stevens in a glide slope to a rolling landing followed by an immediate take off.

This time, he expanded the circuit and turned clockwise so he could get a feel for the immediately surrounding landscape while he practiced his right turns. The whole area was agricultural with a variety of farm fields, all plowed under or wild grass for the winter. The fields seemed small compared to Minnesota, but he guessed that was to be expected. Southwest Minnesota was wide open prairie. France was old and everything was smaller.

They executed another touch-and-go landing and this time climbed to the left for some time. He had heard they needed almost twenty-five minutes to climb to six thousand feet. As they climbed, he could see farther out, but not enough to make out the front.

After they made it to about thirty-five hundred feet, Captain Stevens started a series of rather sharp maneuvers, obviously expecting him to follow suit. First, they did steep turns and sudden reversals. Then, they did some wingovers and even rolled the airplanes. It grew hard to stay on his tail as he increased the suddenness and severity of his movements. It was almost like he was trying to lose Jimmy on purpose. He caught on. Of course, he was trying to lose him, just as an enemy aircraft would try to throw him off.

Stevens finally did lose him. He dove and looped. Jimmy followed, but he had not built up enough airspeed so he stalled into a spin before he peaked. By the time he had recovered out of the spin, the captain was nowhere to be found. Jimmy looked all around but could not find him.

Then Stevens was on his tail, wagging his machine around aggressively. He charged him until Jimmy swore his undercarriage was going to take his tail off. "Of course, James, you fool," Jimmy said to himself out loud. It was his turn to evade him if he could. Jimmy banked, slipped, skidded, reversed his turns, and even did a split-S, but Stevens stayed glued to him. Nothing he tried did any good. After giving it his best effort for a few minutes, he just levelled out and Stevens flew up beside him. He gave Jimmy a thumbs-up and headed back to the airfield.

After they landed, Stevens came up to him for a chat. "You did okay, boy. You have plenty to learn, but at least you know how to handle your airplane. I am going to put you on Phillips' wing tomorrow. No matter what happens, I want you to stay glued to him just like when we were playing around upstairs. It can get horribly chaotic if we get in a dogfight, so your best bet is to follow a good pilot. He is a smart-arsed Cassandra, but a good pilot. Very well, go wash up for dinner." Whew! He had made it through his first test okay.

B Flight was getting ready for take-off as Jimmy walked back to the hut. When he got there, Jack Bailey was sitting on his bed reading a book by the light of the oil lamp. He looked up, "Welcome, James! I see we are to be roommates. How did it go with the captain?"

"Well, I think it went okay, thanks. I hadn't expected to chase him all around the sky, but I'm glad I did. I got a good feel for the plane. I even managed to stay with him for most of the time! Oh and, please, do call me Jim. James is what my mother calls me when I am in trouble!"

"Fair enough!" Jack was friendly and unassuming. He had a shock of strawberry blonde hair sitting atop his head with tightly tapered sides, a big, toothy smile, and bright blue eyes. He seemed about 20 or so. As they chatted, Jim learned he came from Salisbury, where his father ran a shoe store. Jack had repaired shoes right alongside his father in his teenaged years. He had got bitten by the flying bug in much the same way Hank and he had. He attended an exhibition north of Salisbury and had a chance to fly in an early airplane. It was all he had wanted to do ever since.

At Jack's suggestion, they dressed for dinner and headed to the mess in the chateau. Jimmy had much to learn about the pomp and circumstance of the officer corps.

The pilots gathered in the downstairs parlor of the chateau. The orderlies supplied drinks for all from behind a makeshift bar in one of the room. Jimmy had ale. He still wasn't used to all the alcohol consumed. The strongest drink he had at home was hard cider. He had grown to enjoy a good English ale, but some of this stuff really packed a wallop. Whiskey seemed to be a favorite.

They joined Phillips and Campbell, who were already there. "Well, well, well. If it isn't the newest grist for mill, young Arneson. You appear to have survived your orientation whipping, I trust?" Phillips had gotten a head start on them.

"Yes, thank you." Jimmy grinned at Phillips' choice of words. "It caught me off guard at first. For the life of me, I don't know how he got on my tail. I followed him into a loop and then he just disappeared!"

"Yes, we've all been there. I say, you talk funny. Are you an American?" Phillips asked.

"Why yes, I am. I'm from Minnesota. I enlisted in Canada, however." He had never thought of being American as a negative or something to be ashamed of. And yet, Phillips seemed to think so rather strongly.

Phillips eyed him over again, this time with disdain. "Bloody Hell, a Yank to boot. Trenchard must be scraping the bottom of the barrel to take in Americans. Still fighting the Indians out there, aren't you, Yank?"

"I'm surprised you're not wearing your six guns and a ten-gallon hat," Campbell snickered. Jimmy drew an instant dislike to Campbell. He seemed in it for himself, and the type of guy that would pull the legs off a fly just for fun.

"We haven't had any trouble with the Sioux for 50 years now." They just smirked at him. He began to wonder what was going on here.

Phillips continued. "What types of planes have you flown?"

Jim took a sip of his ale. "We flew Maurice Farman Shorthorns at Farnborough to begin with. They were quite difficult. At Gosport, I flew an Avro 504, a BE2, and a DH2."

"How many hours on the DH2?" Phillips was a bit more interested.

"Only a few," he replied. "I learned a few more acrobatics and I was able to try a little gunnery practice in it. It was hard to aim the gun and fly the plane at the same time."

"Right, well the FE8 is about the same as you now know. We tried the swivel gun at first as well, but now we lock them in place and aim the plane. How many hours total?" Phillips was doing all the talking. Bailey stood attentively but quiet. Campbell feigned disinterest.

"I'm up to fifty-five now, fifteen or so on the Farman and the rest split between the others." He hoped it might be acceptable.

"Right. Well, you'll soon be tripling that or else fertilizing some farmer's fields." Then he said, "I'll wager you'll be dead in two weeks."

"What do you mean?" he asked.

"Quite simple, really," Phillips said. "You barely know how to fly, let alone fight. The Hun's plane is faster, more heavily armed, more maneuverable than yours, and he fervently wants to kill you. Save us all the bother, Yank, and don't unpack your kit."

Jim was growing weary of this guy and about to counter with words he probably shouldn't say when Uncle called them to dinner in the dining room upstairs. He sat next to Jack toward the tail of the table. New pilots start at the tail and work their way up, apparently. It seemed an awfully formal affair for the eighteen of them. Major McAllister welcomed them all with a toast to their health. He followed this with another toast to Lieutenants Exeter and Barnes from C Flight, who had also been lost that day. Raising his glass to the pairs of boots occupying their chairs, he quickly moved on. To Jim's surprise, he introduced Jim to the squadron as the newest member of A Flight. When he mentioned he was an American from Minnesota, there was a noticeable groan from the table with much murmuring. Jim had never felt so affronted by a group of people in all his life! What was it about Americans these people were so put off about? Captain Hargrove had warned him of this, but still, it hurt to the quick.

Captain Hargrove quickly rose to add his own words to the introduction. "Gentlemen, I had the great privilege of riding with young Lieutenant Arneson from Boulogne to our comfy little home here this morning. I know many of you resent America's hesitation to join the war, and we have all heard the accusations of America profiteering while British and French soldiers die every day. However, I want you to know, whatever your feelings about

America's position may be, this young man, who is half-English from the Cotswolds I might add, has joined us in our fight voluntarily of his own accord because in his heart it is the right thing to do. He has an impressive understanding of the situation and, if you give him half a chance, I believe you will find him to be an excellent addition to this esteemed body. I urge you to welcome him into our fold."

Jim was indeed honored by Uncle's remarks. He hoped it made some difference in the minds of this surprisingly hostile gathering. He was met with mumbled whispers.

They sat back to dine on a wonderful pork roast dinner with corn and potatoes. They even had a delicious apple tart dessert accompanied by brandy. He had a few sips but feared intoxication. His brave brethren shared no such concerns.

Jimmy retired early from the party that followed dinner. He did not feel like getting drunk the way so many seemed in a hurry to do. Why did they do that, he wondered?

9

TREIZENNES, FEBRUARY, 1917. Phillips had told Jimmy he'd be dead in two weeks. Jimmy thought to himself, "What kind of jerk says that to a new pilot?" It had disrupted his sleep all night and he dwelled on it as he prepared for his first patrol in the cold, pre-dawn darkness of France. He had that jittery feeling like he'd drunk too much coffee and his gurgling stomach betrayed his anxiety. Phillips' comments worried him, but also angered him to defiance and a determination to beat the odds. He was a naïve, Minnesotan farm boy about to fly straight into the maelstrom.

"Steady, sir!" Wilson called out. Jimmy wet his hand with frosty dew as he rested it against the wing to steady himself and he wanted to pee even though he had just emptied his bladder. Wilson and Stewart each hitched up a leg of his crotch-high, sheepskin, fug boots.

"These things are so warm, I'll melt!" he exclaimed.

"Trust me, sir," Wilson said, "You'll be mighty glad you have them at eight thousand feet!" No doubt he was right. Jimmy's nostrils stung in the cold air and his breath crystallized here at ground level, but he knew it would be even colder at altitude.

Steps crunching in the grass signaled Captain Stevens' approach. Stern and weary, he was impatient with others like a teacher tired of unruly children. "Lieutenant Arneson, to recap this morning's briefing, we will head due east to the front, patrol south to Arras, and retrace our steps home. Campbell will fly echelon on my left with Bailey on his left. Phillips will fly on my right and you fly echelon on his right. We'll circle up to fifteen hundred and form up. You got that?"

"Yes, sir!" Jimmy replied.

"Stay glued to Phillips and keep your bearings so you can get back on your own if you have to, okay?"

"Yes, sir."

"I expect Archie to find us, Arneson. He always does. Try to ignore him. He rarely hits anything. If you spot the enemy, waggle your wings and point at them to show the rest of us, then follow my lead. Any questions?"

"No, sir!"

"Good. We'll be off shortly." He slipped on his leather flying helmet as he walked away to his plane.

"Right, lads, shall we continue?" Jimmy tried miserably to sound nonchalant, but his stomach was turning somersaults. Wilson and Stewart glanced knowingly at each other, but politely ignored it.

They completed the pre-flight inspection together, including operation of the Lewis gun in the front of the FE8's cockpit, storage of extra ammunition drums, stick, rudder, ailerons, elevators, rigging, oil level, and fuel level. All was well. "She's a good ship, sir." Wilson was proud of his work. The plane belonged to him more than its pilot.

"Why do you suppose we always refer to planes in the feminine?" Jimmy pondered out loud. "Is it because we ride them or is it because they carry us?"

Wilson and Stewart chuckled as they helped Jimmy don his flying gear. First, they held up his heavy, knee-length, fleece-lined flying coat for him and buckled the belt for him because he couldn't bend his arms enough to do it easily himself. Next came the thick gloves, more like mittens than gloves with only the thumb and index finger singled out. Finally, they slipped on the fur-lined, balaclava flying helmet and goggles. He felt like a stuffed animal. "How am I supposed to fly with all this stuff on?

Wilson chuckled again as he gave Jimmy the once over from head to toe. "Seeing as the FE8's a pusher, sir, we can't have any loose items hanging out. Otherwise, they might fall off and hit your propeller." The antiquated and ungainly FE8 had its engine behind the pilot with the propeller facing to the rear. This resulted in the propeller pushing the aircraft through the air rather than pulling it as in a tractor arrangement. To make room for the propeller, a wire-braced, drag-inducing, cage of tail-boom struts connected the empennage to the trailing edges of the wings.

Stewart supported Jimmy as he climbed into the cockpit—right hand on the inboard strut, right foot on top of the left wheel, left foot into the fuselage stirrup, left hand on the cockpit rim, right foot over and into the cockpit, and left foot into the cockpit, all the while avoiding the control cables running from the nose to the trailing edge strut. He felt like a polar bear squishing down into a little gray bathtub as he squirmed into his seat.

"Ready to start, sir?" Wilson asked.

"Ready!"

"Right, then." Wilson bent over and side-stepped into the tail-boom cage to begin the start-up sequence. "Switch off, petrol on, sir?"

"Switch off, petrol on!"

"Suck in!" He sat as he rotated the propeller through two full revolutions to inject some petrol into each cylinder.

"Switch on!" he called out.

"Switch on!" Jimmy called back after flipping the magneto switch into the firing position.

"Contact!" Wilson yelled, and Jimmy responded in kind. Wilson cranked the propeller with all his might. The magneto fired and the engine sputtered to a rough start with a burst of smoky castor oil. Wilson jumped away from the propeller and crawled out of the tail-boom cage. Jimmy adjusted the air and fuel mixture to keep her running and then pressed the blip switch periodically to keep her from rolling away. Because the FE8 had no brakes, Wilson joined Stewart at the wing tips on opposite sides to hold the plane back.

Phillips, Campbell, and Bailey did the same with their ground crews. Dawn broke as they watched for the signal from Captain Stevens. When he raised his hand and motioned forward, Jimmy yelled, "Chocks away!" Out they went from either side with a tug of the ropes by Wilson and Stewart and the plane trundled away to the west.

The tail rose and she sped up quickly. With a little right rudder Jimmy teased the stick back slightly to lift her into the air. "She'll fly on her own if you let her," he remembered from his flight instructor and resisted the temptation to pull back too much for fear she would stall. He had seen too many cadets lose their lives at Farnborough doing that.

More powerful than the old Maurice Farman, his FE8 lifted up quickly. He felt the odd sensation of weight in his tailbone that always came with take-off, as his organs pressed down on his behind. The Effie immediately crabbed to the right in the cross-wind. He straightened her out with a little left rudder and right aileron at first, but then let her go to crab her way up.

Airborne, the wind took charge and the Effie came alive under his hand. His soul took flight as two dimensions became three, detached from the flat world below. Jimmy felt the air through the stick and rudder in a constant, three-dimensional contest with the wind as each of his corrections was met by another shift in the air currents. His spirits rose with the plane as he breathed in a big breath of fresh air.

He took up the rear in a single-file, climbing spiral to the right to get to fifteen hundred feet. The sun climbed with him. The faint aroma of farm animals below him filled his nostrils and he looked down to see pigs and chickens in the farmyard as he passed over it. Flying a pusher meant no engine smells invaded his senses. By the time he came around over them again, they were half the size. By the third circle, they were little more than dots and the sun showed itself full and bright on the horizon.

The flight formed up ahead of Jimmy. He leaned his mixture to maximum revolutions and settled in behind and to the right of Phillips to complete the V formation as instructed. Once he positioned himself to Captain Stevens' satisfaction, they headed east in a zig-zag fashion, climbing steadily. Their ties to earth faded. They became creatures of the air, bobbing about on the winds.

Jimmy surveyed the broadening expanse of territory as they climbed and tried to pick out landmarks he could remember to retrace his steps home. Canals, rivers, towns, church steeples, bridges, roads, and distinctive copses of wood all helped. Unfortunately, he soon found himself overloaded and began to lose track. He could only hope to remember when he needed to.

They flew up through the first layer of wispy clouds and a fierce onslaught of frigid air blasted Jimmy's face. The tiny, makeshift windscreen attached to the Lewis gun provided his only shield from the cold headwind. He yearned for an engine in front of him to provide some warmth. The heavy flying gear made perfect sense now, absolutely mandatory to avoid frostbite. He thought he knew cold from Minnesota winters, but flying at seventy-five miles per hour at eight thousand feet over France in February was a daunting experience.

He began to make out the front lines ahead of them through breaks in the clouds. A vast, grotesque, brown scar marred an otherwise serene patchwork of verdant fields and woods. It stretched north to south as far as he could see. Below him, Frankenstein scars of trenches stitched the mudscape. Barely discernable from their altitude, men scurried like little ants from crater to crater and puffs of brown mud blossomed periodically as artillery shells exploded. In the distance, ground and air faded together into hazy blue nothingness. The hairs on the back of his neck rose in apprehension. That brown strip of ground had known so much death it felt sinister, like the fields of hell spread out below them.

Captain Stevens levelled off and the others followed suit. The little, five-plane formation flew east beyond the trenches and turned southwards about half a mile east of the front line.

Boom! Boom! Bang! Explosions erupted all around their flight. Archie greeted them with a hail of explosions. Boom! Jimmy's left eardrum pounded from the concussion, his eyes blinked reflexively, and his nostrils stung with cordite. His airplane bucked out of control, jerking the stick from his hand. He grabbed the stick to right his plane. Bang! Before he could regain control, another shell exploded. Boom! Any one of the dirty, brown blasts of shrapnel and smoke might blow him out of the sky. It was like large fireworks missiles exploding in his face. Bang! His head recoiled as his plane rocked violently to the left, almost colliding with Phillips. Boom! Whizz! Shrapnel pierced his wings. Fear choked him as he gasped for air and his heart raced. The explosions came so fast he couldn't think straight. Bang! The randomness terrified him.

The captain changed course and altitude abruptly. They all mimicked his movements, maintaining enough separation for each of them to bounce around in reaction to the shell bursts. The change in direction and height threw Archie's aim off and it took him a couple of minutes to adjust. Jimmy was relieved to see the explosions below and behind them. Captain Stevens changed course and altitude again in a minute, staying ahead of Archie's ability to adjust his aim each time. "Thank heavens!" Jimmy gasped aloud.

After a few minutes of this maneuvering, they flew out of the range of the battery tracking them and the shell bursts subsided. They flew on southwards on their patrol. Jimmy tried to look around constantly as he'd been told. He craned his neck to look to the left, right, back, front, up, and down searching for enemy aircraft but saw none. The heavy, fur-lined balaclava and the thick goggles made it all but impossible to see anywhere but straight forward. The bright sun rising in the east blinded him. All the while, he tried to stay in formation, fend off the freezing cold, and pay attention to where they were so he could head home alone if needed. Overwhelmed, his heart pounded and his hands shook with fear an enemy aircraft might dive on him at any time and shoot him out of the sky.

Five or ten minutes passed by like this and another Archie battery targeted them. They repeated their evasive tactics and flew beyond Archie's range as before. Still, Jimmy was scared out of his wits when the anti-aircraft fire first erupted all around them at once. This was so dramatically different from the serenity of his training flights over England. Death hammered constantly.

The whole flight banked sharply in front of him to the right. As the rightmost plane at the rear of the formation, Jimmy thought he might collide with them and banged his stick to the right and pulled it back to turn as tightly as he could. Captain Stevens dove steeply away to the west. They descended down through the clouds at four thousand feet and continued down to two thousand feet before they levelled off.

Ground fire erupted all around them as they crossed over the trenches. Jimmy could see soldiers scurrying around muddy shell holes. Many trained their rifles on the flight. Tracer bullets streamed toward him from a machine gun emplacement. A bullet zipped through his right wing. The fire of bullets died down as they crossed over no man's land and passed over their own trenches. The round, bowl-like, Tommy helmets in the trenches were a welcome sight. Thankfully, they were over the trenches quickly and the muddy ground below transitioned to dormant farm fields.

They turned north-northwest. They appeared to be headed for home, but why so early and dramatically? Jimmy must have missed something, but he saw no reason.

The ground below was completely foreign to him, a continuous patchwork of fallow farm fields pocked with shell holes. Occasional roads had destroyed villages at their crossings. They continued for twenty minutes before they began a gradual descent. Jimmy knew that meant they were close to home so he started looking for landmarks but remained hopelessly lost.

The town and the copse of woods Captain Stevens said to look for came into view. True to form, they approached from the southeast to land into the prevailing wind. The flight changed over to line astern formation with Jimmy in the rear as they flew over the airfield. Each pilot peeled off to the left for individual 360-degree turns for landing. Jimmy came in last.

As he came around and settled into his approach, he adjusted the air pressure to reduce engine speed, pressed the blip switch down repeatedly, and felt with his stick for the proper angle of attack to slow his airspeed and maintain a steady glide slope in the bumpy air. He was tempted to hold the blip switch down longer, but Wilson had warned him against it to avoid an engine fire when he let up. Gradually, the ground approached as he jockeyed his stick and rudder to keep her lined up. What an odd sensation it was sitting out in front of the aircraft, like sitting in a bathtub on the end of a diving board. He gently nosed up for the flare but miscalculated and hit the ground too hard. Up she bounced. He had to quickly adjust his attitude to avoid a stall and she came down again for another bump before settling down. "Whew, I'm down!" he said to himself. The tail skid dug in to slow her down but it hit a rock and he almost nosed over into the ground.

Playing the blip switch and adjusting the fuel mixture to an idle, Jimmy taxied into the hangars. Captain Stevens was dismounting as he approached. Wilson and Stewart were waiting for him and helped him get his plane turned around into the ready position in line with the others. He was relieved to lean out the mixture, switch the engine off, and catch his breath. "Thank God!" he whispered to himself.

"Welcome home, Lieutenant Arneson!" Wilson helped him unbuckle his harness and step down to the ground. "Have a good flight, sir?"

"Why yes, thank you," Jimmy said. They chuckled, knowing full well he was lying. His trembling hands and wobbly legs undermined his attempts to make light of his fears. With their help, he removed his goggles, helmet, flying coat and fug boots. "Glad to be home though!"

"Yes, sir. Stewart and I will see to her now, sir. I expect you'll be heading to the ready room in Paddington to debrief with the captain now, sir." The hangars were all affectionately named after London train stations, including Waterloo, Victoria, Marylebone, and Charing Cross. Having sent Jimmy on his way, they both set to work to refuel the aircraft.

He wobbled his way along and gradually got his land legs under him again after having flown in the freezing cold for so long. It was only about eight thirty in the morning but he was starving. A hot cup of tea sounded awfully good.

Phillips led the short walk to Paddington, A Flight's hangar. Campbell walked behind him while Bailey and Jimmy walked together after them both. The duckboards ended at the tarmac and the dew on the grass wet the toes of their boots. A fine mist lay softly on the expansive grass of the aerodrome, but the sun shone down through breaks in the clouds to burn it off. A dove cooed in the trees.

An FE8 sat in Paddington with the engine removed, its hoses, tubes, and cables sticking out of the back like squiggly twigs. The smell of castor oil, grease, and petrol hung thickly in the air. They walked to the rear of the hangar. The back corner of Paddington served as their ready room. It had the perfunctory accommodations of a school room with a briefing board and a table with a few chairs around it. This morning, they stood around the briefing board. It showed a large map of the area. Captain Stevens was waiting for them there.

"You damned near pranged your kite on landing, boy," Captain Stevens hissed at Jimmy.

Phillips and Campbell snickered, their skepticism reinforced. Phillips piled on, "Damned Yanks, all bluster and no substance."

"Arneson, you need more practice," Stevens continued. "Give me at least five good landings this afternoon. And spend some more time familiarizing yourself with the countryside. Now, how many aircraft did you spot on patrol today?"

"Why, none, sir." Jimmy realized he should have seen some, but he had not. He was too frightened by Archie and struggling to stay in formation.

"God's truth! You must learn to spot the enemy before they spot you!" he barked. "Most chaps go down never knowing what hit them.

For your information, we flew over two enemy observation planes by Béthune and almost got bounced by a flight of six Albatros scouts waiting up in the sun. Did you seriously not see them? Didn't I tell you to keep your head on a swivel?" Jimmy felt like a teenager being scolded by his father again.

He stammered, "Y-yes, sir! I mean, no, sir! I did not see them. I looked up to the sun but I was blinded."

"Yes, well, next time, close one eye, put your thumb up right over the sun and look all around it. That may help you survive another day."

"Sir, I could have taken one of those observation aircraft easily while the rest of you headed home," Campbell chimed in. He was chasing his score.

"I will not tolerate solo bounty hunting in my flight, Campbell!" Stevens knew the limitations of the FE8 all too well. Singletons often ended up as Albatros fodder. "Now, get on with you – all of you." They all left and headed back to their huts.

Bailey walked along with Jimmy. "Don't worry, old boy. You'll quickly get the hang of it. He would have chewed me out if you hadn't been there. There's always something to learn."

"Thanks, Jack. I'm glad I could be of service!" Jimmy walked back to his hut with his tail between his legs. This day was not turning out the way he had hoped. This was so different from training school, where he did everything right. Today, he felt he had done everything wrong.

10

TREIZENNES, FEBRUARY, 1917. Bang! Bang! Bang! The dilapidated door shuddered on its loose hinges. "Lieutenant Arneson! Lieutenant Arneson! Time to rise and shine, sir," the orderly bellowed.

Jimmy startled awake. Before he could reply, the orderly moved on to the next hut to wake his neighbor. Gathering his senses, he realized he must have slept after all, but he certainly didn't feel like it. He lay awake all night bursting with anticipation for this morning.

It was forecasted to be a decent flying day, the first after three days of bad weather. February had not been cooperative thus far. Featureless gray skies brought snow, sleet, or cold rain most days. It may not have been as cold as Minnesota in February, but it still kept them grounded. At least the downtime allowed him to get his journal up to date.

He threw on his pants and ran shivering out to the latrine, clattering on the duckboards. Puddles from yesterday's rain lay half-frozen alongside the walkway. The moist dawn air raised goose bumps on his forearms and the fresh morning sun peeked through the clouds, painting the frosty grass with bright yellow rays. Hurrying back, he washed up in his room, shaved, and donned his RFC uniform complete with starched-collar shirt, tie, tunic, muffler, breeches, and puttees.

The broken cloud layers promised a good day for flying, but made for a chilly morning. He walked briskly across the silvery grass to the officers' mess in the chateau and was greeted there by the Captain Hargrove. "Good morning, young man. Ready for another outing are you?" he asked, resting part of his weight on his cane as he patted down the tobacco in his pipe. Everybody was a young man to him, even Major McAllister. Uncle was now well past fighting age, but duty to King and Country called him to serve yet again and so here he was, handle-bar moustache and all.

"Am I ever, Uncle!" he replied.

"Well, have yourself a good breakfast and a cup of hot, strong tea. Nothing like a good cuppa to get the blood flowing on these cold mornings, eh, old boy?

"I'm starving!"

"Yes, well the rest of A Flight is in there. Sit yourself down with the chaps. Breakfast is on its way," he said.

He walked in and the aroma of bacon, warm beans, and freshly toasted bread welcomed him. He stepped over to the table and joined Phillips, Campbell, and Bailey, already there. "Good morning, gentlemen!"

"Morning, Yank." Matthew Phillips took a sip of tea and looked him up and down with a skeptical, raised eyebrow. "Are you ready to meet your maker?"

"I always am, sir. Are you?" He had yet to figure out if Phillips was merely being sardonic or if he was serious, or some mix of the two. He had learned at dinner on his first night here that Phillips did not care for Americans, whom he resented for not being in this war yet.

"We shall see. We have our briefing in a minute so don't take long." Phillips shoved a forkful of beans into his mouth. From the way he fisted his fork, Jim knew he came from sturdy working stock.

Campbell on the other hand had a cocky, disdainful air about him. He carried his nose a little too high for his blood. "You'll do well to listen to your senior officers, Arneson. You may think you know how to fly a plane, but I guarantee that you don't know the first thing about flying in combat. If you are lucky enough to survive your first few patrols, we may share some pointers with you. However, you will have to prove yourself first." It seemed a little odd to get this from Campbell, who didn't look to be any older than Bailey or himself.

"Damned Yankees think they know everything," Phillips muttered. "Let's hope you improve on the dismal performance you gave on your first patrol."

Talbot, the mess orderly, brought out a steaming mug of tea and a plate of bacon and hot beans piled high on thick toast. "Here you are, sir." Jimmy tucked in mightily, famished.

Jack was the friendly one of the bunch. He must have risen this morning on his own and dressed quietly to not wake him. "It should be a good day for flying, anyway. It will be cold though. These FE8s don't offer much protection from that."

Jimmy shoveled some beans in his mouth. It was a simple breakfast, but it was hot and it tasted good, especially with the rasher of bacon mixed in.

"Look at him," Campbell quipped. "He doesn't even know how to use a fork." He had not yet bothered to follow the English custom of holding the fork with the tines facing down. He had always used it the other way around back home. It just seemed to make more sense to him unless he was stabbing a piece of meat. The English, however, never varied, even when piling food up on the back of it. He just ignored Campbell and kept shoveling. He had always been one to do what made sense to him rather than following a rule just for the sake of following a rule.

"What are we going to do today, do you know?" Bailey asked Phillips.

"Photo reconnaissance escort, I think. The captain will tell us, of course."

"I wonder if we'll see any Huns today. I should love to add another kill to my record." Campbell had shot down an observation plane the week before, giving him two victories on his record.

"Let's get going." Phillips, Bailey, and Campbell rose from their chairs. Jim grabbed a slurp of tea and followed suit.

Three consecutive days of bad weather without any observation of the front lines meant they needed to escort two Sopwith 1½ Strutters on their patrol to look for changes up and down the front line from here to Douai. B and C Flights were to do the same with other Strutters later in the day. They were soon on their way.

The Sopwiths levelled off at three thousand feet with Stevens, Campbell and Bailey flying close escort just above and behind them. Phillips and Jim flew a thousand feet higher in reserve in case they got bounced. They flew in and out of the remaining clouds at that altitude. A thousand feet above them, the clouds formed a solid gray overcast. To the west, they could see darkening storm clouds working their way toward them. Self-doubt crept in as they flew along. Jimmy's stomach turned as he thought of the danger. Would he measure up? Would he ever stand even with his peers? Would he stand against the Hun?

Archie opened up on the lower formation shortly after they reached the front line. Five minutes later, they saw a flight of three German biplanes with large black crosses on their wings dive toward them from the east. Phillips maneuvered to dive behind them and Jim followed right along. This was to be his first dogfight!

They seemed intent on hitting the Sopwiths and ignored Phillips and Arneson. Stevens obviously saw them as he and the others turned into them. However, the Huns would not be distracted and continued to dive straight for the Sopwiths.

They fired on the Sopwiths and dove on through. Then they zoomed and one of the Sopwiths appeared to get a strike from the forward-firing Vickers. Their zoom to the east brought them back up over Stevens but set them up for Phillips and Jim to hit them.

They had their speed up from the dive and came at them on their left side. Phillips fired off a long burst in front of one and looked to get a hit but it flew on unharmed. Jimmy fired his gun too, but came nowhere close to them.

The Huns spun around to their left in train and they entered a tight left turn after them. Jimmy had his hands full just staying with Phillips. He slammed his stick over to the left until his wings were vertical. Then, he centered it and pulled the stick back as far as he could to hold the turn as tightly as he could. He grunted and tensed his stomach muscles as the g-forces climbed. He had to let up a bit to keep it in the flutter and avoid a stall and apply opposite rudder to maintain altitude slightly above Phillips. All the while, he was trying to keep his eyes on Phillips and the Hun airplanes. The Effies were able to turn inside them and after a couple of turns around the circle they were in a good position behind them. Phillips got off another burst and Jimmy saw one of them start to trail smoke.

The number three Hun rolled out of the turn and dove to the west. Jimmy's mind raced. What should he do? He was told to stick to Phillips like glue, no matter what. But the Hun could be headed for another pass on the Sopwiths. Jim couldn't just let him dive on them. He remembered Lt. Higgin's advice, "You must learn to be a hunter if you want to survive." He needed to follow Phillips but he also needed to go after this Hun to protect the flight below. He froze for an instant in hesitation.

Jimmy rolled to the right to give chase. The German dove away much faster than him. He could not keep up. The Hun stretched out his lead and zoomed. Jim zoomed too following him skywards. His little kite did not have the Hun's powerful engine, however. He started to stall. He stalled off to the left and dove to regain airspeed. The Hun did a wingover and was on his tail.

"Oh, God! What do I do now?" he screamed out loud. In no time, the Hun caught up to him. He could hear his machine gun, "Rat a tat, rat a tat." He could feel the bullets whiz by his ears. Jimmy jammed the left rudder to skid inside of him. The Hun's bullets veered right of him, but only temporarily.

His world slowed. Everything took place in slow motion. Jim rolled left and pulled back to split-S away from him. The Hun pilot followed him right through it. In moments, he was shooting at him again. Jimmy could see bullets ripping though his wing on the right as he turned to the left. Instinctively, he centered his stick and pulled up violently. Then, he slammed his stick back and to the right and jammed right rudder. His plane flicked into a tight roll. He almost stalled and spun out but just barely recovered in a diving turn to the left.

It worked. The Hun tried to follow but could not. He ended up in a half roll out in front of Jimmy in a sharp left turn. Jimmy stabilized his plane and tried to line up for a shot. Before he could get close, the Hun dove quickly away to the east. He tried to follow but quickly fell behind.

Alone in the sky, Jim shook violently. His hands trembled, his head shook from side to side, and his shoulders shuddered. Fear gripped him and would not let him go. He had kissed death and survived. He just flew on. What else could he do? The shakes gradually eased.

He looked around for Phillips. His Hun had rolled out of his turn and dove steeply away to the east. His companion joined him. Like Jim, Phillips didn't have the airspeed to catch them so he headed back towards Jim. He saw his guy dive away so he changed course and headed back to Captain Stevens and the Sopwiths. Jim saw him diving to the southwest and flew to join him. It was all over in an instant. He had survived his first dogfight. He was still alive, but his heart raced as if it would explode. His hand shook on the stick so badly he had to switch to his left hand so he could shake his right violently to calm down. He took deep breaths, rolled his neck, and shook his head.

While they were turning with the Germans the Sopwiths and the others had regrouped. Their turns dropped Phillips and Jim a thousand feet so they were almost at their level. They flew down alongside Stevens for a moment and began climbing to return to their high escort positions. They plodded on and the observers returned to taking pictures of the German territory below.

The rest of the patrol was uneventful. The lousy weather must have kept most of the Germans grounded. The ceiling closed in on them and they found themselves flying in the ragged bottoms of the thickening cloud layer. As it lowered, they dropped altitude to keep the rest of the patrol in sight. By the end of the patrol, they were all down to five hundred feet. The fearsome anti-aircraft fire got more accurate down low. The flight zigged and zagged a lot to keep them off their mark.

They got back to the aerodrome around lunch time. Theirs was the only patrol that day. They were socked in the rest of the afternoon. At least the Sopwith observers were able to get some good pictures of the German positions.

Back at Paddington, Captain Stevens led a quick debrief. Afterwards, he asked them all for thoughts. Phillips was gruff as usual. He said, "The fledgling screwed up and left me with two Huns to deal with on my own."

Before he could say anything, Stevens spoke up. He didn't argue with Phillips, but he didn't add on to it either. "Yes, he did, Phillips. Leave it to me. I'll speak with you later, Arneson. You're lucky to be alive."

They left. Jack and Jim headed back to their hut to get cleaned up. One advantage of a pusher prop plane was the pilot didn't get smeared with castor oil like they did in tractors, but they always sweated from the stress and from the thick flying suits.

"Well, Arnie, you got a little action today, eh what?" Jack said. He washed his face in the blue porcelain wash basin on their shared dresser as they spoke. Jimmy waited his turn.

"I'll say. It was over so fast. Are they all like that?"

"I don't think I can say. I haven't been around enough myself to know. I've got my hands full just trying to stay with my leader!"

Jimmy wanted to ask him about the German planes they saw. "Do you know what kind of planes those were that dove on you?"

"I'm not certain, no. They might have been DII or DIII Fokkers, but those are almost all gone now a days. More likely, they were Halberstadt DIIs. I can't say for sure as I've not seen many of them. They're older than the Albatros scouts, so they can't maneuver as well."

"That explains our ability to turn inside them," he said.

"Well, partly, I suppose."

"It was frustrating to not be able to keep up with them when they dove away." The FE8 was slow.

"It's the bloody wires. These FE8s have so many wires holding them together. It's what kills our airspeed. Each one of them causes drag. We can turn inside some of their planes, but we just can't keep pace." Jack seemed to know a bit about that.

After Jim finished washing up, Jack asked, "Shall we head over to the officers' mess"

"You go ahead, Jack," he replied. "I think I'll write Ellie a letter and do some reading. Perhaps I'll join you later."

"Okay, mate. It should get right jolly by four o'clock. Pop over and we'll have a pint."

Jack headed over to the chateau to join the others. There was never much to do around the field when they weren't flying. Most of the guys hung out in the officers' mess in the chateau. Jimmy was a more solitary type, but the huts they lived in were pretty cold so he went there often as well.

After the events of the day, he wanted to relax a little first. He needed to unwind from the patrol and clear his thoughts. He lay down in bed and reread Ellie's latest letter.

January 20, 1917

My dearest Jimmy,

I know you are not allowed to say much about what you are doing, but you are probably still in England from your last letter. It sounds like your training is both exhilarating and scary at the same time. I pray for you every day and every night for your safe return. You are in my thoughts each and every day. I love you so much.

Your mother, Meg, and I have become close friends. She is such a comfort to me and I am so very grateful for her taking me in. Meg joins us almost every evening after work. We speak of you often and she tells us tales of her life in England. It helps me to imagine your life there. I am so glad you were able to visit her home town.

Our little angel grows more every day. I am at four months now and can feel him move! He turns over from time to time now and occasionally stretches out an arm or a leg. I cannot describe the miracle to you. We have a child growing in my womb. I am sure it is a boy. No girl would dare kick me the way he does!

It's cold here as always in January, but I stay warm by the fire and wrap myself up tight in the wonderful woolen throws your mother makes. Life here is otherwise the same as every year. Winter is a time for rest and reflection this year as always.

Stay safe, my love. I look forward to your next letter and will write again soon.

With all my love and affection,
Your devoted Ellie.

He wrote to Ellie by the light of the oil lamp. There was so much he couldn't say about where he was and what he was doing because of the censorship, but he wanted her to know he was okay. He let her know he had received her letters and he told her about his new friend, Jack, and Captain Stevens. He called him Captain Roger as he didn't want to divulge his name. He was a good man. Jim respected his ability and he sensed that beneath his gruff demeanor, Stevens really did care for each of them.

He wrote to his mother also to let her know he was all right. With his writing out of the way, he tried to take a nap, but he couldn't sleep. He just lay there replaying the morning's patrol over and over. What he did well, all the things he did wrong, and what he should have done better.

11

GRESHAM, FEBRUARY, 1917. Elizabeth Anne Johnson, known to everyone as Ellie, possessed classic nordic beauty with fair hair, light skin and clear blue eyes. Her beauty combined with a genuine sweetness in her personality to melt the hearts of the men and endear the women in Gresham. Everyone in town knew her from her job at Peterson's General Store running the cash register and stocking shelves, where she became the heart of Gresham. All of the townsfolk looked forward to her sweet hellos and gentle, friendly conversations when they shopped there.

Sadly, Ellie developed her sweet disposition as a defense mechanism to help her survive a terrible home life. She feared punishment each day from her father, Osvald, who worked at Smith's Grain Mill in town. Osvald Johnson drank heavily every day on the way home from work and he got mean when he got drunk. Ellie and her mom, Viola, always tried to have the house in perfect order with a delicious dinner ready for him when he got home, but nothing was ever good enough. A shelf remained undusted or the potatoes were cold. Any little thing would send him off on a tirade. He would throw things at them and storm out of the house on a good night. On bad nights, he would beat the offender, either Viola or Ellie.

Ellie tried to keep it a secret, but her best friend, Margaret Lassiter, found out one day at the playground. Ellie was climbing on a gym toy in her little yellow dress ahead of Margaret, and Margaret saw the angry red whip marks on the backs of Ellie's thighs. She confronted Ellie about it and Ellie broke down, cried, and sobbed her story to her friend. Ever after, Margaret sought to protect Ellie. She wasn't big enough to do anything about Ellie's dad, but Margaret stuck to her friend like glue.

Margaret was with Ellie the day Ellie fell head over heels for Jimmy Arneson. To Ellie, Jimmy was her knight in shining armor who would free her from her difficult home life. He showed true to those dreams one day at the park.

There was a central park in Gresham right on the corner of Main and Norway streets, the two largest streets in town. It had some sandboxes, slides, swing sets and climbing bars for the kids. Parents liked to bring their families for picnics on nice Saturdays in the summer. Mothers brought the kids on other days to let them burn off some energy while they visited in the shade of the pavilion.

A little older than most kids there, Jimmy and Hank were on their own one Saturday goofing around on the climbing bars along with some of the others. Fred and Maria tagged along. Hank liked the set where you had to swing from one bar to the next and used to imitate a monkey when he did it. He made a bet with Jimmy he could do it faster than him. Jimmy took him up on it and they did it several times to see who could do it quickest.

Seeking Jimmy's attention, Ellie tried swinging from one bar to the next just like the boys did when she lost her grip and fell. "Ow, my foot hurts!" she yelped. She had landed on the side of her foot and turned her ankle. When she tried to get up, she couldn't walk and started to cry. Her friend, Margaret Lassiter, came over to try to help but couldn't.

Jimmy immediately swung down from his perch on another gym set to help her up. He put his arm under hers and lifted her up. "It's okay, Ellie. You'll be okay. I'll help you," he said.

He coached her to try to walk but she just couldn't. "It hurts too much!" She did try, but not too hard, because she liked the attention she got from Jimmy.

"Well okay, then," Jimmy thought for an instant. "I can go get my bike and you can sit on it while I walk you home. Would that be okay?"

"Ooh, okay I guess." She milked it. Margaret rolled her eyes.

He suggested she sit on the handle bars while he rode, but she said, "Oh, I can't do that. My bottom hurts too much." So, he propped her up on the seat of his bicycle and walked her all the way home. She leaned into him and got all google-eyed over him.

Jimmy liked it, too, but it wasn't just because he thought Ellie was cute. He was actually sincerely kind to people. He just naturally tried to help people out. He walked her all the way home and rode his bike back to the playground where Hank waited for him with Fred and Maria.

From that day on, Ellie's one goal in life was to marry Jimmy Arneson. He would save her when she was in distress. He would keep her from harm. He would take her away from her miserable home life.

So, when Jimmy decided to go off to war, Ellie was devastated. She saw her dreams potentially shattered. She needed to keep Jimmy in her life somehow, and having his baby seemed like a possible way to do so even if he didn't make it through the war. It was for this reason she made love to him that afternoon before he left. She had no regrets.

She also found herself relieved to be out of her father's house. When Osvald kicked her out, she did not know where she would go, but she knew she would no longer be beaten by him. She worried for her mother, but she was glad to be gone from there.

For Edith Arneson to take her in was a dream come true. Ellie thrived in the Arneson household. She continued her job at Peterson's General Store, but she also helped out with the Arneson farm however she could. She woke early to feed the animals, just like Jimmy used to do. She helped with the cooking and thoroughly enjoyed learning how to cook from Mrs. Arneson. Margaret came by frequently as well. The three of them got on famously. They cooked up fabulous meals together. Mr. Arneson was gaining weight as result.

Edith Arneson also taught Ellie and Margaret how to knit. They sat in front of the fire together often in the evening during the winter gabbing away while Harald Arneson snored in his rocking chair.

Life was good. If only Jimmy were home from the war, life would be ideal.

12

TREIZENNES, FEBRUARY, 1917. It was no use trying to relax in his hut any longer. It was just too cold. Jimmy gave up and decided to walk over to the chateau. He turned up his collar against the cold. As he half-jogged his way along the duckboards from his hut, the misting rain muffled all sound save for the incessant rumbling of cannons far off to the southwest. The duckboards led to a delightful flagstone patio running across the backside of the chateau. The formal front of the house faced the road on the other side and was reserved for use by the owner of the chateau. Three stone benches adorned the patio, which was lined with small shrubs to close it in. It looked like it would make a great gathering place in finer weather.

Today however, frigid as it was, he made a beeline for the French doors that opened into the anteroom of the officers' mess in the rear ground level of the chateau. The mess itself was one flight up. The anteroom was warmly furnished with a couple of well-worn settees, several comfortable lounging chairs, some game tables, an old piano, a warm fire, and hot tea with biscuits. One or two cricket bats lay around as well. There was always a newspaper to read, as well as RFC updates and news from the front. There were a fair number of books available on the bookshelves and comfortable chairs to curl up in. Trophies from past victories adorned the walls. A broken propeller from an unknown airplane and a rudder with a large black cross caught his attention. He wondered what the story was behind that. And, of course, the center of focus in the anteroom was the makeshift bar at the far end of the room.

The atmosphere was subdued today. So many times a raucous tune was being played on the piano while the pilots crooned along off key. Only a few pilots were there. He saw Jack up by the bar chatting with a couple of other blokes. As he made his way to join them, he was intercepted by a lieutenant sitting in an easy chair with a newspaper in hand, "Well, if it isn't the virgin from A Flight."

"How do you do, sir? I'm afraid you have me at a disadvantage," Jimmy replied. "You are?"

"I am Basil Kincaid of B flight. I hear you have actually survived two patrols now. How rare!"

"Well, yes, but just barely. I had a Hun on my tail for a bit. I think it was a Halberstadt biplane. I thought I was a goner!"

"And you got him off your tail?" asked Kincaid.

"Yes, but it wasn't easy. I was scared to death! I tried skids, slips, and a split-S to no avail. He followed me through all of those, but I did a snap roll to the right. He couldn't follow me through it and I managed to reverse positions on him. However, he dove away and I lost him."

"Beginners luck, I'd say." It was obvious Kincaid had already been drinking for a while.

"Well, pleased to meet you, Lieutenant Kincaid. My name's Arneson, Jim Arneson."

"I don't much care, to be honest with you. I make it a rule to not learn a body's name until he's been here a month. That means I don't bloody well know many names around here." Kincaid flapped the pages of his newspaper and raised it up like a shield between them.

"Well, sir, good day to you, then." Dismayed, he made his way to the bar where Jack stood.

Jack was chatting with Mike Phillips and Alfie Campbell when he walked up. "Hello, Jimmy. Glad you could make it," Jack said.

"Well, if it isn't the fledgling birdie back from his nap," quipped Phillips. "You screwed up out there today, you know."

"How so?" He was afraid he might get this from him.

"You know damned well you were supposed to stick to me like glue, especially since you don't know what the hell you're doing." Phillips was always intense, but even more so now. "You're lucky to be alive, you fool! You're not riding a bucking bronco in your wild, wild, west, you know."

"I was only trying to keep the Hun from attacking the Sopwiths. I thought that was our mission." He was growing tired of this constant harangue.

Naturally, hotshot Campbell piled on, "Look here, Arneson, new pilots don't last long around here. This was only your second patrol. You're supposed to do what you're told, not fly off and chase Huns around the sky. Fly five and live, they say. Until you've flown five patrols, you're nobody."

This was not a conversation he cared to continue. Fortunately, Jack came to his rescue. "What say I introduce you to a few of the other chaps here, Jimmy?"

"Love to!" he replied. They turned around together and made for the piano where a few pilots were beginning to gather while one of them began to play a tune.

Hank tapped on the shoulder of a pilot turned away from them. "I say, Roger, there's a new fellow I'd like you to meet."

Lt. Roger Marsh of C Flight turned around and caught him by complete surprise. His nose and cheeks were dark reddish brown, and the skin around his eyes was entirely light pink scar tissue, giving him an eerie reverse-Raccoon effect. Jimmy's shock was evident.

"How do you do young fellow? Roger Marsh here. I see my appearance has you flustered."

"I'm sorry. I d-don't mean to be rude. What happened, sir?" He stumbled over the words.

"Got a bit cocky, I'm afraid. You see, I can't stand those damned balaclavas they make us wear. I can't see a bloody thing when I have them on and I feel I shall suffocate. So, I went up without one a couple of weeks ago. Got so cold my skin froze in flight. It burned deeply and my skin froze to the rubber of my goggles. My skin went with them when I took them off, you see."

He shuddered at the thought. "It must have been horribly painful!"

"Yes, quite, but it's getting better. Still not on flying duty though. So listen to me, old boy, don't you make the same mistake!" he said pointing his finger at him while holding his whiskey glass.

Continuing to the piano, Jack introduced him to Kincaid, MacCairn, and Malone, all three with B Flight and standing at the piano, pints in hand, singing, "Keep the Home Fires Burning." They all raised their glasses to him without skipping a beat and Jimmy returned a gallant bow (at least he thought it was).

Jack next introduced Jim to Lt. Arthur Hughes of C Flight. "Call me Artie, old chap. Everyone else does," Hughes offered. Rusty haired and freckled, he had a nervous, twitchy demeanor, sucking on his cigarette a little too hard and squinting his eyes against the smoke as he exhaled while speaking. He winked his right eye far too often for comfort.

Jack whispered in his ear as they moved on. "Flying Sickness D, don't you know? Poor sod's about had it." He had heard of this term at Gosport. The D stood for debility.

A fellow could get sent home for it or, if he was unlucky in his assigned flight surgeon, he could get drummed out of the corps, labeled with Lack of Moral Fiber. LMF they called it. Fortunately, most doctors were more sympathetic and would prescribe a break from the action with less derogatory names such as Flying Fatigue or neurasthenia.

They came across another lounge chair occupied by a newspaper with a pilot behind it. Jack peeked around the corner of the paper. "Ah yes, Lieutenant Brentworth, allow me to introduce my new roommate, Jimmy Arneson."

Lt. Brentworth, head tilted back, looked down his long, aquiline nose at him. "Arneson. Hmm. Northumbrian?"

He didn't know where Northumbria was, but he assumed it was a place. "No, sir. Minnesota!"

"Oh dear, a Yank. It's bad enough they let commoners in the corps. Now, they're letting in bloody Yanks."

"Lieutenant Brentworth is the second son of the Baron of Bowland Wood," Jack offered.

"Wow, I never thought I would meet royalty in the RFC!" Jimmy was a babe in the woods, totally out of his element.

"No, no, dear boy. Not royalty. Royals are related to the King. Nobility, if one must. It actually just means we're on the peerage. My ancient ancestor was a knight for King Henry II. We've held the title in the family since then. I am merely the second son, which makes me nobody really, unless my brother dies. And I do hope that doesn't happen. He's a good man. Major in the Royal Fusiliers, you see."

"Still, it's pretty special in my book. Does it afford you with special privileges?" Jimmy asked.

"More responsibility than privilege, I should say. Collectively, the peerage of England once owned England. While it's no longer the case, we do still feel a strong sense of duty to our King and our Country."

"It is my honor to meet you, sir. Should I address you in any special way? Your highness or something?"

"Let's go with David, shall we? Or lieutenant, perhaps?" He smirked.

Just then, Bertie O'Brien burst into the room with a big hamper of goodies in his hands. "Look at what me mum sent!" he exclaimed. "It's another of her fabulous bespoke hampers from Fortnum & Masons!"

The hamper's contents were soon dumped out on one of the card tables. The hamper was filled with digestive biscuits, oatie bits, chocolates, jams, a tin of Assam tea, and some fine looking wines. Bertie grabbed the wine and ran to the bar shouting, "Garçon! Garçon! A bottle opener s'il vous plait!" The rest of them tore into the contents. Jimmy managed to snag a digestive. Quite good, actually. It would go well with some of that Assam tea, which was his favorite.

Wine flowed from Bertie's bottles and got the drinking started. "C'mon chaps! What are you going to have?" cried Bertie as he poured, one bottle from each hand, alternating pouring and drinking from the bottles. Drinking was a nightly event around here. Not much of a fan of wine, Jimmy decided to have an ale. He figured he could make it last awhile. The more determined drinkers favored whiskey, but he couldn't stomach it.

Once the drinking started, it just kept going until dinner and beyond until most of the men staggered home to their huts. Not for him. He nursed his ale, had the obligatory glass of sherry after dinner and called it an early night.

Monday the twelfth was another gray day that washed them out of flying. The ceilings were so low they almost felt like they were living in the clouds themselves. A fine mist condensed out of the air, wanting to be but not quite achieving a drizzle.

On those days, they were a lazy lot. Those who drank heaviest the night before didn't rouse until mid-morning. The rest of them tended to rise whenever they saw fit. Jimmy awoke around half past seven, dressed and walked over to the mess for some brekkers. As he walked, the mist moistened his face and uniform. The scent of wet wool rose to his nose.

He was surprised to find Captain Stevens and Major McAllister seated at the breakfast table with no one else around. It would have been unseemly to not join them. "Good morning, sirs. May I join you?" he asked.

"Yes, please do, young Arneson," Major McAllister replied. "I hear you had a bit of an encounter on patrol yesterday. Halberstadt DII, I heard. We don't see many of them around anymore. Mostly Albatros scouts now. Tell me about it. I'll be interested to hear your account."

"Yes, sir. Well, we were escorting two of the Sopwiths from 43 Squadron." He nodded to Captain Stevens, who remained quietly listening. "Captain Stevens, Jack Bailey, and Alfie Campbell flew close escort while Lt. Phillips and I flew higher up."

The orderly brought out some eggs, beans, toast and tea for him. He also filled up the cups of Captain Stevens and Major McAllister.

"Yes, continue, Arneson." Major McAllister took a sip of hot tea while Stevens added milk and sugar to his.

"Shortly after our first round of Archie, three Germans dove on the lower formation from the east. Phillips and I pursued but couldn't catch up. They dove straight through the Sopwiths and zoomed. That helped us get close. We circled with them. I think Lieutenant Phillips got a few hits on one."

"Good. Did you fire?"

"Yes, sir, but I was far off lead."

"At least you fired. I'm glad to hear that. Tell me what happened next."

"Well, sir, the third German rolled out to attack the Sopwiths again so I followed him. He dove so fast I couldn't keep up but I think he saw me behind him because he zoomed again. I tried to follow but stalled out and fell off. He got behind me then. I tried everything I could think of but couldn't get away." He thrust a forkful of eggs into his mouth.

"You left your leader?" McAllister raised an eyebrow sternly.

He gulped down the eggs. "I wasn't sure what to do, sir. I didn't want him to get another chance at the Sopwiths."

"Hmm, I see. Laudable motivation perhaps, Arneson, but the Sopwiths had Stevens and two others looking out for them whereas you left Phillips alone against two others." McAllister took another sip of tea, this time with a furrowed brow. "Listen, have another bite of eggs, young man. This isn't an inquisition. Take your time and continue."

"Yes, sir." He took a bite of beans. "He was shooting at me. I didn't know what to do because I couldn't slip or skid away from him. I was awfully scared. He put some bullets through my wing. I was running out of ideas, so I snap-rolled to the right while we were turning. Thankfully, he couldn't follow me. I was able to get behind him, but he dove away, once again too quickly for me to follow."

"You snap-rolled an FE8?" Stevens interrupted.

"Well, of a sort, yes, sir. It rather mushed out at the edge of stall towards the end," he replied. "I had to dive steeply out of it before it broke into a spin."

"FE8s don't snap roll," Stevens said. "At least, I've never seen it. Where ever did you learn to do that?" Stevens asked.

"Gosport, sir. My instructor, Lieutenant Higgins showed me. I practiced them on the DH2. Spins, too."

"Rusty Higgins?" Stevens asked. He had a look of surprise on his face.

"Why, yes, sir. I believe so, sir. I only ever called him lieutenant, but I think I heard some of the other instructors call him that."

"Well, I'll be a monkey's uncle." Captain Stevens exclaimed. "I flew BE2s with Rusty Higgins with No. 3 Squadron last year over the Somme. He's a good man. We lost touch after I got reassigned. I am glad he's still alive. You were lucky to have him as an instructor. He knew how to bend an aeroplane better than anyone I've ever flown with."

Jimmy shoveled in another quick couple of forkfuls of food.

"I'd say that was just the beginning of your good fortune, young man. You're lucky to be alive. This was only your second patrol, was it not?" McAllister resumed his questioning.

"Yes, sir."

"Damned lucky. By rights, you should have been shot down, abandoning your leader like you did. We have some rules of behavior in His Majesty's Royal Flying Corps, young man. And those rules apply to you bloody upstart Americans as much as they do to the rest of us."

"Yes, sir!" He braced.

"Relax young man. Staying with your leader is one of many rules you need to learn and you need to follow, clear?" McAllister was stern but somehow he sensed he was not truly angry.

"It's for your own good. Stay stuck to your leader until you learn to survive on your own. You should not have left Phillips yesterday."

"Yes, sir. I'm sorry, sir. Are there other rules I should know about, sir?" he asked.

Captain Stevens cut in. "You have now seen our FE8s are slow. They were built to fly against Eindeckers, but those aeroplanes haven't been around for a year now. Even those old Halberstadts are faster than us, let alone the Albatros. They can out-dive and out-climb us, and they can run away at will."

Major McAllister added, "They will dive on you and keep on diving past you knowing you can't catch them. When they are well

94

out of range, they will climb above you and dive on you again. They can do that all day long and there's nothing you can do about it. Your best bet is to get them to turn with you. Then hopefully, you can out-turn them."

"But even then, the FE8 rolls slowly, so roll into a vertical turn as quickly as possible and haul the stick back." Captain Stevens took turns with McAllister. "You see, son, this is all the more reason to stick with your leader. You have a better chance of survival in pairs. If you get one behind you, go into a tight turn and your leader might be able to get around the turn to get on his tail."

"When you shoot, get in really close, twice as close as you think. Our most successful pilots get in to twenty yards or less. You only have ninety-seven rounds in the new Lewis ammunition drums, about twenty seconds of fire. Use them wisely. Fire only one to two bullets at each trigger pull. Believe me, you don't want to have to change drums in the middle of a fight."

"Go all in, boy. Either go all in or get out. You can't hesitate. If you do, you're a goner," Stevens added.

"Are the Albatros scouts as good as I hear?"

"Yes, I'm afraid so, Arneson. They are stronger, faster and better armed than our aeroplanes. We can handle their two-seaters, but when the Albatros scouts are out, we always end up on the defensive. I hear there are new British scouts in the works that will put them in their place, however," McAllister replied.

"Now, get on with you, boy. Go write your sweetheart a letter. And, when the weather clears, we'll go up again for some practice." Captain Stevens loved to call him boy. Jim couldn't say he minded. It made him feel like he cared about him.

Jim swallowed a last bite of eggs and headed back to his hut. Still misty, the aerodrome lay quietly awaiting its next opportunity to launch its birds into battle. The only sounds discernable above the distant, muffled cannon were the mechanics sawing, hammering, and clanking away on their birds, trying to keep them serviceable for the pilots. Walking along the duckboards, Jim redoubled his resolution to be the best fighter pilot in the squadron. Otherwise, he was going to have a short life.

13

Sᴛ. Oᴍᴇʀ, Fᴇʙʀᴜᴀʀʏ, 1917. Hank Jacobs learned all he could about automobile mechanics working in the motor pool at St. Omer. Working behind the back of his anti-Semitic nemesis, Sergeant McBride, Hank gradually learned almost everything his fellow mechanics could teach him. Unique among his peers, Hank had the whole picture in his head. After a few months, the other mechanics began to ask him for advice when they got stuck on something.

McBride still gave Hank all the lousy jobs like cleaning up oil spills, but Hank was gratified to know he had the respect and support of his peers. None of them liked McBride either. Together, they conspired to harass and debase him. Sometimes, it was just a little play on his ginger-hood like leaving an empty box of ginger snaps on his desk. Other times it was a little more prankish.

In mid-January, one of the mechanics intentionally spilled some oil on the floor near McBride's desk in an area he walked through frequently. As he walked to his desk shortly after, he slipped on the oil and landed flat on his keister. Much to McBride's chagrin, everybody chuckled and no one had any idea how it got there.

Another day, somebody glued his pencil to his desk. Probably once a week, someone would put used motor oil in his coffee when he wasn't looking. Little pranks like these remained anonymous. It was Hank sometimes, but he was not alone. Three or four of the fellows joined in the fun. The thing that frustrated McBride the most was he could never figure out who did them.

One day, Hank decided on the fly to do something a little more public. The maintenance squadron commander, a Major Phillips, came through the maintenance hangar for an impromptu visit. Sergeant McBride escorted him around the shop, pointing out each of the different repair stations. It was one of those visits where they were all supposed to continue working while the major and Sergeant McBride came around. Hank happened to be helping Frank Cutler with a camshaft replacement when they came by. On a lark, he asked Sergeant McBride to help him figure out how to find top, dead center for the first cylinder so they could set the timing. As Hank suspected, McBride had no idea and was incensed he would ask him a question like that in front of the major. It didn't take much to set McBride off.

McBride came around after the major left and chewed Hank out royally. He just stood there with a smirk on his face while McBride got all red-faced and spitting drool while he yelled. The other mechanics enjoyed the show.

The next several months were passed in drudgery doing menial jobs in the shop. Hank jumped at the chance to work on a different vehicle just for the change of pace. Most of the other blokes felt the same way, but they just seemed to settle into what was asked of them. They usually worked on tenders, staff cars, ambulances and lorries.

In early 1917, they began to get more frequent requests to support the Phelon & Moore 3.5 horsepower motorcycles used by the RFC for courier duties. Simple oil changes and tune-ups could be handled by most of the mechanics in the motor pool, but requests for more difficult maintenance jobs started to come in to the shop. The motor pool did not have any motorcycle experts so McBride asked the group of mechanics if any of them had motorcycle experience. Hank Jacobs stood up and said he did.

Skeptical, McBride challenged him, wanting to know what kind of experience Hank had. Hank told him he used to own an Indian motorcycle before the war and he had rebuilt it himself from the frame up. Begrudgingly, McBride made Hank the motorcycle specialist in the motor pool.

Hank's work life picked up a bit after that. He had the opportunity to build deep expertise in the bikes. He enjoyed it thoroughly. Once again, he found himself grateful for experience he had gained back in Gresham. He found himself reflecting on the occasion when he and Jimmy were able to acquire their Indian bike.

Hugh Smith was three years older than Hank and Jim. They knew of him but that was all, really. Gresham was a small town so everyone knew of lots of people beyond their immediate circles of friends. He seemed to be a friendly fellow who smiled a lot. He was the richest kid in town because his folks owned the grain mill where all the farmers stored their grains until the market was right.

Hugh went to work for his dad right out of school and started making good money right away. After a year or so, he bought himself a brand new Indian motorcycle. Hank used to watch him ride it in town, full of envy. There weren't any automobiles in town to speak of. The Smiths had a 1910 Buick Model F they took out for Sunday drives in the summer and once in a long while, a Model T might drive through town on the main highway, but that was about it. The motorcycle stood out and grabbed everyone's attention as Hugh drove through town.

Tragedy struck one day in March, 1912. Spring was blooming, but the roads were still slick with mud. Apparently, Hugh took a corner too fast and crashed the bike. When it slid into the berm at the side of the road, it flipped, threw Hugh off, hit him in the head, and killed him.

The whole town mourned Hugh's death. The Smiths had his body on display in the newly opened funeral parlor. Hank and Jimmy went through the visitation line along with most of the town before the funeral service. There were flowers everywhere. They had never seen a dead body before and couldn't help but stare. It was eerie. He looked pale and peaceful, but his hair was matted down like it was glued to the side of his head and his face had lots of makeup on it. Afterwards, the whole town attended an open-air funeral service in the pavilion at the town park. Pastor Olson gave a short speech about God's mysterious ways. Then, Hugh was laid to rest in the Gresham Cemetery in the Smith plot.

About a week later, Hank saw a notice at Peterson's General Store saying Mr. and Mrs. Smith were selling the motorcycle Hugh had been riding when he was killed. They said it was damaged but it could be bought for fifteen dollars. Hank knew this was a real bargain from his readings at the library of *Popular Mechanics*. Used motorcycles usually sold for forty dollars or more.

That afternoon Hank discussed it with Jimmy and determined they could probably scrape together fifteen dollars between them if they did a few extra chores around the house in the next week or so. A week later they had the money in their pockets.

They walked over to the big Smith house near the grain mill. Mrs. Smith answered the door when they knocked. "Good afternoon, ma'am. I'm Hank Jacobs and this is my friend, Jimmy Arneson. My dad runs the furniture repair shop in town. Maybe you know of him?"

"Why yes, I do know your father and mother. Nice people they are, too. How do you do, young Master Jacobs? Would you like to come in?" Mrs. Smith was dressed all in black in mourning. She probably would be for months.

"Thank you, ma'am." They both walked into the front parlor. It was big and opulent. "Ma'am, may we first express our condolences to you over the loss of Hugh? We didn't know him well, but he was always nice to us around town. I'm sorry."

"Thank you, Hank. That's kind of you. It is difficult for my husband and me."

"Ma'am, we've come to inquire about the motorcycle you posted for sale at the general store. Is it still for sale?"

"Yes, it is. I just want to get rid of it. It cost my son his life and I don't want to see it around here anymore. If I sell it to you, however, you must promise to be careful on it. I would not want to hear Gresham has lost any more young men to such carelessness. Will you promise me?"

"Oh, yes, ma'am, we promise," Hank said.

"Yes, we promise, ma'am," Jimmy added.

"Well then, it's yours. It's around back. You go 'round the house to the back and I'll join you there."

They left through the front door and walked around the house to the back yard. The bike was sitting on its side back by the barn. Mrs. Smith joined them momentarily.

"As you can see, it's badly damaged. I don't know how you'll get it fixed. There isn't a motorcycle dealership for miles all the way up in Marshall." Mrs. Smith scowled at the bike. It took her son away from her.

"Yes, ma'am, I am confident I can fix it up. I've been reading up on motorcycle repair in *Popular Mechanics*," Hank said.

"Well then, take it away," Mrs. Smith said.

"Do you want the fifteen dollars you advertised it for?" Hank asked.

"Well, you seem like nice boys. Just give me five or ten dollars or whatever you have. I just want it gone."

Hank couldn't believe his luck. "Yes, ma'am. I understand. Here's ten dollars then. And, thank you, ma'am. Once again, please accept our condolences."

"Run along, you two. Don't do anything stupid with it. Please, please, please be careful."

"Yes, ma'am. We will be." They both reached down and righted the bike. The front wheel and the handle bars were badly bent, but they were able to walk it out of the yard and on up the street to Hank's house and put it in the shed in back. They contained their excitement until they were out of sight and sound from Mrs. Smith's home.

They went to the library to find out how to repair it. They knew *Popular Mechanics* sometimes had articles about motorcycles in it, but it was overwhelming trying to find them. Miss Jensen helped them with her copy of the Guide to Periodicals. They found a few articles but not close enough to what they needed.

However, Miss Jensen looked around for them as well and found a 300-page book on motorcycle repair from *Popular Mechanics*. She bought a copy for them out of the library budget. It was fantastic. He checked it out again and again until he had absorbed everything he could.

They boys also checked the advertising sections at the back of every issue of *Popular Mechanics*. They found a dealer in Indiana for Indian Motorcycle parts pretty cheap they could mail order from, so they bought a new front wheel and handle bars.

With the instructions on the motorcycle repair book, Hank was able to figure out how to replace them both, including the headlamp cables. He had to try to bend the front forks back into line so it was always a little wobbly. And, they discarded the fender over the front wheel.

What the repair book didn't tell them was how to ride it. It took quite a lot of trial and error on their parts. He had a hard time keeping his balance, but Jimmy seemed to take to it like a natural. Eventually, they both got the hang of it, but he was always a little tenuous.

His crowning achievement however, was figuring out how to build a sidecar to attach to the side of the motorcycle. *Popular Mechanics* came in handy once again. Now, they could both get around in it or, even better, they could take girls for rides.

14

TREIZENNES, FEBRUARY, 1917. Grudgingly, Old Man Winter began to yield to the maidens of spring in mid-February, allowing a little blue sky to peep through his cloudy cloaks a few days here and there. The morning frost covering the grassy expanse of the airfield still greeted them at dawn each morning, but quickly melted away with the increased smiling of the sun. Spring sirens beckoned them into the skies with increased fervor. At altitude, Jimmy Arneson welcomed the exceptional visibility of the frigid, crystal-clear air between the clouds, the depressing nine-tenths skies thinning to broken clouds covering a mere four- or five-tenths of the sky.

The gods of war flew in with the improved weather as well. The boys of 40 Squadron flew more, fought more, and died more. Operationally, A, B, and C Flights rotated the sequence of patrols for the day. Sometimes, A Flight would take the dawn patrol followed by B and C Flights in intervals later in the morning. Other days, B or C would take the early patrol. It depended on the missions they received from wing HQ the night before. The orders were posted on the operations board in the mess for all to see each evening and, occasionally, Major McAllister or Captain Stevens would gather them together to brief them on the next day.

Their missions were usually offensive patrols, meaning they flew over a section of the front looking for enemy observation planes or other aircraft to attack. Other days called for strafing missions, artillery spotting, or escorting their own observation planes.

Jimmy's flying proficiency grew rapidly with the increased flying schedule. At first, he had to think of what he wanted to do with the airplane, then translate that in his mind to what his hands and feet needed to do with the controls to get there, and then do it. As he learned the FE8's quirks and flew it often enough, the transition time from thought to doing shrank to instantaneous. He didn't think about what to do. He just did it. It became instinctual.

With the mechanics of flying burned into his muscle memory, he began to concentrate on other aspects of flying, like aiming his machine gun. When he joined the squadron, his aim was horrible. He couldn't keep the enemy aircraft in his sight long enough to actually take aim. As he improved, he learned to kick in just the right amount of rudder or apply just enough aileron to keep his enemy in his sights. Then, he could tweak it just a bit more to take a lead and shoot. Still, he hadn't shot down any enemy aircraft yet. He was eager to do so. Every scout pilot wanted to become an ace. He felt he would not prove himself until he had one or two enemy aircraft to his credit.

Unfortunately, the FE8 was outclassed by the German scouts. The Halberstadts he saw earlier were gone now, replaced by Albatros scouts. Jimmy began to see them in the second half of February. They were beautiful in a most deadly way with their sleek fuselages. They sliced through the air like sharks on the prowl. Fast and heavily armed, their one weakness was their slowness in the turns. The FE8s could out-turn them but the

Albatros scouts would just dive away quickly whenever one of the British pilots got close to getting a bead on them. These new enemies cost 40 Squadron three pilots from B Flight on the seventeenth of February and another two from C Flight on the twentieth.

Major McAllister called them together in the mess for a briefing one morning. "Gentlemen, you will have undoubtedly noticed our air operations have stepped up dramatically in the last week or so. We can expect this to continue for the foreseeable future. You will find fatigue setting in so I recommend you make every effort to get a good night's sleep. Avoiding excessive alcohol will help in this matter." A round of chuckles rose up. Bertie O'Brien slapped Malone on the back of the head, mussing his oily hair.

He let the laughter die down and continued, "Wing intelligence has informed me we shall be facing a new enemy in our sector. I have learned that Jagdstaffel 11, or Jasta 11 as they call it, has arrived in Douai with a brand new model of the Albatros, the DIII. The group is led by none other than Baron Manfred von Richthofen." Loud, serious murmurs rose up this time. Von Richthofen was a famous German aviator. He was a protégé of the legendary Oswald Boelke and considered his heir after Boelke was killed in 1916.

"Gentlemen, gentlemen, please!" The major waved the noise down with his hands. "The new Albatros is faster and more maneuverable than the DIIs we have seen so far. You will notice the struts are now a V-type strut and the bottom wing is thinner than the upper wing, similar to the Nieuport scouts. Indeed, one might surmise the Hun copied the idea from the Nieuport.

"The Jasta tactics are also new. You should expect to see them out in larger numbers, sometimes even in squadron strength. In response, we will be flying our patrols in greater numbers as well. Be aware doing so will increase your flying hours significantly. Captain Hargrove has published the new patrol schedule on the bulletin board for your review.

"Now, I am as aware as you are our FE8s are not equipped to handle the Albatros scouts. The DIIs have us bested already. I fully expect the DIII to be an even greater challenge for us. The flight leaders and I have discussed this at length. We believe the best course of action will be to meet them in numbers and to draw them into a turning fight. We will be slower but we think we will still be able to turn inside them. You will also need to watch each other's tails. If you see a friend in need, get in there and shoot the Hun off of him. Even if you can't down him, send a shot or two across his nose to scare him off. Now, are there any questions?"

Stinky Kincaid spoke out quickly, "Sir, when will we get better planes?" He spoke the frustration of the whole squadron. Everyone knew the FE8s were hopelessly outclassed.

"I wish I could say for sure, Kincaid," Major McAllister responded. "I know of two new scouts in the works. Sopwith is said to be coming out with a replacement for the Pup and the Royal Aircraft Factory is bringing out a new scout from the Farnborough works. I don't know how long it will take. No one does. They must pass rigorous testing."

"Yes, and we continue to die while we wait for their bloody testing!" Kincaid spoke too quickly for his own good.

"Lieutenant Kincaid, are you or are you not a loyal subject of His Majesty, the King?" McAllister responded curtly.

"Yes, sir!" Kincaid knew he had gone too far.

"Then you will do your duty to your King and your Country. If it means you must die for your King and your Country you will have the very great comfort of knowing you served both well and honorably! Is that understood?" McAllister's voice cut like a sharp-edged sword.

"Yes, sir! Thank you, sir!"

McAllister took a breath to calm down and straightened his tunic. "Any other questions?"

The squadron pilots remained silent but for a few whispers among those in the rear. A chair creaked as someone shifted in his seat.

"Very well. This briefing is over."

"Attention!" Uncle Hargrove shouted.

The squadron rose to attention as the major strode for the door.

"Dismissed!" shouted Uncle and they all dispersed.

Jack and Jimmy walked back to their hut together. "Wow, McAllister was a bit testy, wasn't he?" Jack asked.

"I'll say. Everyone seems awfully tense about the FE8 situation. Are they really that bad?" Jimmy had not known other planes well enough to complain. He could see they flew at a severe disadvantage in them, but he didn't know how strongly they were vilified by the pilots across the squadron.

"They've been at it longer than we have is all," Jack replied.

"Well, please do let me know if I become so cynical, eh?"

Jack shocked him with his uncharacteristic response. "Yes, if we should live that long."

True to his word, McAllister had them step up their patrols beginning the next morning. They flew two flights together now, averaging about eight planes per patrol depending on aircraft serviceability.

Sometimes, A Flight flew with C Flight, commanded by Captain "Scruffy" Adams. He was an aggressive hunter. Whenever the opportunity arose, he climbed as high as he could stand it in the frigid winter air to position himself for a kill. He had shot down four aircraft this way, but nowadays, the mission profiles and his added responsibility as Flight commander generally precluded such forays for him. Because of this, he often took off on his own after returning from patrol to go hunting.

Captain Stevens was his senior, so A Flight often flew ahead of C Flight. Both flights flew in V formations of five. Jimmy continued to fly off of Phillip's right and Jack flew off Campbell's left.

They flew twice a day, once in the morning and once in the afternoon. The times would vary, but they generally had a light lunch between jobs. Sometimes, they escorted the Sopwith Strutters in their observation duties, but more often they flew offensive patrols over their appointed section of the front between Arras and Douai.

Jimmy continued to stay glued to Phillips, not forgetting McAllister's advice. As his proficiency grew, he found this easier to do. Phillips could tell, too, and his own flying grew bolder and quicker. He no longer felt the need to watch Jimmy and could be more aggressive. He still treated Jimmy gruffly, but didn't criticize quite as much. Jimmy took this as progress.

The twenty-third of February was a bright, sunny, and cold day. A Flight was assigned with C Flight to a dawn offensive patrol to Douai and back. Jack and Jimmy rose early and were already awake when the orderly came around to beat on their door at five o'clock. By now, the morning drill had become routine. A quick breakfast was followed by their briefing in Paddington Station.

Wilson and Stewart, his stalwart ground crew, helped him get his flying kit on, balaclava and all. Up into his kite, through the start-up routine, and off they went into the still dark sky.

The sun was crowning over the eastern horizon as they crossed over the lines near Arras and turned south at about eight thousand feet. Any higher and they froze. Archie blasted at them as soon as they turned southwards. Jimmy could never get used to Archie. The initial salvo always shook him to the core. The mere thought of it sent chills up his spine. The planes jigged, jagged, and changed altitude as soon as the shelling started. Archie could never keep up or anticipate their corrections.

The pilots also knew Archie alerted the enemy of their presence, so they were especially watchful after they passed through an Archie barrage. Today was no different. They soon saw a flight of four enemy airplanes above them heading north off to the east. They expected them to come round and dive on them but the Germans kept going so they did, too. Perhaps the Germans failed to see them. There was no way the British would be able to climb to the Germans' altitude in time to catch them.

Halfway down to Douai, the rising sun glared fiercely into their eyes. Blinded when they looked in its direction, they had to half-glance around it to watch for enemy aircraft. Too late, Stevens saw a flight of six aircraft diving on them out of the sun like screaming Banshees. Stevens waggled his wings and pointed towards them, warning the combined flights of the Germans' approach. They all scattered. Phillips took the high road, climbing to meet the enemy. Jimmy followed as closely as he could, reacting to Phillips' movements with only a split-second delay. Phillips often tried to gain altitude whenever he could and often charged directly at the enemy. He was a fearless pilot and a good, if critical, instructor to Jimmy.

As the opposing formations closed, Jimmy could see the German planes were Albatros DIIIs with V struts. His heart raced and the adrenalin kicked in. Brightly colored with bright white squares showing off the black German crosses, they approached at an alarming speed and dove through the British like a hail of bullets. Phillips and Jimmy fired their machine guns in a head on pass but the Germans just flew through. A couple of the Germans returned fire in the head-on pass but nothing connected either way.

Phillips, with Jimmy in tow, wheeled around to his left as fast as he could but the Germans were long gone. They had no hope of catching them. Well out of range, the Germans zoomed up again and turned left, climbing as they turned to prepare for another slashing pass at the Brits from above. There was not going to be a turning fight today. At this rate, it would just be a matter of time before the Germans' slashing attacks started taking out the British.

Phillips and Jimmy climbed for all they were worth. In the climb, Jimmy looked around for the rest of their flight. Most of the other FE8s had followed the Germans down as the enemy scouts dived away. It looked like Campbell and Bailey had turned to the left after the first pass and were coming around, climbing to engage the Germans. The two of them climbed to the place they thought the enemy might go and were not too far below them when the DIIIs came around again to dive on the Brits below.

Phillips dove to intercept and managed to get off a few rounds in front of a couple of the Huns. Two DIIIs came up out of their dive and turned towards him. They closed up for a head on pass with Phillips and Jimmy and all planes fired at once. Again, nothing connected but this time Jimmy heard a few bullets whiz past his head. Why they didn't hit his propeller was beyond him.

After the pass, Phillips and Jimmy broke to the right while Campbell and Bailey broke to the left. The Germans broke to their right, which brought them around to Campbell and Bailey. Campbell and Bailey turned to get on the Germans' tails and a turning, downward spiral commenced.

Phillips and Jimmy charged for them, watching the fight ensue as they went. One of the DIIIs climbed in a tight turn and did a wingover back into the whirling circle. This brought him down behind Jack Bailey for just a long enough moment to get off a good burst. Jack's plane shuddered and he fell off his turn, flattening out somewhat. The Albatros flew over him and climbed again.

Alfie Campbell was still turning tightly with the other Albatros and gaining on him when Phillips and Jimmy joined in. Phillips fell in line behind Campbell's plane and Jimmy fell in line behind Phillips, three FE8s turning with one Albatros. They were turning slightly inside of the Albatros and getting closer to getting a bead on it with each revolution.

The German obviously saw it, rolled sharply to the inside in a split-S and dove away to the east. Alfie tried to follow him but it was useless. The Albatros was just too fast in a dive. These Albatros scouts, with the advantage of speed, could engage the FE8s when and how they suited, and if they wanted to, they could just run away.

Jimmy looked all over for the others. The Albatros that had fired on Jack saw the other German dive away and followed suit. Stevens and the C Flight boys were nowhere to be seen, nor were the other four Germans.

Phillips, Campbell and Jimmy joined up with Jack Bailey, who was in a steep descent to the west. He was in obvious peril. Dark black smoke trailed out of his engine and large flaps of his upper wing fabric fluttered in the airstream as he dove.

Jack waved to them as he dove away. They followed him down. He made it across the British lines but never came fully out of the dive to level off. About halfway down, Jimmy watched in horror as flames erupted from Jack's engine. Fortunately, being a pusher, the flames were behind Jack. However, the fire grew in size as he dove, turning his plane into a flaming torch.

When Jack got close to the ground, he tried to level off but the plane seemed to stall on him before he could flatten out. It did at least reduce his airspeed so when he crashed he wasn't going more than thirty miles an hour or so. However, it was enough. A Flight watched him hit just over the allied lines. He was fighting to flare but stalled and nosed in. The engine plowed into the gas tank behind his cockpit and it exploded in a ball of flame. His roommate, Jack, his friend, was gone.

Jimmy painted the spot in his mind's eye and marked it on his leg map as best he could. Phillips and Campbell flew over low and slowly but then turned southwards in a steady climb. Jimmy joined them, lagging behind and looking over his shoulder at the burning heap that was once his best friend in 40 Squadron.

They climbed all the way back up to 8,000 feet heading south. Phillips was obviously intent on finishing the assigned patrol route. Shortly after regaining altitude, they came across Stevens and the remnants of C Flight heading back north on their return leg. C Flight was also short a plane with two others smoking heavily. They turned a bit to the west to head home in the shortest possible route.

15

TREIZENNES, FEBRUARY, 1917. The six remaining FE8s straggled into Treizennes about half past seven and taxied to the tarmac in front of Paddington hangar. Jimmy ran up to Captain Stevens in turmoil.

"Captain Stevens, I have to go get Jack!" he pleaded.

"He's dead, boy. Let him be and move on," Stevens replied.

"I can't, sir. I have to go get him."

"Arneson, this is war. People die. Grow up and get over it. It will happen again and again and again." Stevens was losing patience.

"You don't understand, sir. I made an oath to Jack I would see to him getting a proper burial. I must do this. You must let me do this!" Jimmy's eyes watered up.

"I don't have to do anything you tell me! Do you understand, boy? I will not hear anything more of this. Now, go away!"

"Then I will do it without your permission. I swore an oath to my friend and I intend to keep my oath." He turned around and walked away.

"Arneson! Arneson! Get back here!" Stevens was livid. Jimmy took a few more steps. "God damn it to hell!" He threw his flying helmet down and stomped into Paddington Station.

Jimmy broke down into tears as he walked away. He had no idea how he was going to get Jack. He had flown over the area many times, but he had never been away from the aerodrome on surface roads at all. He didn't even know how to drive a car.

He saw Captain Stevens stomp into the back of Paddington where they always de-briefed after patrols. Jimmy stopped and turned around. He overheard Stevens say, "Phillips, you saw where Bailey went down?"

"Yes, sir, I did. Just this side of the lines down by Vermelles," Phillips responded.

Stevens weakened. "Damn it all. I hate doing this, but go with young Arneson and wet-nurse the lad, will you? Have Wilson or Stewart drive the Crossley and take a canvas tarpaulin for Bailey's remains."

"Yes, sir," Phillips replied. Jimmy knew both Phillips and Stevens were jaded. He knew it was their defense against insanity. They had seen many young men die. They were tired and cynical and they knew it. But this told Jimmy they also had hearts themselves.

Phillips walked slowly towards Jimmy. "Come on, lad. Let's go get your friend."

They walked over to Private Stewart, who was helping Air Mechanic Wilson wheel Jimmy's aircraft around to the ready position. Phillips addressed them, "Stewart, we have a job for you. Wilson, can you get on by yourself for a bit?"

"Aye, sir," Wilson responded. "What do you need?"

"We need Stewart to drive us to Vermelles in the Crossley to pick up Bailey's remains."

"Ah, very well, sir. I can get on all right. Thank you for asking, sir, and good luck to you," Wilson replied.

They headed to the motor pool tent with Stewart. Phillips requisitioned the Crossley while Stewart filled the gas tank and checked the fluid levels.

The road from Treizennes to Vermelles took them to the southeast through Lillers and Béthune. Béthune had surprisingly been spared from the intense bombardments that obliterated most of the little towns they encountered along the way. Several times, they had to pull over to let a supply convoy go by. They also passed columns of soldiers marching to the front.

As they got closer to Vermelles, the roads became harder to navigate. Stewart had to search for the clearest and driest path through an increasingly pockmarked landscape, often driving around bombshell craters and large patches of mud.

Vermelles itself was a bombed out ruin. The only thing marking it as a town was the rubble from what were once buildings. A large, bombed-out chateau stood prominently on a hill. Portions of its walls remained standing like an empty shell. They passed by it solemnly on their way to the front.

Still closer, the debris of war thickened. They left behind all sense of civilization as they threaded their way through destroyed trucks and carts. Dead horses lay where they fell and the stench rose up so badly they could hardly stand it. Shelling, which had been a distant rumble at Treizennes, was much more ominous. Shells blasted within a couple of miles. They could see the plumes of dirt from their explosions as they approached the front.

They passed an aid station bustling with activity, even in these supposed quiet times on the front. They had to slow to a crawl to make way for the ambulances that drove up hurriedly. Orderlies offloaded stretcher after stretcher of dead and wounded soldiers. Orderlies triaged each arrival, vectoring them to different tents for treatment. Outside one tent, twenty or so soldiers sat smoking cigarettes while they favored their bandaged wounds. In another open area, nurses, like humming birds, flitted from one stretcher to another, checking on more seriously wounded soldiers waiting for transport to rear hospitals or for further treatment. Outside another tent, the dead were lined up like matchsticks side by side. Tarps or blankets covered the more mangled bodies.

Just southeast of the aid station, they came upon a headquarters of sorts. A collection of tents surrounded the remains of a farmhouse alongside the road. They stopped to ask about Jack's crash site. Phillips spoke for them, "You, soldier, what outfit is this?"

"This is the regimental headquarters of the Queen's Bay Regiment, 2nd Dragoon Guards, sir!" The soldier braced as he replied. "We are part of the 46th North Midland Division, sir!"

"Can you direct me to the intelligence officer?" Phillips asked.

"Yes, sir. That would be Lieutenant Strickland, sir. His tent is right over there." The soldier pointed to a small canvas tent about twenty yards away.

"Thank you, lad," Phillips replied. "Stewart, stay with the vehicle, please."

Phillips and Jimmy walked over to the tent. It was open and they could see a solitary officer hunched over some papers on his makeshift desk. "Are you Lieutenant Strickland?" Phillips queried.

The officer looked up from his work. As is the case in the military, he first looked for their ranks to determine his response. Seeing two other lieutenants, he remained seated, responding casually. "I am indeed, lieutenant. With whom do I have the pleasure?"

Phillips grinned ever so slightly. "We are Lieutenants Phillips and Arneson of the Royal Flying Corps, 40 Squadron. How do you do, sir?"

"Very good, thank you!" Strickland rose and shook their hands. "Welcome to my humble abode. How can I help you gentlemen?"

"We have come looking for a comrade of ours, at least what may be left of him. He crashed near here this morning at around seven o'clock this morning. We saw his plane crash and burn. It was about a hundred yards behind the rearward British trench."

"Hmm, yes, I think I did see a dispatch about a plane crash nearby." He returned to his seat, donned his eyeglasses, and began leafing through a stack of papers on his desk. "Yes, here it is. There was a crash this morning about three quarters of a mile from here. It was reported by the Nottinghamshire and Derbyshire Regiment, the Sherwood Foresters."

"Good! Can you direct us to the location?" Phillips asked.

"Follow this road east," Strickland replied. "You'll come to an intersection in about one-quarter mile. Turn right there and head south towards Loos. After about one-half mile, turn left at the remains of an old farmhouse. All that's left is the foundation, really, and even that is pocked with craters. You'll be getting close to the lines, so you'll need to park your vehicle and continue afoot. The Notts and Derby boys have an HQ set up a bit east of there. Look for that and get someone there to help you find it."

"You have been immensely helpful. Thank you so much!" Jimmy said.

"Yes, thanks awfully, old chap. Stay safe, will you?" Phillips added.

"Indeed, I shall try to do so. Good luck, gentlemen. For King and Country!" Strickland replied.

"For King and Country!" they replied, and headed out of the tent.

They found their way as Strickland had indicated. The roads were like paths through the muck and the shell holes. Plumes of dirt from incoming shells exploded around them. Not only did the sound become deafening, they could feel the concussion from the shock waves they sent out.

They abandoned their vehicle within sight of the Notts and Derby HQ. To say the roads became impassable would be an understatement. They disappeared in a sea of water-filled craters. Phillips had Stewart carry the canvas sheet they had brought along. They trudged their way through mud along a footpath and approached a sentry standing guard outside the regimental headquarters tents.

"Soldier, we are RFC pilots from 40 Squadron looking for our fallen comrade," Phillips said. "Who should we see to find the wreckage?"

"Sir, I should think that would be Captain Stuyckes. He is the operations officer of the day in the main tent just over there, sir." The soldier pointed their way.

"Thank you, young man," Phillips said as they exchanged salutes and passed the sentry on the footpath headed to the tent.

Stuyckes was helpful. He knew of the crash and detailed Sergeant Woolery to escort them to the location. Woolery grabbed a shovel and led them south along some communications trenches and across open land to the site of the crash. Rifle fire and occasional machine gun bursts interspersed artillery explosions. They instinctively ducked as they ran between trenches. Woolery chuckled quietly as he led them, knowing they were virgins to life at the front.

There wasn't much left of the plane. A few struts and longerons remained unburned, as did the tips of two of the wings. Everything else was a pile of broken, burned pieces of wood and tangles of control wires and braces. The propeller stuck up at an odd angle, still connected to the engine which lay half in the mud, its top cylinders also sticking up at an angle. In front of the engine, they could see a burnt, crumpled layer of sheet metal where the gas tank had been.

As the nose of the plane crashed into the ground, the weight of the engine drove it right into the gas tank, squashing it like tin foil and causing it to explode. Everything was burned. They saw the charred remains of Jack's right hand sticking up out of the mud ahead of the gas tank. As they looked closer, they also saw Jack's burnt skull, adorned with a few unburned bits of his flying helmet.

Jimmy reeled away in shock and immediately vomited. His eyes welled up with tears and he cried out in anguish. Phillips scolded him like a child, "Get hold of yourself, boy!"

The gas tank had been directly behind Jack and exploded right into Jack's back and drove his body into the mud in a burning pool of fuel. The engine pressed on through that and halfway into the ground. If Jack had not already been dead, he would have immediately been knocked unconscious and burned to death quickly.

Stewart and Woolery stepped to either side of the engine and tilted it back upright, uncovering the rest of the gas tank. Tilting it back further, they pulled the crumpled, metal tank off, leaving clear access to Jack's corpse. Jimmy could see why Woolery had brought the shovel. He must have been through this before.

Stewart laid out the canvas sheet alongside the body. Woolery began delicately shoveling Jack's remains out of the mud and onto the canvas sheet. Most of his limbs broke free. The underside, what would have been his chest had remnants of cloth and flying gear unburnt, but he was essentially just a jumbled mass of bones and charred flesh.

Jimmy could not believe his eyes. Just a few, short hours ago, this had been his roommate, Jack Bailey. Jack had laughed his happy laugh, joked with Jimmy about his apprehension, and merrily climbed into his airplane just a little while ago. Once again, Jimmy turned away in revulsion. How could this have happened?

Woolery and Stewart completed their grisly task quickly and efficiently. They rolled the canvas sheet in on itself to hold the bodily remains neatly together.

Stewart slung the canvas roll over his shoulder and they walked back to the HQ tent. Jimmy followed along in the rear, stumbling his way along, hardly able to see through the tears filling his eyes.

Woolery said goodbye and the rest made their way back to the tender. Stewart placed Jack's remains in the bed of the truck and they all climbed in for the long drive back to the aerodrome.

Jimmy sat in a sullen funk on the way home, not saying anything. He had seen death before, going all the way back to his primary flight training, but this was his friend, with whom he had shared his fears, his joys, his hopes, and his sorrows.

Jack was a good pilot. He knew what he was doing. If this could happen to Jack, it could happen to Jimmy, too. No matter how good a pilot he was, Jimmy too could end up a pile of charred, unrecognizable bones and flesh.

They passed by the 2nd Dragoons tent, the aid station, and were passing through Vermelles before Phillips spoke. "Listen, lad, I know you were good friends with young Bailey. It's never easy. We have all watched our friends die. You were lucky to recover as much as you did. Normally, they just disappear somewhere behind the lines only to be blown to smithereens in the next artillery barrage. Often, we never know what happened to them. Surely, you've seen this yourself already."

"Yes, I know," Jimmy said without looking up from the floorboards of the tender.

"This is war, boy. War means death. It happens. You never get used to it, but you do get numbed to it. Now you know why I have not wanted to be your friend. I never know which of you new boys will make it and which will not. Most of you are gone far too soon." Phillips was trying to show him his kinder side. He didn't like to talk much about anything, let alone death.

"I think I see what you mean, Phillips. I just wish Jack had made it."

"Me, too, boy. Me, too."

Jimmy sat in silence the rest of the way, wondering how long he had before his turn came.

They returned from Vermelles around half past two that afternoon. Captain Stevens was waiting for them in Paddington when they arrived. He watched silently as they unloaded the folded canvas from the back of the tender knowing full well what it contained. Uncle took over and had Stewart carry it to the infirmary.

Phillips and Jimmy approached Stevens to debrief him. Phillips did all the talking, thank God. He provided a perfunctory, toneless report of the journey and what they found when they got there.

Captain Stevens nodded solemnly. "Very well, men. I'll make arrangements with Uncle for Bailey's burial and let you know when it will be. Arneson, please collect his personal belongings and get them to Uncle. Oh, and bring his riding boots to dinner and place them on Jack's normal chair in his memory."

Jimmy sat on his bunk staring at Jack's side of the room. Jack had only a few things of his own. His razor with shaving cup and brush, a few underclothes, his three uniforms, a pair of dress boots, a package of letters, a writing tablet, a pencil, and a picture of his family taken at the seaside when he was younger. He stared at the picture. His parents beamed with pride in their handsome and happy little family. There was Jack, the crown prince looking after his little sisters. Jimmy cried thinking how they would crumple in grief when they got the news. Knowing Jack's family would go through these few things, Jimmy reviewed all his letters to be sure there was nothing that would embarrass them or cause them to think anything less of Jack. There was nothing. Jack was a fine young gentleman. A gentleman whose life has just been burnt to a crisp in a rickety old aircraft that should no longer be in service.

Jimmy thought to himself. Was he next? Dear God, what had he gotten himself into? This was turning out totally unlike what he thought it would be. Knights knew no fear. He was afraid every time he went up. Knights rode boldly into battle to vanquish the evil foe hindering their noble quest. He was no knight. He was a quivering weakling. He lay back on his bed sobbing.

Dinner was a somber affair for Jimmy. He arrived as late as he could without being tardy, not wishing to partake in the pre-dinner drinks and banter.

Major McAllister acknowledged the passing of Jack and the lad from C Flight with a toast. He referred to Jack as the darling of the squadron, a lad who will be missed. He said no more than he had times before recognizing lost pilots, but his words were kind and heart-felt. One thing he said struck home, however. "Life is short. Death is certain. This is our life. Let us live it to the fullest while we are still here."

Jimmy walked home and sobbed himself to sleep.

16

TREIZENNES, MARCH, 1917. A field across the road to the north of the Treizennes aerodrome lay freshly plowed. Straight furrows of fertile soil awaited spring planting and promised renewal. Hedgerows to its west and south buffered the field from intrusions and provided homes for wrens, swallows, rabbits, and an occasional hedgehog. A peregrine falcon soared above, hunting for its next meal.

Recovering from a wound he received a few days ago, Jimmy limped over to the field to sooth his soul while his body healed. He crawled through a gap in the hedgerows and sat in the southwest corner of the field, looking over the bucolic expanse, listening to the bird songs, quietly observing the wildlife, and writing in his journal. The peacefulness reminded him of home. The hedgerow shielded him from thoughts of war and gave him respite.

He knew he would recover from his wound, but he couldn't fly for a while. The bullet entered his leg from below and exited out the top of his thigh. It passed right through and didn't hit any major nerves or blood vessels, which was a good thing according to Major Milne, the flight surgeon. "No Blighty for you, laddie," he told Jimmy.

Jimmy found himself reflecting on the incident. They had been flying frequently with the advent of March and the improved weather accompanying it. Activity had increased all along the front, so they were flying four hours a day or more, hunting enemy observation planes, escorting the Sopwiths for artillery spotting and photography runs. It had been exhausting. Every time they had gone up, they had stared into the face of death, who waited out there for all of them.

Jimmy had started hanging around in the mess longer than he used to. The alcohol helped him get to sleep, but it wore off and the nightmares returned. Along with the alcohol came tobacco. He swore he would never do either, but was doing both after only a few weeks at the front.

His new roommate, Freddie McGruder, was a short, stout young fellow from York. He was so full of cheer and patriotism, it made Jimmy want to vomit. He was a good kid, but he just didn't get it. He flew on Alfie's wing, but Jimmy tried to look after him when he could. He occupied Jack's space, but he wasn't Jack.

A few days ago, Uncle interrupted the squadron in the evening mess to give them their orders for the next day. "Attention, gentlemen!" Uncle yelled. "Attention!" Everyone immediately stopped talking and snapped to.

Major McAllister followed Uncle into the room with his grim, purposeful look as usual. "Alright, gentlemen, at ease," he said. They all relaxed, but continued to stand there anxiously. "Tomorrow we shall have a busy day as usual. As for A Flight, on early patrol you are to take out an observation balloon at Lens command says is going to see troop movements we have going on over there. B Flight, you have a mid-morning and late afternoon offensive patrol over our usual hunting grounds, and C Flight, you will do the same at dawn and in the afternoon. Then A Flight, you get to stand down tomorrow afternoon."

This was new to Jimmy. He had never been on a balloon-busting mission before. He had heard they were dangerous because of all the ground fire. Alfie played it up as usual, "I've never gotten a balloon before. I shall look forward to blowing him out of the sky." Jim swore Alfie's blustering drove him nuts sometimes. At least he was a good pilot. Jimmy had to hand that to him.

Young McGruder, always on Jimmy's heels like a little puppy, chimed in, "Oh my, this should be quite the adventure!"

Phillips added his cheery contribution as usual, "Adventure my arse. We'll be lucky to come back alive. Don't you know anything, Shorty?" At least he had a new target for his derision besides Jimmy. They all walked up to the bar to get another drink.

Death haunted Jimmy that night. He started having nightmares after Jack died. Sometimes, he saw Jack's charred body stuck in the mud with the engine smashed down on top. He startled awake with an Archie shell exploding in his face. Jimmy sat there shaking for some time, staring into the dark void, desperately trying to wipe the images out of his mind.

The next morning, they had their dawn briefing from Captain Stevens. Shorty McGruder was to fly on Alfie's left and Jimmy would fly on Phillips' wing as usual. They would climb to five thousand and head over the lines, then all dive on the balloon in single file from the east heading west. If they didn't get it on the first pass, they were to climb out to the right for two more passes or until they ran out of ammo and head home. Lens was the hunting grounds of Jasta 11. A flight of Nieuports from 60 Squadron was supposed to be patrolling that sector above them to keep them occupied, but they were all nervous about getting jumped.

The flight took off at half past seven and headed for the front. The sky had scattered cumulus clouds all around, giving them about a three-tenths sky. Archie waited for them as they crossed over the lines. They kept their eyes peeled as they headed south a half-mile behind the German lines.

Captain Stevens waggled his wings when he saw the balloon and they all fell into a straight line formation behind him. Alfie and Shorty went ahead of Phillips and Jimmy. Jimmy took up the rear.

They dove toward the balloon as fast as their old crates would take them. They were spotted soon by the gun emplacements protecting the balloon. Archie opened up first with the most intense barrage Jimmy had ever seen. Explosions blackened the sky all around them. It was all he could do to keep lined up on the target with his plane getting slammed left and right by the explosions.

When they got down to two thousand feet, the machine guns joined in. Jimmy saw two bursts lace his wings and elevators. One bullet hit a strut and splintered it halfway through.

Jimmy could see the planes in front of him taking hits also. However, the guns were all fully sighted on Jimmy by the time he came over in the tail-end position, so he was getting peppered.

One by one, they came within range of the balloon and opened up on it. Stevens, Campbell, and McGruder all fired as long as they could before they had to pull up. Phillips pressed his attack even longer than the other guys and, just as he broke off, the balloon ignited.

Jimmy flew on towards it, firing himself, but soon saw it was a goner and broke off his attack early. The flames grew quickly and it exploded, rocking his plane over on its side. Jimmy had to roll away from the explosion to regain control.

Just as he did, he saw a flight of four Albatros scouts diving on them from the north. So much for the Nieuport diversionary tactic. The Germans concentrated on Captain Stevens, who turned aggressively into them, and the rest of A Flight followed suit.

The planes broke up into individual combats. Jimmy tried to stay with Phillips but lost him in a tight left turn when he dove after an Albatros. He looked around and saw a blue Albatros making for Alfie's tail. Alfie was turning tightly to the right but the Albatros zoomed into a wingover and got back on his tail.

Jimmy saw an opportunity and took it. Rolling right, he slammed into a dive for the blue bastard. Jimmy almost had him in range and fired off a burst in front of the German, hoping he would fly into it. Jimmy thought one or two of the bullets might have found their mark because the German broke off and turned toward Jimmy.

They passed head-to-head within a few feet of each other. Jimmy was climbing to the right and the Albatros was diving inverted to the left. Their landing gears almost collided. On his back, Jimmy pulled the stick back heading for the dirt.

Just as Jimmy was rolling back out of inverted flight, he heard "Ping, Clank!" sounds as bullets hit his engine. A split-second later, he felt the impact of the bullet in his leg. It was the worst burning sensation he had ever felt, like someone stabbed a hot poker right through him. He had been hit!

Jimmy cranked his neck all around and saw no enemy plane. It must have broken off. He righted his plane and dove for the British lines. Then, he looked down at his leg and saw the blood soaking his flight suit, dark red on tan. He grabbed for it and it hurt so bad he thought he would pass out.

Jimmy tried to get his bearings. He saw the other four members of his flight ahead of him. It looked like they had all taken similar actions and all dove for their lines over the trenches. Fortunately, the British anti-aircraft guns were on the job and scared the Germans away.

His engine started clanking and clunking and making an awful, vibrating ruckus threatening to tear the airplane apart. Jimmy pulled out the fuel mixture and the engine jerked to a stop. He looked ahead to see if he had enough altitude to make it over the trenches. It looked close. Without power, he was dead-sticking his airplane.

Jimmy started to lose consciousness from the loss of blood. He tried to keep pressure on his wound but it hurt so badly he couldn't do it. His eyes got blurry and he struggled to stay with it. He put both hands on the stick to focus.

The ground came rushing up as Jimmy grazed just barely over several shell holes below him. His mind flashed on Jack's charred and crumpled body. Jimmy couldn't let his engine slam into him like Jack's did. Jimmy jammed the right rudder pedal all the way in and slammed the stick over to the left, putting his plane into a severe side slip. He knew he would lose height rapidly but he hoped it might bring him in almost sideways. That way, maybe the momentum of the engine would go sideways instead of straight into him.

Bam! Jimmy hit the ground! His left wing splintered and the nose crumpled in a mess. He was thrown out of the cockpit ahead of the plane. He crawled away as fast as he could into the next bomb crater and his plane blew up in flames. Jimmy peeked his head over the edge of the crater and immediately jerked back down as bullets whizzed by, spitting up the dirt. As he lay on his back in the shell hole, the sky faded into blackness and Jimmy lost consciousness.

"Lieutenant! Lieutenant!" Jimmy felt someone shaking him. He clawed his way up to consciousness to find a young Tommy soldier shaking him awake.

"Lieutenant, wake up! We need to get you out of here!" the young Tommy pleaded.

"Wha' what?" he mumbled.

"We need to get you out of here! Harry, grab his shoulder and let's go."

The two Tommies, each grabbing a shoulder of Jimmy's tunic, dragged him over the rim of the shell hole into the next one. Bullets sprayed dirt over them as they hit the rim of the crater.

"Are you a Canadian, lieutenant?" one of the soldiers asked him as he looked at his Canada shoulder patch.

"Mmm, 'merican," Jimmy mumbled.

"Harry, did you hear that, he's a bloomin' Yank!" the soldier exclaimed.

They pulled Jimmy, one shell hole at a time, back to their trenches. Each time they lunged over the rim of a crater, the German machine guns raised dirt all around them in near misses. After several such lunges, they dropped into the British trenches in a muddy, slippery crash.

"Well, well, well, look what the cat dragged in!" Sergeant O'Brien exclaimed. "You all right there, lieutenant, sir?"

Jimmy gradually regained consciousness. "Thank you! Thank you!" was all he could muster.

"Let's have a look at your leg, lieutenant." Sergeant O'Brien lifted Jimmy's leg to examine his wound. Jimmy leaped a mile in pain when he did so. It was excruciating. "Blimey, sir, you may have just got yourself a Blighty there. There's many a lad here in the trenches would love to get a wound like this. You may just get to go home to merry old, sir!"

"No, I can't!" Jimmy grimaced through his teeth. "I can't do that!" He honestly didn't know why he even said it, but he did.

"Looks like the bullet went clean through your leg. Can you move your foot?" O'Brien asked.

Jimmy rolled his ankle around. "Yes, but it hurts like hell!" he said.

"Yes, it probably does. But it's a good sign you can move your foot. It means there's no nerve damage and probably no significant bone damage either." O'Brien had obviously seen many wounds in his time in the trenches. "We'll get you on a stretcher back to the aid station, sir. I thinks you'll be right as rain in no time, sir."

"Thank you so very much, gents. You've saved my life!" Jimmy owed a great debt to these men. Looking at how they lived, he could understand why they were called 'PBI' for poor bloody infantry by the RFC.

"Did you 'ear that, Harry?" The young Tommy laughed. "He called us gents!"

Chuckling, Sergeant O'Brien replied, "That's all right, lieutenant. Nothing we wouldn't do for one of our own. If you don't mind me asking, sir, why did you join the suicide club anyway?"

"Suicide club?" Jimmy asked.

"Yes, sir, that's what we call the Flying Corps. You blokes seem to be falling like flies, sir!"

It certainly seemed to fit lately. "Now you mention it, I'd say you're spot on!"

They loaded Jimmy up on a stretcher and the men cheered him off. Two kind lads carried him back through the communications trenches, dropped him off at the aid station and wished him well before returning to their unit. Jimmy never did find out what outfit they were from. He owed them his life.

Judging by the other soldiers being treated at the aid station, Jimmy found himself feeling fortunate. Some of those men, even if they lived, were going to be horribly maimed and disfigured. He watched an orderly draw a blanket over a soldier's face on the cot next to him. To his other side, he looked down to see the foot of the soldier next to him lying next to his lower leg. The soldier grimaced in constant pain.

The doctor gave Jimmy a quick look over when his turn came. Jimmy never even knew his name and he doubted the doctor knew his. He was just another patient in a long succession. The doctor jammed a swab in his wound on both entry and exit points and stuck a metal prod down the hole and looked around. It hurt like hell. Speaking to his assistant, Jimmy heard him say, "Bullet passed through muscle tissue alone. No major blood vessels, nerves or bones hit. No fabric in the wound. Lucky man. Give him a single dose of morphine, cauterize entry and exit points, sew him up, notify his unit to pick him up, and send him on his way." The doctor moved on to the next in line.

The morphine took effect quickly and deadened Jimmy's pain. Then, the orderly set about his work quickly and efficiently. "Looks like you'll be in good shape in no time, sir. You're quite lucky."

In a matter of an hour or so, Jimmy had been treated and placed in a waiting area to await his transport. The morphine kept him in a dreamy state so the time passed imperceptibly.

A couple of hours later, Uncle came along with a driver in the Crossley to retrieve Jimmy. "Young Arneson, so very good to see you, laddie! We were afraid you had gone west on us, old boy!" He and the driver loaded Jimmy into the truck and padded him all around with blankets to make him as comfortable as possible. "I see you got it in the leg. Is it painful?"

"The shot of morphine took the pain away but it's wearing off now," Jimmy replied.

"I hope you don't end up on a cane like me. You recall that's where I got it in the Boer Wars."

"I'm too young to be an uncle, Uncle!" Jimmy laughed. He tried to hold the proverbial stiff upper lip, but the pain was beginning to roar back. "Do you think I'll be able to fly again?"

"From what I heard, it sounds like it. We'll have Major Milne take a look at it when we get back." Uncle was wary, but seemed confident enough. "I want you to know, Arneson, the flight was truly saddened to see you go down. There was nothing they could do, of course."

"Of course. It was a hornet's nest up there."

"Campbell, especially," Uncle said. "He knows what you did for him up there."

That got to Jimmy. His eyes watered, "I'm glad, Uncle." He looked away and they stopped talking while Jimmy dealt with the pain.

The ride passed quickly enough. Jimmy's leg continued to hurt badly, but the searing pains were replaced with throbbing aches. He tried to move it around to find a more comfortable arrangement, but it was no good. He just resigned himself to it.

Jimmy wondered if he would be able to fly again and how long it would be before he could get back up. Just like the cowpokes back home, having been knocked off his horse he couldn't wait to get back up again. He was scared to death of it, but he was driven to it.

Inside, he descended into darkness for a while. Jimmy had been extremely lucky, but he had indeed been shot down. He never knew what hit him. He never saw the German who did it. His number may not have been drawn this day, but it came close. "How long will it be before I don't come back?" he asked himself. He tried to not think about it, but those thoughts always lurked under the surface. They came up too often.

They bounced their way back into the field around three o'clock. Jimmy was tired and sore, but his spirits leapt when he was greeted by a small welcoming committee as they pulled up. McGruder cheered out, "Hurrah!" and the other fellows laughed. Even Phillips had a grin on his face. Ales in hand, they passed one his way and patted him on the back.

Captain Stevens was even there and said, "Welcome home, boy!"

Campbell pushed his way past McGruder, "I'm glad you made it, mate. Thanks for what you did up there. You saved my life!"

Jimmy was gratified. "It was nothing!" "Ha!" he thought to himself. It may have been the best tankard of ale Jimmy ever had.

17

TREIZENNES, MARCH, 1917. Jimmy awoke groggily the next morning. His head was thick from the excessive amount of ale he consumed the night before. No one had tried to wake him, fortunately, so he slept in quite late.

He was grounded from his wound. Major Milne looked it over thoroughly later. He would be okay. The wounds would heal but it would take some time. In the meantime, he would not be able to fly because he wouldn't be able to operate the rudders adequately.

His flight had taken the early patrol without Jimmy, so he had a late plate of beans with a couple of the boys from B Flight. They were due to make a big, two-flight patrol shortly thereafter with C Flight.

He hobbled in on crutches and was met by Stinky Kincaid. "Well, if it isn't little Arneson the cripple! I hear you took a bullet up your arse yesterday. Did it remind you of me?"

"Oh, shut up, Stinky!" Bertie O'Brien chimed in. "He hasn't even had his morning cuppa yet. Give him a chance!"

"Thanks, Bertie!" Jimmy said. "Say, the PBI sergeant that helped me in the trenches yesterday was named O'Brien. Any chance you're related?"

"Well, that's interesting, isn't it? I don't know a PBI O'Brien, but there certainly is a chance. My grandfather Charlie was said to be very well-endowed like myself, so he could have sired many little O'Briens!"

"Ha! Takes you half an hour to even find the little thing!" Kincaid was in rare form this morning.

"Anyway, sit down old boy. Tell us all about your great adventure. Do you get to go home to Blighty?" O'Brien asked.

"Doc Milne says I'll be okay, but I'll probably be laid up a few days before I can fly. I wouldn't be able to handle the rudder very well with this." He tenderly patted his thigh.

"You can't handle a rudder worth a damn without the bullet. At least you have an excuse now." Kincaid again.

"Bah, don't listen to his guff. Glad you made it back, old boy. I've got to get off to study the charts before our big do. Enjoy your time off while you can!" O'Brien and Kincaid both got up and trotted off.

Jimmy took his time enjoying his plate of beans and cup of tea in solitude. He was glad to sit it out for a bit. Afterwards, he decided to sit on one of the benches behind the chateau for a little while and take in the sun. It was looking to be a nice day with only a few, high wisps of stratus off to the south.

While he was sitting there, the big patrol took off in a roar. It was rather impressive to see nine airplanes taking off all at once. This was a new thing for them. They were flying in greater numbers to better counter the larger flights from Jasta 11. Their entrance into 40 Squadron's sector had made their lives miserable. The PBI did have one thing right. RFC pilots were dropping like flies. Jimmy rather doubted all nine would return.

He hobbled back to his hut and took a nap, tired from the exertion. Shorty McGruder woke him up a couple of hours later. "I thought I would let you sleep for a bit. A Flight got back a little over an hour ago."

"Thanks," Jimmy said, wiping the sleepers from his eyes.

"The big patrol is due back anytime. Think you can walk over there to see how they made out?" Shorty asked.

"Sure, let's do that. Just give me a minute to get dressed."

Jimmy hobbled over to Paddington with Shorty. Phillips and Alfie Campbell were there as well, catching some sun in the lounge chairs off to the side of the tarmac. Wilson and Stewart were working on the rigging of Phillips' plane in front of the hangar.

"Hullo, Arnie." Phillips was unusually nice today. "How's your leg today?"

"All right, I guess. I had a lovely lay in this morning and a nice little nap just now. It still throbs quite a bit. The pills Doc Milne gave me help keep the edge off." Truth be known, Jimmy was feeling a bit groggy still from the nap and the pain pills.

"Any news of the big patrol, then?" Shorty added.

"Nothing yet," Alfie replied.

Shorty rounded up a couple of chairs for Jimmy and him and joined Phillips and Campbell. The sun felt so good. Jimmy snoozed again while they all sat there.

"There, I see one!" McGruder startled him awake. "Look, he's smoking!"

A single FE8 was working its way in, bobbing around like a bumble bee, trailing a thin line of smoke out the rear of the plane. It rose and fell, slipped right, corrected, and slipped off to the left again. The pilot must be hurt or have had his controls shot up to be bobbing about like that.

In he came, lining up for a landing straight in from the southwest. He side-slipped a little, just enough for Jimmy to make out the red numeral 3 on the side of his cockpit, then righted himself just before touching down. Red 3 was Bertie O'Brien.

Bertie landed hard and bounced back up. Then, suspended in air momentarily, he stalled and the nose pointed down too sharply to recover from. He crashed.

As was too often the case, the plane plowed on in, its engine drove into the gas tank, and lit it up before driving Bertie into the dirt, just like Jack. The plane exploded in flames as everyone ran out to it.

Jimmy couldn't run with his leg, so he sat there, stunned. How lucky he had been just yesterday to avoid the same fate. Images of poor Jack welled up in his mind's eye.

The crowd gathered around the plane, but there was nothing anyone could do. After ten minutes or so, they all came back in, leaving the clean up to the wrecking crew. Bertie was gone.

They sat there speculating. Where were all the other planes? Usually, they all came in together. Maybe Bertie came home early with engine problems or something. They waited for a good hour or more before deciding to hit the mess for drinks.

Captain Stevens joined them an hour or two later. He looked more somber than usual as he approached the men. "We've been getting calls from artillery emplacements near where the action took place. They also got a call from 60 Squadron, who was there, too. They joined the fracas late. None of them made it, boys. All nine planes and pilots are lost."

"Oh, my God!" exclaimed Shorty. "What happened?"

"From what we've been able to piece together, they got jumped by Richthofen and his bunch from Jasta 11. Four planes were shot down in the initial swarm behind their lines. Five planes, including Bertie, straggled home, chased by the Albatros scouts. They fell, one by one, on their way back. Only Bertie made it back to the field, and we all know what happened to him. The rest are strung along their path home."

"Jesus H. Christ," Phillips said. "These damned planes are going to kill us all."

"Major McAllister will address us at dinner. In the meantime, we will be trying to get a better picture put together. That's all I have to say for now. It's a black day for 40 Squadron, men. It's a black day." Captain Stevens put his cap back on and walked upstairs to the Squadron office.

Phillips, Campbell, McGruder, and Arneson made their way to the mess. "God almighty." Alfie Campbell was shaken like he had never seen before. "Who all was on the mission?"

Shorty chimed in. "B Flight had Ridley, the flight commander of course, Stinky Kincaid, and Eugene Malone. Bertie flew with them too, obviously."

"Scruffy Adams would have led C Flight," Phillips added. "Fatty Dunn and Puffy Hughes were supposed to go up as well. I don't know who the others would have been."

"Brentworth and Marsh," Jimmy added. "I know because I had tea with Bertie and Stinky before they left. They mentioned Brentworth and Marsh were going with C Flight."

"I guess the aristocracy die in this god-awful war right along with the rest of us sods," Alfie said.

"Sods is right," Phillips said. "Our lives matter so little to those blokes who run this flying corps. We're just numbers to them. They just do their math every day. Four more lambs for the slaughter to 40 Squadron, two to 60 Squadron, and so on, and so on. All they care about is filling the empty chairs the dead leave behind every day."

"Just look at the crates they expect us to fly," Campbell added. "These old FE8 clap trap piles of shite may have been adequate in 1915 against the Eindeckers, but things have moved on since then.

What kind of incompetence in the government allows them to send us out to fight in such deathtraps?"

Phillips said, "Well, those Froggies know how to make better planes. Their little Nieuport scout can handle those Albatros buggers. I don't see why our government doesn't just buy some from them."

"Motivating, isn't it?" Alfie said. "Get up there, do your job, get home and do it again the next day. Hooray for the next man to die!"

"Blast, we don't even have Fatty Dunn to play us a tune." Phillips was getting inebriated quickly. Normally unflappable, he was bothered by this, bothered deeply.

Shorty, ever the optimist, raised his glass high, "Here's to the brave men who gave their lives for King and Country today!"

They all raised their glasses and tossed down as much alcohol as they could take, each of them wondering if they were next.

Needless to say, dinner was a somber affair. They all took their usual places, but nine chairs had empty boots on them. Half of the squadron had been wiped out in a single day.

Major McAllister and Uncle joined them shortly after they had all taken their seats. Uncle gave his perfunctory, "Attention!" order and they all stood. The senior officers looked tired and drawn.

Wordless, the major waved them back to their seats. "Gentlemen, I assure you we feel this loss deeply, just as you do. Ridley and Adams were as close to me as friends as all of you are to each other. Each and every one of you is important to me. I have the deepest respect for your bravery in the face of death. I have further news to share with you tonight, but first, let us raise a glass to the intrepid spirits of nine brave and honorable brothers who have gone west today."

They all stood, raised their glasses, and downed their contents. Most of them were pretty drunk already, so they plopped down heavily afterwards.

"Gentlemen, first I want to share with you what we know about today's fateful patrol. Then, I will convey what I have been able to glean from several discussions I have had with my superiors today. I realize most of you are inebriated. That's all right. I shall be joining you as soon as I discharge my duties as your squadron commander this evening.

"Richthofen and his pilots have been coming out more boldly in larger numbers, as you well know. It has not been unusual to see ten or fifteen of their number in a single flight. In response, we hoped to match them by flying in larger numbers ourselves. Such was the intent of today's 'big patrol.' However, it merely served to highlight, even more profoundly, the inadequacy of our FE8 aircraft to do battle with Jasta 11's Albatros DIII aircraft."

"Here, here!" a few of the men half-grumbled.

"Our men were patrolling east of Béthune at ten thousand feet when they were jumped by Jasta 11, diving from fifteen thousand. You all know their tactics well, I am sure. They ripped through our formation, took out two of our number on the first pass, and zoomed back up on the backside to line up for another pass.

"Try as we might, we could not rise to meet them and lost two more in the second pass. Nieuports from 60 Squadron saw this action from a distance but were not able to get to our men in time to avert the slaughter. They dove on the melee as our remaining aircraft were diving away to get out. Several of the DIIIs followed our aircraft and were able to catch up to our pilots and eliminate them one at a time. We have received eye witness accounts from both members of 60 Squadron and from artillery and infantry outfits on the ground.

"Our men fought bravely, just as each and every one of you do each and every day. However, we suffered greatly. Ever bright and cheery Bertie O'Brien was the only one to make it back to the field, but he too, died in his attempt to land his broken plane. My heart is heavy with today's loss, just as yours are, I am sure.

"Captain Hargrove and I have also been having a running string of conversations with Wing and Brigade headquarters today. The news of our losses and the reasons for those losses have been forcibly conveyed to our superiors. They have at last listened.

"Effective immediately, 40 Squadron is to stand down from air operations until further notice. In the morning, you are to fly our remaining FE8s to Wye Air Station in Kent and turn them over to Number 51 Reserve Squadron for use in pilot training there. Once you have completed this task, each of you is granted four days leave to briefly visit with your families in England. Upon your return, I have been assured we will have replacement pilots in place and a full complement of Nieuport Scouts built under license by British factories. I do not know the specific models, but we should find out shortly."

Alfie Campbell stood up and yelled, "Three cheers for Major McAllister!" They all stood and joined in, "Hurrah! Hurrah!

Hurrah!" This was great news. At last they would be given a plane capable of taking on the Albatros scouts. Somehow, it seemed to give some meaning to the deaths of their friends.

"Having now conveyed that information, and fulfilled my duties as your commander, please pass the nearest bottle forward!" Major McAllister sat down and proceeded to get drunk along with the rest of them. Fortunately for all of them, Uncle remained somewhat sober to care for them all and see them into bed.

18

TREIZENNES, MARCH, 1917. Jimmy would have the slept the entire next day if his bladder hadn't forced him to wake up. His mind was thick, resisting thought as he crawled out of bed and stumbled across the room to the piss pot in the corner. His mouth felt like a PBI had marched through it caked with mud, and his head felt like it was clamped in a vice.

He pried open his eyes to see Shorty sprawled on his bed with an arm and leg hanging over the side. Shorty would be in the same shape soon. Indeed, the whole squadron awoke with massive hangovers. The breakfast mess was like a hospital ward, filled with pilots who had been poisoned with alcohol. Their attending orderlies rather enjoyed the show.

The good news was, for the first day in weeks, they did not have to fly into battle. They could afford to be hung over. For the first day in weeks, they could rest for a while. After late breakfasts and gallons of hot tea, they all packed their kits for a few days leave. By eleven o'clock in the morning, on a crystal blue, clear day, they were all ready for take-off. The nine remaining FE8s of 40 Squadron took off into the skies of France for the last time.

They headed across the English Channel at Calais at eight thousand feet. It was a beautiful, calm day. The sun warmed the backs of their necks as they flew north. Captain Stevens led the triple vic formation. Soon, they were approaching the white cliffs of Dover. What a beautiful sight it was. They veered to the left and found Wye airfield within a few more minutes. It had taken them less than two hours to fly from Treizennes to Wye. What a treat it was to fly without Archie exploding all around and Germans diving out of the sun to take your life.

The turnover of their aircraft to the training squadron was strangely bittersweet for Jimmy. He suspected it was true for most of the men. These planes were outclassed by their enemy and claimed the lives of too many of their friends. The men hated them for that. However, they had been 40 Squadron's means of fighting the enemy for months. Jimmy's original plane ended up a crumpled wreck in no man's land, but still, he had the sentimental attachment to the type one gets after having survived stressful times together.

As soon as the turnover was complete, Captain Stevens released the pilots for their leaves. Joyously, they all headed to the train station to purchase tickets and one-by-one and two-by-two, they all scattered to the four corners of the kingdom with slaps on the back and well wishes.

Jimmy decided to go to Salisbury to visit Jack Bailey's parents. He knew there was nothing he could say to comfort them, but he felt he owed it to his closest friend in 40 Squadron. It took the better part of a day to get there by train. He had to transfer trains at Waterloo Station in London.

Jimmy arrived unannounced the following day. Mr. Bailey answered the door. "Hello, can I help you?"

"Mr. Bailey, my name is Jim Arneson. I shared a hut with your son, Jack, with 40 Squadron in France."

Mr. Bailey's kind face transformed to one of intense sadness. He looked down at his shoes, then slowly worked his way up. His eyes were full of tears when they met his once more. He blinked them away and tear drops fell onto the entry way rug. "Why of course, you're Jimmy. Jack spoke of you in his letters. You were good friends, he said. Please, please come in."

"Thank you, sir." He entered their small, warm, and tidy home. The smell of home-baked bread wafted in from the kitchen. A couch and two well-worn wingback chairs surrounded a dark wooden coffee table in the reception room. A sidebar covered with pictures of friends and family showed a large portrait of Jack prominently in the center, the position of honor, wearing his RFC uniform. It took Jimmy's breath away to see Jack's face again.

"Mother, come, look who's here. It's Jimmy, Jack's friend from France!"

Mrs. Bailey hobbled out from the kitchen, favoring her right hip and drying her hands on her apron as she walked. "My Lord, it is you. Welcome to our home, young man. Please, welcome. Will you have a cup of tea?"

"That would be kind of you, ma'am." Jimmy walked into the reception room and sat on the sofa. Mr. Bailey sat in his easy chair.

"Cigarette, Jimmy?" Mr. Bailey offered.

"Thank you!" He reached out to retrieve a smoke from the smoke box. Mr. Bailey struck a match and lit his and Jimmy's alike.

"Tell me, Jimmy, what brings you here? Do you have something to tell us?" Mr. Bailey asked.

"I have no special information to convey, Mr. Bailey. I was here in England turning in our old planes and just had to come here to meet you, I guess to honor Jack. He was my best friend at 40 Squadron. Such a good man and such a help to me when I first got there."

Mrs. Bailey brought in the tea tray and poured him a cup. "Milk or sugar, Jimmy?"

"No, ma'am, just black, thank you." He had learned English families were rationed tightly and milk and sugar were expensive rarities.

"Well, thank you, Jim. We were devastated when we heard of Jack's death. He was our only son. I had hoped he might take over the shoe shop when he returned. Now, I don't know what I shall do. One carries on, doesn't one?" The old stiff upper lip of the British, he thought. "Tell me, Jimmy, were you with Jack when he died?"

"In a way, yes, sir. We were each alone in our own aeroplanes, but we were on the same patrol when he got hit."

"Yes, we received a nice letter from a Captain Stevens. Tell me, Jimmy, did Jack suffer?"

Jimmy squirmed. "He, he died quickly, Mr. Bailey. He died quickly." His voice tailed away. He couldn't tell them the awful truth. He just couldn't. It would not be right. "Jack was a hero, sir. He fought bravely all the way to the end. He received a military burial with full honors and lies in the cemetery by the aerodrome in Treizennes."

Mrs. Bailey began to weep quietly into her tea. She bowed her head and couldn't look up. Mr. Bailey was trying to put on a good show, but Jimmy could tell they were both shaken by his presence. It brought back to them such painful memories of the bad news they received.

He took a sip of tea. "I just wanted you to know he meant a lot to me, Mr. and Mrs. Bailey. He was such a good man and a good friend. I am sorry for having freshened the pain you must have felt."

"Please, don't feel bad, young man," Mrs. Bailey spoke up. "We loved our little Jack so much. Of course, it is painful to revisit it but we are so grateful for you to stop by."

"I must go, I am afraid. I need to get back to the squadron." Jimmy had more time, but he couldn't stay any longer. He would not know what to say and he thought it best to leave them alone in their grief. It had been a mistake to come here, he realized. Jimmy stood, replaced his tea cup on the saucer and made for the door.

They rose with him and escorted him. "Thank you, Jimmy. Thank you," was all Mr. Bailey said. He shook his hand goodbye and Mrs. Bailey gave him a warm hug. Jimmy took his leave.

There were few places more tranquil than the English countryside and there were few ways better to take it all in than a ride on the train. Melancholy from his visit to Jack's parents, Jimmy treated himself to a first class ticket and stared out the window at the rolling fields and forests of Wiltshire, Hampshire, and Sussex on his way to Folkestone. The next morning he arranged passage to France on a crowded troop ship. A river of green, there were always thousands of Commonwealth soldiers headed to the meat grinder in France. Jimmy knew better now what they were in for and it saddened him. So many fine young men snuffed out so early. Once across the Channel, he hitched a ride in a tender to Treizennes from Boulogne-Sur-Mer.

He was one of the first men back. When he arrived, Jimmy quickened at the sight of a long line of Nieuport scouts waiting to be flown. They were beautiful. Compared to the FE8s, they were small but sleek with their silver-doped sides and so muscular with their rotary engines up front. The hangars were abuzz with mechanics getting others ready to go.

Jimmy checked in with Uncle, threw his kit into his hut, and immediately headed to Paddington to see what Wilson and Stewart were up to. He found them there as he expected, working on the rigging of one of the new airplanes.

He was surprised to find Captain Stevens working right alongside them. "Well hello, sir! How do you do?" Jimmy said as he walked around the nose of the Nieuport.

Stevens was in good humor, perhaps better than Jimmy had ever seen him. A smile grew on his face. "Arneson! Welcome back, boy. Where did you go on leave?"

"I visited Jack Bailey's parents in Salisbury," he replied.

"Ah, how did that go?" Stevens asked, turning somber.

"It was terribly awkward, I'm afraid," he replied. "They were so sad. I couldn't tell them much. They received your letter and said it was nice."

"Yes, well I'm glad they got it. Visits like that always are awkward, Arneson. I went on a few myself at first."

"Yes, sir." Changing the subject back to a brighter topic, "I see you are getting to know our new birds!"

"Yes! They're marvelous!" Stevens had his sleeves rolled up and hands covered in grease. A black slash of grease across his forehead showed where he had apparently scratched an itch. "We're tuning the rigging on this one. I think these aircraft will make a huge difference for us against the Hun."

"Have you flown one, yet, sir?" he asked.

"Oh yes. They're magnificent. Go pick one out for yourself and get up there to try it out. It will be like nothing you've flown before!"

"Any one I like?" Jimmy said.

"Any one you like! None have been assigned yet. This one's mine. We'll paint flight markings on them after the rest get settled in. Get a briefing from Captain Newcombe first. He's been assigned here temporarily to help us settle in on the new birds. I think you'll find him in Waterloo."

Like a schoolboy at Christmas, Jimmy walked among the planes on his way to see Newcombe, trying to decide which he might want. He knew he couldn't make a good choice without flying all of them, but he also knew it was impractical. He found Captain Newcombe in Waterloo just as Captain Stevens had thought. Newcombe was a nice enough fellow. Jimmy explained what he was after in a plane and Newcombe walked him though the instrumentation, pre-flight checks, and startup procedures. He explained what to expect in the way of performance. His biggest caveat was to avoid over-stressing the bottom wing. It could break off in a high-speed dive or high g-force maneuvers.

Jimmy picked one of the Nieuports at random and took it up. It was a dream. The big, 120 horsepower Le Rhóne motor roared powerfully after warm-up. Jimmy lurched forward when Wilson pulled the chocks out, and was airborne in an instant.

Climbing out to the west, Jimmy simply could not believe how quickly he gained altitude. When he got to seven thousand feet, he started experimenting with maneuvers. At first, he did fairly simple things like S-turns and stalls. As he got more accustomed to the incredible responsiveness of the controls, he advanced to more difficult maneuvers. He did steep turns, wingovers, Immelmanns, rolls, loops, and spins. The roll rate into a tight turn to the left was fantastic, not so much to the right. He also found he could almost do a flat turn on a dime with the rudder alone and the snap roll was split-second. The speed in a dive was good, but he held back for fear of losing his lower wing. This little plane did his bidding at the mere touch on the controls.

He liked the tractor arrangement of the engine. Having the engine in front instead of behind meant that engine warmth worked its way back into the cockpit. It was significantly warmer at altitude than the old pusher FE8 setup. There were two downsides however. First, the castor oil expressed by the engine came right back in his face. The windscreen deflected it a little bit, but he could tell he would get smeared with oil every flight. A more sinister negative of the tractor-engine arrangement was the gas tank right in front of him. If a bullet set the tank on fire, he would get burned to a crisp.

It felt strange to not have the machine gun right in front of him. The Nieuport had a single Lewis gun, like the FE8, but it was situated on top of the upper wing to get its line of fire outside the propeller arc. A gunsight in front of the windscreen helped to aim the gun. The gun was mounted on a rail allowing it to be pulled down toward the pilot to change ammunition drums. It could also be used to fire up above the pilot if desired.

Overall, the difference from his old plane was so dramatic Jimmy realized for the first time that he never knew just how obsolete the old FE8s were. Perhaps that was a good thing because he might have revolted. It's tragic to think the English government's slow bureaucracy sent so many pilots to their deaths in such inadequate aircraft.

The rest of the pilots and the replacements showed up later that day and the next, so they were at full complement again. Jimmy was still rooming with Shorty McGruder, but most people had new roommates to get to know. Drinks in the mess were chaotic as no one knew anyone else. He found himself considered one of the old hands, which he found rather odd. He had only been at the front for a month!

Major McAllister pulled them together for a squadron briefing before dinner. He welcomed them all and told them of changes he was making to the squadron leadership. Two new flight commanders were needed for B and C Flights. He appointed Colin 'Fritz' Walker to Flight commander for B Flight and moved Nathaniel Brown from B Flight to C Flight as their new flight commander.

Jimmy could tell from his expression that Alfie Campbell resented not being chosen. However, he was glad to hear he was assigned to the number two spot on B Flight. At least he got some form of recognition.

Phillips, McGruder and Jimmy all stayed with A Flight, which was good news to Jimmy. He liked Captain Stevens immensely. Phillips remained at number two spot but he was to have a new fledgling, Geoffrey Clark, while Jimmy was advanced to number three position with Shorty in his tow.

Major McAllister shared missions for tomorrow. "Okay, A Flight, you're up for an offensive patrol at dawn from here to Laon. B Flight, you have the same at noon, and C Flight, you're on the same run at four o'clock. That's all, gentlemen. Tear up the sky with your new birds tomorrow. Good night!" He turned and left the room while they all stood at attention.

When the orderly banged on the door at four o'clock the next morning, Jimmy awoke fresh and glad he had retired early to get a good night's sleep. They were all eager to get into the sky with their new planes, but he still had the sense of foreboding that preceded every flight. Archie would still be out there gunning for him, and the Albatros scouts were still the fastest plane in the sky.

They mounted up and took off at half past four. Their climb out went quickly as they no longer needed to zig-zag their way up and could climb to ten thousand feet in a straight line to the front. They continued to climb to twelve thousand on the first part of the patrol. The warmth from the engine was welcome at this altitude. It was still frigid, but not nearly as bad as it had been in the old FE8.

The air was thinner at twelve thousand. It would take some getting used to. He felt a little lightheaded up there. They had all been briefed on hypoxia, but they feared it nonetheless, as the onset was deceptive. They had been told it got better over time as they got used to it more.

Archie was waiting for them as usual. The flight flew higher and faster now, but Archie still came awfully close. Jimmy took a close call at his ten o'clock that rocked him almost vertical. He thought he would die from an Archie shell, one of these days, when he least expected it. He often dwelled on it in moments of silence. Oddly enough, he found it therapeutic to accept the inevitability of his own death. It made it easier to go on. He would miss his darling Ellie and he would never see the baby she carried, but it was too late now.

His new spot at number three position was a bit of a change for him. He now formed behind Captain Stevens' left wing instead of Phillips' right, as before. Also, McGruder was formed on him to his rear left. He was sandwiched between the two now. He had to count on McGruder to react to his adjustments quickly.

Jimmy also knew, for the first time, he would be leading another pilot when they engaged with the enemy, instead of focusing on staying with Phillips. Would he know what to do or would he freeze, killing both McGruder and himself? He did not have to wait long to find out.

Stevens spotted two Roland observation planes heading for their lines over Béthune. They were flying at about five thousand feet, little more than dots a mile and a half below them. Stevens signaled for Jimmy and McGruder to stay high to watch for Huns while he, Phillips, and Clark went after the Rolands.

Jimmy watched them dive out of the corner of his eye while he scanned the skies for enemy fighters. The scattered puffs of cumulus made excellent cover for anyone playing hide and seek. Sure enough, halfway into Stevens' dive, Jimmy saw four brightly colored Albatros DIIIs start their dive after them from the southeast.

Jimmy and Shorty aimed to intercept them before they could disrupt the attack, but they didn't think they would be quite able to get to them in time. They dove as fast as they dared. Jimmy could feel the bottom wings flutter a bit and had to blip the engine a bit to slow down. It would be close.

He was sure Stevens saw the Germans but Stevens pressed his attack on the Rolands. The German aircraft started to turn to the left in their dive to get behind the three attackers. It was a stupid thing to do. It gave Jimmy time to get close enough to fire deflection shots at the lead. Shorty stayed with him as he dove, fired, and rolled right to come around behind them.

The lead Albatros, a bright blue and white color, instinctively pulled up to the right when Jimmy's shots hit his wing. The other three Germans followed their leader in chaotic fashion. Jimmy had jumped the jumpers!

When he came out of his roll, Jimmy was almost on the tail of the tail-end German aircraft, a yellow and green number. All four airplanes were in a climbing spiral to the right. Jimmy was ecstatic to not only be able to stay with them in this maneuver, but to even start pulling lead on the yellow and green bird.

Jimmy fired, but too soon. His lead was not sufficient and the bullets fell away behind him. He stayed with the German, pulling his stick ever tighter, trying to pull lead on him. Then, without warning, his wing stalled and he fell over into a spin to his right. "Damn!" he yelled aloud. He recovered as soon as he could but he had lost several hundred feet with no opportunity to catch up again. McGruder had slacked off the turn when he saw Jimmy break and stayed close. The two rejoined and made for the rest of the flight again.

Stevens and the other two had completed their first pass and smoked one of the Rolands. It was diving to the east while they lined up for another pass on the remaining observation plane. Stevens had seen Jimmy spin and knew the Germans were headed his way. He broke off to engage them while Phillips and Clark pursued the Roland.

Stevens took them head on and got one of them in the head-to-head pass. He spun his Nieuport around so quickly he was on the Germans' tails again before they had even entered their turn back to him. He was turning inside of them and was gaining on them when McGruder and Jimmy made it back to him. The Germans saw three Nieuports on three of their own and dove away to the east, abandoning the remaining Roland.

They dove after the Germans and stayed with them so much better than they could have in the FE8s, but the DIIIs were still faster in a dive and they soon knew they were going to get away.

They broke off and headed back to join Phillips and Clark. Phillips had hit the second Roland on his second pass. It was trailing a thick line of black smoke and diving away to the east when they rejoined.

Wow! It was their first victorious engagement with the DIIIs. These Nieuports were absolutely the best. If only Jimmy had felt the stall before it took over, he might have had a kill.

They joined up on Captain Stevens again and climbed back up to twelve thousand feet. They had lost nine thousand feet in the scuffle. It took them no time to get back up in these beautiful machines. The rest of the patrol was uneventful and they headed back home energized and proud of their new birds.

As soon as they touched down, Jimmy had to bolt for the latrine. Sadly, Jimmy found this to be a regular occurrence, having ingested more oil than healthy from the engine spray.

19

VIMY, MAY, 1917. Hank Jacobs had worked in the motor pool for nearly eight months when Sergeant McBride strode up to him with a most satisfied, smug look on his face. "I have a new assignment for you, Shylock. Since we are experiencing a shortage in tenders at present, I have been ordered to begin retrieving damaged tenders from the front and bringing them back here to repair. You, Jew boy, are the lucky one who gets to go to the front lines today to recover the first one."

"What do you mean?" he asked.

"I mean you go get the tow truck, load up the tools you think you'll need and go recover vehicles I send you to. If you can fix a vehicle there, do so, and make it available to the nearest headquarters. If not, hook it up and tow it back here."

"How will I know where to go?" he asked.

"Because I will tell you, idiot. Look here at this map." He laid out a map on a nearby table. "This here 'x' is the location of several vehicles damaged in the last battle out near Vimy Ridge. You go out there and fix what you can and bring one back. It's located south of Lens. See there? Don't come back empty-handed."

Hank looked at the map. It looked to be about 40 miles to get there. He could see it was quite close to the trenches of the front line. "This looks dangerous. Are you sure it's worth it?"

"It is dangerous. That's why I'm sending you. If you get killed, I get rid of one big pain-in-the-arse Yid." McBride grinned a big, ruthless smile.

"What about the motorcycles? Who will take care of them?" Hank asked.

"Who cares about the motorcycles? This is way more important!" McBride bristled.

Hank proceeded to load up the Thornycroft J-Type lorry they had rigged up as a tow vehicle. When he thought he had all contingencies covered, he headed east through Béthune.

The road to the front became less of a road and more of a path through the mud as he got closer to his destination. Towns were no longer towns. Repeated shelling had mostly levelled them. The remnants of buildings stood as skeletons. Parts of a cathedral spires stood precariously in remembrance of better days. Most towns were now piles of rubble with paths for vehicles cleared through the middle of it all.

Further on, the road jammed with horse-drawn carts, abandoned vehicles, and lines of soldiers. Replacement soldiers marched on one side of the road heading towards the front. Their green uniforms sparkled like clean, spring leaves. In stark contrast, the opposite side of the road was lined with soldiers marching back off the line. The soldiers were covered in mud. Their faces were dirty with mud caked on their cheeks, hands, and clothing.

Mud was everywhere, making everything brown. Roads, walkways, even the ruins of buildings blended into the same mud brown. Vehicles mired in it. Men and horses stomped through it leaving their imprints in the muddy clay filled with rain water.

Overhead, Hank heard the unmistakable sound of an airplane engine. First one, two, three, and then four. He looked to the sky. The clouds obscured the planes at first, but then he saw them circling down out of the clouds in the distance, three chasing one. The one was green with a tan underbelly, apparently British. The three in chase were each uniquely and brightly colored. They must be the Albatros fighters he had read about.

The British pilot threw his plane about with abandon. Hank watched him turn tightly to the right, roll over inverted and dive through a half-loop straight into the ground. A ball of flame erupted from the crash while the Albatros fighters hovered overhead like vultures circling the dead. The pilot must have miscalculated his altitude in a panic fearing his life. Now it was over.

Hank thought of Jimmy. Jimmy would be out here by now. Hank hoped it had not been him. How Hank wished he were with Jimmy instead of here on the ground, in the mud, under the thumb of an anti-Semitic asshole of a sergeant.

The three German fighters formed into a straight line and began heading toward Hank and the road he was driving on. The soldiers on both sides of the road dove off to either side of the road, the bright green uniforms getting their first tastes of mud. The drivers of the horse carts dove off their rides as well. Hank figured he had better do the same instead of continuing to sit in his large truck, a most appetizing target for the approaching airplanes.

The Germans came down on the soldiers along the road one at a time, each one firing their machines guns at the road as they passed over. A horse was hit and screamed its death throes. One or two soldiers were shot as well. Their friends rushed to help them. Hank's truck was hit several times. Fortunately, the engine remained intact, but the canvas coverings were riddled with bullet holes. The Germans made one strafing pass and disappeared in an instant.

Collecting his thoughts and wiping the mud off his uniform, Hank realized he was approximately at the place McBride had pointed out on the map. So, he found a place off the road dry enough to park his truck and began taking inventory of the truck situation. Five trucks lined either side of the road within a stretch of about one quarter of a mile on the road.

He approached each one in turn completing a sort of triage of each vehicle. Two were lost causes. Artillery shells had hit them or landed quite close because various wheels, fenders and axles were missing completely from the trucks. One of them lay on its side to boot. There was no way he could repair them. Two others were damaged but appeared to have drivetrains intact. Of these two, one had almost completely lost its driver's compartment and cargo bed. The other one had been hit by shrapnel in the engine compartment, so it was a loss. The last of the five trucks was in the best shape. Its chassis, engine, and drivetrain all looked pretty solid. One wheel had been knocked off its mounting and the fender over it was mangled, but that was about all.

Hank thought about cannibalizing parts from the other trucks to make this one whole, but in the end, he decided to try to tow the last vehicle back to St. Omer and forsake the others. Hank retrieved his truck, backed it up in front of the damaged one and connected the chains to the raised arm and winch on his truck. The winch raised the front of the truck up about two feet, high enough to enable towing it. Hank crawled underneath and disconnected the drive shaft, stowing it in the bed of the truck.

He began his long, slow trek back to St Omer. He could only go a few miles per hour for fear of having the truck fall off its hooks. It was close to midnight by the time he got back to the motor pool. He left the truck combination out in front and returned to his bunk where he quickly went to sleep, exhausted.

In the morning, he received another letter from Meg in the mail call. She was all fired up this time.

April 23, 1917

Dear Henry,

You'll never guess what happened here at the bank. Haraldson, the bastard, still won't let me get involved in other stuff at the bank besides working as a teller. Even when I spoke with Daddy, he said he would not override Haraldson just for my sake.

Well, anyway, I am not one to let this kind of crap stop me, so I made secret arrangements with my brother, Russell, to look over his work so I can learn from it. He has been working in the commercial loans department and was working on a big loan to the land development company owned by Mr. Fleming, from Marshall.

Mr. Fleming is planning to build a new housing development in Marshall and wants Father to loan him some of the money. Russell did a financial analysis of the expected profitability of Fleming's proposal and let me look at it. Russell had transposed one of the numbers in one of his tabulations. The idiot would have caught it if he had done a good foot and balance, but he didn't. As a result, the analysis predicted sales of 90 homes more than it should have. Russell was going to recommend this big loan that would have ended up being a really bad business deal for our bank.

When I was going through his work, I found his error and pointed it out to him. He was shocked but grateful. He changed his recommendation at the last minute and we avoided a major problem. But here's the real rub. He took the credit saying one of the junior clerks had made the error and he found it. Can you believe it? I was livid, but what could I say?

141

I am going to get even with my brother if it's the last thing I do.
Damn him!

By the way, I love you.
Margaret

Meg said she loved him! And, she said it in a most Meg way, "By the way—" So Meg. Hank enjoyed Meg's feistiness. She wasn't about to let old man Haraldson get in her way. He lay back down in his bunk, closed his eyes and remembered the day Meg had told him of her aspirations with the bank.

Jimmy, Ellie, Hank, and Meg used to gather at Peterson's General Store late on Saturday mornings. During the week in summer, they were all occupied otherwise. Hank worked at his dad's furniture store and Jimmy always had lots to do at the farm. Meg helped out at her father's bank, the Gresham City Bank, and Ellie got a job at Peterson's running the cash register and stocking shelves. None of these jobs paid much but did provide them with some spending money. Hank's dad paid him $5.00 per week, more than any of the other three.

So, Saturdays were the best time to meet up. Hank usually met Jimmy at the store mid-to-late morning. Jimmy always went in to buy a cinnamon roll from Ellie and chat with her until she got off work at eleven. Meg would usually show up about eleven as well.

Ellie Johnson had a huge crush on Jimmy Arneson. Sixteen now, Jimmy liked her back. They made a beautiful couple. Jimmy was a little taller than most, handsome, blonde, lean, and muscular. He was the hero type, larger than life, a cut above. They all looked up to him. Leadership came naturally to him and they followed him easily. He was always the one with the ideas, the plan, or the great moment.

Ellie was a gorgeous little blonde that made people look twice, but she was also sweet and caring. She cared for her parents deeply, even though her father was a pretty stern man. The world seemed to not conform to his expectations of propriety. Ellie helped her mom around the house and the lovely flower gardens she maintained.

As for Hank, he was definitely not tall, handsome, or blonde. He was shorter than Jimmy. Not so much to be a shrimp, but a couple of inches shorter. He wasn't athletic, but he had strong hands and arms. He worked with his hands a lot, helping his father with the business, working on the motorcycle, and helping farmers with broken farm equipment they brought in.

Hank had his eyes on Margaret Lassiter. She was growing up to be an attractive brunette. She still hung out with Ellie as best friends, so it was sort of natural the four of them would go on outings together. She appeared to like Hank, but she certainly did not exhibit the goo-goo eyed adoration toward him that Ellie exhibited towards Jimmy. He called her Meg and she did not object to it.

One Saturday in June, Jimmy suggested they picnic out by their favorite stretch of the Dogwood River. Naturally, everyone went along with his idea. Jim and Ellie decided they would walk together out to the place while Margaret and Hank would ride the motorcycle and bring a picnic lunch.

After pulling a lunch together, Hank and Meg rode out to the bridge over the Dogwood and turned off the road, driving along the river a few hundred feet. They came to a grove of Dogwood trees. It stood next to a grassy field not far from the river's edge. They laid out their picnic blankets and sat down. Overhanging Dogwoods provided partial shade. A gentle breeze cooled them as they sat and relaxed. Little birds tweeted and twittered about. Dandelion seeds blew in the breeze.

Before long, they saw Jim and Ellie walking across the field, hand in hand. They were totally absorbed in each other and didn't even notice Hank and Meg watching them. They were destined to be together. Meg and Hank just watched in silence. Meg sensed the specialness of the moment, too. "Those two are head over heels in love." She observed with a touch of envy in her voice.

"Indeed, they are," he agreed.

They started setting up for lunch as Jimmy and Ellie approached. Soon, Jimmy and Ellie joined them on the picnic blanket. "What a lovely walk!" Ellie said.

"Everything go okay with the bike?" Jimmy asked of him. He was a bit embarrassed, Hank thought. His face was quite red.

"No problems," Hank replied.

Lunch was delicious. They inhaled it in a few minutes of silent munching. They killed a pie, too. Afterwards, they stretched out to let the food digest. Jimmy laid his head on Ellie's lap as she stroked his golden locks.

Meg and Hank lay down next to each other as well. A bit awkwardly, they looked up to the sky and talked about the puffy clouds forming to the west, trying to make animal shapes out of them. They enjoyed each other, even liked each other, but they weren't over the moon like Jim and Ellie. They were extensions of the couple more than anything.

Still, there may have been signs. Meg surprised Hank with, "Henry (she insisted on calling him Henry), what do you want to do with your life?"

Feebly, he replied, "I dunno. Maybe work on cars. I like to make things work."

"Humph," Meg grunted. "I'm going to run my father's bank."

"What about your brother, Russell?" he asked. "Isn't he first in line for the throne?"

"You can take your throne and toss it in the river, you smarty pants. As for Russell, he can't find his way out of a paper bag. Mind my words, he's going to screw up one of these days and Daddy will put me in charge."

"Hmm, well, good luck with that," Hank said.

Meg leaned forward, eyebrows scowled, chin out, and fists clenched. "You think I can't do it because I'm a girl, don't you?"

Hank leaned back. "Hey wait, no, I didn't mean that at all!"

"You better not, you big oaf!"

A hawk flew overhead, catching Jimmy's eye and causing the rest of them to look up, rescuing Hank. Jimmy always looked at birds as they flew around. He would even, on occasion, end a conversation so he could watch. "Wow, just look at him soar. It's like he's floating on air. You can see the air currents in his wings. Look how he adjusts his feathers to compensate, ever so delicately at times."

"Looking for dinner if you ask me," Hank said.

"Maybe, but he sure is doing it majestically!" Jimmy smiled his big wide smile and everyone chuckled.

A little while later, Jimmy stood up and announced he was going to take a little walk, but he would be right back. They all looked at each other quizzically and shrugged their shoulders. "Okay, if you say so," he said. "See you in a little while."

Hank, Meg, and Ellie lazed away in the sunshine letting the noonday sun warm their faces. Times like this, doing nothing, were luxuries to be savored.

Jimmy returned ten minutes later. He held his right hand behind his back as he approached. When he arrived at the picnic blanket, he pulled out from behind his back a beautiful little bouquet of periwinkle-blue Forget-Me-Nots and handed them to Ellie.

Ellie visibly melted into him. "Oh, Jimmy. Don't ever lose the sweet, little boy inside of you I love so much." Ellie caressed Jimmy's blond hair, imploring him with her beautiful blue eyes. They kissed. Hank and Meg blushed. Meg rolled her eyes.

20

VIMY, MAY, 1917. McBride had Hank continue excursions to the front for several days. On the fourth such trip, events took place that were to change Hank's life.

McBride once again sent Hank to Vimy to recover vehicles. Hank found one alongside a typically muddy road and was in the process of disconnecting the drive shaft to tow the truck back when he heard an airplane approaching. He knew by now to be vigilant for fear of another strafing attack and crawled out from under the truck to see what was happening. He could see a biplane approaching him head-on, but he could not tell what kind of plane it was or if it was friend or foe. He clambered behind his truck just in case it was a German.

As it approached in a steady shallow glide, the engine cut out. The plane was completely without power as it glided over him at a mere thirty feet or so. Now, Hank could see it was a French Nieuport. The pilot brought it in for a dead-stick landing in the field alongside the road. At least it used to be a field. The pilot had found a stretch of ground relatively unblemished with shell holes so he was able to roll to a complete stop without incident.

Fearing the pilot might be wounded, Hank hurried up to the plane to see if he was okay. As Hank ran toward him he could see the pilot unbuckling his harness in a hurry. He stood up in his cockpit as Hank came close and turned around. He lifted the goggles off of his face and said in a cheery voice, "Good afternoon, old man! Lovely day to get shot down, don't you think?"

"Good afternoon, sir!" Seeing the crown on his epaulette indicating he was a captain, Hank braced to attention and saluted him. The captain was not particularly tall, but not short either. His hair was brown and curly but it was his eyes that were dramatic. They were a piercing blue, as if he looked right through you when he made eye contact. He raised his hand to his forehead in casual reply and asked Hank to help him down, which Hank gladly did. "Are you okay, sir?"

"Yes, yes, I am fine, but my bloody engine has gone on the fritz. It started sputtering after I passed through that last bit of Archie on my way back over the lines and lost power steadily afterwards. It gave up the ghost just as I was gliding in. I don't suppose you would know if anyone around here knows anything about engines, would you?" His accent was refined, indicating a moneyed background.

"Why yes, sir. I am a mechanic. I was just hooking up that truck over there to tow it back to my motor pool."

"Jolly good, old bean. Would you mind taking a look at my plane?"

"Why, I would be happy to, sir! I've always loved aeroplanes. I even built a few gliders before the war. I tried to become a pilot myself but my bum leg kept me out. I'll just go get my toolbox."

"Excellent! So, you're a Canadian, are you? I see your Canada shoulder patch. I am a Canadian, too." The pilot was genuinely curious.

"American, sir. I hail from Minnesota." They walked along together back to his truck. "My best friend and I signed up together in Winnipeg. He's a pilot for the RFC somewhere abouts."

"You don't say? What's his name?" The pilot asked.

"Jimmy Arneson, sir," he replied.

"Sorry, don't know him. I'm from north of Toronto myself. I've been over here two years already. The name is Harrison, Cecil Harrison. Pleased to meet you," the pilot introduced himself, extending his hand.

"Private Hank Jacobs, sir. Say, are you the famous ace, Captain Harrison?" He reached out to shake his hand.

"I don't know about how famous I am, but yes, I have achieved some modest success so far, Jacobs."

"Pleased to make your acquaintance, sir! Now, if you'll excuse me, I'll take a look at your aeroplane for you." Hank opened his toolbox and removed the cowling from around the engine.

Hank had never worked on a rotary engine, so much of it was new and confusing to him. He looked it over in general, trying to make sense of how it worked. He had read about them in *Popular Mechanics*, but had never seen one up close like this. It was a fascinating piece of machinery. He knew from his reading that rotaries were popular for airplanes because they offered more horsepower per pound than water-cooled engines.

When he took off the cowling, Hank noticed a bullet hole in the left side. Strangely, it looked like it came out of the cowling rather than going into it. This seemed rather odd to him. He looked around at where it might have come from. Looking over the back side of the engine, he noticed a drip coming down from just behind one of the engine cylinders. He traced it back to its source and found a brass fuel line had been severed. It appeared a bullet had ricocheted off of the engine cylinder and hit the fuel line on its way back out. The cylinder itself seemed okay with just a surface crease from the bullet, but the line had been cut clean through. Fortunately, it dripped away from the hot cylinders. Otherwise, it might have started a fire.

"Ah, look here, sir. This fuel line has been severed by a bullet. I think you must have been quite lucky, sir. The bullet hit the line on its way out, away from the engine. If it had cut the line on its way in, it might have squirted the fuel onto the hot engine. You would have most likely been a flamer."

Harrison watched and listened intently. "Lucky is right, Jacobs. Catching fire is a pilot's worst nightmare, you know. We even carry handguns to end ourselves quickly if we have to. No parachutes, you see. They won't let us have them."

"Oh, my," Hank said. "Well, I think I can get you on your way in no time, sir. I can cut a piece of rubber tubing and attach it to the fuel line on either side with worm clamps. It will get you home, sir. You best show your mechanic what I did when you get home so he can apply a more permanent fix to it."

"Fantastic!"

Hank set to work straight away. It didn't take long. He trimmed up the brass tubing, cut a length of rubber tubing close in size and tightened the clamps down. "You should be in fine shape, sir. I suspect you'll need to re-prime your pump, however."

"I can't thank you enough, Jacobs. Without you, I would be consigned to a night in the trenches and a long, bumpy ride back home to 60 Squadron. If there is anything I can possibly do for you, just say it. I am immensely grateful."

Hank's heart jumped and he swallowed hard. Time to go for the brass ring. "Umm, sir, there is something, actually, if you don't mind. I have always wanted to work on aeroplanes rather than trucks in the motor pool. Is there any way you could put in a good word for me to become an air mechanic?"

"Can I ever!" Harrison exclaimed. "I can do you one very much better than that. However, I must place a condition on it."

"What, sir?" Hank asked.

"As it turns out, I am not particularly happy with my present mechanic. So here's my deal. I will get you transferred to my squadron as an air mechanic on the condition you become my personal mechanic!" Captain Cecil Harrison puffed out his chest a bit, obviously quite pleased with himself.

"Absolutely!" Hank rejoiced. "That would make me very happy, sir!"

"Consider it done, then. It will take me a couple of weeks to get the papers pushed though the depot, but you can expect orders to 60 Squadron soon. Now, write down your name, rank, service number and present assignment. I'll get started on it right away."

Hank got a notepad and pencil from his truck and wrote everything down for the captain. His heart was racing. Could it be? Could it really be? Hank might be out from under McBride and get to do the thing he had long wanted! "Here you go, sir!"

"Excellent. I shall be glad to see you at 60 Squadron before a fortnight gives out. Now, let's get me started so I can be on my way."

Hank and the captain spun the aircraft around so he could retrace his path for takeoff. Then, Hank took position ahead of the propeller and followed Harrison's lead. Hank cranked the propeller around by hand to lube the cylinders and prime the fuel. Then, on Harrison's command, Hank cranked the propeller hard to start the engine. It sputtered at first but then roared to life.

Captain Harrison gave him a big thumbs up as Hank jumped out of the way. Harrison rolled away, quickly gaining speed to a fine take-off. He waggled his wings as he climbed away. Hank literally leapt for joy!

Hank found himself whistling "Shine on, Harvest Moon" as he finished hooking up the damaged truck for the tow home. He wasn't sure he could believe what had just happened. His mom always used to say good things come to those who help others. Maybe today proved the point for him.

All the way back to St. Omer, Hank daydreamed of what it would be like to be Captain Harrison's personal mechanic. Would he be working on his Nieuport or would he soon be switching over to a Sopwith Camel or SE5 as the newest British aircraft in the war? He would soon be working on state-of-the-art aircraft.

He dare not say anything to anyone in the motor pool. He could just imagine McBride finding some way to ruin it for him, just to spite him. Hank vowed to himself to not say a word and let the orders come in first. He also vowed to himself to not get too hopeful about this. It was a bit too good to be true.

His mind settled on McBride for a moment. Hank looked forward to saying good-bye to him and began rehearsing the speech he would give to him, putting him in his place once and for all for all of the grief he had suffered from him.

As he did this, a thought occurred to Hank that surprised him, not from its great insight but because he should have thought of it months ago. All these months of derision from McBride and he hadn't seen it before. McBride, too, was being persecuted by all of the mechanics in the shop as a ginger. Hank had heard them joke about McBride ruthlessly behind his back but also muttering the word just loud enough for him to hear as he walked by. McBride derided Hank because he himself was being derided. Indeed, McBride had suffered derision all his life just as Hank had, just for different reasons.

Hank had not turned to deriding others as a way to cope with the derision he received as McBride had, but he could certainly see how a person might do so as a defense mechanism. McBride ridiculed others to make himself feel better about himself.

Understanding spawned compassion. Compassion spawned forgiveness. Hank actually found himself feeling sorry for McBride on his way home to the base. His impassioned speech to whither McBride's ego gave way to wondering if he should discuss this with him.

This realization gave Hank new strength. Hank felt he had risen above the situation through this new understanding. Perhaps he need not mire in the muck of it with McBride, but just let it go.

Hank found he need not carry that baggage around with him anymore.

21

BRUAY, MAY, 1917. Puffy, white cumulus clouds dotted otherwise clear blue skies with the advent of May. Earth celebrated the warming sun with colorful blossoms and verdant fields. The breathtaking beauty only served, however, to make even more tragic by contrast, the great scar of the western front.

Bruay was fourteen miles south of Treizennes. It was easy to find because the mining southwest of the town created large slag heaps that served as prominent landmarks, visible from miles away on a clear day. Still guilt-ridden from having killed his first German, Jimmy Arneson relocated there with 40 Squadron to support the large-scale battle raging around Arras, less than twenty miles away.

Major McAllister let them know, however, that the battle was winding down now and the British were consolidating their gains. "Senseless gains," Jimmy thought to himself. Thousands of men died for the capture of a mile or two of territory at best. The trenches remained, just a tiny bit east of where they were before.

Jimmy's flight flew every day, usually twice per day. Their missions were focused on providing support to the PBI by strafing enemy positions, convoys, German reinforcement columns and machine gun positions. Those were hazardous missions. Below two thousand feet, the airplanes were within range of the machine guns and rifles on the ground in addition to Archie.

In fear for his life, bile rose in Jimmy's throat every time he climbed into the tiny cockpit of his Nieuport. When would death come? Would it be today? Would it be on this patrol? Would Archie finally get him or would it be a bullet from a German soldier's Mauser? The danger of providing support to the ground troops was worse than fighting enemy aircraft because it was so random. When he fought an opponent in the air, Jimmy could sense how the fight was unfolding. He could tell if he had an edge or if he was losing the battle and needed to run away. Flying low-level missions near the front lines, he never knew when he might get it. He heard and felt bullets whiz by. He could see and hear bullets rip through the fabric of the wings and chip away at the ribs and spars. But he never knew when one might hit him.

The flight lost Clark to ground fire. B and C Flights took losses as well. Clark's replacement was named Hughes. He flew under Jimmy's tutelage, but Jimmy steered clear of him on the ground. Jimmy didn't want to know him. He, too, would die. The better Jimmy knew him, the more his death would bother him. Best to not know him.

Phillips, killed in April on the same mission when Jimmy shot down his first German, was replaced by a lad named McKenna, but Jimmy chose to ignore him as well. Oddly, Jimmy wanted to tell McKenna what Phillips had told him when he started, that he would be dead in two weeks.

Every evening, Jimmy drowned his fears with whiskey. It burned his throat but it dulled his brain and spared him his own thoughts. He stumbled into bed and slept until the nightmares returned. They came almost every night. Jimmy fired his guns at the Hun and saw the German's head split apart. His brains splattered his windscreen. Jimmy was hit himself and his plane caught fire. He burned and in the flames the devil came for him. Just as the devil grabbed for him, Jimmy startled awake in sweat. His roommate, Shorty McGruder, heard Jimmy and tried to comfort him but it was no good. Not just a dead man waiting for his appointed time, Jimmy was destined for the fiery depths of hell when the time came.

Jimmy lost his edge. He knew what to do, but he flew mechanically without fervor and held back in combat. Hughes stayed with him but Jimmy didn't engage the enemy. He could not bring himself to shoot at them. Jimmy killed once. He didn't want to kill again. McGruder had been promoted to fly number three with his own rookie, McKenna, to worry about. Shorty carried them more than he should have needed to. He began to come along beside Jimmy to fire when opportunities arose. Jimmy was waiting for his time to die.

Jimmy could tell Stevens was watching him. Stevens said little to him, but he could tell from the captain's sideways glances he was growing skeptical of Jimmy's performance. "Go all in, boy. Either go all in or get out. You can't hesitate. If you do, you're a goner," Stevens had told him weeks ago. Jimmy heard him and yet he equivocated. Jimmy knew it and Stevens knew it, but still, Jimmy hesitated.

Due to graces unknown to him, Jimmy was to find new hope on an offensive patrol a few days later. They were east of Béthune at twelve thousand feet and he was flying number two on Stevens' right, as was usual now that Phillips was gone. They saw a flight of six Albatros scouts above them to the east, at about fifteen thousand feet, heading their way.

Stevens immediately put them into a steep climb heading directly toward the Germans. They didn't see the British patrol at first because the Nieuports were rising up beneath the noses of the Albatros DIIIs. Jimmy's heart raced and his adrenalin started to pump.

Jimmy could tell when the Germans saw the British flight because their wings rocked and the leader dove steeply to meet them. So often, dogfights began head-to-head. This would be no different. They all made it through the first pass without losing anyone and Stevens banked sharply to the left, taking McGruder and McKenna with him.

Jimmy broke to the right and almost hit Hughes' wing with his own as he climbed, spinning his plane around sharply. He got a height advantage over the Germans and began to pick his target. Hughes fell behind him but was beginning to catch up. Jimmy singled out a lozenge-camouflaged Albatros climbing to the left. He had a lot of power but was turning rather flatly. Jimmy thought the Hun was a novice. Jimmy got behind him and turned inside of him within two turns. The Hun continued to spiral up but Jimmy had no problem turning inside him and keeping up with his climb.

Jimmy lined the Hun up in his sights but once again he fell off, not willing to take the German's life. He pictured a young, blonde kid scared to death like he had once been himself and could not bring himself to kill the enemy. The German reversed his turn and fell off into a dive to the right. Jimmy followed him, but let him get away.

Looking back to the rest of the flight, Jimmy climbed again, swiveling his head around to spot the enemy and looking for an opportunity to engage. He saw a Nieuport below him climbing back up to the fray from the south. To his terror, he also saw a black Albatros above the Nieuport getting lined up to pounce on him.

Instinctively, Jimmy dove for the Albatros with Hughes in tow. Jimmy thought he might be able to intercept him before the German got lined up, but he was wrong. The Hun was behind the Nieuport.

Jimmy now saw the Nieuport was McGruder. Shorty must have lost McKenna. He was alone. McGruder was jinking, slipping, skidding, and reversing his turns rapidly and unpredictably. The Albatros was closing on him, firing short bursts. Fortunately, none of the shots were connecting, at least not yet.

While he couldn't intercept the Hun, Jimmy was able to get on his tail. They had a train going, the Hun on Shorty's tail, trying to get a bead on him and Jimmy on the Huns's tail, trying to fire. Hughes took up the rear, barely holding on to them all.

Jimmy closed on the Hun. The German didn't see him, obviously concentrating entirely on Shorty. Jimmy hit the German's engine with a short burst from his Lewis and watched as a thin black line of oil grew into a black plume of oily smoke. Jimmy knew the Albatros would soon flame up. The Hun knew this too and immediately spun his plane for a race to the ground before that happened. McGruder would live to fight another day. Jimmy had saved him.

This felt right and just. Jimmy didn't know if the German was going to die and he didn't care. What he cared about was his roommate. Shorty was still alive. He remembered Stevens' words, "If you don't kill him, how many of your friends will he go on to kill because you didn't get him when you could?"

He also remembered what Major McAllister had once said, "The guys who go down are the ones who never see it coming." Jimmy decided at that moment to be an extra set of eyes for his friends, to see it coming for them, to fend the bad guys off for them, to save them. That was worth killing for, to save lives of others.

Jimmy, Shorty, and Hughes found Stevens further down their patrol route. Stevens had apparently taken McKenna in tow when he got separated from McGruder. The flight reformed and continued the patrol southwards.

Nothing of significance took place for the remainder of the patrol, which gave Jimmy an opportunity to reflect on what had just happened. Everything fit together like a jigsaw puzzle. Jimmy was a dead man already. He just didn't know when. But if it was to be, Jimmy could make some sense of his death by devoting himself to saving his fellow pilots. A grim determination came over him to fulfill his just mission to the best of his abilities.

When the flight arrived back at the aerodrome, Jimmy was grimly pleased to hear Captain Stevens had confirmed a kill for him of the German he had shot off Shorty's tail. They were just in time to head over to the mess after cleaning the oil off their faces and changing into their evening uniforms. McGruder beat him to it and headed over before him. Jimmy sat quietly in the hut and thought further on his newfound focus. It still made sense. It gave him purpose. It gave him a reason to fight. It gave him a reason to live. It gave him a reason to die.

When he finally arrived at the officer's mess, McGruder, ever the optimist, and ever the partier, was waiting in celebration. He welcomed Jimmy with a whiskey and a slap on the back. Before Jimmy even got a chance to find a seat and loosen his tie, Shorty raised his glass in a loud toast to Jimmy, "Here's to Jimmy Arneson! This man saved my life today. I owe this man my life! He is my saving grace!" The crowd raised their glasses to Jimmy in cheer.

Alfie Campbell raised his as well shouting, "Here's to Gracie!" Jimmy was sincerely honored, raised his own glass in return, and swallowed it in one gulp.

His new name was to stick. No longer was Jimmy called 'Arnie' by his compatriots. His new nickname was 'Gracie.' He didn't mind. Not only that, but the next morning, when he went out to mount his plane, he saw Wilson and Stewart had painted 'Saving Grace' diagonally on the side of his airplane just ahead of the roundel, black on silver in a nicely done italic cursive. Wilson was apparently a man of many talents.

Seeing this, Jimmy asked him to paint two small roundels on the left side of his fuselage down by the bottom edge. He told Wilson this was the important count for him. Jimmy wanted to have a roundel painted thusly for every save he made. These first two were for Alfie and Shorty. He intended to add more of these.

Major McAllister and Captain Stevens stopped by on their way to Steven's airplane. They saw the name on the plane and the roundels. "Saving Grace," Stevens said. "I like that. Now, what's with the roundels? Are you shooting down British pilots now, Gracie?" Stevens had already picked up on Jimmy's new nickname. When Jimmy explained the roundels to them, they rather liked the idea. After all, Stevens and McAllister were also in the business of trying to keep their pilots alive. Jimmy overheard Stevens say to McAllister as they walked away, "Not only is he a great pilot, he's now got the right attitude. We could use more like him." Jimmy's heart swelled.

June brought with it another big push north of Bruay near Mesen in Belgium. They provided support to the effort with offensive patrols, but the units stationed further north bore the biggest brunt of the fighting. It was surprisingly quiet for 40 Squadron on their sector of the front.

In early July, Jimmy received wonderful news in a letter from Ellie.

June 20, 1917

My darling James,

    I have wonderful news. We have a beautiful and healthy baby boy, born on the fourteenth of June. We named him James, Jr., just as we had discussed.
    It was quite a full day as you might imagine. My labor started shortly after breakfast and lasted until midafternoon. Mrs. Jensen helped as midwife for James' birth and I had invaluable help from your mother and dear Margaret. Everything went well and I have had a week to recuperate.
    Little Jimmy is so precious. He is the spitting image of you, bright blue eyes and wisps of white blond hair. He has your nose and chin, too. Really, I don't think he has any of me in him! Please find enclosed ink prints we made of his little hands and feet. Isn't he just adorable? We will strive to have a photograph taken and send it to you soon.
    He feeds and sleeps well. We are just fine. I have so much help from your mom and Meg I couldn't ask for more. They both want to hold him as much as I do, so I get a "baby break" any time I want or need.
    Life is so delightful here nowadays, my darling. The only thing that could possibly improve it would be for you to be here, too. Please take care of yourself, darling, and come home safe and sound. We all love you and miss you. I am forever yours, my love.

    From your darling son and loving wife,
    James, Jr. and Ellie

His heart sang to this wonderful news. He had a son! It gave him new hope and something to look forward to. It made him want to live so he could see his little boy. If fate should take a different turn, at least now he knew there would be a son to live after him if he should die.

22

FILESCAMP FARM, JUNE, 1917. After three weeks of intensely worrisome waiting for his orders to come in, McBride walked into the shop one morning and informed Hank of his emancipation. McBride's face was contorted with suppressed antagonism as he came up to Hank to tell him he had received orders for him from brigade headquarters. Hank was to travel to Filescamp Farm aerodrome to report to 60 Squadron.

Hank could barely contain his joy and made haste to fulfill those orders. He left the shop as soon as McBride was done with him and packed his personal belongs. Within an hour, Hank was ready to find transport to the St. Pol area. He found a truck heading towards there, threw his kit bag aboard, and climbed in after. Hank looked back at the shop as he left. He had no regrets. Hank had learned to control himself in new ways, he had freed himself from McBride's reign of terror, and he had learned a lot about automobile and truck maintenance. It was time for a new beginning.

The aerodrome was not far off the route Hank had taken to Vimy Ridge, about halfway between St. Pol and Arras, south of the main highway there. His anticipation boiled over as they drove. The ride took forever. Hank had to trade trucks in St. Pol. They finally arrived and he found the adjutant's office. The adjutant referred Hank to the first sergeant who set him up in a canvas tent barracks and introduced him to the sergeant he would report to for aircraft maintenance. "Sergeant Acker, this is Ack Emma Henry Jacobs, your new protégé."

"Ack emma?" Hank asked.

"Yes, lad, that's A and M for Air Mechanic in the Royal Flying Corps phonetic alphabet. Perhaps you've heard of it?" The first sergeant asked sarcastically.

"Oh, yes, I have heard of that. We just never used it in the motor pool. My apologies!" He sought to ingratiate himself.

"You an American?" asked Acker.

"I am. Minnesota is where I am from," he replied, bristling a little.

"Well, I'll be. And, you're the fellow Captain Harrison asked for personally?" Sergeant Acker asked.

"Yes, sergeant," he replied. How would they view this situation, he wondered?

"Have you ever worked on aircraft before?" Acker queried.

"Well, I built a few gliders at home before the war, but no, I have never worked on real aircraft before." He wanted to be honest and not inflate himself in any way. "I've been working on engines and motor vehicles for eight months now."

"You've got a lot to learn then! I shall have to pair you up with a more senior ack emma to teach you the ropes." Acker was okay with this, Hank was glad to see. "Ned Cole will do that. He's a good man. Pay attention to him and learn everything you can as fast as you can. We shall soon see if Captain Harrison's faith is well placed. Plan on starting at six o'clock tomorrow morning."

"Thank you, sergeant!" Hank could handle that. He had always been a quick learner. He was gratified to see there was no indication of interest in his Jewish background from these two men.

Hank had an opportunity to settle into his bunk and catch up on letters. One he got was from Meg.

May 12, 1917

Dear Henry,

There has been a wonderful development at the bank I want to share with you. Mr. Haraldson called me into his office the other day. I went in loaded for bear, expecting another big fight with him. Turns out, it was just the opposite.

He told me he reviewed the Fleming loan analysis before filing it away. He does that with all major transactions. While he was looking over Russell's calculations, he saw the notes I had written on it for Russell to see. He could tell from the notes Russell had been the one that messed up, not the junior clerk, and I was the one who discovered the error.

First, he chewed me out a little bit for going around behind his back to review Russell's work. But then, he apologized for his attitude toward me and thanked me for saving the bank from a major mistake! He might be a misogynist, but he's at least forthright enough to apologize when he should.

He said, however, that it was going to have to stay between us. Russell is still the heir apparent and Haraldson doesn't want to upset the apple cart. However, he said he would be watching him a lot more closely from now on. And, he said he would work with me to rotate me through some other jobs at the bank so I can officially learn more about the whole operation.

Happy day! I am so excited, Henry! This is what I had hoped for.

Oh, by the way, I love you, you foolish man,
Margaret

"Well, what do you know, Meg got her vindication," Hank thought to himself. "I'm happy for her. She deserves it."

"Oh, by the way—" There was his smarty pants Meg again.

Ned Cole turned out to be a great mentor, workmate, and friend. The stocky fellow from Yorkshire was a blacksmith before the war. He showed Hank a whole new life as an air mechanic. There were so many aspects of his life here that were dramatically different from the motor pool, Hank felt he was reborn.

First, he had few problems with Anti-Semitism. For the most part, no one cared. Oh, there were a few instances where someone said something, but Hank now had the self-confidence to stand up for himself. All he had to do was tell them to their face he did not appreciate their insults and they would pay a heavy price if they kept it up. In one instance, it did result in fisticuffs but, having bested the bully, Hank was left alone by everyone else.

The evening after that scuffle, Hank reflected on the unconventional way he had learned to box. Once again, it was something for which he was indebted to Jimmy.

It was the morning after the big fight when Jimmy beat up Bjorn Nelson. Hank and Jimmy headed to their fishing hole in the Dogwood River, which wound its lazy way north and east through Gresham on its way to join the Mississippi. Dogwood trees lined stretches of the slow and shallow river, giving it the name.

Their fishing poles were little more than a branch with a string tied to one end and a hook tied on the other end of the string. They dug up earthworms for bait but usually lost them in the water. They hardly ever caught anything, but they liked going there just on their own, no brothers, no sisters, and no parents.

Most of the time, they talked about their lives at home and school, girls, or their dreams for the future. Their friendship was close that way. Hank never worried about what he said or how he said it with Jimmy and neither did Jim.

Jimmy's defense of Hank at school the day before drew Hank one step closer to Jimmy. He was deeply grateful. "I want to thank you again for stepping in yesterday, Jimmy. I feel like I should have stood up for myself better. How did you get so confident in yourself?

"Gosh, I don't know. I just did what seemed like the right thing to do, you know? I didn't think about if I would win or lose. That wasn't the point, you know?"

"You acted like you knew what you were doing in the fight. Did you take lessons or something?"

Jimmy tried to wink at him but his eye was swelling up and getting darker. "Ouch!" he said. "Do you really want to know where I learned about it?"

"Yeah, you bet I do."

"I read about it in a book at the library!" Jimmy sniggered. "Then, I practiced all the stuff in the barn, hitting a hay bale with a burlap sack draped over it."

"You're kidding! You are kidding, right?"

"Honest Injuns, Hank."

Jimmy and Hank had been going to the library together for a while now. He just never saw him reading about boxing.

"I checked it out when you weren't around. I didn't want to look silly."

"Have you checked it back in yet?"

"Oh yeah, some time ago."

"Show me. I want to read it, too. Let's go there now."

"Sounds good to me."

The library was located on Main Street about two blocks east of Smith Street. It was red brick and had four white pillars spread across the front if it, giving it an imposing look like a bank.

Miss Jensen greeted the boys when they walked in. "Good morning, boys. How is your Saturday shaping up?" Hank had a hard time keeping his eyes off of Miss Jensen. She was maybe twenty years old, shapely, and pretty with freckles and cascading locks of strawberry blonde hair.

Jimmy leaned over and whispered in his ear, "She's beautiful!"

Hank pushed him away. Miss Jensen blushed. Jimmy sniggered. "We're good, Miss Jensen. Thanks."

"My, that's quite a black eye you have there, Jimmy. I heard all about the big fight yesterday. Are you both okay?"

"Yes, Miss Jensen. Thank you. It weren't nothin'," Jimmy replied.

"It was nothing," Miss Jensen said, correcting Jimmy's grammar. "Well, there's no one else around this morning so you have your run of the place. Anything in particular you want to look at today?" She saw them there regularly and always tried to help them. If they did ask for something she didn't have, she always tried to get hold of something on the topic for a future visit. She had several publications listing lots of different kinds of books and magazines she could get.

"Nothing special today, Miss Jensen. Thank you. We just want to look around for a bit," Jimmy said.

"Very well, gentlemen. Enjoy!" Miss Jensen replied.

After digging around for a few minutes, Jimmy pulled the book off the shelf and showed it to Hank, *The Science of Defense: A Treatise on Sparring and Wrestling*, by Edmund Prys. Hank flipped through it and decided he wanted to check it out.

The boys split up afterwards, each going off to his favorite sections. Hank headed to the transportation section to see what was there about automobiles. They fascinated him. Miss Jensen had arranged to get the *Automotive Times* for him to read. The latest edition had a great article on the Model T from Ford.

Jimmy headed to the history section. He liked to read about the exploits of cavalry officers like J. E. B. Stuart and George Custer. They were his heroes. If he wasn't reading about cavalry, he read about knights and King Arthur. His mom had told him all of the King Arthur legends. She enjoyed them herself, having grown up near the parts of England where Arthur was said to have lived.

Hank wanted to be Henry Ford and Jimmy wanted to be King Arthur. What an unlikely pair they made. They both checked out a couple more books and went to Hank's house for the afternoon to read.

For the next several weeks, Hank read about boxing in his book. Each afternoon, he would head over to Jimmy's and they would practice in the barn together. Those lessons served Hank well.

Hank thrived learning about aircraft maintenance. Life at 60 Squadron was ideal compared to the old motor pool. Another dimension different here was the teamwork. In the motor pool, most of the guys kept to themselves or whispered in secretive circles that kept others out. Perhaps it was a result of McBride's terrible leadership. Here, Hank worked among a whole community of air mechanics who helped each other out all the time. He could approach anyone in the group for help when he wanted to without fear of rejection or shaming. Even the non-commissioned officers helped out. Sergeant Acker was one of the best mechanics they had. He was a great leader and they all respected him for his abilities, regardless of his rank.

The ack emmas enjoyed a healthy comradery as well. They knew their work was important and it motivated all of them to do the best job they could. The lives of their pilots depended on their ability to keep their airplanes in tip-top shape. They were directly contributing to the war effort. Air Marshall Hugh Trenchard even said once, "... these men are the backbone of all our efforts."

The pilot officers the airmen supported were most appreciative of their work and treated them with kind respect even though they were of other ranks. Both officers and other ranks kept fraternization regulations in mind, but they all developed a close bond with their pilots and traditional formalities of saluting, "Sir"-ing, etc. fell by the wayside. Captain Harrison felt the same way. The first time Hank saw Captain Harrison off on a mission out on the tarmac the captain said to him, "Jacobs, I am most glad to see you here. I will fly with greater confidence knowing you have taken care of my aircraft." Hank's heart burst with pride. He would never let this man down. However, they might have differed about whose aircraft it really was!

They were a generally happy lot and grateful for their good fortune to be working on an aerodrome well back from the front lines. Most of them could have just as easily ended up in the trenches were they not so lucky. They slept in warm beds at night, showered regularly, and ate good food.

Some of the men had even made the transition to flying crew as observers or gunners. However, most of that was in the early days of the war and the ack emmas were now considered to be of more value maintaining the aircraft than flying them. Some even observed it took longer to train the mechanics than it took to train observers or gunners.

Their lives weren't all benefits, however. They worked incredibly long hours sometimes. If the fighting was heavy or they were taking heavy losses, they spent twenty hours a day keeping the aircraft serviceable. They often cannibalized parts from one aircraft to keep another going. This is where Sergeant Acker would get involved. He didn't want them creating "hangar queens" of aircraft that never flew because so many parts had been robbed from them. As a result, he tried to personally supervise this activity.

When they weren't working on aircraft, the squadron had them work on improving the hangars and other facilities on the aerodrome.

A month or two after Hank arrived, the squadron began the process of transitioning over from Nieuport Scouts to the new SE5a fighter from the Royal Aircraft Factory. Captain Harrison had the choice of switching over to the SE5a early on but he chose to stay with his Nieuport for a little while. He figured any new aircraft would have teething problems that need to be worked out. He was more intent on fighting the Hun than on being a test pilot in combat. In addition, he felt the Nieuport handled better than the SE5a in some ways.

As a result, Hank continued to work on the Nieuports longer than some of his peers. He didn't mind. Sure, he was eager to learn about the new aircraft but more eager to support his pilot. Harrison was a good man and successful at his craft. He was up to twenty five victories now.

Perhaps the hardest part of being a ground crewman was the wait for the pilot's return from a mission. They always feared their pilots might not return. Many did not. When they went west, the ground crew often never knew what happened to them. They would always ask the other pilots if they knew anything and they always checked with the first sergeant to see if any word came in from elsewhere. However, all too often, there just was nothing anyone knew. A horrible void set in that they had to put aside to get on with the work of supporting a replacement airplane and a replacement pilot. Sometimes, it was a bloody awful parade.

Hank got a happy surprise in a letter from Meg in July, dated the middle of June.

June 15, 1916

Dear Henry,

 We have wonderful news to share with you today. Ellie gave birth to a lovely and healthy baby boy. We have named him James, Jr. after his father and our friend, Jimmy.

 Her last weeks before giving birth were stressful for her. She was always uncomfortable and complained of backaches frequently. Then, on the morning of June 14, Flag Day, after we had all enjoyed breakfast at the Arneson's, her water broke while she was doing the dishes. She was standing at the sink when a trickle of water ran down her leg. She said she felt like she was peeing her pants but couldn't stop. As the trickle grew to a small stream, we realized her water broke.

 Mrs. Arneson sent Fred after Mrs. Jensen, the midwife. She and I tried to get ready for the birth in Jimmy's bedroom. We laid down a layer of newspapers and an old sheet on top of the bed, boiled water, got lots of towels ready, and made sure we had a big bowl. I'm so glad Mrs. Arneson was there because she was calm through the whole process and knew what to do while I was a nervous wreck. I felt so out of control and you know how much I like that!

 We situated Ellie on the bed and waited for Mrs. Jensen. Ellie said her backaches started turning into a squeezing sensation. It started up high but gradually moved lower as they grew stronger. All we could do during this was try to keep Ellie calm and comfortable. I say we, but it was really Mrs. Arneson.

 Mrs. Jensen joined us in about an hour and we all breathed a sigh of relief. Ellie's labor lasted all morning and into mid-afternoon. The contractions grew in frequency and intensity. Mrs. Jensen could tell the baby was moving down the birth canal. Ellie said she felt like her whole abdomen was being squeezed tight.

 When Mrs. Jensen thought it was time, she had Ellie start pushing. She was lying on her side and pushing for all she was worth. I held her hand and tried to encourage her.

 The baby's head came out first and you could see him squirming to get his shoulders out. Then, all of a sudden, he just squirted out the rest of the way. It was a miracle!

Mrs. Jensen lifted the baby by the feet and spanked it to get it crying and then laid him down and rubbed him. He spit out some fluid and she laid him on Ellie's chest to get him nursing.

I watched as Mrs. Jensen expertly tied off and cut the umbilical cord. Pretty soon after this, Ellie flushed out the afterbirth and lay back exhausted. Things began to calm down and we all cried tears of joy while we cleaned up. Ellie was so strong through all of this. I have never seen her so strong. I was scared the whole time but she just did what she was supposed to do and persevered through it all. She was incredible.

Oh, Henry, I can't begin to tell you how miraculous it all was. I wish you and Jimmy could have been here. Little James, Jr. is just adorable. He's the spitting image of Jimmy.

I hope to God you are okay over there. I think about you every day. Please take care of yourself and come home to me.

With deepest love and affection,
Your Margaret

Holy smokes! Jimmy and Ellie had a brand new little boy. Hank was sure Jimmy would like him being named James, Jr. He wondered if Jimmy knew yet. Hank hadn't heard from him for a month or two. He hoped Jimmy was okay, too.

There were basically three jobs among the mechanics. Riggers maintained the airframe, cabling, control surfaces and fabric of the aircraft. Fitters maintained the engines. Armorers maintained and loaded the machine guns and rigged bombs. Hank started out as a rigger because he was already fairly well versed in engine work.

Hank threw himself at this with abandon. He wanted to learn everything he could and do the best he could out of gratitude to Captain Harrison for the lucky break the captain gave him. Ned Cole helped him get started, but Hank soon learned who the expert was in each part of the job and went directly to him for the best guidance. Ned was fine with this and even encouraged it.

His experimentation with gliders when Jimmy and he were teenagers proved to be useful to Hank. From those studies and experiments, he already knew the basics of airframe construction, control surfaces and cabling. It was a joy for him to see how the professionals did it in state-of-the-art aircraft. Hank quickly ramped up to a level of proficiency where he could work independently and continued from there.

Hank especially enjoyed working with Captain Harrison to find ways to tune his aircraft's handling characteristics to suit his flying preferences. Hank learned the nuances of rigging the cabling to do this. By loosening some of the cables ever so slightly, he could tighten others to trim the wings and elevators, and to adjust the dihedral of the wings slightly up or down. Captain Harrison liked responsiveness more than stability so reducing dihedral gave him a little more of that.

Hank also developed expertise in armaments, learning how to minimize machine gun jams and to aim the gun in alignment with the Aldis sighting tube.

Sergeant Acker watched Hank's progress and let him know how he was doing. Acker was pleased with Hank's progress and so was Hank. After he was satisfied with Hank's abilities as a rigger, Acker switched him over to fitter duties working on the engines. Hank quickly learned how to tune the engines, clean the valves, and keep the engines running smoothly. From there, he advanced into more of the heavy engine repair and overhaul work. Hank learned how to remove the engine from the aircraft, tear it apart, put it back together better than new, and install the engine back onto the aircraft. Much of his experience from the motor pool applied directly to the fitter's job.

Before long, there wasn't anything Hank couldn't do for the aircraft. When he wasn't working on perfecting Captain Harrison's airplanes, Hank helped out other mechanics to get exposure to other types of repairs and to extend his own knowledge.

Before long, other mechanics began approaching Hank for assistance when they were stuck. He was deeply honored by this. Helping others deepened Hank's expertise even further. To help others, not only did he need to know what to do, but he had to be able to explain how to do it and why it needed to be done one way and not another.

Hank grew to understand the impacts of certain kinds of combat damage, what could be allowed to continue with minor patches, what needed to be repaired, replaced, or sent back up the line for overhaul, or needed to be scrapped all together.

He was brought in to consult on decisions about whether or not they could repair an aircraft at the field or if they had to send it back to depot for further work. At 60 Squadron, they had a strong maintenance team and good repair facilities so they could do most of the work right there at their airfield. Other airfields, Hank was told, had fewer facilities or less advanced mechanics and had to send more work back up the line to heavy repair stations.

Over time, Hank was recognized by Sergeant Acker and others for his efforts and promoted through the ranks to Air Mechanic Senior Class. Even more significant to Hank, Sergeant Acker mentioned to him that the overall reliability of the aircraft at 60 Squadron had risen significantly since Hank's arrival.

23

BRUAY, JULY, 1917. Harry Henderson, an unusually tall man for a pilot, rubbed his temples and pushed away his plate of beans and eggs on the morning of the twenty-third of July. His sour stomach from too much whiskey the night before seemed to sour his mood as well. "I don't know about the rest of you chaps, but I tire of playing the fool for the wealthy bastards back home. We face death every day and the warmongers who run the aircraft, weapons, and munitions factories keep getting richer. We die, they grow fat. We are the fertilizer for their profits. They betray us to become rich."

"Fertilizer," Grimes piped in. "You mean manure!"

Floozie Curtis, the squadron's provocateur, asked, "What about your patriotism, Harry? Aren't we here to preserve our freedoms and our way of life against the threat of the Kaiser?"

"Bah!" Henderson exclaimed. "They have the same warmongers on the German side. I swear they have colluded with the English gentry to invent this war just to line their pockets. They're all cousins, after all."

Larson had a different beef, "You can have your warmongers. I just want to go home. I miss the rolling fields of Yorkshire. I want to hold my Nel again and feel her warm flesh against my own."

"Ah, you're just horny. You know how to take care of that, I assume?" Shorty McGruder got a good chuckle from the lads. Jimmy appreciated his attempt to lighten things up a bit.

"Yes, yes, yes. Ours is not to reason why. Ours is but to do and die. Into the skies of death we fly!" Alfie Campbell chimed in, twisting Tennyson to suit his purpose.

"Fokkers to the left of them. Fokkers to the right of them. Fokkers in front of them. Spandaus thundered. Stormed at with Archie's shell, boldly they flew and well into the skies of death and into the mouth of hell!" Alfie knew his Tennyson. "I think I shall have to work on it!" They all laughed the wretched laugh of the battle weary.

Captain Stevens popped his head into the mess, "All right gentlemen, enough grousing for now. It's time we mount up for King and Country. A Flight, I'll see you in Paddington in five minutes." As always, the captain brought them back to reality.

They disbanded their gripe session to prepare for their patrol. "Come on, Gracie, we have work to do," Shorty said. Jimmy's new nickname had stuck. For three months now, his mission had held true. He sported seven roundels on his fuselage now, one for each save, a score that gave him pride and purpose.

Today, they were going to escort RE8s spotting for artillery to the east of Armentieres. Shorty was to lead McKenna, who was still with them. Jimmy had lost Hughes however, and had a new pilot, Lieutenant Malone, as his junior. The morbid parade of names and faces continued.

Stevens, McGruder, and McKenna flew low escort over the RE8s at about three thousand feet while Jimmy and Malone flew above and behind them at six thousand. Cumulus cloud formations covered a little over half the sky. Above and around them, the sky was crystal clear blue. Darker clouds were headed their way from the west, however. It would be raining this afternoon.

Jimmy kept his eye out for Huns who might be playing peekaboo behind the clouds while they maneuvered to gain a better attack position. Jimmy and Malone scanned the skies all around them, above, below, left, right, behind, and in front. Jimmy remembered how hard it was to see anything with the old balaclava helmet when he flew the FE8s and was grateful to be rid of it, now unnecessary with the Nieuports.

He liked flying the high position because it was not targeted by Archie. The planes below them took the brunt of the Archie barrages. Jimmy could see them exploding all around the RE8s and three low Nieuports. Artillery spotting was a hazardous mission because the airplanes had to fly low, making them easy targets for Archie, and because they had to stick around in one place for long periods of time while the artillery sections zeroed in on their targets.

Jimmy watched from on high as one of the RE8s took a direct Archie hit. It exploded right next to the fuselage behind the wing and blew the right wings clean off. Jimmy doubted the pilot knew what hit him. The observer in the back survived the blast but had to sit in the plane while it broke apart and drilled into the ground. Jimmy couldn't imagine a much worse way to go than to know you're going to die but not be able to do anything about it. No parachutes. Crazy policy if you asked him.

The other RE8 completed its mission and started heading southwest for home. The three low Nieuports stuck with him as he went. Just then, Jimmy saw a flight of six Germans dive on the lower formation from behind a cloud to the east. They were diving at high speed. He would not be able to intercept them before they engaged. Jimmy waggled his wings to get Malone's attention and rolled over into a steep dive. As he rolled back out of inverted flight, he just hoped his Nieuport's wings stayed with him.

Jimmy saw Malone following him but not keeping up. He couldn't wait for him. He dove toward the lead Albatros. Stevens and the others saw them, fortunately, and turned to climb into them. The Germans fell in mass on the RE8. It went down in the first pass. They zoomed on the back side of their pass into a climbing right turn. Jimmy had expected this and was waiting for them. He made a head-on pass at them and spun around to the left to get on the tail of the easiest target. The formation broke up as they turned. Jimmy picked out a yellow and green bird making for the other Nieuports. The lower formation was approaching the Huns head on now. Jimmy watched them slice through each other and saw the individual fights taking shape.

The yellow and green Hun went after McKenna. Shorty and Stevens were each occupied in their own fights. McKenna was a pretty good pilot and saw the guy getting into position on him. He rolled into a split-S and the Albatros followed right along after him. Jimmy continued to dive after the Hun. McKenna jinked, slipped, skidded, snap-rolled, and climbed vertical as best he could. The Hun was good and stayed with him.

Jimmy dove right at the Hun to get in a shot to distract him. He had to save McKenna. He concentrated his entire energy on the Hun and squeezed off a burst from his Lewis gun. Gladly, Jimmy watched the Albatros break away. McKenna would survive this fight.

Just as Jimmy was beginning to look around for Malone, he heard bullets whiz by him. He saw bullets rip through his lower left wing and watched in horror as the stream stitched its way towards him. Two hot pokers stabbed into his left thigh and he knew he had been hit. Then, another ripped through his left shoulder. He rolled to the right while the fourth bullet found its mark. It felt like it was right in the middle of his back between the shoulder blades. Jimmy lost control of his airplane and it spun towards the earth.

He bled a lot and felt his consciousness drifting away as he righted the plane out of the spin. Only half aware, Jimmy remembered putting his plane in a shallow dive to the west. He don't even know if the engine was running. His world began fading out and he had to fight it back.

Jimmy slipped in and out of focus for the next minute or two. The ground approached quickly and he fought to keep the plane from stalling. His body screamed in pain and his stomach rose up in his throat so he thought he would vomit. Jimmy tried to remain focused but his head bobbed about as he flew on the edge of consciousness. He barely managed to glide it in for a landing, but it nosed over and everything went black. Jimmy vaguely remembered hanging from his straps. He heard voices yelling but he didn't know what they were saying. He passed out.

Next thing Jimmy knew, he was blinded by the glare of a surgical lamp. He saw a man bend over him in silhouette. He looked left and right and realized he was on a table. Everything hurt. Out of nowhere, a gauze pad covered his mouth and nose and he passed out again.

He remembered rain rattling on a tin roof, almost as if in a dream. Four people stood around him grabbing for his legs, arms and head when he stirred next. He thought they were moving him to another bed or a stretcher. A young man said something to him, but he couldn't make it out clearly. He think he said something like, "We've done all we can here. We're moving you to a better hospital farther back." He blacked out again.

He woke up in a glaring white hospital room. He was groggy and everything was a blur. Gradually, he regained focus. He had a needle stuck in his arm and looked up at the bottle of liquid hanging from a hook with a tube coming down to his arm. He couldn't move. When he tried to grab for the tube, he realized his wrist was strapped down to the bed. He tried to lift his head and couldn't. He yelled, "Help!" but his throat was so sore it came out as little more than a whispery whimper.

A nurse strode up to him, all dressed in white with a big, funny looking hat on her head. "You must stay still, Lieutenant. You are not to move. We have strapped you down for your own protection."

"Where am I?" he asked, still having difficulty focusing.

"You are in Hospital for Officers, Hyde Park Place, in London," the nurse said calmly.

"London? What am I doing in London?" He was thoroughly confused.

"You were wounded and they sent you here. Don't try to talk too much just yet. I will send for a doctor who can explain it all for you. Take this little sip of water and please lie quietly." The nurse turned and walked out of the room.

His mind raced. London? Why would I be sent to London? They have plenty of capable base hospitals in France. All he could do was wonder and wait. After what seemed like an hour, a doctor came into the room.

"Lieutenant Arneson, yes?" the doctor said. He stood over him, bespectacled in a white lab coat.

"Yes," he responded. "Why am I in London?"

"Your wounds were quite severe, Lieutenant. You lost a lot of blood. The field hospital dressed two wounds in your left thigh, one wound in your left shoulder, and a hole in your back." The doctor spoke clinically. "All of these were handled in France, of course. You were brought here because of the injury to your back."

"What do you mean?" he asked.

"It appears you are paralyzed from the waist down. We have not been able to fully determine the extent yet, but it looks like one of the bullets hit your spine and ricocheted off to exit your body through the right side of your rib cage. One of your ribs was broken as the bullet exited. We cannot tell for certain, but it appears your spinal cord was not severed. However, one of your vertebrae was damaged. Let's try some exercises to see if anything has changed, shall we?"

The doctor prodded Jimmy and asked him if he could feel anything in several places. Jimmy didn't feel a thing until the doctor stuck a little needle in his side, just above his waist.

"Your condition has not changed since our last check," the doctor said. "However, it has only been a week since your injuries were sustained. Luckily, you were evacuated quite quickly. I believe you may have a case of spinal shock, so we have restrained you to minimize the risk of further damage to your spine."

"Spinal shock?" he asked.

The doctor continued, "It is normal for severe swelling to occur around a spinal injury as is the case with your wound. This swelling can cause the loss of nervous sensation below the injury. With spinal shock, your paralysis should go away as the swelling subsides. This normally takes place within the first two weeks, though some rare cases take longer. I want to monitor this for the next several days to see if you begin to develop any feelings below your waist."

"So I'll get better, then?" he asked.

"There is no guarantee here, Lieutenant. Your injuries may be permanent or they may not. Only time will tell us which it is. You must lie still to give yourself the best chance of recovery. I will have the nurses take care of your needs. You'll do that for me, won't you?" The doctor asked.

"Yes, sir, I will," he replied.

"Good man. I'll check in periodically. Good day to you." The doctor turned and left the room.

The days crept by. The nurses dressed his other wounds regularly, helped him with his bodily functions, and tried to keep him company as best they could in the small amount of time they had.

Most of the time he was alone with his thoughts. Not knowing was tortuous. Would he heal or not? What would Ellie think of him as a cripple? Would she leave him? He would be left alone as a cripple the rest of his life, cared for by an aging mother and father until they died, and then what? Destitute and unable to care for himself, he would end up in some home for invalids, left to rot out the end of his days. It was a future he could not allow to happen. He would kill himself first.

Saints be praised, Jimmy started to feel the doctor's pin pricks after four days! Even the doctor, to whom Jimmy appeared to be an unnamed case, smiled when Jimmy jerked at his pin prick. "Excellent!" the doctor exclaimed. "This is exactly what I had hoped for, Lieutenant. We will keep checking more often now. I would expect to see you recover feelings in all your extremities within a day or two. Then, we should see your reflexes return with a vengeance. Hypersensitive reflexes are part of the normal progression. It is time to rejoice, young man!'"

Each time the doctor came in, Jimmy could feel things farther down until even his little toes felt the doctor's pin pricks. On that day, the doctor and nurses removed his restraints and helped him stand. Jimmy was horribly wobbly and weak, but he could stand!

Now, the nurses began working with him tirelessly to help him recover full mobility and strength. As predicted, Jimmy did indeed have sensitive reflexes for a while as well. It was like his nerves were surprised by feelings. Before a week had passed, he was able to walk with the help of two canes, one in each hand. He walked the halls until he couldn't walk any longer.

After a week of this, the doctor came in to discuss his discharge from the hospital. "Well, Lieutenant, you have made an excellent recovery. Your wounds are healing nicely and you have recovered your sense of feelings from the spinal injury. I think we should discuss next steps."

"What will happen to me now? Can I go back to my squadron?" he asked.

"Perhaps one day, Lieutenant, but not too soon. All of your wounds need to heal completely. They have progressed to a point where outpatient care will suffice. The larger issue is your recovery from the spinal injury. While your basic nervous sensations are progressing nicely, your body needs more time to fully recover. You have noticed, I am sure, you are still quite wobbly when you walk. This is normal and will get better over the course of a couple of months."

"Do I have to stay here the whole time?" he asked.

"No, you do not, Lieutenant. I plan to prescribe convalescent leave for two months. You are going home, Lieutenant!" The doctor smiled again.

"Home, to Minnesota?" he asked disbelievingly.

"Yes, home to Minnesota." The doctor smiled. "Provided you have a physician at home who can monitor your continued recovery, I see no reason why you can't do so at home."

"When can I go?" he asked.

"In the next few days. We have paperwork to complete and orders to get processed for you. After you feel you have recovered fully and with your doctor's concurrence, we will reexamine your case to determine whether or not you can return to duty and in what capacity."

"You mean I may not be able to fly?" he asked.

"It all depends on your recovery, Lieutenant. It is not certain either way. I think the odds are good you will recover fully, but time will tell. Good luck to you, Lieutenant."

"Thank you, doctor." Jimmy teared up. He was going home.

"Very well, Lieutenant. Rest up now. I have asked the nurses to keep you as comfortable as they can while you remain with us." With that, the doctor left the room.

24

STE MARIE-CAPPEL, OCTOBER, 1917. Hank Jacobs and the other air mechanics of 60 Squadron were busy keeping their airplanes in tip-top shape, performing overhauls of engines and conducting other heavy maintenance. Spare time in the evening was spent playing cards, writing letters, or drinking.

It was during one such lull when the entire air base was shocked into wakefulness one night in October by the explosion of a bomb. Hank leapt out of bed in a state of frenzied confusion. Before he could get his pants on another bomb exploded and shook his tent. He rushed out to see what was happening, but it was the thick of the night so nothing much could be seen. Ned Cole ran up to him with a torch to help them see. Others lit torches as quickly as they could. Hank could hear the engines of the planes but couldn't see them.

Two more bombs fell as he and Ned ran for one of the two searchlights they had on base. They started up the generator and the light came to life. Not long after, the other light started up and soon their two light beams were crisscrossing each other in the night sky. Still, they could see nothing but the low ceilings of the clouds overhead. The anti-aircraft batteries were quickly manned and fired into the air in the blind hope of hitting something.

By the time they were all in place to defend themselves, it was over. The planes had dropped their bombs and headed back home.

None of them had any idea what kind of planes they were or where they came from.

After an hour or so, Sergeant Acker came around to their searchlight and told them they could turn it off and go back to bed. They followed instructions and turned off the light, but there was no way any of them could get back to sleep with their adrenalin rushing as it was. They ended up just sitting around in the mess hall speculating about what had just happened. Luckily, no one had been hurt in the attack and no buildings had been hit. Work parties were formed to fill in the craters left in the tarmac by the bombs, so Hank and Ned helped out with the shoveling for the rest of the night.

The next morning, the aerodrome was abuzz with tension. The observation planes on base were rigged with bombs to retaliate against the German aerodrome near Courtrai and took off at dawn. Scout flights accompanied them to their targets. Captain Harrison was flight commander for A Flight. Hank prepared his plane, saw him off at five o'clock, and returned to repairing bomb damage.

It had been a long night. After seeing Captain Harrison off and helping to fill in the last crater, Hank went to his cot and slept. He asked Ned to wake him up before A Flight returned. At least he could get a couple hours of sleep.

Ned woke him at eight o'clock to tell him A Flight was overdue. Hank got up, dressed quickly, and headed to his hangar to await their return. It was a dreary morning, the sun unable to break through the deep and low overcast. Hank dragged himself out of slumber as he walked along the duckboards. When he arrived, he was glad to see hot tea and biscuits waiting. Ned had returned before him and was having a cuppa himself.

"Sergeant Acker was saying he heard the mission was taking longer than expected," Ned said.

"I hate waiting," Hank replied. "How many have we lost recently?"

"Only two so far this month. It's been a light month what with the weather."

"Only two. Two lives gone, two families heartbroken," he answered.

"What's the latest with your Meg back home?" Ned asked.

"Oh, she's doing well. She worked through her problems at the bank and is now doing fine," he answered.

"What was it she does again?" Ned asked.

"She works in the commercial lending department in the town bank," he said.

"Sounds pretty heady to me," Ned exclaimed. "I'll go back home to the family smithy. You go home to a financial banker. You're going to be well set, eh mate?" Ned smirked.

"I guess so," Hank answered, "I haven't really thought about it."

"I look forward to seeing my Bessie. I expect we'll get married and raise a couple of little Coles."

"Hey, listen!" Hank said. "I can hear the engines, can you?" The buzz of the engines was unmistakable. Distant at first but growing in anger as they approached.

"Aye, that'll be them all right," Ned replied.

They got up from their chairs and walked out of the hangar to the tarmac. All the other ground crews began to emerge from their activities as well.

The planes first appeared as specs in the distance. No semblance of order or formation, just a gaggle of planes. Hank counted four. Someone was missing. He knew A Flight sent out five this morning. Of course, they had no way of knowing who at such distance. As the flight came over the field for their landing circuit however, they could see the position numbers on the sides of their planes. The only one missing was number one, Captain Harrison.

Hank's heart sank and his head slumped. "The captain's missing, Ned."

"Yes, he is," Ned said. "But you know, Hank, this is the captain we're talking about. He's always going off on his own chasing a Hun all the way to Berlin if he needs to. He'll turn up."

Ned was right, he knew. The captain was often the last one back from a mission. Those were often the days he had a victory to report. Hank had an odd, sinking feeling in his gut, however. Something wasn't right. He felt it in his stomach and his neck. "Right. You're right of course, Ned. He'll turn up. Let's help the other blokes, shall we?" They went over to the next hangar to help the ground crew with their plane.

Hank asked the pilot from the number two plane, a Lieutenant Lapsley, if he knew anything about Captain Harrison.

"No Jacobs, I'm afraid I don't," the lieutenant said. "Captain Harrison was with us early on. The Germans hit us on the way in with the new triplane we've heard about. Those things are wicked maneuverable. And they can climb incredibly fast. Six of them jumped us and went for the bombers. They fought them off but got separated as usual. Captain Harrison never rejoined our flight. Last I saw him, he was pursuing a triplane heading east."

"Thank you, sir," he said.

"Look, he'll turn up, Jacobs. He's always gallivanting off by himself. He knows what he's doing." The lieutenant was conciliatory. The pilots felt the losses even more than the ground crews did, so they understood how Hank felt.

Ned and Hank helped the other ground crews get their planes settled back into their places, refueled, rearmed, and ready to go. An hour or more went by doing all this, but still no sign of the captain. Ned decided to head back to the tent while Hank chose to hang around the hangar for some time longer. Hank puttered about trying to keep busy but his sense of impending doom grew as time went by.

The weather began closing in around ten o'clock. By noon, the sky was dark gray with a thick layer of low flying clouds, misting all over the field. The grass glistened with moisture on the tips of the blades.

Still no sign. Hank knew by now, the best bet for hearing something would be by phone calls from anti-aircraft batteries, other squadrons, or ground troops near the lines, so he headed over to the adjutant's office to check with the first sergeant. He walked into the flight office and approached the first sergeant's desk.

"Ack Emma Jacobs reporting, sergeant." He stood sharply, not quite at attention. Other ranks did not salute each other.

"Yes, Jacobs, what can I do for you, son?" The first sergeant was a father figure for all of them.

"Any word on the whereabouts of Captain Harrison, sergeant?" Hank asked. "He hasn't returned from this morning's patrol."

"Haven't heard a word, Jacobs. But then, I don't always hear of every update from the field. Let me check with the adjutant for you." He stood and walked into the office where the adjutant and the squadron commander worked.

The sergeant was in there for a few minutes and came back out. "No one has heard anything about Captain Harrison. But look here, boy, it's not at all unusual with the captain. Why I remember days when he wouldn't show up until after dinner and be just fine. He sometimes stops at other fields to visit old friends, you know. I'm sure he's up to something like that. Mustn't worry, lad. Give him time."

"Yes, sergeant. Thank you, sergeant. You don't mind if I check back in from time to time, do you, sergeant?" he asked.

"Not at all, boy. Not at all. Now run along and write a letter back home. It'll get your mind off it." The sergeant then returned to the paperwork on his desk and Hank left.

Hank tried to follow the sergeant's advice. He returned to the tent he and Ned shared. Ned had gone off somewhere else. Hank sat down at the little table they shared as their desk and began to write a letter to Meg. He couldn't concentrate, however. In fact, he couldn't concentrate on anything.

Hank went back to the aircraft hangar and putzed around. He cleaned all his tools and toolbox drawers, reorganized his tool boxes, and cleaned them again. Then he organized the parts shelves and storage bins, anything to kill time.

Hours went by with no word or sign of the captain. The day faded into afternoon and evening. Nothing. Hank's sense of impending doom grew into a void, a terrible feeling of loss, an emptiness in his soul. He stopped in at the squadron office again just before dinner. Still no word. Eventually, Hank fell into a fitful sleep, exhausted.

The next day brought no further news. Hank queried the other pilots who had been on the patrol. They knew nothing additional. He checked in at the squadron office. They knew nothing more.

Sergeant Acker asked Hank to help out some of the newer mechanics and teach them the ropes, as he put it. Hank did as he asked, of course, and it helped pass the day. At least it kept his mind occupied.

The following day, the base awakened at dawn with the firing of anti-aircraft batteries. Ever since the bombing, the airmen kept the guns manned at all times in fear of another attack. Ned and Hank jumped out of bed and ran outside the tent to see what was happening.

They could hear the buzz of a rotary engine and knew there was at least one plane about, but they couldn't see anything. A Fokker triplane popped up from behind a nearby tree. He was obviously hedge-hopping to confound the Ack-Ack guns and headed for their aerodrome. As he got closer, the machine gunners opened fire on him. He jinked and threw them off easily enough. The little tripe bobbed all over the sky on its way into the airfield.

On he came relentlessly to the tarmac. They all expected a bomb to fall next, so when the German dropped something off the side of his plane, they all ducked for cover. It did not explode, however, and off he flew into the nearest trees to hedge-hop his way out of the range of their guns. He was come and gone in a flash.

They all ran over to see what the German pilot had dropped. Ned got there first. He picked up a wreath of branches. It had broken up a little bit in the fall, but was still largely intact. Tied into the middle of the wreath, Ned found a leather-wrapped package.

Ned dropped the wreath and looked at the package in his hands. It was not overly large nor heavy. The leather was oil-soaked and pliable. It was tied up with a leather strap wrapped around it.

Several officers ran up to them as well. "Careful there!" one of them yelled. "It could be a bomb, you know."

"Hand it over to me, airman," a lieutenant ordered. Ned complied but they all remained huddled around the lieutenant to see what it was. He unwrapped it carefully. Inside the leather wrapping, the lieutenant found a pair of aviator goggles with a note folded up inside them.

The lieutenant unfolded the note and read it to all of them. Written in impeccable English, the note read, "The Imperial German Air Service regrets to inform you of the loss of a great aviator, Captain Cecil Harrison, of 60 Squadron, the Royal Flying Corps. This brave and honored pilot, known as a hero to friend and foe alike, was shot down by Oberleutnant Hans Althof, flying a Fokker DR1, near the town of Menen. Captain Harrison was buried in the cemetery by the large cathedral in town. He was given full military honors in his burial service. We offer our condolences to you over the death of a fine airman and hero to all."

They all stood there in stunned silence. Hank could not believe his ears. "May I see it, sir?" he asked.

The lieutenant handed it over to him, saying, "Just for a moment, airman. I will need to give this to the major straight away."

Hank read through it again slowly, hoping he had misheard what it said. When he was through, he handed it back to the lieutenant who headed toward the squadron offices. Hank stood there stunned as the crowd dispersed into twos and threes muttering away about the captain's death and the chivalry of the German pilots.

The void hit him like a stomach punch. Hank sat down on the grass right there, put his head in his hands, and wept. Ned came back shortly afterwards and sat on the grass with him. "He was a great man, he was," Ned said.

"I wouldn't be here without him," Hank said. "Ned, what if something I did or didn't do to his aeroplane contributed to his death? What if his plane wasn't rigged properly or what if his engine cut out on him just when he needed it most?"

"Now you listen here, mate," Ned said. "You put that thought right out of your mind, do you hear me? You are hands down the best air mechanic in this squadron. There isn't a man in this outfit who doesn't respect your abilities. Captain Harrison had the utmost confidence in his aircraft because he knew it, too."

"Thanks, Ned." Hank's eyes dried up a bit. Ned was a good man and a good friend. After dinner, one of the mechanics recited Requiem, by Robert Louis Stevenson, in honor of the captain. It was quite fitting:

Under the wide and starry sky
Dig the grave and let me lie:
Glad did I live and gladly die,
And I laid me down with a will.

This be the verse you 'grave for me:
Here he lies where he long'd to be;
Home is the sailor, home from the sea,
And the hunter home from the hill.

25

GRESHAM, AUGUST, 1917. Jimmy's brow beaded with sweat just sitting still on the sparsely populated train watching the hot and humid Minnesota prairie pass by. His woolen RFC uniform was hardly the clothing for such heat. He moved over to the other side of the train to get out of the sun. Soon after, the brakes screeched through clouds of steam as the train slowed coming into the Gresham train station. Jimmy's eyes welled up to see home again, but his apprehension rose also. What would it be like? Would he adjust? Much of his soul remained in Treizennes, pulling him back.

"Jimmy! Jimmy! Over here, Jimmy!" Ellie was waving one hand high, holding little Jimmy in the other, smiling broadly and running towards him as he hobbled off the train. He had to take it slow to avoid stumbling down the train's stairs with his two canes. A porter helped him with his kit bag.

Jimmy tried to put up a good front as she rushed into his arms. "Careful, I'm not very steady on these things yet!" She didn't care, rushed up to him, and raised her lips to kiss him passionately. He stumbled back and fell on his butt, his canes flying through the air as he tried to catch himself with his hands. Pain shot up his spine as he struggled to hold in an agonized scream.

Ellie jumped back, horrified, "Oh, Jimmy! I'm so sorry!"

The porter stepped in and slipped his arms under Jimmy to help him to his feet and Harald, Jimmy's dad, rushed in to help. Jimmy regained his footing with their help and the porter gave him his canes. Jimmy's face flushed in embarrassment as he straightened his uniform. His dad helped brush him off on his back and legs.

Ellie approached again, more tentatively this time. "I'm sorry Jimmy. I'm just so happy to see you again!"

"It's okay, Ellie. I'm fine. It's good to see you, too!" He pulled her in to him with one arm and kissed her while he supported himself with one cane.

"Oh, Jimmy, you're home!" Ellie squealed, unable to contain herself. "Look, here's your son, James Jr.!"

"My son!" He was a beautiful little fellow. "How old is he?" Jimmy asked.

"Just eight weeks," Ellie replied.

"He looks like me, but he has your nose!" Jimmy exclaimed.

"He's you, darling, all you," Ellie modestly replied. "Oh, Jimmy, I've never seen you in uniform before. You look so dashing!" She saw his uniform, Jimmy saw his canes.

Edith, Jimmy's mom, came up and kissed him on the cheek and hugged him. "Welcome home, son! I'm so glad you're alive. Oh my, you've lost so much weight. We'll have to fix that!"

Ever the stoic, Jimmy's dad shook his hand, but Jimmy could see genuine warmth in his eyes. "Yes, welcome home, James. Let me get your bags for you." His dad carried Jimmy's bags for him as they headed to the buggy for the ride home. Gwen, the family horse, nickered to welcome him home, too. Jimmy hugged her and petted her nose. He felt strange, as in a dream. Gresham was still small, quiet Gresham. Nothing had changed here, but he was not the same person. A lifetime had passed in less than a year.

At home, Jimmy's dog, Smoky, ran up to him and almost knocked him over jumping up on him and licking his face like crazy. Smoky wiggled and wagged his tail with a huge smile on his face.

Edith and Ellie set to making some dinner for them all while Jimmy and his dad sat on the porch. Smoky curled up at Jimmy's feet and Dad packed his pipe. "I'm glad you're home, son. Now, explain to me again your situation. You're on leave for a while, right?"

"They call it convalescent leave," Jimmy explained. "The easiest way to explain it is to say my wounds still have some healing to do. I have to work on rebuilding my strength in the meantime and return for examination in two months. If they feel I am ready, I will go back to France then."

"Where were you wounded?" Harald asked.

"Over Armentieres," Jimmy replied.

"Ah, yes. I'm sorry, I meant what part of your body was hit?" Harald explained.

"Oh, sorry. I took two in the left leg, one in my left shoulder, and one hit my spine and broke a rib on the way out."

"Oh my! Four bullets?"

"I was quite lucky, actually. The leg and shoulder wounds were clean shots without any bone damage. Those are the tough ones," Jimmy explained. "Even luckier, the bullet that hit my spine bounced off and did just a little bone damage. The problem has been the swelling around the spine. I couldn't walk for a while."

"Lucky indeed. I would say someone upstairs is looking out for you." Jimmy's dad was a deeply religious man.

"So, Ellie and little James live with us now, right?"

"Yes, they do. Sadly, Ellie's father could not bring himself to accept Ellie's pregnancy out of wedlock," Harald explained. "They've reconciled now, at least cordially, but Ellie chooses to remain here and we welcome her."

"I'm sorry about the out-of-wedlock thing, Dad," Jimmy apologized. "How do you feel about it?"

"You know our beliefs, son. But we also understand the urges of youth. You were going off to war, after all. She is welcome here," his dad explained. "However, I insist you marry her as soon as possible."

"I couldn't agree more, Dad," Jimmy acknowledged. "I have a few things to process first, however."

"What do you mean, son?"

"Umm, it's hard to explain. War is not what I expected, Father," he stammered.

"Hmmm. Very well. But you will maintain separate rooms until you do." Jimmy's father was adamant.

"Yes, Father. I will," Jimmy replied. "Tell me of Karl and Fred."

"Karl left shortly after you did," Harald explained. "He's gone to China as a missionary with the Lutheran church. We don't hear from him often, but he does write occasionally. He is teaching English in a school over there. I can never remember the name of the village. I think he said it's in the Hunan province."

"So he decided to do it after all," Jimmy remarked. "I always thought he would."

"I think your departure spurred him on, actually," Harald said. "He is doing God's work. I pray he will be successful over there. It is a brave thing he is doing."

"And Fred?" Jimmy asked.

"Young Freddie enlisted in the Marine Corps a few days after the announcement was made about the United States joining the war." Harald was concerned about Fred. Fred had always been hot tempered and easy to set off. "I hope he makes it. Maybe the Marines can instill some responsibility in him."

"So you're running the farm all by yourself now?" Jimmy asked. His dad was getting up there in age. He must have been 47 years old, Jimmy reckoned.

"Yep. I could sure use the help while you're here. Harvest time is coming up for the beans and the sweet corn. We'll certainly get your strength built back up." Harald smiled.

There was plenty to do around the farm all right. Jimmy had difficulty doing much at first. It was hard enough to walk with two canes. Forcing himself to do without, he quickly discarded one so he could carry little things. Within a couple of weeks, he had discarded both canes. He was unsteady and his legs ached badly, however. Ellie rubbed them with ointment for him at night.

Ellie worked hard at the farm, too. Edith often watched little Jimmy while Ellie helped out. Jimmy was impressed by her persistent, dedicated energy. She never let up. She essentially took over everything he used to do before he left, plus more. Ellie milked the cows, fed the animals, mucked out the stalls, did laundry, helped with the cooking, and cleaned house. Sweet and innocent little Ellie was turning into a fine and strong young woman. She retained her natural beauty, but added on to it strength, competence, and determination.

Jimmy started out helping her with his old chores. It was difficult at first. He would knock things over with his canes and get angry when he couldn't do something that once was easy. Too often, he took it out on Ellie, like the time they milked the cows together. She was milking Mayfly when he came up. Jimmy took his pail over to Junebug to start milking her. When he went to sit down on the stool, his left leg gave way and he kicked his pail with his foot sending it across the barn and landing him on his keister. Both cows spooked, which in turn spooked the horses and sent the chickens flying and cackling. The barn erupted into a cacophony. Mayfly stepped to the right and bumped him when he was down. He was afraid she was going to step on him and he yelled out, "Control your animal, dammit!"

Ellie giggled.

Jimmy screamed at her, "What the hell are you laughing at? Just get your damned animal away from me!"

Ellie recoiled from his outburst, sprang up, covered her eyes, and ran away in tears. Jimmy just sat there fuming.

He tried to keep himself busy, but he couldn't settle down. Jimmy still had nightmares and startled awake in the middle of the night, screaming. Ellie would be at his side from the room next door in an instant, stroking his hair and telling him it's all right.

Pastor Olson came by twice a week to speak with him about the war. Jimmy shared his guilt over killing men. The pastor tried to tell him it was okay to do so if you were defending your own life. What he said mattered little to Jimmy. He thought the pastor just wanted him to feel happy. Maybe his words would help, Jimmy didn't know. He would have to chew on them for a while. While his father was deeply religious, Jimmy was never sure what to make of it all.

Working on the farm was the best thing Jimmy could have done to rebuild his strength. It came back to him steadily. Each night he was physically exhausted, which helped his sleep. Getting better sleep helped his disposition. He began to see hope in life again. The simple, hard work of the farm brought the old Jimmy back to the surface. Jimmy began to actually feel good about life. He still had nightmares, but not every night.

Jimmy helped with little James, Jr. as well. He started calling him 'JJ' for short. He hoped it would stick. Changing JJ's diapers, feeding him, dressing him, and bathing him renewed Jimmy's hope for the future and a desire to see it. JJ was such an adorable, lovable little guy. He relied on Jimmy. JJ and Ellie were Jimmy's responsibility. He wanted to be responsible for them. He loved them and they loved him in return.

By the end of the first full month at home, he had almost recovered from his wounds. The feelings in his legs and extremities were getting back to normal.

Reflecting on how quickly he had recovered, Jimmy realized the one constant support through it all had been Ellie. She provided him with all the love and support he could have asked for. Even when he yelled at her, she persisted in her gracious love for him.

Jimmy took Ellie out for a picnic at their favorite place by the Dogwood River, just like they used to do. After their meal together, he gathered a bouquet of periwinkle-blue Forget-Me-Nots and gave them to her. She remembered the last time he gave them to her and cried little tears of joy.

Jimmy proposed to her. "Ellie, my darling, will you marry me?"

"Oh, Jimmy, yes! Yes, yes, yes, a thousand times, yes!" she squealed in delight.

They embraced. He kissed his Ellie more deeply than ever before. He kissed her with his heart as well as his lips. He wrapped his arms around her and held her close, luxuriating in the warm softness of her breasts. He loved her truly. They lay down on the picnic blanket, kissed some more, arm in arm. And then they made love.

"Ladies and gentlemen, allow me to introduce to you for the first time, Mr. and Mrs. James Arneson!" Pastor Olson beamed.

"You may kiss the bride." Ellie lifted her veil and leaned forward. Jimmy stepped toward her, hugged her, and kissed her on the lips. They were married!

It was a small ceremony. They had invited family and few friends. Meg was Ellie's bridesmaid, of course. Jimmy would have had Hank as his best man, but Hank was still in France. Jimmy's father stepped in for Hank as his best man.

Ellie and Jimmy walked down the aisle to the buggy waiting in front of the church. They headed home to his parents' house to change and depart for their honeymoon. A friend of the family lent them the use of his cabin at Lake Pepin. They would spend a week there alone together.

After their honeymoon, Jimmy moved into his old room with Ellie and JJ. He continued to help his dad on the farm. They fell into a routine. It was good work, but it was monotonous. Day after day Jimmy went through the motions, but something was awry. Jimmy got antsy every afternoon as the day wore on. France crept back into his consciousness and undermined his joy of life. He took up smoking again.

Ellie was so sweet and loving. She cared for Jimmy selflessly, she was devoted to him, and she cared for JJ with all the love and affection anyone could ask for. And yet, Jimmy grew unhappy at home, too. He still struggled too much inside to have any normal sense of emotions at home. When JJ cried, he bristled. He often had to get up and leave the house to settle down.

Jimmy began to spend too much time at the bar in town. At first, people struck up conversations with him, but after a few sullen exchanges, people left him alone. He sat in the corner alone, staring off into space, knocking down drink after drink like he was in the officer's mess at Bruay. Ghosts of his fallen comrades tugged at him from France. He was torn and it showed, distracted in conversation, unable to fully engage. He wasn't all there. Part of Jimmy was still in France. He was irritable and flew off the handle far too often for no good reason.

Jimmy felt uncomfortable in his own skin. On the surface, everything was idyllic. He had good work, a loving wife, a handsome son, and a good situation at home. What more could anyone ask for? Under the surface, however, Jimmy was a mess. In quiet moments, he returned to the skies over France. He flew through Archie barrages and flinched when a shell blasted too close. People around him just saw him quietly staring and suddenly he would jump out of his chair with a crazed look on his face.

Nights got worse. He lay in bed wide awake staring at the ceiling and sweating. After hours of this, he fell asleep in exhaustion only to startle himself awake when an Archie shell exploded in his face. Sometimes, Jimmy would see the faces of the men he had killed. His guilt kept him from church even though his whole family went every Sunday. In fact, he couldn't go near the church without being overwhelmed with guilt. Pastor Olson tried to soothe his guilt but Jimmy could no longer stand to talk with him.

Why was he the one who lived? Jack Bailey, Mike Phillips, Hughes, and so many others deserved to live so much more than Jimmy, but they were all dead. He saw the men he failed to save die in his mind's eye over and over again. Nothing was ever right. He found himself needing to be back on the aerodrome. He wanted to know about his friends and fellow pilots. Was Shorty McGruder still around? What about Captain Stevens? He never saw or heard from them after he was shot down. He did not know if they were alive or dead. He knew they were still dying, the men in green. His mission was not complete. He had to complete his mission, to save as many as he could.

It came to a head one night when he jumped up in bed, startled by the blast of an Archie shell. "I can't take it anymore!" Jimmy yelled.

Ellie startled awake. JJ cried. She had seen him do this too many times. "It's all right, Jimmy. You're safe here with me. You're at home, darling," she pleaded. "Oh, sweetheart, it's okay. I love you. You're home in Gresham."

"I have to go back," he said. "I have to go back to France. I can't handle it! I can't stay here knowing men are dying there every day. I have to go back."

"But Jimmy, you did your service. No one expects you to do more. You've already done everything a man could do. Stay here with us," Ellie pleaded.

He cried. He put his head in his hands and sobbed. Ellie tried to comfort him, but he couldn't stop. He cried and cried and cried. "If not me, who?" he pleaded. "Who will save them?"

In the morning, he was certain he must return. He could not stay any longer. He had to go back. His physical wounds had healed. It was time for him to get re-examined by the RFC to go back to France. He packed his kit bag, said his farewells to Ellie, JJ, his mother, and his father and got a train ticket to Winnipeg. It was time to return to duty.

The northbound train retraced the steps Hank and Jimmy took the year before when they embarked on their journey. Rumbling along the tracks, Jimmy stared out the window and reflected on lost innocence. He remembered his youthful exuberance for adventure. He was going to be a knight of the sky, riding his steed into courageous battle to vanquish the evil foe. His thoughts returned to the day they enlisted.

Jimmy and Hank headed to the center of Winnipeg assuming the recruiting offices would be there. Sure enough, they found them right off the town square.

"Good morning, gentlemen!" The sergeant rose and stepped forward to shake their hands. "Flight Sergeant Adams here. How can I help you?"

"We want to be pilots in the Royal Flying Corps." Jimmy stepped right up to it.

"Well, that's grand!" said Sergeant Adams. "Are you Canadian citizens?"

"Nope. We're Americans," Jimmy said. "We heard you were looking for pilots and were accepting volunteers from the States."

"True enough, absolutely true," Adams agreed. "Of course, you'll have to qualify for it, but you both look like fine, strapping young men. Do you have any questions of me or shall I just draw up the paperwork right here?"

"What kind of qualifications?" he asked.

"Well, there's a physical examination and a battery of aptitude tests to see if you're fit for duty as a pilot. We sign you up here and send you off to Toronto for evaluation and assignment." Sergeant Adams seemed a good man, straight and tall, articulate, and pleasant looking enough in a rugged sort of way.

"What sort of pay do we get?" he asked.

"Well, it depends on your rank, of course, but I must tell you, people don't enlist for the great salary. A lieutenant makes about fifty pounds per month. That's about $250 U.S. dollars."

Hank looked over at Jimmy and caught his eye. Jimmy raised his eyebrows and nodded, inclining it to the papers being gathered by Sergeant Adams. He was ready to go.

So, they did it. After they answered all the questions on the attestation forms the sergeant had for them and signed them, he stood them up at attention and had them swear their oath to King and Country.

"I, James Arneson, do make Oath, that I will be faithful and bear true Allegiance to His Majesty King George the Fifth, His Heirs, and Successors, and that I will, as in duty bound, honestly and faithfully defend His Majesty, His Heirs, and Successors, in Person, Crown and Dignity, against all enemies, and will observe and obey all orders of His Majesty, His Heirs and Successors, and of the Generals and Officers set over me. So help me God."

They were in the Royal Flying Corps! The sergeant gave them directions to the train station and the Testing and Evaluation Center in Toronto. He also gave them vouchers for an overnight stay in a nearby hotel, meals, and train tickets to get them to Toronto. Their great adventure had begun!

Now, making the journey for his return to duty, Jimmy rode with a grim reality. He knew he would not find peace until he had seen this thing through, fearful though it might be.

Sergeant Adams snapped to attention when Jimmy walked into the Winnipeg recruiting office wearing his officer's uniform. "Sir!" Adams exclaimed.

"How do you do, sergeant?" Jimmy asked. "Do you remember signing me up in September, 1916?"

"By Jove, sir, I believe I do! How are you, sir? You're looking grand!" Adams was a bit overfriendly and Jimmy doubted he actually remembered him.

"Lovely, sergeant. I have been on convalescent leave after getting wounded over Armentieres. It's been grand, but the time has come for me to return to duty. I trust you can assist me?" he asked.

"Why yes, I can, sir. Let's see, I think it's 'Return to Duty,' form B-210. Let me pull one out and we'll fill it out, shall we?" Adams retrieved a blank form from his file cabinet and placed it on his desk in front of him. Donning his glasses, they went through the form together.

The form had a question calling for duty station and unit. "Number 40 Squadron at Bruay, France," Jimmy stipulated.

"Very good, sir. Number 40 Squadron is a fine outfit. Nieuports, yes?"

"Indeed! I was flying one when I was shot down," he replied.

The form also included a section for return from convalescence calling for a medical exam. "We shall have to send you to Toronto for the flight surgeon to give you your medical examination, sir," the sergeant added. "The RFC can process the request to return to 40 Squadron while you're in Toronto."

"Request?" he asked.

"Yes, sir. There's always the chance His Majesty may have need of you in another squadron, sir," the sergeant said apologetically.

"Oh well, it is the government, isn't it?" Jimmy replied.

"There is one other thing, lieutenant, sir," Sergeant Adams added. "As you are an American, the Royal Flying Corps has an agreement with the United States Army that flying officers such as yourself can transfer to the U.S. Army, Aviation Section Signal Corps, if you prefer. You can keep your full rank and get full credit for time in service and time in rank, sir. Would you be interested?"

"No, thank you, sergeant," Jimmy replied. "I looked into it already. The US is still far, far behind in aviation. They are still mostly in the formation stage and I am a pilot, not an organizer." The US took a long time to gear up for the war. Even though war had been declared in April, the Signal Corps was still little more than an organization on paper. The few airplanes they had were not adequate to the task and were hopelessly outclassed by the airplanes of the primary combatants. Jimmy knew he would likely be put behind a desk or assigned to instructing new pilots and that was not what he wanted or needed to do.

"Very well, sir," the sergeant replied.

Jimmy was off to Toronto again. It was a different experience from 1916 however, because he was now an active duty officer, with better food, a private cabin on the train, and better quarters. Rank did have its privileges.

Jimmy passed his medical examination just fine, but waited impatiently for his assignment. A week after his examination, he received orders to proceed to 56 Squadron in France. He was disappointed he was not to return to his old outfit and his friends there, if any of them still lived. However, he was also happy to see it was 56 Squadron, which was reputed to be the best squadron in the entire RFC.

Jimmy packed his bags and headed out as soon as he could arrange transport.

26

STE MARIE-CAPPEL, NOVEMBER, 1917. Following Captain Harrison's death, Hank Jacobs helped out the other mechanics wherever he could. Operations slowed down as winter set in. However, in place of air operations, they learned the hard way that this airfield was a target of long-range German bombers. The squadron experienced midnight bombing raids all too frequently. It was rumored among the mechanics the Germans were building up for a big offensive.

They also got a new Commanding Officer for the squadron, Major Percival Grenford. He was later to learn he was the third son of some baron or other, making him part of the aristocracy.

Shortly after his arrival, Hank was informed he was being assigned to maintain the major's aircraft, a new SE5a. The two men met when Grenford took his new airplane up for a test flight. "Air Mechanic Jacobs, is it?" he asked.

"Yes, sir, how do you do, sir?" Hank replied in a brace as expected of other ranks when speaking with an officer.

"I hear you're the best mechanic on the airfield. Is that so, Jacobs?" Hank immediately disliked Grenford. The major spoke with a condescending tone reminding Hank of the motor pool days.

"So I am told, sir. I do my best. I love everything about aeroplanes," Hank replied.

"Good. See to it this aeroplane is always in tip-top shape and ready to fly. I shall not fly with all the missions, but I do like to keep my hand in. Understood?" he said.

"Yes, sir!" Hank snapped to.

"Good. Now, let's see how this bird flies." Grenford climbed in the cockpit and donned his goggles and scarf.

They walked through the standard start-up procedure. With, "Contact!" Hank cranked his propeller and his engine started right up. The SE5's V-8 engine was so different from the old rotaries. Good engines, though. Grenford rolled away to take off and Hank watched him shrink to a dot off to the south.

Their relationship was formal and strained at best. The major frowned on fraternization with the other ranks and only begrudgingly acknowledged Hank's existence. Quite naturally, Hank's loyalty to his pilot diminished. Fortunately, Grenford didn't fly very often, so Hank continued to help out the other ack emmas whenever he could.

Hank received a letter from Margaret in early November advising him of Jim's condition.

October 21, 2017

Dear Henry,

I don't know if you aware of it, but Jimmy has been badly wounded and has been sent home to us for convalescence.

I am sorry to say he is not in very good shape, Hank. He is barely able to get around on two canes. Apparently, according to Jimmy, this is a vast improvement as he was temporarily paralyzed from the waist down. He said he feared he might never walk again.

He is at home now being cared for by Ellie and his mother. He exercises every chance he gets, trying to build up strength in his legs. He's skinny as a rail, too. He's lost a lot of weight since we last saw him.

He told me he had been shot down by a German pilot and was shot in the leg, shoulder and back. He says he is lucky to have lived and was rescued from his crashed plane from British soldiers in the trenches.

I know you are unable to come home to see him, but I wanted you to know of his situation. He is healing, albeit slowly. I am sure you will want to write to him and let him know how you are doing.

I hope you are doing well, Hank. I miss you and want you to come home safely.

With love and affection,
Your Margaret

Hank was surprised by what he read. Jim was wounded! He was taken aback to hear how badly Jimmy had been shot up, but he was glad to hear he was alive. Hank immediately wrote Jimmy a letter himself to let him know he knew, wishing him the best, and how he was doing, himself.

The bombers generally flew overhead in the middle of the night. The squadron might get alerted from a field unit calling in a sighting, but more often the Germans came without warning. Hank and Ned would always jump out of bed and dash to their positions. They usually headed out to help a machine gun position on the eastern end of the field.

About three weeks into December, they were surprised by a daylight strafing attack by German scouts. Hank and Ned were working together on a problem-child SE5a that wouldn't run smoothly no matter what they did to fix it. They were about to pull the heads off the engine so they could change the camshaft when they heard the Germans approach. The angry buzz in the distance sounded different than their own birds.

They could see five or six dots off to the east coming straight for the airfield. The Germans were hedgehopping as they came. Their planes would pop up for a moment and then drop down out of sight. They would arrive in an instant. Ned ran to the hangar to yell, "Air raid!" Soon, everyone was scrambling.

Hank and Ned immediately scrambled for their usual post near the machine gun emplacement on the east end of the field. They were running for it when the Germans reached the airfield. Six abreast, they came in with guns blazing. The machine gunners Hank and Ned were assigned to support had gotten on their guns just before the planes reached the field. The twin Vickers were firing away and the gunner was spinning his guns around to get a lead on the aircraft as they flew by.

As they fired their Spandaus, the Huns' bullets hit the ground in straight lines advancing to their targets. Ned and Hank could see one of them was stitching his line of bullets straight toward them. They veered off to the left together. Hank tripped in a rut in the field and went head over tea kettle. Ned, right behind him, tripped over him and went flying, too.

The Hun adjusted his aim to bring his bullets over to them, but they scrambled just out of his sights before he whizzed by. The bullets hit the ground within a few feet of their tumbled mess.

They ran for the machine gun position and got there in a few more seconds. The German planes had completed their first pass over the airfield. They set alight the SE5 that Hank and Ned were working on. It blew up in a blaze of flames. The Hun climbed and turned to the left to come in for another pass.

The gunner yelled to them as he tried to line up his gunsights, "I need more ammo!"

Ned yelled back to all of them, "I'll go! Hang on. I'll be right back!" He took off for the hangar.

The aircraft were on top of them before they knew it. Their main targets were the aircraft on the tarmac and in the hangars. The machine gun emplacement was in their sights when they had completed their strafing and were heading east at the end of their second pass.

One of the Germans lowered his nose as he approached and squeezed off a burst from his guns. Hank watched in horror as the line of bullets headed straight for the machine gunner and his ammo feeder. Hank saw the bullets rip into the sandbags first and then the two men who threw their arms up into the air as the bullets hit them. They fell lifelessly back into the gun emplacement.

Hank reached them a moment after the Hun aircraft flew overhead on its way to prepare for another pass. He jumped over the side of the sandbag wall and landed between the men. They had both been hit several times and were dead. He looked down at the gunner. His eyes were open but there was no life in them.

The gunners were blocking the space Hank needed to operate the gun so he first had to quickly lift and drag them over the side of the emplacement.

Hank took up position to fire the twin Vickers machine guns and spun around to look for the German aircraft. They were completing their sharp turns to come around again when he saw them. He could see there were not many bullets left in the ammo cans for his guns. He just figured he would do what he could until Ned got back. Hopefully, Ned would be able to help feed the guns continuously.

As the Huns completed their passes, their formation gave way to a loose staggering of aircraft. Hank picked one out headed his way and aimed his gun. He waited until he thought the German was close enough and pressed the triggers. The guns roared and his whole body shook with the vibrations. It was much more difficult to aim than he thought it would be, but he tried his best. He saw the plane whiz by him and could make out the pilot's head as he flew by. He spun around to fire after him, but he didn't know if he hit him or not.

Hank could see Ned off in the distance running toward him with a couple of ammo cans in his hands. He was running as fast as he could with the heavy containers. Hank began to spin around to see if he could get a bead on another of the Germans as they went by.

Before Hank could make it all the way around, he was hit. The burning pain was unlike anything he had felt before. He knew his bum leg was hit because he was thrown off balance and fell to the ground. Another bullet hit his left arm as he went down. He never knew where the plane was that shot him.

Hank tried to get back up but was knocked senseless for a bit. As he regained his senses, he leaned over to his right side and pushed himself up with his right arm. He was about to reach for the gun handle to continue pulling himself up when Ned arrived.

Ned threw the ammo cans into the emplacement and ran to Hank's side. "Hang on, mate! We'll get you taken care of!" Hank could feel Ned grabbing him under his arms and dragging him a few feet away. He looked up to see Ned's face as he strained. Ned set him down and Hank watched as Ned fed the ammo belts into the machine guns. Ned was just finishing up and getting ready to fire when Hank's world went black and he lost consciousness.

27

LAVIÉVILLE, DECEMBER, 1917. Every bump in the road telescoped up his spine as the roughly sprung tender bounced its way south from St. Omer on muddy, half-frozen roads. Snow fell most of the day and eddied its way into the canvas-covered cargo area of the tender where he sat huddled against the cold along with a sergeant and an air mechanic first class, also headed to 56 Squadron at Laviéville. Forty miles south of Bruay, it took them almost all day to reach the 56 Squadron airfield, a dreary start to his next assignment. Fortunately, things were about to look up.

"Lieutenant James Arneson reporting as ordered, sir!" Jimmy introduced himself to the adjutant of 56 Squadron, Major Townsend.

"Ah yes, Arneson. We've been expecting you," Major Townsend replied. "Allow me to introduce you to our commanding officer, Major Baldwin. Follow me."

They walked through the open door into Major Baldwin's comfortable office. He had heard their conversation outside, "Lieutenant Arneson. Good to meet you, lad. We've heard a lot about you."

"Me, sir? You've heard of me?" Jimmy was shocked to hear this.

"Yes, we have a bit of a surprise for you!" Major Baldwin was genuinely enjoying this.

"Welcome back, Gracie!" Captain Stevens said as he walked through the door.

"Captain Stevens! This is a great surprise. You're here at 56 now?" Jimmy was amazed.

"Flight commander of C Flight!" Stevens replied. "I saw your name on the recruitment lists and asked for you here. I hope you don't mind."

"Goodness no, I don't mind. I am so glad to see you!"

"How are you doing? I mean, you look well. We heard you had some nasty scratches. Everything heal okay?" Stevens asked.

"Yes, I'm fine now. It was a bit rough for a while," he explained. "I took two in the leg, one in the shoulder, and my back was hit on a vertebra. It was a bit scary at first. I was paralyzed for a week or so. I got excellent treatment though."

"Oh my, I'm glad you're all right now," Stevens said.

"How are the boys at 40 Squadron?" Jimmy asked.

"Alfie Campbell is now flight commander of A Flight, been promoted to captain and still chasing his score. I think he's up to fifteen last I heard," Stevens said. "Shorty McGruder is still around as well. He's Alfie's deputy flight commander."

"Glad to hear it," Jimmy said. He was glad they were alive.

Stevens continued. "Listen, Gracie, we can use you here, that's for sure. The good major here has assigned you to my flight. I hope you're okay with that."

"Am I ever!" he exclaimed.

"Good. Well, let me show you around," Stevens said. "'Okay with you, major?"

"By all means. Welcome aboard, lieutenant. You're in good hands. I'll see you around the mess hall, eh, old boy?" The major said.

"Thank you, sir!" Stevens and Jimmy saluted, spun round, and walked out together.

They walked to the Nissen hut where Jimmy would bunk. "Thank you so much, captain!" he said. "I am honored you asked for me."

"You're a good pilot with a good attitude, Jim," Stevens said. "That's why I asked for you. You'll find it quite different here. This is a top-notch squadron with the best aeroplane in the air right now. We hold the advantage with the SE5a and can pick our fights, just the opposite of the old FE8 days with 40 Squadron."

"Is McCudden here?" Jimmy asked. "Is he as good as they say he is?"

"Indeed, James is flight commander of B Flight. I see him every day," Stevens replied. "He's a good man and an extraordinary pilot. He rather keeps to himself, however, and often goes out alone. I can't say I care for it, but who am I to argue with his success?"

"I look forward to meeting him!" Jimmy replied.

"I'm sure you will soon," Stevens said. "Here's your quarters, Gracie. Take your time to settle in and come find the officer's mess. I'll see you there and introduce you to the rest of C Flight."

Lavieville was a major step up from both Treizennes and Bruay. The officers bunked in a little grouping of well-appointed Nissen huts sleeping four to a hut. They each had their own nice little section to call home. A pot-bellied stove in the middle provided heat for the hut. Jimmy unpacked and reflected gratefully on his good fortune.

The officer's mess was especially nice. When he walked in, he saw Captain Stevens immediately, standing with a group of three other officers, and walked up to say hello.

"Gracie! I see you found the place. Allow me to introduce you to the rest of C Flight." Stevens tipped his tankard to the three fellows. "These are Lieutenants Pieter Steenkamp, Liam Buckley, and Sanjay Murthy. They call Pieter 'Blondie' for obvious reasons, Liam is 'Bucky', and Sanjay goes by 'Sandy.'"

They all seemed to be fine chaps and reflected the international membership of the squadron. Jim was pleased to see every member of the Commonwealth represented. There were pilots from England, Ireland, Scotland, Canada, South Africa, and even India.

He was astounded to learn they even had a little orchestral quartet that entertained the officers every Wednesday with such fun songs as "Oh, You Beautiful Doll!" and the "Mysterious Rag."

There was much to learn here. New people, new planes, new tactics. Jimmy had never seen a more organized, efficient, and motivated team. He looked forward to it.

As it turned out, Jimmy was one of five new replacement pilots to arrive on the same day. At five o'clock, Major Baldwin pulled the squadron together at the officer's mess to give a squadron briefing.

Most of them were already gathered at the officer's mess when the major walked in. True to form, Major Townsend announced his entrance with an order to attention, "Attention!"

The major got right to the point. "Gentlemen, we have several new pilots joining us today, so I thought it would make a good occasion to update everyone on the war efforts and 56 Squadron's situation. Further, I thought I had better get this over at five o'clock before too many of you are soggy with beer!" Cheers and guffaws followed.

"The Battle for Cambrai is now in its second month and beginning to wind down. We are no longer being called upon to support Army attacks or to defend against the German counter attacks. However, there is still lots of air activity, even in this lousy weather we've been having.

"You can expect most of our missions to be deep, offensive patrols to find and destroy enemy aircraft, especially two-seaters observing our movements or bombing our troops. Common types include white-winged Albatros C-type two-seaters, as well as AEG, DFW, LVG, and old Roland aircraft. Get the two-seaters. They are the eyes of the enemy. Keeping them from completing their missions is why we are here.

"Watch out for their counter-fire. As our dear Captain McCudden has demonstrated so well, get underneath and behind them to get into their blind spot and evade their rear gunner's machine guns. Then, fire up into them from below. Also, beware of cooperation between two or more of them. Do not focus too heavily on one without watching out for the other getting into a position to fire back at you.

"Of course, the Hun does not want you to shoot down all of their two-seaters, do they?" Another round of chuckles among the pilots. "They still fly the Albatros DV V-Strutters and Pfalz DIIIs more than any other type. Our Essies can handle them well. We can out-turn, out-dive, and out-climb these types so choose your fights accordingly. If you get into a jam, dive away to get out of their range. Tight climbing turns can also be effective evasive maneuvers. We see several black-tailed Huns regularly and believe them to be from Jasta 5.

"The Fokker DRI triplane is showing up more frequently lately. These little Sopwith copies can be deadly so be careful. You can out run them in level flight and out-dive them, but under no circumstances engage in a climbing or turning fight with these little buggers. They climb like bandits. Your best tactics here will be to get above them and dive through their ranks in a slashing attack and zoom back up only after you have got out of their range.

"You can also expect to be called upon to escort Brisfits and Airco DH4s on their observation and bombing missions. The Bristol Fighter can be counted on to fully engage with the fighters as well. They are surprisingly strong and maneuverable.

"Lastly, I have received notice that commanding officers are now officially forbidden to fly in combat. All I have to say to this is, 'I won't tell if you won't tell!'" The pilots all cheered the major, then.

"That's all, gentlemen. Enjoy your evening. Major Townsend has tomorrow's assignments. Good night!" As the major left the room, Major Townsend posted orders for the next day. Everyone gathered around to see what the day would hold and rushed the bar for refills.

The next day Jimmy jogged out to the tarmac to meet his new airplane and ground crew. Captain Stevens introduced him to both. "Good morning, Gracie! Let's go meet your new crew, shall we?"

"Yes, please!" he replied. They walked over to hangar number 3 together.

Waiting out in front were Air Mechanics Brooks and Moss, making a few adjustments on Jimmy's new plane. "Ack Emma Brooks and Moss, sir! Pleased to meet you, sir!" They looked like fine young men. Everyone at 56 Squadron seemed to dress well, even the mechanics. Jimmy thought it must have been a matter of squadron pride.

"And I you!" Jimmy said. "This my new bird?"

"Yes, sir," Brooks replied. "She's a fine aircraft, sir!"

"Might I ask for a look around her, Brooks?" he asked.

Stevens interrupted, "Take her up and get comfortable, Gracie. You'll be going up for real tomorrow."

"I will, sir. Thank you!" he replied. As Captain Stevens turned and walked away, Jimmy threw up a hasty hand salute.

"Now then, where were we?"

Brooks and Moss gave him a thorough briefing on the airplane as they completed the pre-flight checks. She had a large white stripe on the fuselage ahead of the vertical stabilizer to designate 56 Squadron and a large "N" call letter painted aft of the RFC roundel.

"We'll need to embellish a little here, gents," he added. "I would like a name painted on here in front of the roundel, if I can."

"Why yes, sir. Several of the pilots do. What would you like?" Brooks asked.

"'Saving Grace,'" Jimmy said. "Painted in white on a diagonal in cursive. And eight small roundels painted on the bottom edge of the fuselage underneath the name."

"Very good, sir. May I ask the significance?" Brooks asked.

"The boys back at 40 Squadron named my Nieuport 'Saving Grace' while I was there. You see, my personal mission is to keep my compatriots alive. I count saves, not kills. I have eight so far."

"Marvelous!" Brooks said. "I shall be honored to help you in any way I can, sir!"

"Thanks! Now, let's get on with this."

Jimmy's first impression of the SE5a was its big, boxy front end to accommodate the huge, 200-horsepower, Wolseley Viper V-8 engine. It made for a long nose that would be difficult to see around while taxiing and would take some getting used to. Both the FE8 and Nieuport had rotary engines that took up far less room. This bird had almost twice the horsepower. The SE5a looked and felt like a more serious, business like aircraft than either of the others. More gravitas, in effect.

Jimmy climbed up into the cockpit and found himself at home. Four months had not taken away the spirit of flight. He was eager to fly, but first he had to acquaint himself with the instrumentation, some of which was new, and some of which was no longer there, such as the blip switch. The SE5a had a proper throttle to advance or retard the power of the big V-8 without having to always manually adjust the air and fuel pressures. Also new was a fuel selector to select the tank to draw fuel from. A lever on the left side opened and closed the radiator shutters to optimize power in different temperature ranges.

The Vickers machine gun, which was positioned part way down on the left half of the fuselage, protruded into the left upper corner of the cockpit. Interrupter gearing had improved to now provide reliable fire through the propeller.

A second machine gun, a Lewis, was positioned above the upper wing on a Foster mounting, just like the Nieuport. This would be easy to accommodate. An Aldis sight provided for aiming of the Lewis while the Vickers used a ring bead site. Two drums of ammo for the Lewis were stowed in the cockpit. The control stick was crowned with a leather-covered ring enclosing two firing triggers, one for each gun, side by side. It would be easy to fire with either gun, or both. A small, glass windshield, as well as struts and bracing wires framed his view down the long nose to a large, four-bladed propeller.

Jimmy let Brooks know he was ready and they commenced the start-up sequence. He turned the magnetos off and so Brooks could prime the cylinders. Brooks did so, rotating the propeller by hand and then calling for contact. At Brooks' direction, Jimmy turned the switches on and Brooks cranked the propeller to start her up.

The bird came alive. The V-8 felt so much smoother than the old rotaries, but still hugely powerful. Its power reverberated through the frame, the cockpit, and the pilot. This airplane was powerful. He kept the radiator shutters closed for a bit to let the engine warm up.

Once warm, he signaled Brooks and Moss to pull the chocks and advanced the throttle to taxi to the take-off point. A steerable tail skid helped ground maneuvering. Nice touch, he thought.

Opening the throttle for take-off, he felt as much as he heard the engine roar. At 50 mph, the Essie lifted off effortlessly. He immediately felt comfortable in this plane.

Its stability made it easy to fly. Its added strength was evident in the air currents. The old FE8 and Nieuport floated on the wind. Flying was a constant adjustment of the aircraft in response to air currents. The Essie floated on air currents also, but the feeling with this bird was more like powering through them. Also, the balanced offset of the cylinder firing order in the V-8 eliminated much of the gyroscopic effect and resulting wicked-spin problems of the old rotaries.

The Essie climbed quickly, nearly as rapidly as the Nieuport. At altitude, Jimmy began basic maneuvers to get a feel for her handling characteristics. As he expected, there was a trade-off between stability and maneuverability. She was a bit heavy on the controls compared to the agile Nieuport, but not so heavy he couldn't get used to it.

He started with gentle S-turns and added steep turns, lazy eights, and wingovers. It was a piece of cake to do these in the SE5a. He added slow flight, stalls, and spins. Climbing back up to four thousand, he advanced to rolls, barrel rolls, snap rolls, loops, split-esses, Immelmans, full-power level flight, high-altitude flight, and high-speed dives. He was struck by the speed of 130 miles per hour or more. In a dive, he reached 180 miles per hour and knew she would do more. The air rushed by his head, tucked behind the windscreen, faster than he had ever experienced. It was exhilarating.

This plane would outrun anything the Germans had. It was a remarkable advance over the early aircraft he had flown. The SE5 would be excellent for young pilots who hadn't had much training.

Jimmy set his mind on familiarization with the territory. Laviéville lay significantly south of Bruay, his last base in France. They were also farther west of the front, which turned to the southeast south of Arras. Jimmy found landmarks for the airfield. The easiest was the road from Arras to St. Pol. It would mostly be a matter of finding this road and following it to the field, which lay just a mile south of the road.

The last thing he tried out on his inaugural flight was gunnery. Here again, the Essie performed well, providing a nice, stable firing platform. He was always skidding and slipping the Nieuport while firing. Here, he could concentrate more on his aim and count on the plane to fly steadily. He thought this might also allow for longer-range shooting. All in all, he was impressed by this bird. Combat would tell, of course, and that came soon enough.

28

SOMEWHERE IN FRANCE, JANUARY, 1918. Hank woke up in a hospital somewhere in France. How he got there was a hazy dream. The nurse told him he had to have somewhat delicate surgery because one of the bullets hit his femur and he almost lost his leg. Apparently, the surgery went well, because he still had his leg and he was told he could expect to walk again. His leg was elevated and covered in a tent for the first few days. Later, they took the apparatus down when it was clear he would keep the leg.

It was his right leg, the same one he had injured on the motorcycle years ago, so he knew he would now have an even more pronounced limp. As he faded in and out of awareness, he found himself back in Minnesota when he banged up his leg to begin with.

Hank and Jimmy were sixteen and had to help out more with family stuff on a regular basis. Hank's dad insisted he work at the family furniture business full days during the summer, Monday through Friday. He was either the floor salesman during the day or helped with furniture repairs in the back workroom.

Jimmy's dad wanted him working all day on the farm. Jimmy's older brother, Karl, was on a summer study program at St. Olaf College in Northfield. He was set on becoming a Lutheran pastor and a missionary, so Jimmy had to pick up the slack. There was always something he had to do all day, every day.

Not surprisingly, the two boys looked for ways to escape their drudgery whenever they could. The Indian motorcycle they had bought together was running pretty good now, so that was their main escape every chance they got.

The county roads were all arrow-straight and dusty as all get out, but it didn't stop them. They used to run the bike up as fast as they dared, barreling down the straight away at fifty miles an hour. When they got really brave, they would see how fast they could take the right-angle corners from one dirt road to the next.

That's exactly what they were doing that fateful September day in 1912. They used to take turns between driving and riding in the sidecar Hank had jury-rigged. Usually, they took corners to the left so the sidecar helped keep the bike righted, but today, Hank felt especially daring.

Jimmy was in the side car on Hank's right and Hank was driving. They sped out county road number 18 to the east. Three miles east of Gresham, Hank decided to turn a sharp corner to the right to head south on the dirt road. The side car prevented him from leaning in to the turn like he normally would have without the side car attached. It started to roll to the left violently, lifting Jimmy and the side car up in the air even though Jimmy was leaning out as far as he could. Instinctively, Hank reversed out of the turn to try to bring it back down, but he ran out of road.

The front wheel hit the ditch on the east side of the road and turned the bike head over heels. Jimmy was thrown out of the side car and Hank was vaulted out over the handlebars of the bike, with the bike following him in its somersault. The motorcycle landed right on top of Hank, crushing his right leg under the hot engine. He screamed like crazy. His leg snapped at the knee and he thought it would burn right through with the heat of the engine. Hank jerked his leg to try to pull it out but the pain was excruciating. He tried to lift the bike off his leg but he couldn't get any leverage. Tears flooded his eyes so he couldn't see. Every movement caused intense pain in his leg. Hank leaned back to catch his breath but when he came forward to try again, his head pounded with a pain so intense he lost consciousness.

Next thing Hank knew, he was slung over Jimmy's shoulders as he walked back into town. Jimmy had been hurt, too. Hank could see Jimmy's arm bleeding badly from a cut below the elbow. When Jimmy turned to look at Hank's face, he could see Jimmy's eyebrow had been split as well. Blood trickled over his right eye. Hank could feel Jimmy limping as he carried him, so he must have hurt his leg, too. Hank slipped in and out of consciousness as Jimmy carried him back to the hospital in Gresham.

An hour later, they stumbled into the hospital waiting room. Jimmy laid him down on the couch and pretty much collapsed on the floor. Nurse Fjellstad rushed out from behind her desk to treat them. Hank remembered looking up through pain-hazed eyes at her lovely face looking down on him with great concern, but blacked out.

Hank awoke the next day in a hospital bed. Meg was sitting in the visitor chair reading a book. She was the first thing he saw when he opened his eyes. He just lay still there for a bit, trying to gather his senses. His hands were bandaged and his right leg was hung in traction with a large cast on it. His leg hurt, but not too sharply. He wiggled his toes. It hurt to do it, but he was grateful to see them move. He looked around, moving only his eyes. The basic hospital room greeted him with cold welcome. Meg read quietly concentrating on her book.

She glanced up and saw him looking at her through downcast eye slits. "Well, hello, Henry, you stupid fool."

He managed weakly to whisper, "Hi."

"I am greatly relieved to see you awake, but I am angry at you, so be careful, you idiot." Her lip trembled little bit and her eyes teared a little, betraying her concern. Doctor Norberg will come around shortly to check on you. The nurse said I could give you some water if you wanted it."

"Yes, please," he murmured.

Meg got up and walked to the window. She poured a glass of water out of the pitcher on the table and brought it back over to him. Hank tried to lift his head but was instantly clobbered with a pounding headache. He collapsed back onto the pillow, grimacing. She reached behind his head to lift it for a drink. "This should help you feel a little more awake anyway."

Hank took in a few sips. It tasted delicious in his desert-dry mouth. "Thanks, Meg." He took a few more sips and laid his head back down.

Meg returned to her chair at his bedside. "Tell me everything you remember."

Hank recounted the tale as best he could. There were a lot of holes in his memory following the accident. He had spent a lot of time passed out.

"Jimmy carried you on his shoulder three miles to get you here. Apparently, he had a gash in his right thigh that bled a lot while he walked. They had to give him some blood. He broke his right arm, too. It was a compound fracture they said, and he had lots of cuts and gashes. He looks as bad as you, but at least he can walk on his own. He'll probably come by before long. They still have him here in a room down the hall. Ellie is with him, surprise, surprise!"

"What happened to my leg?" he asked.

"Doctor Norberg said you tore several ligaments in your knee and broke your femur, the big thigh bone. He also said you were burned pretty badly there. They put a window in your cast so they can clean the burns while your bones heal. Your hands were badly burned, too, and you have a bunch of scrapes and cuts all over your face and forearms. That's why you're all bandaged up."

"I hurt all over," he mumbled.

Meg gave him another drink of water. "We're all worried about your head, too. Nobody knows what might have happened there. You've got some huge bumps. Doc is worried about a concussion."

The door nudged open and Jimmy walked in, escorted by Ellie. "Hey, old man. How are you doing?" Jimmy smiled, but Hank could tell he hurt, too. He used a cane in his left hand to help him walk. His right leg was all bandages and his right arm was in a sling with a cast from his fingers to his armpit with a big right-angle bend at the elbow. His left forearm and head were also bandaged and he had a huge black eye. "Looks like this is the second black eye I have gotten because of you!" He laughed.

Jimmy laughed, but it made his ribs hurt too much. It turned into a groan. "Holy buckets, Hank. We were just about goners, don't ya know."

"How's the bike?" Hank asked.

"No idea. Apparently, your dad took a wagon out to bring it back. I would guess it's pretty banged up. That was quite a flip we did in it!" Jimmy replied.

"Yeah, I imagine it was." Hank's head hurt.

Margaret chimed in. "The doctor said you would be laid up for a long time, maybe several months. He doesn't think you'll ever get full strength back in your leg. The ligaments in your knee will heal, he said. But they won't be as strong. I guess the knee got wrenched pretty badly. He doesn't know how much flexibility you'll get back."

Needless to say, old Doc Norberg was right about most all of it. Hank was laid up at home all through the fall and well into the winter. During December, he rebuilt his strength, walking up and down the halls and stairs of his home with a cane. By the end of January, he could get around pretty good, but his knee was extremely weak. It hurt to walk on it and he had to be careful to not twist it lest he crumple to the ground in a heap of agony.

Hank never was able to run well at all afterwards. Short spurts in a straight line were about all he could manage. He dared not turn sharply when running. Nor walk fast for that matter. He was to be a man with a limp for the rest of his life. Still, he didn't let it get him down too much. Lots of guys had suffered worse from motorcycle accidents. Adventure was the spice of life, they said. He had his first that September day.

Gradually, Hank returned to full wakefulness in the hospital in France. As he looked around, he realized he was better off than many of his ward mates. He lay on his cot for hours on end, listening to them moan in pain. Some were going to be horribly disfigured from facial wounds. There were many amputees in his ward as well. Still others were not going to make it. The nurses, dressed all in white, reminded him of angels flitting from one cot to the next tending to those poor guys.

The fellow on his left was bandaged all around his head and upper torso. He was unconscious most of the time and only roused once in a while to moan and call for a nurse. He was in bad shape. The fellow on his right was more alert. His name was Patrick Sykes. Pat was a corporal with the Fifth Grenadiers. He had lost most of his right arm in an artillery barrage a week ago. Still, he was remarkably accepting of his situation,

"Look at it this way," he said. "I'm left-handed!" Hank chuckled. "More important," Pat said, "I'm done. The nurses say I'll heal okay and then I go home for good. No more trenches, no more lice, no more mud, no more living in terror."

"You're a stout man, Pat," Hank said. "So many men are dying. Does anyone come out of the trenches unscathed?"

"You might be surprised," Pat said. "If there's a push on, you stand a good chance of getting it, but most of the time, it's just living in misery. We don't have so many raids anymore and the patrols don't go out as often anymore. Of course, there's always the shelling. You never know when you might get it. That's what got me, a shell landed five feet away and took me arm clean off. My buddies got all broken up. One fella, we never even knew what came of him. He just scattered to the winds."

"Where are you from, Pat?" Hank asked.

"A little ironstone-mining town in South Staffordshire called Oakengates. I guess I won't be going back into the mines either. I hope his Majesty provides a pension for us folks. Otherwise, I don't know how I'll get by."

"I hope you do, Pat. I hope you do," he replied. "Do you have a girl back home?"

"I do indeed. Her name is Victoria, named after the queen," Pat replied. "She's a right strong gal with a good heart. I hope the loss of my arm won't send her away. I'm sure she has other suitors."

"Don't worry," Hank replied. "She knows a good man when she sees one, I'm sure, and she'll want to keep you around."

"How about you, Corporal Jacobs?" he asked. "Where's home for you?"

"I come from Gresham, Minnesota," Hank replied. "It's a tiny farming town in the southwest corner of the state. Minnesota is in the United States, as you probably know."

"Right!" Pat said with wonderment in his voice. "I've heard of it, but I can't say as I know much of anything about it. What's it like over there?"

"Flat, grassy plains as far as the eye can see," Hank said. "We mostly grow corn, wheat, and soybeans on the farms around town."

"You a farmer then?" Pat asked. "Hank, is it?"

"Yes to Hank, no to being a farmer," he replied. "My dad runs a furniture shop in town. We make tables, cabinets, chairs, and the like for the townsfolk and the farmers around us. My passion is around mechanical things, however. I like to work on engines and such."

"That's a good thing to know," Pat acknowledged. "Them automobiles is showing up everywhere nowadays. Why I bet after the war, every town will need someone to keep them running and fix them when they breaks. You oughta think about setting yourself up in a garage or some such. I bet you could make a good living with it."

"You just might have something there, Pat," Hank said. "I'll have to think about it."

"You have a girl, Hank?" Pat asked.

"Well, yes, I do, sort of," he replied. "Her name is Margaret. She's best friends with my best friend's girlfriend."

"Okay, let me think about it. Right, so you and she just sort of fell in together because of your friends. Is that right?"

"You got it!" Hank replied. "She's smart and has a good head for numbers. She works at the bank in town, which is owned by her father."

"Now that's a match made in heaven!" Pat said. "Why she could get you all set up in your own business. You do the work and she manages the money for you."

"Hmm, I'll have to think about that, too," Hank said. "You're a pretty smart fellow yourself there, Pat!"

"Why, thanks, Hank! Guess I'll have to use the old noggin more now I ain't got no arm."

"I think you'll do just fine, Pat, just fine."

Hank had a lot to think about now, and lots of time to think about it, lying in bed all day long.

After a week in the hospital, Hank was discharged with a three-week rest and recuperation leave to England. They billeted him in a fancy hotel off Piccadilly Circus called the Regent Palace. Large parts of this quite new hotel had been commandeered by the British government. Hank figured he just got lucky as most of the space was given to officers.

At first, Hank couldn't get around easily, relying on unwieldly crutches, so he spent most of his days in bed except for meals and bodily functions. After a week or so, he found he could limp around okay with a cane in his right hand.

Piccadilly Circus was a great place to stay, as he learned from walking around during his second week of recuperation. There were plenty of pubs and restaurants. He found himself a regular at The Queen's Head, next to the Piccadilly Theatre on Denman Street. Hank was smitten by ale, London Pride becoming a quick favorite. Same with the food there. He had heard pubs had terrible food, but the steak and ale pie at the Queen's Head was hard to beat.

As the healing progressed, Hank decided to fan out and from Piccadilly and see some of the mainstay tourist attractions in London. He visited the Tower of London and the Tower Bridge one day. The next, he stopped in at St. Paul's Cathedral and Buckingham Palace. Finally, he walked around Trafalgar Square and Parliament. Each day, his leg wore out but by the end of the day, but it grew stronger. Thank heavens for London cabs and buses.

29

LAVIÉVILLE, JANUARY, 1918. Jimmy had to watch his step on his way to the latrine. A thick layer of frost covering everything in sight made the duckboards slick. His nostrils froze when he breathed in and thick clouds of vapor formed in front of his face when he let his breath out. He felt like he was walking through his own fog. On days like these, he was grateful for the thick woolen scarf his mother had sent.

The ceiling looked to be about four hundred feet this morning. The formless gray skies looked like snow. There would be no flying once again. They might be able to take off, but they would have a dickens of a time finding the field to land with such a low cloud layer. He had heard of many pilots who descended through the clouds blindly only to plow smack into a tree or church steeple. Such was the case most days in January. Snow, sleet, or misty freezing rain made up Old Man Winter's repertoire.

When they could fly, they did, but there wasn't much fighting going on, either on the ground or in the air. Everyone hunkered down to stay warm. The pilots of 56 Squadron spent a lot of time training in makeshift classrooms set up in the hangars. The seats close to the wood stoves were the most popular. They talked at length about formation flying, flight maneuvers, and air combat tactics.

Captain McCudden shared his methods with them for attacking two-seaters. The good captain personally got 14 of the 17 kills for 56 Squadron in December, including four kills on one day. He obviously knew what he was doing. He liked to fly high and alone, popping in and out of clouds to avoid detection and waiting until he had a clear tactical advantage. Ever the hunter, this was a key element of his success. Jimmy wondered if they could follow similar strategies in patrol strength. It would be much harder to stay undetected in a group, he thought, but still worth trying.

When McCudden saw a target down below, he positioned himself to dive below and behind the aircraft so he could zoom up underneath it to shoot at it. This way, he avoided the rear gunner who was always looking for attacks from the rear but could not fire below his own aircraft.

The gunner often saw him and warned the pilot, who would steer his plane sharply left or right to give the gunner a better shot. McCudden compensated for it by staying below the target's belly. He always closed to 50 yards or less before firing if he could and then aimed first for the gunner and second for the wing spars where they joined the fuselage. Like Albert Ball, McCudden liked to pull his Lewis gun down on the Foster mounting to fire upwards.

With the stresses put on the airframe during wild, evasive maneuvers, it didn't take much damage for the main spars to give way. Once that happened, it triggered a domino effect of structural failure and the wing collapsed. The wings fell off and down she went. He repeated several times that the steadiness of the SE5 helped him aim more precisely. This was an impressive man who studied his hunter craft well.

The other thing he taught them about was the cooperation between two observation aircraft and how it complicated things. The German two-seaters often flew in pairs for mutual protection. If one was attacked, the second aircraft maneuvered to get gunfire on the attacker. McCudden concentrated on one aircraft at a time and tried to keep his target between him and the other airplane. Doing so discouraged the second gunner from firing for fear of hitting his companion.

McCudden also shared that both the Vickers and Lewis guns jammed frequently. His first recourse was to switch to the gun that wasn't jammed and if that didn't work, to break off the attack, get clear of enemy fire, and then try to fix it. He stressed it was better to break off an attack than to press it home and get shot down.

In other briefings, Jimmy learned that nowadays four- or five-plane fights sometimes turned into multi-level melees of fifty or more aircraft whirling around in chaos. An attack on observation aircraft might start the fight but then other flights or squadrons often joined in. The upper-level escort might get tied up with a second flight and then others joined in above them as combatants dove, spun, zoomed and climbed in their attempts to gain the upper hand. There were many more aircraft in the skies over the trenches than when he flew with 40 Squadron. Fortunately, the British now had the edge in numbers. Everything was new again.

Ellie wrote him a letter with more good news, which he received in January.

December 15, 1917

My dearest Jimmy,

Low and behold, I have more good news to share with you my darling. I am once again pregnant! It would seem our little honeymoon at Lake Pepin has borne fruit!

The baby is due in early July, according to Doctor Fjellman. We seem to be prolific, you and I! I believe I shall have to curb your enthusiasm when you return (just kidding my darling). Wouldn't it be nice to have a little girl next? I would love to dress her up in all the finest baby clothes and raise a little sweetheart.

Little James, Jr. has grown like a weed since we saw you last. He is six and one-half months old now. He rolls over on his own, sucks his thumb, and squirms around like crazy when we put him down on the floor on his little blanket.

Your mother and Meg continue to be godsends in caring for little JJ. He can be a handful when he wants to be. He likes to get his own way, of course. He continues to be your spitting image. His hair is longer now but remains white blond, just like yours was when we were young.

We are all grateful we got to see you here during your convalescence, my darling. Of course, I wish it could have been permanent for you to stay here with us, but it was simply not to be. I hope and pray you are getting on well with your new outfit. Do write us all when you get a chance.

Please come back home safe and sound,
Your devoted Ellie, James, Jr., and ?

Jimmy thought to himself, "Another child, oh my!" It was such a blessing and a joy. He wondered if this one would be a girl. It would be nice to have one of each. He immediately wrote back to her and filled her in on his life at 56 Squadron as best he could, knowing the censors would be reviewing it.

The training 56 Squadron had was put to the test on the 19th of January. C Flight was sent on an offensive patrol between Cambrai and Douai, a hotbed of German airfields and patrols well behind the German lines. They were to fly high looking for enemy aircraft that might seek to disrupt the Sopwith Camels from 24 Squadron or others who were attacking observation and bomber aircraft on their way to or from the German aerodromes further behind the lines.

Jimmy was assigned number five in the five-plane flight. Captain Stevens led the flight with Blondie Steenkamp leading one pair and Bucky Buckley leading the other. Sandy Murthy flew with Blondie and Jimmy flew with Bucky. Before they mounted up, Captain Stevens pulled him briefly to one side. "Gracie, I know you have more experience than your flight mates, but I have you flying number five because you're new to the squadron and you've been off action for a few months. I have every confidence you'll move up quickly once you're back in the swing of things. Don't let it throw you off your game, okay?"

"No problem, captain. I understand and I appreciate your kind words," Jimmy replied.

Brooks and Moss helped Jimmy strap in and get started, "Switches off, petrol on," Brooks called.

"Switches off, petrol on," Jimmy complied and replied.

"Air closed. Suck in."

"Air closed. Suck in." Jim closed the radiator flaps.

Brooks slowly turned the engine propeller two full revolutions. Then, he called out, "Contact!"

"Contact!" Jimmy replied.

Brooks cranked the propeller hard and she started up in a cloud of smoke from the exhaust pipes.

Jimmy let her warm up, waited for the captain's signal, and yelled out, "Chocks away!"

His bird rolled out smartly to taxi to the take-off point. They all took off together as was the practice at 56 Squadron, turned east and began a straight climb to fifteen thousand feet on their way to the front.

Once over the front, they continued to their assigned patrol height of seventeen thousand. The air was mighty thin up there. Jimmy was not as used to it as his compatriots were. It had its definite effects on the pilots. They had to build a tolerance for it. Jimmy used to get bad headaches at first, but they subsided after repeated flights to high altitudes. In addition, the pilots were advised to loiter around 10,000 feet before further descent in order to avoid leg cramps. Jimmy hunkered down in his cockpit to keep his fur lined facemask and goggles behind the little windscreen, grateful for the heat from the big Viper engine.

It was new to him strategically to fly higher than the enemy. At 40 Squadron, they were always at a height disadvantage against the better German airplanes. Now, the British had the performance advantage. It was a good feeling.

They all kept their eyes peeled and heads rotating all around as they watched for other patrols or Archie bursts indicating air activity. As number five, Jimmy was especially focused on the airspace above and behind them, knowing they could get bounced themselves at any time. At the same time, he had to watch Bucky out of the corner of his eye. Even though they flew a loose vic of five, Jimmy needed to form on Bucky.

The planes of C Flight flew through and around several large cumulus cloud formations as they patrolled their territory. The cold grew intense. Jimmy found himself wanting some action, just to warm up. He should have thought twice before asking, because Stevens waggled his wings moments afterwards. Stevens then rolled onto his left side and dove away quickly.

The rest of them followed suit quickly in turn. Levelling out in the dive, Jimmy looked ahead to see what they were going after. He saw German Archie bursts far below and assumed that was their target. As they got closer, he saw a flight of six DH4s headed west back towards the British lines. What Jimmy didn't see, but fortunately what Stevens saw, was the flight of ten Huns diving on them.

Stevens dove hard and fast, trying to get to the Germans before they got to their bombers. This was where things got crazy. As they were diving, they saw a flight of five Camels heading towards the Germans as well and another flight of five Huns diving on the Camels. Stevens wagged and gave Bucky a hand signal to go after this second Hun flight.

Bucky and Jimmy veered off from their flight and made for the Camels' attackers. They soon saw the Hun flight they were about to engage was a mix of aircraft types. Two of the new triplanes were accompanied by three Pfalz DIIIs. Jimmy was relieved to see Bucky start a shallow, high-speed climb in response to this, obviously remembering their training to gain altitude advantage.

The Huns saw them coming. The two Fokkers turned sharply and began climbing toward them. The Pfalzes followed behind, less agile on the turn and the climb. Bucky maintained their climb as they approached right up until the point of contact, then dove for the triplanes in a head-on pass. He picked the green Fokker on his left and Jimmy picked the other one, painted mostly blue. Jimmy's adrenalin kicked in. He could feel it in his gut as his stomach tightened. His heart raced. His focus honed in on his target.

The Hun and Jimmy fired on each other as they closed. Jimmy pressed both buttons in the middle of his yolk to fire both the Vickers and the Lewis guns. Kicking in a little rudder and a slip to keep his fire aimed as precisely as he could, Jimmy tried desperately to ignore the reflex to duck down in his cockpit and hide.

He felt no hits as they passed and pressed on in his dive hoping for a shot at a Pfalz. Bucky did the same. They closed on the slower German planes head-on as well. In a pass like this, their planes and the Huns were equally deadly. Once again, he fired both guns and aimed as best he could. He thought he may have gotten a hit, but could not be sure.

After the second head-on pass, Jimmy watched for Bucky's lead. Bucky zoomed sharply to gain altitude. Jimmy pulled back on his stick and followed. His SE5a climbed beautifully! Jimmy could see behind him, however, that the Fokkers climbed, too. Bucky's airspeed bled off in the climb and he rolled left into a tight left turn to bring them around for a second pass.

The Fokkers climbed as well and were even with them as they came at each other. Another head-on pass brought similar results. Jimmy was amazed to observe, as he passed his opponent, the German was turning onto his tail in a sort of flat turn even as they passed. The Hun must be using rudder alone to do this. He got his guns on Jimmy before he could get fully by and Jimmy felt some hits on his airframe behind him.

Bucky dove straight out after this pass. They gained speed quickly. The three Pfalzes were still climbing but away from the Fokkers and the British. Bucky continued to dive away until they were out of range and climbed.

Bucky made a decision in the dive to go after the Pfalz aircraft instead of the Fokkers. Good idea, Jimmy thought. The Essies could outrun the tripes if they had to. Bucky dove on the formation of three Pfalzes from behind them. He went for the back right aircraft, a white bird with a blue nose and a big, blue diagonal stripe around the fuselage and on the top wings.

The Germans saw them coming and broke, two to the left and the blue one to right. Bucky followed his prey easily. He throttled back to avoid overshooting his target as the Hun rolled right as sharply as he could. Bucky lined up for the shot and hit the fuselage behind the pilot on the first try.

Jimmy hung back and above Bucky on the outside of his turn, looking for trouble from the Fokkers. They were on their way, but Bucky still had some time. Bucky fell in behind the jinking Pfalz. They wove, scissors-like, across the sky, losing altitude as they went. Bucky fired short bursts each time the Pfalz reversed and found his target on the third try. The pilot slumped, the engine smoked black oil, and the plane fell off into a spin.

Bucky and Jimmy pulled up and turned left to see where everyone else went. As they looked, they watched the Pfalz catch fire in its spin, a confirmed kill for Bucky. The Fokkers had caught up with them, however, and were angling to get behind them. Bucky and Jim rolled out level and dove away, knowing the triplanes couldn't keep up even though they tried.

Once again, the Essies outdistanced the Fokkers and climbed back above them. The Germans climbed to match the height of the British planes but were out of range. Bucky's strategy was working. He went for the Pfalzes again. This time, he picked out a green and yellow bird. Jimmy followed Bucky and strained to see what was behind them.

Bucky got up close behind and below the Pfalz. The Hun rolled away in a split-S. Bucky and Jimmy followed. The Hun turned to the left in a tight, climbing turn. It was a bad move that put him squarely in Bucky's field of fire. Bucky and Jimmy were both concentrating on the kill when out of nowhere, the blue Fokker triplane dove straight down through them from above, guns blaring. The German hit Bucky's plane in the rear fuselage. Bucky broke off his attack on the Pfalz, not knowing where the machine gun fire came from.

Jimmy kicked himself. He had failed Bucky. He should have seen the German coming. The tripe pulled up sharply in a crazy, tight turn. Jimmy craned his neck looking for the other Fokker. Sure enough, the other triplane had Bucky targeted and was turning inside him to get close enough for a shot.

Jimmy couldn't let that happen, even though he knew the first Fokker was already coming around to get on his own tail. Jimmy jammed the throttle forward as far as he could and dove after Bucky's pursuer. Thank God for the Essie's speed. Jimmy cut across the arc of their fight and went for the green triplane in a high-angle, deflection shot from the front, about as low a probability shot as you could try.

Bucky turned to the left as tightly as he could. He came around and was pointed in Jimmy's direction a hundred feet below him. The Fokker was hot on Bucky's tail. Jimmy hit the Vickers' button and spewed a stream of bullets in front of the Hun. The German flew right into them and Jimmy saw hits on the Fokker's cowling, top wing, and fuselage. What incredible luck, he thought. The Fokker fell off the turn and skidded out to the right. He levelled off and went limp. Jimmy must have hit the pilot.

Jimmy couldn't follow through or even watch his prey because the German's partner, the blue Fokker, was on Jimmy's tail. Jimmy instinctively pulled up in a tight left turn but quickly realized this was the wrong thing to do. The triplane followed him easily and was tightening his turn on him. "Never turn with a triplane!" Jimmy yelled at himself out loud.

Jimmy rolled over to the left and pulled straight back to dive out of there as fast he could. The German followed his moves easily and Jimmy thought he was a dead man. Bullets ripped through his right wing. He just kept diving straight down for another two thousand feet and found himself clear of the German's guns. He had not been able to keep up with Jimmy.

Jimmy and the Fokker were both well below Bucky and the two remaining Pfalzes after the fast dive. Jimmy didn't know what happened to the first Fokker he had hit. He sped out of the Fokker's range and zoomed back up to join Bucky. By the time he reached Bucky, the two remaining Pfalzes were running away in a steep dive to the east. The triplane was joining them. They let them go because they wanted to see what happened to the rest of their flight. As so often happened in dogfights, the two of them found themselves alone in the sky. The dogfights of their mates had taken them in different directions and altitudes.

They knew a flight of Camels had joined Stevens and the other two SE5s to take on ten Albatros and Pfalz scouts. Where they went was anybody's guess. Jimmy looked all around and saw nothing. The DH4s had been heading west and would have continued to do so if they were being attacked, so the two of them headed off in that direction at about 10,000 feet.

They looked up, down, left, right, and behind and saw nothing for about five minutes. Then, three dots appeared above them to the west. They thought they might be C Flight, so they put their planes in a shallow, high-speed climb hoping to catch them. They didn't catch them until the three planes began their descent into their aerodrome. It was indeed Captain Stevens, Blondie, and Sandy. They had all made it.

After they all got down they debriefed each other. The Camels had been a great addition to the scrap with the Huns and had dispatched three of them. Stevens and Blondie each got one as well before they broke off the attack. One of the bombers had been damaged but looked like it would be able to make its way back home.

Jimmy apologized to Bucky for not seeing the Fokker that dove between them, but Bucky would have none of it. "On the contrary, Gracie. You saved my life with your brilliant intercept of the Fokker on my tail. I would have gone west for sure if it hadn't been for you!"

"Whatever happened to it?" Jimmy asked. "Did you see it go down?"

"No, unfortunately I didn't," Bucky replied. "I think the pilot was dead or wounded but I just couldn't keep track of it. Sorry, mate."

"Ah well, a probable then," Stevens said. "However, Gracie, it looks like you'll need to have Brooks paint another of those little roundels on your plane. Congratulations on the save!"

"That's what I'm here for!" Jimmy replied. It did feel good to know he had made a difference. Bucky was still around and that's what really mattered to Jimmy.

"What say we head over to the mess, chaps?" Blondie piped in. "First round's on me!" He got no argument from the rest of them and off they went.

30

LONDON, FEBRUARY, 1918. During the final week of his leave, Hank Jacobs had pretty good use of his leg back. He still used the cane but could hobble around without too much pain, so he decided to stretch his horizons a little bit.

He caught a train out of Waterloo Station to the town of Battle, the site of the famous Battle of Hastings where William the Conqueror defeated King Harold Godwinson to become the king of England in 1066. It had been a highlight in their history lessons and had captured his imagination at the time, so he wanted to take advantage of the opportunity to see the actual site of the battle. A brochure in the hotel lobby said tours were given each day.

The train ride was delightful. Hank enjoyed gazing out on the pastoral English countryside as the train trundled through Sussex. Dormant fields, rolling over gentle hills and dales were dotted with occasional oast houses. Villages spouted up around square, Norman church towers. He had sprung for a first class ticket, so he enjoyed the peaceful solitude his cabin provided. He also enjoyed the tea service offered by the attractive young maiden pushing her tea cart back and forth up the aisle. He found himself wondering why they couldn't make travel so enjoyable in the States.

Arriving in a few hours, he walked into the town square. Town triangle was a more appropriate term as the roads forked around the plaza from the north. The south side of the plaza was a massive gate house that marked the entrance to the battleground. He paid his tuppence and entered, eager with anticipation.

The gatehouse was impressive to Hank, a country boy from the States. It had been built several hundred years ago and was replete with offices, gift shops, toilets, and a gathering place for the walking tours which started each hour on the hour. He strolled around the place waiting for the next tour to start.

Just before the hour, they were all summoned to gather by a charming young English lass of perhaps 20 years old. Her name was Phoebe and she stood all of five feet tall. Dressed primly in a tartan skirt and navy sweater, her strawberry blonde curls set off her outfit with perfect balance. She spoke with a refined British accent dripping culture, but without the condescension he so often observed in British people who presumed authority.

Phoebe was a scholar of the Battle of Hastings. As they walked around the battleground in a counter-clockwise circle, she stopped to educate them about the battle as a whole and the significance of the particular spot on which they were standing. While her narrative may have been scripted, she delivered it with such élan and delightful humor that she brought the battlefield to life.

Hank could envision the Saxon shield wall at the top of the hill and vividly imagine the Norman knights and troops as they marched up the hill and charged the wall repeatedly. He could see in his mind's eye the feigned Norman retreat on the Saxon right flank that drew them out from the wall in pursuit and spelled their doom.

Walking all the way around the south side of the battlefield, Hank could see the perspective of the Norman army as it viewed the hill before them. To wrap up the tour, they stood around the spot where King Harold was reputed to have taken an arrow in the eye, turning the battle into a rout. Hank was also struck by the destruction of Battle Abbey from the Dissolution under orders from King Henry VIII. How crass it seemed to Hank for a king to destroy such beautiful buildings for the sake of money to pay for his court excesses.

He returned to London by train, his mind filled with images of Norman knights and Saxon shield walls. It had been a good day.

Hank got back to the Regent Palace around six o'clock in the evening and headed up to his room. After freshening up and a change of clothes, he decided to head downstairs to enjoy a cocktail and review the daily news before dinner.

The Regent had a lovely bar frequented by soldiers who were home on leave and others who were billeted in the hotel. Things could get quite lively there in the evenings, depending on who was in town. Hank preferred to take a chair in a quiet corner of the library to enjoy his time more peacefully.

Fortunately, his favorite chair was available so he settled in for a while. The gentleman server brought his Whiskey Mac while Hank selected the first paper to peruse, *The New York Times*. He found only a few articles of interest in the Times, so he picked up a copy of the *London Gazette* to see what news there might be of the war.

Hank read through the casualty lists with somber reflection. Even in these quiet months of winter, the list was far too long. Following that, he reviewed the postings section. Lo and behold, he saw his buddy, James Arneson, listed as being posted to 56 Squadron!

Hank knew Jimmy had been badly wounded and sent home to convalesce from Meg's letter. She had shared with him that he was home for a few months to recover from several wounds, including one to his back. It sounded like there was a possibility Jimmy might never recover full mobility again. Hank was saddened to hear it and worried for his friend. However, he knew he would be well cared for by Ellie and his parents.

Now, to see him posted to 56 Squadron was a major surprise. He was elated on two counts. First, he was happy to learn his friend had recovered enough to return to duty. Second, Hank was excited to think he might put in for a transfer to join him at the squadron. Coming off his own recuperation would be the perfect time to make a change. Hank no longer cared for the pilot he supported at 60 Squadron, so he figured, "Why not?" He decided to go into the Movement Section of the Air Ministry early the next day to submit his transfer request. What a grand day it had turned out to be.

As soon as the government office opened the next morning, Hank was standing in front of the first sergeant. He seemed a good chap but was a bit peeved Hank should be there before he had his first cup of tea brewed. Hank apologized for the inconvenience. The sergeant softened. Hank pressed his case, requesting a transfer to 56 Squadron from 60 Squadron.

Hank told the sergeant of his American lineage and his friend who had just been transferred there. The first sergeant was an old lifer who understood the closeness of military friendships, having served in His Majesty's service for thirty years.

The sergeant provided Hank with a stack of paperwork he needed to complete, a pencil, and a desk to sit at while he filled out all of the required forms. He said he would forward them to the Air Ministry that same day. The sergeant offered no guarantees but mentioned the RFC had come around to view transfer requests seriously if the applicant had provided valorous service in France, which Hank had. The sergeant also extended Hank's leave to stay in London until he found out.

After an anxious week of waiting, Hank received approval of his transfer with orders to report to No. 56 Squadron as soon as his health allowed. He was ecstatic and hurried back to the hotel to pack his things. Hank booked passage for France first thing the next day. At long last, he was to be reunited with his best friend, Jimmy Arneson. Hoorah!

31

BAIZIEUX, FEBRUARY, 1918. Jimmy realized in February that he had arrived in France one year prior. He thought to himself, "Had it been only a year?" It felt a lifetime ago. So much had changed. The number of airplanes in the air, the new types of airplanes, better engine performance, and armament improvements were all new. Jimmy was different, too. He was no longer a naïve farm boy from Minnesota. He had been wounded twice, lost friends, killed enemies, married, and become a father. At times it was more than he could fathom.

Like a year earlier, the weather in February was miserable. Snow showers more often came down as sleet that threatened to become snow. More often, the sleet turned to freezing rain. The frozen ground turned to slimy mud, and the smell of soaked wool from all the uniforms sickened him.

At the end of January, the squadron had flown their mounts two miles to the west to Baizieux. It provided a firmer landing field and had better facilities. As was often the case, the squadron was provided a chateau by a grateful Frenchman for use as their officers' mess and quarters for the senior officers. The rest of the pilots populated the Nissen hut village their ground support put together.

February brought a marked increase in air activity from the Germans, flooding the skies with observation planes. The British suspected a German push was imminent. At 56 Squadron, they stepped up their schedules with confidence from their January training. They flew offensive patrols twice per day, looking for the German two-seaters and shooting them down at every opportunity.

Invariably, the observation planes were escorted by colorful Albatros DVs, Pfalz DIIIs, or Fokker triplanes. To counter this, the British split their flights into two halves. Two or three planes in a flight attacked the enemy two seaters while the remainder of the flight lingered above to counter attacks from enemy scouts. Sometimes, two flights flew together with one flight providing high cover and the other flight attacking the enemy.

Jimmy grew quite comfortable with the SE5a. He could turn much more tightly and engage all but the triplanes in turning battles as well as the dive, slash, and zoom tactics they generally employed. He had even chalked up another save of a pilot from A Flight two days ago, raising his count of saves to nine. Blondie was the big score builder, however. He got two kills in one dogfight.

Change seemed to be the constant at 56 Squadron. In addition to the changes in tactics, they also saw changes in squadron leadership. Captain McCudden, the flight commander of A Flight, and the flight commander of B Flight, moved on to other squadrons with the intent that these fine gentlemen would promulgate the successes of 56 Squadron to other squadrons on the front.

These moves necessitated other changes in the flight assignments to backfill their losses. Blondie took over A Flight and Bucky took over B Flight. That left only Sandy and Jimmy in C Flight with Captain Stevens. C Flight got two new recruits in their place, Lieutenants Watts and Lees. Neither of these lads had more than 25 hours of instruction before joining them. Watts was to fly with Sandy and Lees was to fly with Jimmy.

For the next two weeks, they worked hard to regain their proficiency as a flight. Two patrols a day gave them ample opportunity. They were consistently assigned high escort duty.

Jimmy thought this was intentional so the more experienced pilots could focus on the two-seaters, which remained aggressive.

Between patrols, Jimmy worked with Watts and Lees on maneuvers and tactics. They were bright but naive. They weren't able yet to fly without thinking about it, so they got overloaded easily. Repetition of loops, wingovers, Immelmanns, rolls, spins, and split-S maneuvers was required. Jimmy kept them in the air a lot during those first few weeks.

Watts often got separated from Sandy during a fight. He had trouble keeping up with Sandy's maneuvers. Jimmy showed him how to anticipate his lead's moves. He also taught them basic survival skills such as never flying straight and level for long, and swiveling their heads all the time to see what was happening around them.

Lees also had trouble staying with Jimmy. Jimmy tried to keep his moves simplified as best he could but there just wasn't much he could do. In combat, one moved quickly or died. Twice during these weeks Jimmy had to go find Lees after he had chased a German. Lees had failed to stick with Jimmy and got in trouble with a Hun on his tail.

On another occasion, Watts lost Sandy in a fight and had an Albatros on his tail. Jimmy was able to get there in time to fire across the Hun's nose and scare him off. He counted it as another save, bringing his count to eleven given the save he had gotten for a pilot in B Flight the day before. Jimmy chose to not count the times he cleared Lees' tail. As his lead, Jimmy felt he should have done better to keep him out of trouble in the first place.

Captain Stevens was increasingly tied up assisting Major Baldwin, the squadron commander, as the month progressed. Major Baldwin was called up to Wing HQ often so Stevens had to backfill him with squadron duties. C Flight often flew as a flight of four when Captain Stevens was so detained.

Jimmy was shocked on the 20th of February when Captain Stevens called him into the squadron office. "Sit down, Gracie, please," he said. "As you know I have been called into squadron duties a lot lately. It seems Major Baldwin is having to educate our superiors in how to run flight operations. That's a good thing. Baldwin is a smart, smart man. He made 56 Squadron one of the best."

"Yes, sir," Jimmy replied.

"I called you in here because I want to commend you, Gracie," Stevens said. "I've noticed how much time you've been spending with Watts and Lees, helping them learn how to survive and fight. I want to thank you. No one asked you to. You've done it of your own accord. It's commendable."

"Why, thank you, sir," Jimmy replied. "I'm only trying to help all of us get through this bloody war."

"I want you to be my deputy flight commander, Jim," Stevens said. "I can't fly with the flight as much as I should or would like to. I need someone who can run the flight while I am out backing up the major. Would you do that for me?"

"Oh my," Jimmy replied. "I am honored, Captain Stevens. What about Sandy, though? He has more seniority than I do. Shouldn't he be the one?"

"True, he does have more seniority," the captain replied. "However, I think you're the one who has demonstrated the kind of battle leadership needed to keep this squadron the top squadron in the RFC. Will you do it, Gracie?"

"Yes," he replied. "I'll give it my level best, sir!"

"Thank you, Jim," Captain Stevens said as he rose, indicating the conversation was over. "I'll notify the others straight away."

"Thank you, sir!" Jimmy stood, saluted, spun around, and walked out. "Wow!" he said to himself as he exited.

For the next couple of weeks, Captain Stevens led the flight about half of the time. Jimmy was the flight leader when Stevens was tied up in squadron affairs. A new kid, Freddie Jenkins, backfilled the captain when he wasn't around. Jimmy led the vic, Sandy flew number two with Lees in tow, and Watts flew number three with Jenkins. Their work continued to focus on shooting down observation planes and bombers, which seemed to be coming over with increasing frequency.

C Flight often flew the high patrol while B or A Flights concentrated on the two-seaters. Jimmy preferred it this way. They were becoming more proficient at fighting the enemy scouts. Watts and Lees were getting better every day. They all looked out for Jenkins as the newest member of the flight.

Survival in the air was the first imperative. If a new pilot survived the first two weeks, he had a much better chance of living through the war. Learning how to avoid getting shot down was an art in itself. A new pilot had to learn to anticipate the enemy's attack pattern and react to it in the best way to neutralize it. He had to learn to throw his aircraft around with abandon, and he had to burn the moves into his muscle memory to make flying instinctual.

The British began to fly in greater numbers than the Germans. The RFC had doubled in size since Jimmy joined in 1916. They had better mounts now, too. They were faster and this meant everything. Hotheads charged into the enemy whenever and wherever they saw them. They did not last long. Calmer minds maneuvered for an advantageous position before engaging and then only did so with tactics that provided for an escape if necessary. These were things Jimmy tried to teach the younger pilots.

Thursday, March 7, 1918 dawned like most March days. The morning dew cleaned everything on the ground, but the primary focus of the pilots was always the sky. They had a thin overcast at fifteen thousand feet. The wind blew from the northwest at eight knots with gusts to fifteen, too much for the old Shorthorns, but no problem for their Essies. A thick, stratus cloud layer moved slowly over them at four thousand feet, also from the northwest. The air smelled like rain, but none fell so they flew.

Their mid-morning mission was to escort a flight of DH4 bombers sent to bomb a railroad depot west of Cambrai. It would take them several miles behind enemy lines. B Flight was to provide close escort and C Flight, as usual, would fly high escort at ten thousand feet. Captain Stevens was busy so Jimmy flew as flight leader.

They rendezvoused with the bombers just west of their lines as planned and assumed their escort positions. Archie was lighter than usual and concentrated on the bombers, not C Flight.

They were almost on the target when Jimmy spotted a flight of six aircraft approaching them from the southeast. They looked to be a mix of triplanes and biplanes as was common lately. He turned the flight to the south-southeast in a shallow climb to get some height on them. They surprised him by not diving on the lower formation but instead rising to meet C Flight.

Jimmy tried to maneuver around them but they turned into him each time he banked right. This was very aggressive behavior for the Huns. Jimmy's blood rose and his pulse quickened. The two flights closed at roughly the same altitude. It was going to be a head-on pass.

Jimmy picked the center plane of their formation, a blue and white triplane, as his target. His flight members picked theirs as well. They closed quickly, his heart racing. They all fired on each other in the pass. Jimmy could see his guns closing on his target as they approached. He knew he would strike some hits. At least he thought so until the German skidded to his right and prepared to fire at him in a flat skidding turn. Jimmy climbed to avoid his fire as they passed. Zooming after the pass, Jimmy could see the German behind him. The German climbed as well but had lost airspeed in his flat turn that put him far behind.

Sandy and Lees were climbing to the left as were Watts and Jenkins. They lost sight of the bombers and lower escorts in their melee with the six Huns. Jimmy had to assume the others pressed on while C Flight dealt with these fellows.

Still climbing to the left, Jimmy could see two Fokkers turning inside of Watts and Jenkins. Why were they turning with the Fokkers? They should have dived away. It would not be long before the triplanes got a bead on them, so Jimmy did a wingover to head in their direction. Jimmy's opponent, the blue and white triplane, fired as Jimmy passed over him but missed him. Jimmy knew the tripe would be following him but he counted on his speed to pull away from him.

Jimmy dove, lined up on the lead Fokker attacking Watts and Jenkins and fired. He missed the German, but the triplane broke off the attack. As Jimmy climbed back up, the blue and white Fokker fired on him again. This time, the German connected and Jimmy felt a few bullets hit his fuselage behind him. Jimmy looked around as he continued to climb in a tight spiral and was horrified to see six more triplanes diving on them from the west. C Flight's retreat was effectively cut off by this new flight of Germans and they were now outnumbered twelve to five. The new flight of Huns would arrive soon.

Trying to keep the big picture in his head, Jimmy pulled around tightly and craned his neck to find his flight members. Sandy and Lees were flying together and had just climbed away from a pass they took at two Albatros DVs. Watts and Jenkins were turning with two Fokkers again and losing. Jimmy's opposing blue and white Fokker was trying to catch up to him. Jimmy flew to Jenkins, the new kid. He had fallen away from Watts, was taking hits, and jinking when Jimmy reached him.

Jimmy fired at long range hoping to dissuade Jenkins' pursuer, a black triplane with checkered wings. It didn't work. The Fokker pressed his attack on Jenkins. He lined up behind Jenkins and fired at him. The Hun continued to press his attack even as he looked back and saw Jimmy. The three of them were weaving and bobbing in a line, Jenkins trying to avoid getting hit and the other two behind him trying to get hits on the plane in front of them.

After a few seconds of this, Jimmy hit the Fokker hard. He started smoking and spun out of control. Jenkins flew on, looking to rejoin Watts. Jimmy looked over his shoulder and saw the blue and white Fokker on his tail, closing inside his left turn. Jimmy rolled over and dove away from him to get out of his range.

The other flight of six Fokkers hit C Flight then. They split up as they chose their targets. Jimmy saw Lees go down on their first pass. Lees nosed up and keeled over, stalling into a tight spin and trailing heavy black smoke.

Two Fokkers went after Sandy and two others went after Watts and Jenkins. Watts and Jenkins were diving away with four Fokkers in pursuit now. Sandy had dispatched one of the DVs but was turning with the remaining Albatros when two triplanes attacked him from the right.

Jimmy started to go for Sandy's pursuers when he found himself cut off by the blue and white Fokker plus the two that had shot down Lees. Jimmy now had three triplanes on his tail! He couldn't get to Sandy because he had to turn away from his own pursuers in tight, defensive turns. The Germans surrounded him and came at him each in turn. Each time a German attacked, Jimmy turned into his attacker trying to get a shot in. Sometimes, he succeeded in this and sometimes not. He was taking hits all over.

Jimmy snap-rolled into a spin to get some distance. It worked but wouldn't last long and he lost altitude in the bargain. Jimmy made his way for Sandy, who was also battling three aircraft now. Ramming his throttle forward, Jimmy came up from beneath the four of them and fired at the lead Fokker. He got some hits on the German with a deflection shot and the Fokker started smoking. The German fell off his turn and started diving east, out of the fight and running for home.

Jimmy continued his vertical climb into a half-loop, coming over the top inverted, when he saw Watts and Jenkins battling three triplanes. He yelled at them in futility, "Stop turning and dive!" Jimmy rolled upright and dove in their direction. They were still turning with the triplanes, a sure formula for defeat. Sure enough, a green Fokker scored hits on Jenkins and he blew up. His gas tank must have exploded. Young Jenkins was gone. The explosion threw his attacker off for a moment, but the other triplanes were pressing their attack on Watts at the same time.

Jimmy fired from a few hundred yards away to no avail as he closed on Watts and his attackers. They were turning tightly to the left when he got there. Jimmy shot at the belly of a Fokker and saw it fall off its turn. He must have struck the pilot but he had no time to see what happened.

The blue and white Fokker had been stalking Jimmy and dove on him from above. He hit Jimmy's right wings out near the struts. His top aileron took hits and became sluggish. Jimmy could turn but not as quickly. The situation turned from bleak to desperate as C Flight's opponents pressed their attacks from virtually every point on the compass.

Jimmy tried to take it all in. He saw Sandy in the middle of a Fokker fur ball. Four of them were taking turns on him as they had done with Jimmy earlier. He flew to Sandy as fast as he could. Sandy climbed, dove, rolled, spun, and jinked to no avail. "No!" Jimmy shrieked out loud as he saw Sandy get hit and catch fire, diving away out of control and in flames.

Lees was gone, Jenkins was gone, and now Sandy was gone. It was down to Watts and Jimmy. Jimmy looked around to find Watts. He was diving away to the south with three Fokkers in pursuit. Jimmy dove for him only to be hit out of the blue with a hail of bullets from two Fokkers diving on him from above. Jimmy hadn't seen them coming. His left elevator was hit badly as well as his rudder. It became difficult to turn.

Jimmy continued to dive for Watts. Watts was diving fast and turning tightly to the west when his right wing fell off. He fell out of the sky. Jimmy could not believe his eyes. He was the only one left now. The three Fokkers chasing Watts turned towards Jimmy in what would be a three-on-one, head-on pass. Jimmy hunkered down behind his windscreen, peered through his Aldis sight, focused on the center triplane, and pressed both gun buttons. He got hits on the German's engine and saw him catch fire.

However, Jimmy took hits from the other two Fokkers and saw his right wing struts hit badly. Jimmy feared he would not be able to turn without breaking a wing, so he made a high-speed, shallow turn to the west and dove for home. His speed built quickly and saved him as the Huns trailed farther and farther behind.

C Flight had been wiped out. Jimmy had not saved anyone. They had all died right before his eyes. He had failed. How arrogant he had become, painting his plane with "Saving Grace," Here he was running away for home after having lost his entire flight. What kind of savior does that? He just wanted to die and was tempted to dive into the ground.

His engine smoked on the way home. He must have taken some bullets in his engine. The oil was draining out slowly. Soon, Jimmy's engine would freeze and he would sink to the ground behind the German lines. "A fit end to a wasted life," he thought.

Somehow, Jimmy made it back to the base. He limped in for a landing and his right wing fell off as he touched down. His plane spun in a ground loop and came to a stop in a heap. Jimmy jumped out and fell on his face as he ran away from it. His plane promptly caught fire and burned to a crisp. Jimmy wished he had stayed in it.

That night at dinner, Jimmy placed four sets of boots on the chairs for Sandy, Watts, Lees, and Jenkins. Jimmy sat among them, inconsolable. It had been a disaster. Jimmy berated himself, thinking he should have seen it coming. He should have steered clear of the fight as soon as he saw the other flight of Fokkers. Why didn't he get them all out of there and run for home?

Captain Stevens sat next to him. "I read your intelligence report, Jim. You did all you could. You got four kills, a third of their strength."

"Unconfirmed kills," Jimmy muttered.

"Yes, but you know you took out four Huns who were gunning for your guys. You were outnumbered over two to one. You did nothing wrong, Jim."

"Yes, I did. I let them all down and they died," Jimmy replied. "That's what I did."

"Listen to me, Jim," the captain said. "Any one of us would have had the same struggles. We probably would have fared worse than you. You did the best you could and you should not punish yourself for it. War means dying. We are all going to die sooner or later."

Major Baldwin called the squadron to order and raised a glass in honor of the fallen that night. He said some good words about giving one's all for King and Country, the fortunes of war and how sometimes the winds blow against them. Jimmy didn't get it all. He wasn't listening. He was drowning himself in whiskey.

Apparently, someone led him or carried him back to his bunk. He didn't know. Jimmy woke up the next day with his mouth tasting like the floor of a horse's stall. He was alone in his Nissen hut, his roommates were all gone.

He cleaned out their lockers of their belongings, removed any objectionable bits and packed them up for shipment home to their families. When he got to Jenkins' belongings, there wasn't much to pack. He had only been with the squadron a short time and had not accumulated any of the little mementos most pilots acquired. Jimmy hardly knew him, this latest lamb for the slaughter. These new pilots came in and went down before anyone even found out where they were from.

Jimmy's whiskey bottle was empty. He got another and drained it, too. He thought to himself. "Why do we fight? For glory and honor? Do we think people will praise us and remember us through the ages like Odysseus or Achilles? We fool ourselves. We are just grist for the mill, instruments in a war designed to make rich weapons manufacturers richer."

Jimmy was dead already. The bullet had not yet found him, but it was loaded in a belt of ammunition waiting for its turn. Jimmy knew he would die here in France. He would never again see his mom, dad, Ellie, his son, his unborn child, Hank, or the Dogwood River. Every day brought him closer to an eternity burning in Hell.

Several days passed. Jimmy flew, but not well, and drank himself into oblivion every night. Captain Stevens noticed and called him over as they walked to the hangars after a patrol. "Jim, I'm taking you off flying operations for a while."

"Why?" Jimmy asked.

"You've been off your game ever since your tough luck on the seventh. We all think you need a break."

"I don't need a break. I need to kill the Huns," Jimmy replied.

"Look, Arneson, I know it's been hell on you," Stevens said. "We all do. We can see it in your flying. You've just been going through the motions. It's like you're some sort of lifeless automaton. There's no spark left."

"I'm fine, Cap," he said. "I just need to work it out."

"This war is bloody hell, Jim," Stevens said. "You and I have both seen it time and again. It wears on a pilot. Hell, it wears on me, too. I'm the one who sent you up there, remember. I'm the one who should have been leading that flight."

"I said I'm fine. Just leave me be!"

"No, you're not fine," Stevens said. "The other pilots have even complained about it. They don't want to fly with you anymore. They say you're a liability to them, that you drag them down on the ground and in the air. You're drinking too much and your flying is erratic. You need to clean yourself up."

"But Cap—"

Captain Stevens leaned into him, his face only a few inches from his own. "I'm standing you down for a week to get straight, starting immediately. I mean it. You need to pull yourself together. Any longer and I'll not be able to keep it between us. Even the major is beginning to wonder about you. If you're not careful, you're going to get washed out."

Jimmy went back to his bunk and killed the bottle of whiskey beside his cot. When it was gone, he got another bottle and drank himself unconscious. "To hell with it," he said to himself. "Go on then, kill me. It's just a matter of time."

He realized it was now March 13. "Happy bloody birthday to me," he thought as he passed out on his cot.

For a week, he drank and slept, slept and drank. They moved to Val'heureux somewhere during that time to avoid the German Army that was marching its way to Paris again. The King came to visit. They told him to stay in his hut and not come out.

32

VAL'HEUREUX, MARCH, 1918. Hank could barely contain himself the whole way to France to join the 56th. He trained down from Waterloo to Folkestone and hopped the first ship headed to France. They docked at Boulogne-sur-Mer, the massive arrival point for all British soldiers he had come through his first time over. He took a bus to St. Omer, his old place of assignment in the motor pool. It felt odd to be there again. He was tempted to stop by the motor pool to see if any of his old work mates were still there, but chose not to because he had put that behind him and was more excited to get to the 56th Squadron airfield. He had no need to see McBride again!

Hank found the Movement Section easily and arranged a ride on a truck to 56 Squadron, now stationed at Val'heureux. One of the guys on the truck informed them all it meant "happy valley." To which, one of the old salts observed, "Happy valley my arse!"

The 60-mile ride took over half of the day because they had to drive slowly. They arrived around three o'clock in the afternoon and piled out of the truck. They headed to the squadron office, checked in, and got their quarters assigned.

When it was Hank's turn to report, he asked the first sergeant for the quarters of Lieutenant Arneson. "Arneson, is it?" the sergeant asked. "Let's see now. Yes, here he is, in hut number eight. You know him, do you?"

"Yes, sir, I most certainly do, sir. We grew up together!" Hank exclaimed.

"Well now, isn't that nice?" The sergeant raised an eyebrow and leaned forward to reply in a more hushed tone, "I wouldn't get my hopes up if I was you, Jacobs."

"Oh?" he asked.

"You'll see for yourself soon enough, lad. Get on with you then," the sergeant said dismissively.

How odd, Hank thought. What could be the matter? Had Jimmy been wounded again? Hank hobbled over to his own hut, number 23, rucksack slung over his shoulder, and claimed an available bunk. He hurriedly stowed his gear. Then, he made his way directly to hut number eight to see his old friend. Finding it in the midst of the officers' huts, he knocked on the door, "Jimmy!"

A groggy voice croaked, "Yes, come in. Who is it?"

Hank opened the door, stepped in, spread his arms wide, and yelled out, "Jimmy, it's me, Hank!"

"Who?" Jim said hoarsely, running his fingers through his disheveled hair and looking up at Hank through squinty eyes and a haze of cigarette smoke as he rolled out of his cot.

Hank could not believe his eyes. Was this really Jimmy? The Jimmy he knew was a handsome, fit, smart, bright-eyed, and happy-go-lucky young man. The man before him now was a sullen, chain-smoking skeleton of a man with sunken eyes, a two-day-old scraggly growth of beard, inflammatory breath, and a thousand-mile stare. "Jim, it's Hank, your old friend from back home. Don't you recognize me?" Hank pleaded.

Trying to pry himself up out of a stupor, Jim rubbed his eyes with the backs of his hands and lifted his eyes open momentarily with his forefingers. "Hank, my God, Hank. Is it really you? What are you doing here?" Jimmy's shirttails were half out, his boots were off, and his socks looked like they could stand on their own. He stunk like an outhouse.

"Jim, what's happened to you?" Hank blurted out. "You look like hell!"

"What do you mean? I'm fine!" Jimmy rose up to stand at full height at last, but was uneasy on his feet, his upper body waving back and forth over his hips. "Look here, what kind of way is that to treat your old friend?"

"I'm sorry, Jimmy. You know I think the world of you," Hank implored. "I just can see the war has been harder on you than I thought."

"Hard," Jimmy said. "Yeah, it's been hard. D'ya wanna drink?" he asked as he reached for a glass to pour his own, straight whiskey.

"No thank you, Jim," Hank replied. "I still have to report in to the maintenance hangar."

"Right, what are you doing here, again?" Jim asked through the whiskey as he raised his glass.

"I got a transfer, Jimmy. I'm assigned to 56 Squadron now!" he replied excitedly.

"No kidding?" Jimmy said. "Well, welcome aboard, pal. I guess I'll be seeing you around then."

"Do you have some hut-mates, Jim? It looks like there's a few other fellows who bunk here. Where are they?" Hank asked.

"Oh, on patrol, I suppose," Jimmy replied.

"Why aren't you with them?" Hank asked.

"Yeah, well, that's a whole other story," Jimmy mumbled as he took another swig. "Cap'n Stevens told me to stand down. I don't really know why. You'll have to ask him."

"Got it," Hank replied. "Okay, well listen, Jimmy, I need to go check in and find out what's up with work. I'll look you up again soon as I can, okay?"

"Yeah, sure, Hank," Jim muttered. "See you 'round." Jimmy fell back on his cot and rolled over, not even noticing he had spilled his drink in his lap.

Hank left, dumbfounded, for the maintenance hangar.

Sergeant Knowles headed the maintenance team for 56 Squadron. He was a good sort. He and Hank hit it off well. When Hank told him about his experience at the motor pool in St. Omer and his time as Captain Harrison's personal mechanic at 60 Squadron, Knowles lit up like a candle. He was elated to have a senior mechanic to help out, especially one with such well-rounded experience. Hank shared with Knowles his hope he could work on Jimmy's plane for him. Knowles said he would consider it, if Jim ever returned to duty. Apparently, Jim's troubles were well known at the squadron. At Knowles' suggestion, they walked over to see airmen Brooks and Moss, Jim's ground crew.

"Brooks, Moss, I'd like to introduce you to somebody," Sergeant Knowles said. The men stood up from the wheel they were working on. "This here is Corporal Jacobs. He's a new ack emma what just reported in today. 'E knows Lieutenant Arneson."

"Hallo, Corporal Jacobs!" Brooks replied. He was a broad-faced, curly-headed chap of about Hank's height and weight. "How d'you know the lieutenant?"

"Call me Hank, please. We grew up together in Minnesota!" Hank replied. "I've known Jimmy since we were eight years old. We signed up together in Winnipeg, Canada."

"Wow, I guess you do know him, then!" Moss added.

"Corporal Jacobs was Captain Cecil Harrison's personal mechanic at 60 Squadron before Harrison was shot down. He's got a solid reputation," Sergeant Knowles said. "Hank says he'd like to be assigned to work on Lieutenant Arneson's plane. I know that's one of yours, so I thought I'd better ask you two how you felt about it."

Brooks spoke up. "I got no problem with that at all, Hank. I'll tell you what, though. I think you'll have to work on your friend before you work on his aircraft. The poor guy's a mess."

"Yeah, I saw that," Hank replied. "I met up with him in his hut. He looks like hell. What happened?"

"You'll want to talk to his flight commander, Captain Roger Stevens, as well, but here's what we know," Brooks said. "He came into the Squadron off convalescent leave last December. I guess he and Stevens knew each other from their days at 40 Squadron. Lieutenant Arneson had a good reputation and was well received as near as we could tell." Moss nodded his concurrence with Brooks' opinion.

Brooks continued, "They call him Gracie on account of his plane. He calls it 'Saving Grace.' I guess the pilots at 40 Squadron gave him the nickname because he saved a bunch of them from the Huns."

"So he told me," Hank said.

"He has us paint little roundels on his plane for each save he gets. He counts them instead of his kills. He's up to twelve of them now," Brooks explained.

"Anyway, he's an excellent pilot, we hear. He was doing great and they even made him deputy flight commander of C Flight under Captain Stevens. Stevens has been helping the CO a lot, so Lieutenant Arneson has been leading a lot of the flights himself," Brooks continued.

"Then, everything fell apart earlier this month. He led C Flight on a high escort mission and got bounced by a big bunch of Fokkers. The Germans wiped them out. The lieutenant's the only one that made it back, but he cracked up his airplane on landing. It was a total write off. Burned to a crisp right after he got out."

"The loss of his flight wrecked him, Hank," Brooks added. "I've never seen anything like it in my life. He just fell apart. Hit the booze like crazy and started smoking like a chimney. He could barely climb into his cockpit anymore. We tried to help him as best we could, but there wasn't much we could do."

"Captain Stevens pulled him off flight duty about a week ago. We haven't seen much of him since then. I hear he spends his days drunk in his hut. We've seen pilots get the wind up before, but never fall off the edge of cliff like Lieutenant Arneson. You think you can help him?" Brooks asked.

"I have to," Hank said. "He's my closest friend. I can't let him go like this. I don't know what I'm going to do, but I have to try."

"Good luck, Corporal Jacobs," Moss said. "Me and Brooks will do anything we can to help. He's a good man, the lieutenant. We like him, too."

"Thanks, guys," he said. "I appreciate it. Is this his plane?"

"No," Brooks said. "His is number 2 over there in the hangar. It's in pretty good shape, but it's new to him, seeing as how he crashed the last one. Have at it, mate. Let us know if you need anything from us."

"Thanks!" Hank said. "You've been a big help already. Sergeant Knowles, is it okay if I look over Jim's plane?"

"You go right ahead, Corporal," Sergeant Knowles said. "I'll call on you to help out elsewhere, but for now, dig in on number 2."

"Thanks," he said. Hank walked over to number 2 and looked it over. It was a standard SE5a with no remarkable differences from any other as far as he could tell. It had checkered red wheels to designate C Flight, but was otherwise a standard RFC issue.

Later, Hank looked up Captain Stevens. He had a desk in the Squadron Operations room. Hank and Stevens took a walk together after Hank introduced himself.

"So you say you grew up with Jim, Corporal Jacobs?" Stevens asked.

"Yes, sir, I did," Hank replied. "We've known each other since we were eight years old. We signed up together."

"Fascinating," Stevens said. "And I hear you worked on Cecil Harrison's plane?" he asked.

"Yes, sir," Hank replied. "First on his Nieuport and then on his SE5. He was good man, sir. I admired him greatly. He gave me my big break."

"He was a great man, Hank," he said. "May I call you Hank?"

"Please do, sir! Thank you."

"I knew Cecil well. We spent some time together while I was at No. 3 Squadron. Big loss to us all."

"Yes, sir," he replied.

"You think you can help Jim?" he asked.

"I hope so, sir," he replied. "This isn't the Jim I know. I have to bring him back for my own sake as well as his."

"You're absolutely right. This is not the Jim I have known either," he said. "You'll need to succeed, Hank. And you need to do it soon. I've been covering for him, but I can't do it much longer. He needs to get back on ops as soon as possible. We'll work together to keep him safe up there while you work on him down here, all right?"

"Yes, sir!" Hank replied enthusiastically. "Thank you, sir!"

"Good luck, Corporal," Stevens said. "I'm going to overlook the fraternization regulations for the time being so you can help him. You can even bunk in his hut if you need to. Let me know if you want me to arrange it. Keep it quiet, though. I could get in trouble for it. Just let me know if you need anything."

"Thank you, sir," Hank replied. He had his leeway to work with Jimmy. Now he just had to figure out what he would do. Little did he know Jimmy would help him take the first step.

The next morning, Hank went to Jimmy's hut first thing. Jimmy was still asleep and C Flight was out on a mission. Hank went up to him and nudged him on the shoulder to wake him. Jimmy pushed back with his shoulder. "'Leave me be."

"Come on, Jim. It's past time to be up. The whole airfield is up and going about its business. You need to do the same," he said.

"Bah! Why bother?" he grumbled.

"Good news, Jim," Hank said. "Sergeant Knowles, the chap who runs the maintenance unit, assigned me as your mechanic. Brooks and Watts were okay with it, too. How about that? We get to work together on your plane!"

"Yeah, great, Hank. Now look, go away and leave me alone. Come back around noon or something."

Hank just pressed on. "Jim, I spoke with Captain Stevens also. He filled me in about you. He said it would be okay for me to help you."

"Help me?" Jimmy said angrily. "What's he think I need help with? I'm fine!"

"No, Jim. You're not fine," Hank said. "You're a mess." He tried to remain calm, but Jim was getting increasingly belligerent.

"I am not! What do you know? Get out!"

"No, Jim. I'm not leaving. You need to get up," Hank said.

Jim jumped up, balled his hands into fists and stuck his chin in Hank's face. "For the last time, I said get out!"

"No!"

Jim pulled his right hand back and threw a drunken, wide swing at Hank. Hank parried it easily. Jimmy looked shocked and threw another from the left, followed immediately by a right cross.

Hank ducked his left and pushed his right in on him at the elbow as he faded left. Jimmy was unsteady on his feet and stumbled away. "Jim, calm down!"

Jimmy regained his footing and charged him with a primitive roar, both fists pumped, head down like a bull.

Hank hit him hard right on Jimmy's crown as he charged in on him. Jimmy ran right into it and went down hard on his back, unconscious. Hank's knuckles screamed in pain.

"Jim, Jim, Jim, you sorry bastard," Hank said as he lifted Jimmy up off the floor and laid him on his bed. Jimmy was out for the count.

Hank went to the mess hall and grabbed a pot of coffee and two cups from the orderly. Back at Jim's hut, he sat and waited for Jimmy to come to. It didn't take long.

Jimmy rubbed his head with the heel of his hand and raised himself up on his elbow. "When did you learn to do that?" he said groggily.

"I read the book, remember?" Hank laughed. "Plus I got a little practice in at the motor pool and 60 Squadron."

"Damn, it hurts!" he said. Hank was glad to see the hints of a smile on his face.

"I'm sorry, man, but you were asking for it. Hey, I uh, got us some coffee at the mess hall," Hank said. "Here, have a cup." He handed Jimmy a cup of steaming hot coffee, strong and black. Jimmy sipped at it and grimaced.

"Jesus Christ, Hank Jacobs. It's good to see you, man," Jimmy said. "How the hell did you end up here?"

"I saw you got posted to the 56th when I was reading the *London Gazette* in the lobby of the hotel I was staying at."

"Hotel?" he asked. "Where and what were you doing in a hotel? I thought you were with 60 Squadron."

"I was with 60 Squadron, but I got wounded when we got attacked by the Huns," Hank replied. "They had to do some surgery on my leg and then gave me some leave in London to heal up."

"Wounded, huh?" Jimmy asked. "You, too? Where did you get it?"

"In my bum leg," Hank replied. "Now it's really a bum leg! I still use a cane sometimes, but I think I am about to let it go. It's getting better."

"Must have been a nasty wound."

"It was, cut some ligaments, nerves, and stuff, but it's okay now," he said.

"Glad to hear it," Jimmy replied. "I spent some time in London, too, when I got shot in the back."

"I heard," Hank said. "Sounds like you were almost paralyzed for life, according to Meg."

"Didn't know at first," Jim said. "It was a mess, but it slowly got better. I got to go home for a few months and married Ellie while I was at it."

"Meg told me about that, too," Hank replied. "Great. Congratulations!"

"Thanks!" Jimmy said as he slurped some coffee, wincing again as he did so.

"So, Jimmy, I had no idea you were so messed up," Hank said. "What's going on?"

"Oh, you don't want to hear it, Hank," Jimmy said. "Let's just forget it."

"No, Jimmy," Hank replied. "I can't do that. It wouldn't be fair to me or you. I want to know, straight from you, what led you to such a state? It's so not like you. What happened?"

"It's a long story, Hank," Jimmy said.

"I got all day," Hank replied. "You got all day, too!"

Jimmy chuckled. "Well, let's just say this piloting thing we both wanted so badly ain't all it's cracked up to be, Hank."

"What do you mean?" Hank asked.

Jimmy proceeded to share his story with Hank. He loosened up as he went. Hank listened intently. Jimmy talked about his chronic fear of Archie barrages, and the times he had seen planes blown out of the air. He shared with Hank that he had nightmares about it even still. He tried to describe his nightmares to Hank but froze up. He hit a wall and couldn't go on.

"I need a drink, Hank," Jimmy confessed. "I can't talk about this stuff sober." Hank let him have one, figuring it was better for Jimmy to get things off his chest.

Jimmy took a slug, breathed deeply, and looked for safer ground. He told Hank about the FE8 and its inadequacy against the superior Albatros scouts. Hank was amazed at Jimmy's recollection of some of the dogfights he was in. It was like he was in the middle of it in his mind as he talked. He stared off into space as he spoke, playing the movie reel in his mind's eye. He conveyed the chaos of the fights, the instant decisions, and the terror of having an enemy on your tail.

Jimmy told Hank about Jack Bailey and how they became really good friends. But he also told Hank about Jack's death and the trip to recover Jack's body. Jimmy froze up again when he tried to describe the scene of the crash. His eyes welled up and he looked up at the ceiling of the hut. His voice trailed off. Jimmy sobbed then, dropping his head into his hands, trying to hold it in, but failing.

Hank realized there was only so much he could ask Jimmy to talk about at one sitting. Hank just sat quietly with him and let Jimmy stop talking for a while. He leaned over and rubbed his friend's shoulder. "Maybe you should take a nap, Jimmy," Hank said. "I'll come back a little later, okay?"

"Yeah," Jimmy said. "A little later."

Hank left Jimmy alone for a while then. Hank was stumped. He knew he couldn't force Jimmy to just sit there and talk through all of his stuff. Jimmy would just clam up on him. He needed some kind of diversion. That's when he thought about Jimmy's plane. Maybe they could spend time on the plane together as a way of keeping them occupied while they talked.

Hank went to the hangar where Jimmy's plane was kept. He familiarized himself with the layout, organized his toolbox just the way he liked it, scrounged up some tools he knew he would need, and killed a couple of hours of time.

When he went back to Jimmy's hut, Hank found Jimmy snoring away with an empty bottle on the wooden floor beside Jimmy's cot. Hank decided to let Jimmy sleep. He realized it was going to take some time for Jimmy to get it all out.

33

VAL'HEUREUX, APRIL, 1918. The next morning, Hank was pleased to see Jim awake when he got there. Hank knew Jimmy drank himself to sleep the night before but seeing Jimmy up of his own accord was a step forward.

At Hank's suggestion, they got some take-away breakfast items in their respective mess halls and met up in the hangar with Jimmy's new airplane. Hank had a makeshift table in the back of the hangar where they could sit while they ate.

"Do you like the SE5, Jim?" Hank asked.

"Yeah, it's a good plane," Jimmy replied. "It's fast. That's its biggest plus. I can choose when to engage and when to run away because of its speed. Well, up until my last flight, that is. It doesn't turn like my old Nieuport used to, though."

"Interesting," Hank mused. "Captain Harrison used to say the same thing. If you could change something, what would it be?"

"I would like it to roll into a turn more quickly. Once I'm in the turn, it does okay. That's mostly elevators. However, it's a little slow getting into it."

"Hmm." Hank scratched his chin and looked it over. He thought back to the adjustments he had made to Captain Harrison's plane. "Whad'ya say we see what we can do with the rigging? If we can reduce the dihedral, even a little bit, it might help. It won't fly by itself though. You'll have to be more hands on."

"That's okay," Jimmy said. "That's the way I like it."

After finishing their breakfast, they tinkered with the SE5a's rigging. Turnbuckle by turnbuckle, they loosened here and tightened there. Hank had done this with Captain Harrison's plane before, so he could have done it much more quickly. However, Hank intentionally encouraged Jimmy to make many of the changes himself and to let the job take as long as needed. They talked as they worked, enjoying once again the comradery of doing things together they had always enjoyed growing up in Minnesota.

At first, they reminisced about their childhoods in Minnesota, Ellie, Meg, their parents, and their siblings. They had fun remembering their experiments with gliders and the old Indian motorcycle. Eventually though, Hank introduced Jimmy's experiences in the war into the conversation. Hank knew Jimmy needed to talk about it, to get it out into the open.

He asked Jimmy about the other pilots in 40 Squadron. Jimmy told him all about Alfie Campbell and Mike Phillips and all the grief they gave Jimmy about being an American. Jimmy told them about other pilots, too. Sadly, Jimmy also remembered the deaths of so many of them. He recounted some of those fights for Hank. Hank began to see how it affected Jimmy. Hank could see how the loss of friends left and right sent Jimmy down the path of fatalism, expecting his own death and never knowing when the next fight would be his last.

Hank saw that Jimmy had been through hell. "So, where are you now, Jim?" Hank asked.

"Hell, I don't know, Hank," he replied. "Why did I survive? Why me? Why didn't I die? I'm already a dead man doomed to burn in hell for eternity. They had things to live for, homes to go to, people who loved them."

"So do you, Jim. You have all those things."

"I'm a dead man, Hank. I just don't know if it will happen the next time I go up, or the one after that."

"Yeah, this war has seen so many men killed, broken, or messed up," he replied. "I guess you might as well be one of them."

Jim looked at him quizzically.

"I'm not sure what I mean by that, to be honest with you," Hank said. "There's just so much suffering, it's hard to fathom. We've all seen it to some extent, haven't we? I mean, I guess I've been luckier than most, but I've seen things I wish I hadn't, same as you."

"Have you?"

"Sure, I spent a fair amount of time at the front lines. I've had artillery shells land close enough to knock me off my feet and cloud my head for days. I've been shot at, and I've shot back. I've been shot and spent time in a military hospital. I'll never forget what I saw in some of those, no matter how much I might want to."

"Yeah."

"I do think you've had it worse than most, Jim. It's got to be awfully hard to see close friends shot down in flames."

"Yeah, it is."

"You can't change any of it," Hank said. "Those things happened. They can't be undone. You have no choice in that. But I think you can choose how to respond to it."

"What do you mean?" Jim asked.

"We can't change the past, Jimmy," Hank said. "None of us can. We can let it haunt us, or we can accept it and move on. We did what needed to be done, Jim. We did what was asked of us. We didn't choose to kill people, we did it because we had to."

"But we killed people."

"Yes, we did," Hank said. "Maybe we could have somehow done things differently, but it was what it was. We have to learn to forgive ourselves."

"I don't think I can ever do that, Hank."

"Well, maybe you can try, yeah?" he said. "And even if you can't, maybe you can turn that guilt into a rudder to guide you to wherever you go from here. Use it to set your course here and now. Let it remind you to do better tomorrow."

"It ain't over, Hank," Jim said. "I still need to go up there and kill people."

"I know," Hank said. "It will be hard, but we're together again now. I'll see you through this, pal. I'll help you if you let me."

Jim poured himself another cup of coffee. He didn't say a word, but just stared off into space.

"Think it over, Jim," Hank said. "I'll see you later. Do me a favor though?"

"What, Hank?"

"Stay sober tonight, okay?"

Jim smirked at him. "Yeah, yeah, yeah. All right, Hank."

Hank left him then, and went back to his hut. He thought it helped Jim to tell his story. Hank didn't think he had ever done it before. Hank knew Jimmy had many things to think about. Hank just hoped he would be able to help.

That day established a pattern for them that would last several weeks. Each day, they would meet at the hangar and work on Jimmy's plane together. Hank tried to make one change each day to optimize the plane's fit and performance for Jim.

They worked through the aileron control system, tightening all of the wiring from the yoke to the ailerons. Then, they did the same for the rudder and elevators.

They harmonized Jimmy's guns so they converged at fifty yards to better concentrate his cone of machine gun fire. Hank showed Jimmy how to hand-load the ammunition belts so he had fewer gun jams. They adjusted the Aldis gun sight to line up better with the Lewis gun and adjusted Jimmy's seat height so he could aim more easily.

Then, they worked on the big Viper V-8 engine. Hank showed Jimmy how to tune it so it ran like a sewing machine. Hank installed high-compression pistons and rings like McCudden had to improve performance and even rigged a spinner on the propeller like McCudden's to improve the aerodynamics.

While they worked on Jimmy's plane, they also talked through Jim's issues, a little bit each day. Jimmy finally spoke of killing other people and the guilt he felt over it. He shared the advent of his mission to save his compatriots' lives and some of the successes he had.

Jimmy still drank himself to sleep at night, but over the course of those few weeks, Hank could tell Jimmy was fighting it and making progress. There were some sober nights mixed in there as well. Those grew more frequent and the drunken binges grew further apart.

Jimmy spoke of the common habit of the pilots with their drinking and smoking to cope with the stress. He told Hank his tales of getting shot up on two separate occasions, recovering back home, and coming back here.

Eventually, Jimmy was able to confide in Hank the details of the fateful mission when Jimmy lost his flight. It was the event that sent Jimmy over the cliff and finally talking about it with Hank was the event that helped Jimmy the most to climb back up and out of his funk. Several times, Jimmy fell into tears as he talked. Hank let him get those out, too. Jimmy felt safe with Hank and could let it happen.

Each improvement and each conversation added a thread to the interwoven whole of Jim and his plane. The weave was stronger than any one thread. A living metaphor, Jim's outlook improved as his plane improved. Hank's friend was returning.

Hank and Jimmy completed an inspection of the fuel tanks, pumps and lines one day. Hank took a gamble when they had finished. "Okay, Jim," Hank said. "Let's see if these changes make any difference for you. Take her up and give her a workout."

Jimmy was taken aback. Obviously, their work on the plane would lead up to Jimmy flying it, but he had suppressed those thoughts. He turned away from Hank and walked out of the hangar. He stood at the edge of the tarmac looking out across the airfield. He just stood there, staring off into the distance for a long time. Then, he turned back to Hank and said, "All right, Hank. I'll do it."

Hank filled the tanks and walked through the pre-flight and start-up procedure with Jimmy. The big engine purred after warming up. For the first time in several weeks, Jimmy advanced the throttle and rolled out to take off. Captain Stevens happened to be standing nearby and saw Jimmy head out. He looked over to Hank and gave him a thumbs up.

After about an hour or so, Jimmy landed, taxied up to where Hank was standing, shut her down and crawled out. "Wow!" Jimmy said. "That made a huge difference! I like it!"

"Excellent!" Hank replied. "Glad you like it." He grew bolder still. "How would you feel about trying it out for real tomorrow?"

Jim took off his leather flying helmet and scratched his head. "You mean go up with the flight?"

"Yep," Hank said. "Exactly. You have to get back in the saddle, Jim. Remember when we used to wreck the motorcycle? We didn't let it stop us then, and you can't let this stop you now." Jimmy hesitated once more, but in the end, agreed with Hank. It was time.

Hank let Captain Stevens know he thought Jimmy was ready. Elated, Stevens promised to go easy on him at first.

Hank sent Jimmy off with C Flight the next morning. Hank saw Jimmy's game face, just like when they were kids on the high school football team. He was resolute. It was an escort mission. Captain Stevens had him fly high escort attached to a Lieutenant Finch.

It took forever. Hank was waiting for Jimmy when he returned. No enemy aircraft today, thankfully. Jimmy did okay. Hank knew he would. They had a cup of coffee together afterwards and talked about the flight. Jimmy stuck around with Hank as he cleaned up the airplane. They talked over old times on the Dogwood River.

Over the course of the next couple of weeks, Jim and Hank found a new pattern for their lives together. Hank saw Jimmy off on his missions and welcomed him back on their completion. Each time Jimmy returned, Jimmy would debrief first with his flight, and then with Hank. Their talks continued. If Jimmy had an idea to improve the airplane's performance, Hank would work on it with him that night and they would try it out the next day.

Gracie had returned at last. Hank breathed a sigh of relief each night.

34

VAL'HEUREUX, APRIL, 1918. There was a quiet spot a short walk from the aerodrome where a small river flowed peacefully by on its way to the Atlantic. Fine, April weather ushered in renewal of the plants and wildlife along the river. Rushes lined the banks and made homes for Wrens, Chickadees, and other small birds. Dragonflies fluttered about, looking for insects to eat. In a still, deep pool, ducks raised their young under the overhanging brush, their parental quacking disturbed an otherwise quiet interlude. Nearby brambles housed a warren of hares who dared to feed in the open grass until a falcon flew overhead.

Jimmy went there to be alone, to think, or sometimes to cry. It helped him cope, to sort through issues, to settle his mind on how he felt about things.

He didn't realize how messed up he had been. Hank's friendship renewed his better self, a self who looked to the future, eager to see what each day would bring, and a confidence to tackle obstacles that arose before him.

Jimmy looked back and realized his dreams had always centered on himself, on adventures he would have, and daring deeds of valor. "Well," Jimmy said to himself, "I got my adventure and daring deeds all right, more than I expected." In his dreams, Jimmy had not anticipated the fear of dying, the stress of seeing others die around him, and the guilt of killing other people. He saw now he was a fool to think he could handle this alone. He didn't handle it well. He fell into drunkenness, self-pity, and fatalism.

Jimmy failed to see the love and support of those around him. Hank helped him to see it. Hank didn't need to say it, he lived it. He was Jimmy's friend when Jimmy was shunned by all others. Hank persisted when others gave up. He endured. Their friendship endured.

Jimmy was a fool to think it all revolved around him, that he was the driver, the mover, the shaker. He thought he fueled his own engine, but he was wrong. It was always his friends and loved ones who fueled him. Even as a kid on the dirt streets of home when he fought for Hank, it was Hank's friendship and faith in him that fueled Jimmy to take on others bigger than himself. When they crashed the motorcycle and Jimmy carried Hank to the hospital, it was Hank's faith in him that gave him the strength to do it. When Jimmy helped Ellie in the playground and carried her home, it was her love for him that drove him. When Jimmy was recovering from his wounds and he didn't know if he would ever fly again, it was her selfless love that saw him through.

It was Pastor Olson's kind persistence that helped him deal with his guilt. It was Mrs. Olson's kind and caring instruction that sparked his curiosity and honed his mental acuity. It was Miss Jensen's eagerness to help him explore his interests in the library that spawned his achievement. Love, caring, and friendship of others had bolstered Jimmy all along. He just had never realized it before.

It was hard for Jimmy to accept love from others and he failed many times. With Hank's help, Jimmy saw things more clearly. He appreciated their love. Awakening to this, gratitude propelled him. Each day, he awoke thankful for the love of others, especially those who loved him even though they had seen him at his worst.

He loved his friends and family. Hank was a brother to him. Hank's steadfast love saved Jimmy from oblivion. Jimmy could never repay him. Jimmy's mother and father always loved him unconditionally. They supported him in everything he did. And Ellie had always been the love of his life. Jimmy never realized how much he relied on her and how much she gave him selflessly. She gave him a child, JJ, who lit up Jimmy's life with joy. And she would give birth to another child of theirs.

It had been a momentous month. His life would never be the same. He had much to be thankful for and tried to express it in a letter to Ellie.

April 24, 1918

Ellie my love,

If I could have anything I want, what would I ask for? I would ask for a woman to love who loved me back just as much. Thank you for being that woman. I would ask for children of whom I could be proud. You have given me that, too, with JJ and now, with the new child on the way.

I would ask for friends with whom I could laugh, enjoy, and from whom I could feel appreciated and loved. You, Hank, and Meg have given me this over and over again.

I would ask for the opportunity to make a difference. I hope I have done so here in France. I would like to think some of my friends here will survive this war who otherwise might not have.

By the grace of God and your love, I have all these things. Thank you, my darling.

As the moon settles below the horizon on its journey to the Atlantic, I am heartened to know it will soon adorn the evening skies over my home and you, my darling Ellie. My mind fills with visions of you, my love. My nostrils breathe in the sweet fragrance of your tender skin. I am taken away from the horror of this war to a soft field of grass along the Dogwood River, nestled in your loving arms.

My life is more precious for being uncertain, and richer for having loved you.

I love you,
Jimmy

Jimmy's appreciation for the love of others strengthened his resolve in his mission to save others, to help see them through the war. He flew with renewed vigor. He celebrated each save and was grateful to extend to others the love extended to him. He was gratified to see that, once again, his fellow pilots wanted him with them.

Jimmy was grateful to find Hank waiting for him when he returned from a mission. Hank helped him get through each and every day. When he was scared, Hank comforted him. When they talked about the mission, Hank helped him see how he could improve and he helped Jimmy forgive himself when he failed. Hank gave him peace where he had only felt remorse.

Jimmy saw things in a new light with new hope. He found hope this war would end soon. America, who had declared war a year ago, was finally engaging in full force. The war was changing, with their addition. The Americans were making a huge difference for the war-weary allies. Hope was felt by all again for the first time in years. There was talk of the war ending soon.

Jimmy found himself hoping he would survive to go home. He hoped his fears had been wrong. He dared to hope he would grow old loving his family. And he hoped this war would be the last war. He hoped they would all see the folly of war and work to ensure peace in the world for ever.

35

VAL'HEUREUX, MAY, 1918. Jim and Hank were going over Jimmy's airplane Tuesday night in the hangar on the twenty first of May. Captain Stevens came up to them. "How are you gentlemen this evening?" he asked.

"Excellent, sir!" Jimmy offered. "We're just going over the aeroplane to see if there are any changes we want to make for tomorrow."

"Glad to see it," Stevens said. "I wanted to have a brief chat with you if you don't mind."

"Of course, sir," he said. "What's on your mind?"

"Well, I want you to know I am happy to see you back in the game, Arneson. You're getting back to your old self," Stevens said. "I owe that to you, Corporal Jacobs. You've done well working with your friend." Jim had come back nicely. In the two months they had been back together, he had gotten healthier, stopped drinking excessively, and improved his outlook on life. He was back on regular flying status and seemed to be doing well there, too. He added a couple more saves to his tally, now up to fifteen. Jimmy took great pride in that number.

"Thank you, sir," Hank replied. "I'm glad to have my old friend back, too!"

"I've learned to cherish Hank's friendship more than ever, captain," Jimmy said.

"Yes, yes, yes. It's all good," Sevens said. "However, I think it's time we establish some guidelines for you both related to fraternization."

"Yes, sir," Jimmy said. "I appreciate your relaxation of those regulations so Hank and I could work more closely together. But, I know the need for consistency."

"Exactly," Stevens said. "I am glad to see you two can work together as well as be friends. I don't mind it at all personally, but we all need to keep up appearances, so to speak. I think we need to get back to behaviors more closely aligned to the RAF guidelines. By that, I don't mean strict enforcement of the rules. What I mean is the two of you need to demonstrate respect for those ideas to your peers."

"Yes, sir!" Jimmy said.

"Good. You know why we have such regulations, I assume. Officers and other ranks are not to have personal relationships with each other. It is intended to minimize favoritism and to maintain discipline in a consistent manner."

"Yes, sir," Jimmy said. "What do you suggest?"

"As an officer, Jim, you should eat with the other officers and join in on officers' mess evening gatherings. Jacobs, you should be eating with the other ranks in the enlisted men's mess."

"No problem, sir," Jimmy said. "We'll start immediately."

"Good. Thank you. On another topic, Jacobs, your reputation has grown considerably since you've been here," Stevens said. "The men respect your skills in maintaining their aircraft and maximizing their reliability and performance."

"Thank you, sir!" Hank replied.

"Sergeant Knowles has requested your help in training and coaching the other ack emmas in the squadron," Stevens said. "Would you be willing to do so in addition to your continued maintenance of your assigned aircraft?"

"Why, yes, sir," Hank replied. "I would enjoy it very much."

"Good," Captain Stevens said. "I'll meet with Sergeant Knowles now and you can begin in the morning. Jim, we're scheduled for a nine o'clock patrol, so get a good night's sleep."

"Yes, sir!" Jimmy replied.

"Good night, gentlemen," Stevens said. They saluted and he left.

The next morning, Hank discussed his new assignment with Sergeant Knowles over breakfast. He would start working with two young mechanics while Jim was out on patrol. They decided to work out a regular schedule for working with particular mechanics Knowles felt needed some assistance.

Along about eight o'clock, Hank went over to the hangar to prepare Jimmy's plane for the patrol. He fueled it up, checked out the fluid levels and the rigging, and carefully examined the ammunition belts to make sure Jimmy's guns didn't jam on him. Satisfied that the plane was ready, Hank wheeled it out onto the tarmac.

Jimmy and the rest of C Flight arrived together just before nine. Hank helped him get his flight suit on and get settled into the cockpit. "What's the deal today, Jim? Anything special?"

"Just a routine offensive patrol. We're heading over to the area between Cambrai and Douai to look for two-seaters. There's almost always enemy patrols around so I expect we'll see some action," Jimmy said.

"Well, the weather looks like a good day for flying, anyway," he added.

"Yep, we'll be up around fourteen thousand."

Jimmy got strapped in and they looked around to see how the other guys were doing. Captain Stevens spun his hand around over his head to tell them all to fire up their engines.

"Take care, Jimmy. Have a good flight," Hank said. "I'll see you when you get back."

"Right-o, buddy!" Jimmy was in good humor this morning. "Let's go!"

Hank hopped down off the wing and worked his way out in front of the propeller. They started up the plane and Hank held on until everybody was ready to go.

Captain Stevens waved his hand forward over his head to signal take-off. Jimmy waved his hands for Hank to pull the chocks.

Chocks away, Jimmy pushed the throttle forward and rolled away. He waved to Hank as he left and Hank waved back. Hank stood there for few moments watching the five planes take off and head east. Jimmy waggled his wings as he usually did on the way out.

Hank's work with the two young mechanics went smoothly enough. They pulled an engine out of an SE5a and mounted it on the engine stand. They pulled the heads off the engine and changed the head gaskets. Hank left them to finish up around noon so he could grab a bite of lunch and await Jimmy's return, expected around half past noon.

Several of the mechanics hung out in front of the hangars waiting for their birds to return. It was always a bit tense until they saw the planes and could count the number of aircraft returning.

The patrol was a little late. Around a quarter to one, they saw some dots off to the east they suspected was the patrol. They counted three planes. As they approached, they could see two of those three trailing smoke. It had not gone well.

The planes came straight in and landed together. It wasn't until they taxied up that they could tell who was missing. Jimmy was one of them. Captain Stevens was the other.

An old, sinking feeling came over Hank, reminding him of Captain Harrison's demise several months ago. He went over to the briefing hangar to listen in on the debriefing with the adjutant, Major Townsend.

A first lieutenant named Ford spoke for the three pilots, all of whom were obviously shook up. "We encountered a large, mixed flight of six of the new Fokker DVIIs and four triplanes about ten miles behind the lines. We met at the same altitude in a head-on pass. Captain Stevens was hit by a brightly striped DVII." Ford couldn't tell if Stevens was shot down or just had to dive away. "Last I saw of him, he was diving to the west, trailing black smoke, but there was no fire."

Ford continued. "I saw Gracie engage another DVII with white wings and a grey fuselage. I think Gracie shot him down but things were moving too fast to be certain. Lieutenant Adams here was shot up by a diving DVII, but he split-essed and dove for the ground. Lieutenant Kelly got on the DVII's tail so Adams got away. He took hits though. After a few climbing turns, the positions reversed and Kelly was also shot up and spun out of control. He wasn't followed because Gracie came to his rescue. We last saw him shoot the DVII off of Kelly's tail. Gracie got on the DVII's tail and they dove off to the east. Two of the triplanes followed them.

"I mixed it up with the other two triplanes and was able to shoot one of them down, a blue and white checkered plane. The other one dove away to the east. I let him go because my motor started sputtering and I feared I had taken some engine hits. I dove after Adams and Kelly who were both well below the fight. When I joined up with them, the sky was empty. We don't know what happened to Gracie. We headed for home because two of us were shot up pretty badly. We got mangled."

The adjutant immediately put calls out to all observer posts and nearby squadrons to report any signs of Stevens or Jimmy. Hank hung around the hangar not knowing what else to do. He had been through this before with Captain Harrison and he remembered Harrison often came in later than the others. Hank tried to tell himself that Jimmy would show up but his gut twisted inside. He checked in with the adjutant every hour or so.

The adjutant learned from 24 Squadron that Captain Stevens had made it to their field and was okay. His airplane was a wreck though so he was headed back in a 24 Squadron tender.

There was no word about Jim, however. Afternoon waned into evening without a peep. Hank's heart hung low. Major Townsend tried to console him. "Look, Corporal Jacobs. You have to realize these things happen all the time. A pilot can take hits in a fight and not be able to make it all the way back home. He may land anywhere in between. Sometimes, he has to land behind enemy lines and gets captured. Sometimes he makes it to the trenches and crashes there, and sometimes he sets it down behind our lines. It's not unusual for him to be unable to communicate with anyone for hours or even days. And if he's taken prisoner, we may not hear anything for a few weeks at best. Arneson is a damned fine pilot and would get it down safely if he could. He's probably making his way to a friendly unit somewhere right now. We'll keep checking and listening for some word. All we can do is hope for the best. In the meantime, I recommend you get some rest. Go to the flight surgeon if you need to for some sleeping powders. I'll send a note with you if you like."

"Thanks, Major Townsend," he said. "I'm okay. I'll head back to my bunkhouse." Hank saluted and walked to his cot.

After two weeks of painful waiting, Major Townsend called Hank into the squadron commander's office. Knowing a major would almost never call on a corporal to report, Hank feared the worst. Major Townsend led him into the office and stood by his side as they reported to the commanding officer, Major Baldwin.

"Corporal Jacobs reporting, sir!" Hank exclaimed as he braced at attention.

"Jacobs, please be at ease," Major Baldwin said. "I called you in here because I am aware of the close friendship you have with Lieutenant James Arneson. Am I correct?"

"Yes, you are absolutely correct, sir," Hank replied.

"After two full weeks, we still have not heard any news regarding Lieutenant Arneson's situation, whatever that might be," he said. "In such a circumstance, we are required to change the operational status of the pilot, James Arneson in this case, from 'Missing in Action,' to 'Missing in Action, Presumed Dead.'"

"Yes, sir?" Hank asked.

"I want you to know I am personally sorry for your loss. Lieutenant Arneson was well liked and respected in this squadron. We shall all miss him." Major Baldwin was as uncomfortable with this conversation as Hank was. "I thought, in light of your close relationship with him, that you should be the one to go through the lieutenant's belongings and bring them to the adjutant for eventual shipment to his home. Umm, in my experience, Jacobs, one might find sensitive materials or correspondence that would only hurt or embarrass the survivors, should they receive them. In those cases, I believe one should discard of them discreetly rather than include them with the deceased's belongings. Do you understand?"

"Yes, sir," Hank said. "I will do that, sir."

"Good man, Jacobs. I will leave it to you if you wish to correspond with the family of Lieutenant Arneson. I will be writing a letter myself to his wife and parents."

"Thank you, sir!" Hank saluted him, did an about-face, and left the office. The adjutant followed Hank out the door.

"I am also truly sorry for the loss of Arneson, Jacobs," Major Townsend said after they had left the CO's office. "Gracie was highly thought of by many in this squadron. Not only was he a gifted pilot, his fellow pilots wanted to fly with him because they all knew his top priority would be to help them come back safely. He was a top-notch fellow."

"Major, may I ask you a question?" Hank asked.

"Why, of course, Jacobs. Ask anything."

"Does this mean he's dead, or does this mean there's still a chance he could be alive?" Hank asked.

"The latter, young man," Major Townsend said. "However the chances are significantly less, I'm afraid. He could be a prisoner of war or he may be on the run, evading the enemy, and still trying to get back here. But we may never receive word in either case for weeks or months, if at all. Statistically, in situations like this, the highest probability is that the pilot is dead. So, we must request replacements and it requires an explanation. We will, however, hang on to Gracie's belongings for some time before we send them on, just on the off chance we may hear something more in the next few weeks."

"I must tell you, lad," Townsend continued, "the sad truth is that almost all fights with the enemy take place behind the Hun's front line. If one of our chaps goes down, we have no way of knowing what happened unless one of the other pilots saw it. And, even more sadly, we may never know. Many pilots have just disappeared like this with no resolution ever determined."

"Thank you, sir. I appreciate your insight," Hank said as he braced to attention and saluted the major. Townsend returned the salute and Hank headed back to his bunk.

Hank went to Jimmy's hut that was shared with the other pilots of C Flight. They were, gratefully, all away at the time, either at the mess or some officers' gathering. Hank felt strange being there, doing this. He felt like he was invading a space occupied by Jimmy's spirit. He could feel Jimmy in the air.

As Hank began slowly going through Jimmy's clothes, he could smell him on them, the way any person leaves their scent on clothes they have worn. He held a shirt up to his face and sniffed. It transported him back to their childhood, when they first met in 1904.

The state fair and the Labor Day holiday were over and the tall prairie grasses on the flat plains had baked in the intense summer heat of southwest Minnesota to the point of dormancy. Dust swirled everywhere as Gresham's one-room schoolhouse filled for the first day of school.

"Good morning, class," Mrs. Olson said. Pretty and blonde, she wore her hair pulled back to a little bun. "I would like you to meet our new student, Henry Jacobs. Henry is eight years old and he and his family have just moved here from Pennsylvania. Please welcome him to Gresham."

In rugged unison, the class responded, "Hello, Henry!" A few continued with, "Welcome to Gresham."

Henry felt like the oddball in the room right off the bat. Everybody else had straight hair the color of straw and his curly mess was black as coal. Most of the boys wore overalls without shirts or shoes while he wore a black suit with short pants, tall socks, and leather shoes. Drifting in from the west, a gentle breeze provided welcome, if momentary, relief from the oppressive heat. Henry reached back to wipe away a bead of sweat growing on the hair over his starched collar.

"Now class, would each of you please give Henry your name and age as you go around the room? Let's start with the first row on the left work our way across the rows," Mrs. Olson continued.

Each of the kids in class introduced themselves dutifully. Henry didn't remember many of their names. They were all ages, both younger and older. This was a big change from back home. A one-room school house might be normal out here, but it seemed strange to him.

Fortunately, there were a few kids his age. Jimmy Arneson stood out as one of them. When they got to Jimmy, he said, "James Arneson, age eight, but everybody calls me Jimmy." Then he winked.

At ten o'clock, they got to play out in the dusty schoolyard. Jimmy and Henry gravitated to each other. Jimmy was a little taller with yellow hair like all the rest. But, he had a twinkle in his eyes that was both impish and kind at the same time. "So, you're Henry. Do folks call you Henry all the time or do you have a nickname?" Jimmy asked.

"Grown-ups call me Henry, especially Mom. When she's mad at me, she calls me Henry Joseph. I kind of like Hank instead," Hank said. In truth, Henry had never been called Hank before, but it seemed like a better name for Minnesota than Henry. After all, Gresham was about new beginnings for the Jacobs family.

"Okay, Hank it is. Bet you can't beat me to the fence!" Jimmy yelled as he took off with a start. Hank ran after him as fast as he could. When they got to the fence, Jimmy turned and kept running. Hank caught up briefly and they laughed together. His black suit and shoes were quickly covered in dust. They came upon an old bicycle rim lying on the ground and Jimmy picked it up, rolling it ahead of them and chasing after it all around the school yard.

The two boys became instant friends. After school, they walked together to Hank's home. It was only a couple of blocks. Gresham was a tiny town with farms surrounding a few buildings and homes. The smell of grain from the grain tower permeated the humid, hot air, thick with dust from the dirt roads. The brutal sun baked anything left out in it. The boys got to know each other as they walked, exchanging all the normal questions young boys ask when they meet. "Where are you from?" Jimmy asked.

"A little town near Philadelphia called Germantown."

"That seems like a long ways away. How did you get here?"

"It was a long way. We rode the trains out here. Had to change trains like five times. It took us three days. We mostly slept sitting up on the benches," Hank added. A horse wagon drove by, raising dust on the street with each clop of a horseshoe. Horse dung in street fouled the dust as it rose up to their nostrils. Finches twittered as they chased each other among the Maple trees.

"Why did you come here?" Jimmy asked.

"You mean why did we leave Philadelphia or why did we come here to Gresham?"

"Both, I guess."

"Well, my dad makes furniture and cabinets and stuff. He had a shop in Germantown. He was doing okay, but then some German guys started getting mean to Dad. So, he decided we needed to move away," Hank replied. "Gresham was about as far as the train went." There was more to the story than Hank knew. The anti-Semitism of the German-American residents of Germantown escalated from name calling to threats to physical harm. They beat Gustaf Jacobs badly one night as he was walking home from the grocery store and threatened to kill him if he didn't leave town. Gustaf and his wife, Anna, withheld the extent of the brutality from the children but left town as soon as they could make arrangements.

"Are you German?" Jimmy asked.

"Polish. My dad says we're Masurian, but I don't really know what it means. I think it's a kind of Polish." His dad told him German and Polish people hadn't liked each other for years and years. The Germans and the Russians had vied for control over Poland for centuries. The Polish people had always resented both conquerors but were unable to maintain independence despite valiant attempts.

"We're Norwegian, at least my dad is. My mom's from England," Jimmy said. "Seems like everybody around here is Norwegian. Lutheran, too. Do you go to church?"

"Umm, yeah. You sure ask a lot of questions!" Hank replied, evading the question. Hank's father was determined to avoid anti-Semitism in their new home. He instructed the children to keep their Jewish religion a secret. Too many times, being Jewish had caused the Jacobs family trouble, from Poland to Germantown.

"Sorry, I guess I'm just trying to get to know you better, seeing as how we're going to be best friends!" Jimmy laughed. He hooked his thumbs around his overalls as he did. Hank laughed, too. He thought to himself how nice it would be to have a best friend. "Got any brothers or sisters?" Jimmy asked.

"Yeah, I have a little sister named Maria. She's only six."

"I've got lots," Jimmy said. "Martha is my sister. She's three years older than me. Karl is my older brother. He's only one year older. They were both in school today. I have a younger brother named Freddy, too. He's six as well, like your sister. I had an older brother named Erik, but I never knew him. He died when he was three. Got sick I guess."

A German Shepherd barked and came running at the boys from the side yard of a house they passed on Maple Street. The dog spun around and his head jerked back when he reached the end of his chain. Hank flinched and jumped to the side away from the dog. "Oh that there's just old Blue," Jimmy said. "He barks a lot, but he don't ever leave the yard. They keep him tied up, don't ya know. Besides, my dog, Smoky, would beat him up in nothing flat."

"You have a dog?" Hank asked. He had always wanted a dog, but his mother would never let him have one. She said it would just mess up the house and cost them money they couldn't afford. His mother, Anna Wójcik Jacobs, was a kind woman, but a dedicated penny-pincher. The Jacobs' furniture business provided a decent living for the family, but she nonetheless made it her job to spend as little as possible on all things in order to have money for the important things the family needed.

"Yep. Best dog around," Jimmy replied. "You'll have to come by my place and meet him. He's a good old dog. Follows me everywhere and we do all sorts of stuff together. He'd be here with me now, if Dad didn't put him up in the barn at night and not let him out 'till after I go to school."

"What kind is he?"

"Black with some white here and there," Jimmy sniggered. "Beyond that, who knows? He's a mix. Mom says he's mostly Border Collie 'cuz he's really good with the sheep. That's his job, don't ya know. But he's my dog, really."

"So how did you get here?" Hank asked.

"I was born here," Jimmy replied. "Mom and Dad came here from Canada. Dad came from Norway, same as most folks hereabouts. We live on a farm a half-mile out of town," Jimmy offered. Harald and Edith Arneson had immigrated through Canada in 1890 and settled in Gresham because the government was homesteading 160-acre plots to anyone willing to make a farm. "You want to come see it?"

"You bet. I'll ask Mom," Hank replied.

His mother was sweeping the front porch when they got home. "Mom, this is Jimmy. Can I go see where he lives?" Hank asked.

"Not now, dear. I need you to help me with some chores," she replied. "Perhaps another time."

"Okay, Hank," said Jimmy. "Pleased to meet you, Mrs. Jacobs. See you tomorrow!" Jimmy took off running down Main Street, headed for home.

"Hank?" Mom asked. "Are you Hank now, young man?"

"Yes, ma'am! Sounds like Minnesota, don't you think?" She shook her head and kept sweeping. Hank thought he saw a little smile on her face as he ran past her into the house.

Hank began to sort through Jimmy's belongings to pack them up for the last time. He folded Jimmy's uniforms and opened his desk drawer to pack his writing kit. Every item spoke to Hank of Jim, his pen, his journal, his bedclothes. Hank sat down on Jimmy's cot and read Jimmy's journal with great sadness. It documented his deterioration from an eager, happy young lad into a demoralized and guilt-ridden casualty of the war. It was gratifying, at least, to see his final entries reflecting a new found hope as a result of their final days together. In the middle of Jimmy's journal, Hank found a thick envelope with his name on it. Inside, there was a letter for Hank and another envelope with Ellie's name on it.

My dearest friend Hank,

If you are reading this letter, I have gone west. This war has finally taken my life and I am at peace.

Hank, I confess to you my deepest gratitude and appreciation for your friendship. You brought me back from the edge of a dark abyss that called me to give in to its depths. Before our reunion, I had given up my soul to hopelessness.

You have always been my best friend. I cherish the memories of our times together. I am saddened to think we will not have any more of those. Think of me when you fish in the Dogwood, walk in the summer fields, or lie on the ground reading the clouds while you chew on a stalk of tall, sweet grass. I will be there in spirit with you.

More than I realized at the time, your friendship gave me strength and a joy for life all throughout our youth. Having you by my side bolstered me to think thoughts of grand adventure, to approach life without fear, and go forward full of confidence. All of our boyhood adventures, we did together, side by side. You were the best friend a person could ask for. Your belief in me helped me believe in myself.

This war turned out to be the biggest adventure of my life, but it got the best of me. Things might have been different if we had managed to stay together. Without you by my side, I fell into despair. I let fear and guilt drive me. I wrestled with them daily.

In the end, I decided to fight for my friends. Here, in combat, I fought to keep my friends alive. I believed this was the only way I could justify taking the lives of others. I chose to kill Germans so my friends might live another day. Sometimes I was successful, sometimes I failed.

In the greater cause, I also fought for my loved ones back home, to keep them free from aggression and oppression. I may have been a foolish instrument of wealthy war mongers, but in my heart, I felt I was trying to do the right thing.

Ralph Waldo Emerson said it well, "The purpose of life is not to be happy. It is to be useful, to be honorable, to be compassionate, to have it make some difference that you have lived and lived well." I hope I have made some difference, that my life was not wasted. I hope I lived up to the ideals of my loved ones.

History has shown over and over that the preservation of ideals sometimes requires violence and sacrifice. To love your fellow man, to keep them from harm, sometimes you must be willing to walk into harm's way and sometimes, you must harm those who threaten your ideals.

I resigned myself to death several months ago. I saw my friends die and I knew it was just a matter of time before my turn came. I am okay now. Put my empty boots on my chair in the mess hall and drink a toast to my life.

They say life is most appreciated when one looks back on it. As I have painted the picture of my life in my mind's eye, I have sharpened the memories of my time on this earth. You were always there with me and I will continue to be with you in yours, though only in spirit. My life is now reduced to my soul and my memories.

Hank, my friend, I must ask more from you. You will find enclosed a letter addressed to Ellie. Please give it to her and please look after her, JJ, and my unborn child in my absence. My deepest *regrets are that I did not love Ellie with the appreciation she deserved and I will not be able to watch my children grow up. Thank you for being my friend, Henry Jacobs.*

Your friend,
Jim Arneson

Hank took Jimmy's empty boots to the officers' mess and placed them on his chair. Along with his fellow pilots, Hank toasted the life of his best friend and spoke of his love for them. It was a solemn occasion, but one they all needed. Hank was sure Gracie would have also enjoyed the many drinks imbibed in his name throughout the evening.

Every day immediately following his disappearance, Hank found himself looking out to the tarmac whenever a plane flew in to see if it was Jimmy. As time rolled on, Hank tried to stay busy at his work, but he had a hole in his heart that would not leave him alone. Eventually, he had to admit Jimmy was not coming back. His feelings of emptiness grew into a painful void that consumed him for a while.

Major Townsend let him know he was about to send Jim's package home to his parents and Hank might want to write a letter to accompany them. Hank did so, but decided to hold on to the letter Jim had written to Ellie, so he could give it her in person.

Jim was gone, just gone. They never did find out what happened to him.

36

VAL'HEUREAUX AND GRESHAM, JUNE, 1918+. Major Baldwin offered Hank the opportunity to go home in late June, 1918. Hank declined after giving it much thought. While he missed Jimmy, Meg, and his family, and while he would like to be home, Hank had a reason to be there, too. He had his own part to play in the huge theater of war. He decided to stay on to make a difference with 56 Squadron in his own way and to pay homage to his friend who had died fighting to save these fellows.

American soldiers hit the front lines and the tides began to turn. The missions assigned to 56 Squadron now included more strafing and ground support activity. War was evolving to include coordination of air and ground forces. It was dangerous business as the planes and pilots were exposed to a great deal of ground fire in their low-level flying. Planes and pilots came home riddled. Hank and the ack emmas of 56 Squadron spent long hours keeping them in service.

Many of the old guard were moving on. Captain Stevens was promoted to major and appointed as commanding officer of 24 Squadron. New lambs arrived regularly, young pilots, eager to take to the skies, while young airmen supported them on the ground. Hank's time for the last five months of the war was almost entirely spent teaching and raising up these youngsters.

In August, Hank learned from Meg's letter that Ellie had given birth to twin boys, Joseph and Theodore. She would have a handful raising three boys. He vowed to himself to help her any way he could when he got home.

The war ended in November. Hank stayed on with 56 Squadron long enough to help get the planes back to England and then took his discharge and headed home. At long last, the killing was over.

When Hank arrived at the Gresham railroad station, he was greeted by his folks, Meg, Ellie, Jim's folks, and the three little boys. It was perhaps the most bittersweet experience of Hank's life. He was elated to be home and they were happy to have him home, but his arrival scraped the scabs off their wounds from Jimmy's death.

Hank met with Meg and Ellie as soon as he could after getting settled in at his mom and dad's house. His grief spilled over when the three of them were alone for the first time. Meg and Ellie cried and Hank fought back his own tears as they talked about Jimmy. He told them all he could about Jimmy's disappearance and how that sort of thing was more common than people realized.

Ellie had received the official notice from the Royal Air Force by telegram saying he was missing and presumed dead. A few weeks later they received Jimmy's personal belongings Hank had packed up. Those were accompanied by a nice letter from Major Baldwin and supplemented by Major Townsend.

After sharing all he knew with them, Hank handed Ellie the letter he had found in Jimmy's journal. She read it through in silent tears, wiping her eyes with her handkerchief as she read. After reading it, she shared it with Meg, who read it aloud. It was Hank's first hearing of it. He had kept it sealed the whole time.

My dearest Ellie,

Perhaps wrongly, I never shared with you the difficulties of my days here in France. I wanted to spare you from worry, but my darling, I am sorry to say that your reading of this letter means I have not survived.

Please know I reconciled myself to this possibility some time ago, knowing my odds were slim. Knowing our continued freedom relies upon victory in this war, I was prepared to lay down my life for my loved ones, for my friends, for my country, and for this just allied cause.

I have long taken consolation in something Jesus said, "Greater love hath no man than this, that a man lay down his life for his friends." My love, we will all one day leave this earthly life anyway so, if I am to die, I can think of no better reason than to save the life of a friend. As you know, that has been the purpose to which I dedicated myself in France. I have no misgivings about it. My death is a small price to pay for the lives of others.

However, I regret my duty to this cause conflicts with my deep desire to joyously share our lives together. I am saddened that fulfilling my duty meant I must give up the greatest joys in my life, you, James, Jr. and our unborn child. I regret that my own passing forces you to sacrifice much joy in your own life, only to be replaced with sorrow and strife. I pray you will forgive me for it.

My memories of our time together soften the blow of death for me. I am grateful for the time we had together and I hope you will feel that way also. It is hard for me to give up this life, my memories, and my hopes for the future, a future in which we would have had many happy years together raising our family, but I take solace in the firm belief that we will be together in eternity.

I regret I did not better demonstrate my deep love and affection for you. I have focused too much on my own needs and have been thoughtless and careless of yours. I cannot rectify that in this life, but I shall endeavor to do so from the other side, if in anyway, I am able. My darling Ellie, know that I have loved you deeply and my love for you is eternal. My last thoughts and words will have been of you, my love.

Life is full of farewells, but those we love don't really go away. They walk beside us every day, neither seen nor heard. So will I be with you in spirit all your days. Think of me in the cool breeze, in the fragrance of spring flowers, in the raindrops of fall and the snowflakes of winter. I will be in all those places with you, loving you, waiting for you, and missing you.

May God bless you my darling and keep you in his loving arms until we meet again.

Your loving husband eternally,
Jim

Meg and Hank cried with Ellie. It was a wonderful letter. Jimmy's eloquence came through as he spoke of his love for Ellie, for his family, life, and country. They said a prayer for God to embrace Jimmy and keep him with him in Heaven. Hank vowed to Ellie to help her and to help raise her three boys in any way he could. Meg added her own vow to his. Pastor Olson arrived then to meet with Ellie so Meg and Hank left.

Hank stayed with his mother and father for a couple of weeks, but they all soon recognized the arrangement needed to be temporary. The problem was that Hank would need to make some money in order to rent, build, or buy his own place.

Mr. Elstad owned a barn on Main Street in Gresham. Hank made a deal with him to let him open an automotive garage in his barn. Hank would pay him 40% of his incomes up to $15 per month, approximately what he might have paid in rent.

He opened his garage and waited for the cars to come in. They didn't come. He made a little money but not much, certainly not enough to pay rent on an apartment. He basically lived in the garage for six months and worked on a few cars.

It occurred to Hank it might be good to sell gasoline for the cars. That would bring the cars in, he would make a little money off the sale of the gasoline, and the owners would know about him when their cars needed service or repair. He researched the costs and specifications of how to set up a gas station. They were far more than he could afford.

Hank asked Meg how he could get the money. She told him he could get a loan from the bank, but she said he needed to be more grown up, you know, more establishment, to convince them he was a good business risk. She offered to help Hank put together some numbers to justify the investment from the bank. She also suggested they get married to improve the bank managers' perceptions about his stability.

Hank was elated to be proposed to this way! They got married as soon as possible. It was small, informal, and practical to suit Margaret's tastes.

Meg had started working at the bank during the war and still did. She was in commercial lending at the time so it was a conflict of interest for her to loan him money for his businesses. They got special approval from the board of directors so the conflict of interest was resolved.

When they got word of the loan approval, Hank flashed back to the hospital in London when he was wounded. Good old Patrick Sykes was right all along. He wondered how Pat got along back home with his one arm and if his girl still married him.

With the business loan, Hank opened the first gas station in town. His plan worked and over the course of the next several months, people started coming to him more often to work on their cars as well. Hank became Gresham's one-stop shop for all things automotive. Gresham thrived with the return of peace and Hank's business grew with the increased popularity of automobiles. Meg continued to help Hank with the financial management of the business.

Hank and Meg thrived in the post-war boom and started a family. They had Henry, Jr. in 1920 and Martha in 1921. The two of them mirrored their parents in temperament. Henry, Jr. took up Jake as his nickname. Jake followed Hank in his fascination with all things mechanical and was forever at Hank's side. Two more kids, Dorothy and Benjamin, followed in 1923 and 1924. Ben was a bookworm, along with Dorothy. Walter, their fifth child, came along in 1926 after they thought they were done. Walt and Billy Arneson, Fred's son, became fast friends. Little Walt was a rascal of the first degree, getting into mischief all the time, no doubt influenced by Billy. Five children was quite a brood but they had lots of love among them.

In the early twenties, the automobile industry took off. Everybody had to have a car and the Model T was just the thing. In response, Hank got another loan to open up a Ford dealership in addition to the gas station. The new business grew quickly. Henry Ford was a smart fellow. A few years later, Hank added the popular Fordson tractors and farm equipment to the dealership and eventually spun it off on its own.

Hank was in the right place at the right time with the right skills. His time in the motor pool at St. Omer served him well after all. "Sometimes, adversities are the birth pains of joyous new beginnings." Hank's dad used to like to say that whenever something wasn't going right for the kids. While it always used to irk Hank to hear it as a child, it had proven to be true for their family.

As the businesses grew, Hank split them into three separate companies organized under an umbrella corporation. Meg helped Hank run the financial management of all three. Her business acumen helped immensely. After a while, she quit her job at the bank and managed the centralized corporate operations. Meg's brother, Russell, remained at the bank. He ended up running the bank after all. However, before Mr. Haraldson retired, he had a private discussion with Russell to let him know he knew about the old Fleming loan debacle. Russell came away from it humbled and a lot more serious about work.

Fred was Jimmy's younger brother by three years. As boys, Jimmy and Hank tended to shove young Fred away to get him to leave them alone. Hank regretted to think they had not been very nice to him.

Fred grew up to be handsome but hot-tempered and enlisted in the United States Marine Corps right after America declared war in April, 1917. Fred fought in the battle of Belleau Wood and came home from the war deeply scarred from his experiences. Never the same, he turned to drink, fast cars and gambling. Harald and Fred came to blows over his errant ways.

Shortly after the war's end, Fred started going out with Harriet Harcourt, who was young, beautiful, of questionable repute, and looking for a good time. She joined him in his regular drinking forays.

Fred and Harriet's son, William, born in 1920, was an accident. They got married as soon as Harriet found out she was pregnant. He was named after Harriet's father. Soon after young William was born, Fred died in a car crash while barreling drunkenly down the road one night.

Harriett began looking for a new benefactor, but the baby tied her down, and there weren't many takers to be had in sleepy little Gresham. She didn't hang around long and left town secretly one night. She left young William, still an infant, on Ellie's doorstep with a note attached asking Ellie to care for him. Harriet was never heard from again. Poor Ellie was faced with raising four boys on her own. Meg and Hank could only hope they could help her sufficiently.

When Fred's private diaries were found after his death, they learned of the horrors he experienced in his short time over there in the gruesome, hideous realities of war in the trenches. Fred had made a particularly gut-wrenching mistake in combat that led to the horrific death of friends he held dear. His guilt was never shared and it drove him to drink it away. Fred's tale was all too common.

Hank's father died in 1925 at the ripe old age of 73. His heart gave out while he was working on a chair in his back room. Gustaf had always enjoyed creating a beautiful piece of furniture. He died doing what he loved. Hank's sister, Maria, and her husband, George Bernsen, took over the family furniture business. They turned it into more of a furniture store than furniture building as that was more lucrative. Besides, George was a better salesman than a craftsman. His skills helped the business grow substantially.

Jim's father, Harald, died in 1926. Jim's older brother, Karl, came home from China soon afterwards and worked the farm. Jim's mother, Edith, lived in the family home with Karl and his young family. Edith gave part of the farm to Ellie and Hank built her a little house there. After a few years of farming, Karl decided to pursue a career in education at St. Olaf College and moved to Northfield. Edith continued to live on the farm and helped Ellie raise her children.

Along about this same time, with his businesses operating successfully, Hank took it upon himself to learn how to fly. Ironically, he had never done this before. He had let it go while building his businesses. It rekindled the joyful inquisitiveness of his youth and his love of airplanes.

Ellie struggled to earn a living off the land and raise four kids at the same time. When Hank learned of this, he and Meg got an idea to help her out. Hank had been thinking about buying an airplane and he thought he might rent land from Ellie to store it and build a little runway there. Ellie went along with it.

Hank bought a Curtiss JN-4 Jenny and plotted out a nice little landing strip on her land. His rent of the land from Ellie subsidized her income nicely. Ellie got interested in airplanes as well. She persuaded Hank to teach her how to fly. She grew to love it. Flying was hypnotic and she too fell victim to its spell.

Later, Hank decided to start a new business under his corporation to run the airstrip because aviation was growing as an industry. He asked Ellie to run it for him and she agreed. Hank built a proper airstrip, some hangars, and an office and put Ellie in charge. Aviation grew as others took up flying and passenger and cargo services started. The boys grew up around garages and airplanes. By 1930, Ellie's boys were thirteen and twelve.

Ellie had a lot to learn about airports and running a business. Fortunately, Hank had fun helping her run the airport operations with his rediscovered love of airplanes. Meg, her best friend from childhood, taught Ellie the business side. She was a quick study and before long had turned the airstrip into a growing airport business.

Hank also bought an army surplus DH-4 with the big Liberty engine and restored it as a spare time hobby. He managed to build two seats in front of the pilot's cockpit instead of one.

The Arneson and Jacobs boys helped out around the airport, too. Some worked in the hangars, keeping them clean. Others mowed the grass, took out the garbage, ran errands, and more. They saved their earnings for rides in airplanes and lessons to get their own licenses. Early lessons were just informal when Hank took them up with him in the Jenny or the DH4.

Two of Jimmy's former squadron mates, Lieutenants McKenna and Malone from 40 Squadron, came by one day for a surprise visit. Hank was at the airport when they stopped by. They came to the United States on business and stayed on specifically to find the place where Jimmy had grown up. They wanted to pay their respects to Ellie and to share with her how important Jimmy had been for them. They told her all about Jimmy's mission to save the lives of his fellow pilots, his moniker of "Saving Grace," and how it came to be.

They gathered all the boys around and McKenna recounted the day Jimmy saved his life. Saving McKenna is what led to Jimmy's serious wounds in July of 1917. They expressed their admiration, gratitude, and respect for one of the finest officers they ever knew. "He was the one who saved me, all right. I had an Albatros spraying lead all over me and along came Gracie. He threw his airplane around fiercely to get on the Hun's tail and he saved my life."

Malone shared his experiences also. "When we would get back to base after a mission, he used to chew my tail off. He told me all of the things I did wrong to get in trouble and then he taught me all kinds of things I could have done to get the Hun off of me. He didn't just save McKenna's life that day. He saved many lives, including mine on many days. He taught us how to survive the war. He was a natural born leader. We all looked up to him. We all knew he had our backs and that gave us the courage to carry on."

"Oh, how he could fly," McKenna added. "He knew how to make those old crates do all kinds of things they weren't designed for. He practiced tirelessly to perfect every move and then he made us learn them, too."

They spent the evening sharing memories of Jimmy and were all immensely grateful for their visit. What a great way for the boys to learn about their dad.

37

GRESHAM, 1936. Hank hired general managers to run his businesses while he remained chairman of the board and Margaret ruled the operation. Hank bought a 1933 Beechcraft Model 17 Staggerwing to fly around for pleasure and spent his spare time doing that and fiddling around the airport.

The airport had grown. People were taking interest in flying as a sport in addition to transportation so they started a flying school. Ellie ran it, too. Hank hired a former barnstormer as chief instructor. They purchased a couple of Stinsons as student instructional planes and occasional rentals.

The Arneson and Jacobs families grew as one. Ellie had her four boys and Meg and Hank had their five kids, but they were so close they really were three parents raising nine brothers and sisters. Meg and Hank continued to live in town, but they did most everything together with Ellie and spent a great deal of time out at the airport. Naturally, JJ, Joe, and Ted all got their pilot's licenses. Hank was sure all of their kids would want to do the same eventually. It was such a big part of their lives.

JJ left in 1934 to study at the University of Minnesota. The twins, Joe and Ted, left the following year to attend St. Olaf College in Northfield. They were active in sports and both played on the football team.

All three of the Arneson boys favored Jim, but JJ reflected his father almost completely. He was the spitting image of Jim, not just in his looks, but uncannily in his mannerisms and patterns of speech. There were many times when Ellie and Hank were taken aback by the resemblance. His personality was significantly different, however. Unlike Jimmy, JJ thought pretty highly of himself and was known by his friends to be a bit arrogant.

Sunday, June 14, 1936 was a special day for all of them. Not only was it JJ's 19th birthday, but Hank and Ellie had determined to host their first airshow and fly-in at the airport for Flag Day. As part of the celebration, they also wanted to dedicate the Gresham Municipal Airport as the James Arneson Memorial Airport.

Hank decided to do this to pay tribute to his best friend, a man to whom he was forever indebted. When the two of them headed out for Winnipeg together in 1916, Hank committed to following Jim to hell and back if he had to. Hank looked back on those years with pride, knowing he did just that.

Hank grew into his own during the war. He learned to deal with antisemitism from dolts like McBride and how to stand on his own two feet. He learned the craft that would earn him a fortune, and he grew from being a follower into being a leader. Jim Arneson was his role model in all of this. Jimmy showed him the way, gave him confidence, and helped him appreciate his own abilities. The least Hank could do was name their little airport after him.

They had arranged to have aircraft of all types and sizes displayed on the tarmac and surrounding fields of the airport and a fly-by of four P-26 Peashooters from the Grand Forks Air Base. Local merchants and restaurants set up booths and tents to display their wares and to feed the attendees. Folks from all over the Midwest came in for the show. It cost them a bundle to set it all up, but with luck, admissions fees would defray most of those costs.

At the height of the show, Hank had the mayor of Gresham introduce him so he could give his dedication speech.

Mayor Hansen, distinguished members of the Gresham City Council and Chamber of Commerce, loved ones, friends, and fellow aviation enthusiasts, it gives me great pleasure on this august occasion to dedicate this airport as the James Arneson Memorial Airport.

I want to briefly tell you the story of James Arneson so you understand why this airport is named after him. Jim and I grew up together here in Gresham. He was my best friend and my role model. Always popular, he was athletic, intelligent, handsome, and always ready for a new adventure.

Aviation was in its infancy in 1916. It grew by fits and starts with each new experiment. We yearned to be part of it all. Jim and I enlisted in the Royal Flying Corps in 1916 and found ourselves in France. Jim was a pilot with 40 Squadron and later the 56 Squadron. He had nine victories and seventeen saves. War was hard on Jim. The stress of flying every day and watching his friends die at an alarming rate combined with the guilt of killing other pilots sent Jim into a tailspin.

He pulled himself out of depression when he decided to make it his mission to intervene whenever and wherever he could to save the lives of his fellow pilots. Pilots in the Royal Flying Corps died far too frequently. It is believed that nearly one out of every two British pilots was shot down or taken prisoner by the Germans. Seventeen times, he saved someone else's life. He painted little roundels on his plane to keep track of them. He was admired by his fellow pilots and sought after as a flight companion. His fellow pilots had him paint "Saving Grace" on his aeroplane because they all felt he was their saving grace. They even nicknamed him "Gracie" for this.

Courage is fear that has said its prayers and then does what needs to be done. That was Jimmy. He was afraid, but he had faith. He flew, not to save himself, but to save others.

His health was not good before he died, but he had restored his sense of hope for the future. Unfortunately, on May 21, 1918, Jim failed to return from a patrol. He was never heard from again. Like so many allied pilots, he most likely crashed behind enemy lines and his grave was pummeled by artillery as the allies advanced over the territory. Like dandelion seeds blown by the wind, these men died, never to be seen or heard from again. They were taken by the wind, scattered by the winds of war.

Jim was an unsung hero of the United States in the Great War and my own personal hero. That is I why I choose to dedicate this airport in his honor. Please join me in a moment of silence for the memory of James Arneson. Thank you all very much for coming and I hope you enjoy our first airshow. God Bless you all!

After the big airshow had closed down and all the people had gone home, Meg, Ellie, and Hank sat on Ellie's front porch overlooking the airport. They often sat there in the evening to watch the sun set over the prairie.

"Well, ladies," Hank said. "We did it. We paid tribute to our dear Jim. I once said I would follow him to hell and back. I did and now I can sleep well knowing his name will carry on with the life of this airport."

"You were always a good and faithful friend to him, Hank, just like he was for us," said Ellie. "We will all remember him fondly for the rest of our lives."

Meg spoke up then, "Hank, you know how that war you fought in was supposed to be the war to end all wars?"

"Yes, it was," Hank said.

"Doesn't look to me like that's going to hold true," Meg continued. "When I read the papers now a days, I see an awful lot about this Hitler fellow. He's big trouble. I think he's going to start another war. What do you think?"

"I'm afraid you're probably right," Hank agreed. "I'm sorry to say it, but it doesn't look good."

"Our boys are going to get mixed up in it, aren't they?" Ellie asked fearfully.

"I'm afraid so," Hank said. "If war comes, you know our boys will insist on being part of it."

"Let's hope it doesn't happen," Ellie said.

"Yes, let's hope it doesn't happen," Meg said.

But they knew.

Acknowledgements

Many people helped to bring this novel to life. Please allow me to express my gratitude to each of them.

First and foremost I must thank my wife, Annie, my far better half, whose support made this book possible and to whom I am eternally grateful.

My lifelong friend, Van Chesnutt, a man with whom I would trust my very life, was my choice to be my Alpha reader, the first person to read this. I asked him to be honest with me as he has always been and tell me if I had created a monster. He encouraged me selflessly and gave me several good ideas. Thanks, Van!

I also want to thank my many beta readers: Adam, Bob, Chris, Doug, Jim, John, Mike, Richard, Tim, and Tom. Their feedback was hugely valuable to me in improving the book in more ways than I can mention.

My thanks also go to the Whidbey Writers Group for helping me join my writers critique group. Mike, Renee, and Corlan helped me improve my writing in many ways.

I owe a great deal to my editor, Matt Simon. Matt spent endless hours helping me to refine this book. A great teacher, a fine human being, and an outstanding player of Words with Friends, Matt is a person I hope to work with over and over. I always learn a lot from him and thoroughly enjoy the process to boot.

Many thanks to Keith at How It Works (howitworks.com) for his help with the cover design.

Finally, I want to thank my son, Adam, for encouraging me, offering excellent suggestions, and skillfully creating a thoughtful painting for the cover that touches the essence of the book so very well.

About the Author

Dave Bly has been an inveterate airplane nut since he was seven years old when his dad brought home plastic models of the Mercury-Redstone Launch Vehicle and an F-101 Voodoo for them to build together. As a youth, Dave loved flying around western Pennsylvania with his dad in Cessna 172s and Piper Cherokees. He found his idols not on baseball cards, like his buddies, but in the memoirs of fighter aces from World Wars One and Two. Failing his own military flight physical from color blindness, Dave enlisted in the U.S. Air Force, served with the 366th Tactical Fighter Wing, and later became a private pilot. He now lives on Whidbey Island in Puget Sound.

www.davidably.com